TELLURIDE
Top of the World

TOM TATUM
A Novel

outskirts
press

Outskirts Press, Inc.
http://www.outskirtspress.com

ISBN: 978-1-4787-9237-6

Cover Image by Kathryn Tatum

Outskirts Press and the "OP" logo are trademarks belonging to Outskirts Press, Inc.

PRINTED IN THE UNITED STATES OF AMERICA

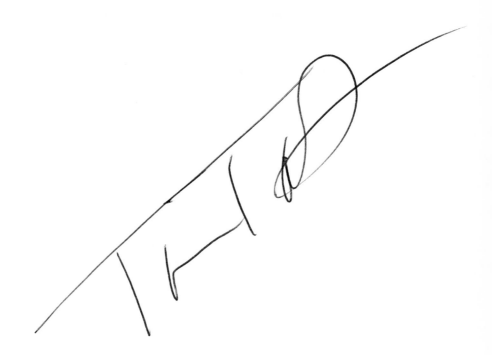

SALT LAKE CITY

LA SALLE MOUNTAINS

GRAND JUNCTION

COLORADO RIVER

MINTURN
GOLD

DELTA
JAIL

MOAB

PARADOX

NATURITA

Ybar C

SAN MIGUEL RIVER

NORWOOD

TELLURIDE

AJAX MOUNTAIN
12,785'

BLUFF

CORTEZ

ANASAZI RUINS

SOUTHERN UTE RESERVATION

MEXICAN HAT

UTAH   COLORADO

ARIZONA   NEW MEXICO

CANYON DE CHELLY

SAN JUAN RIVER

MONUMENT VALLEY

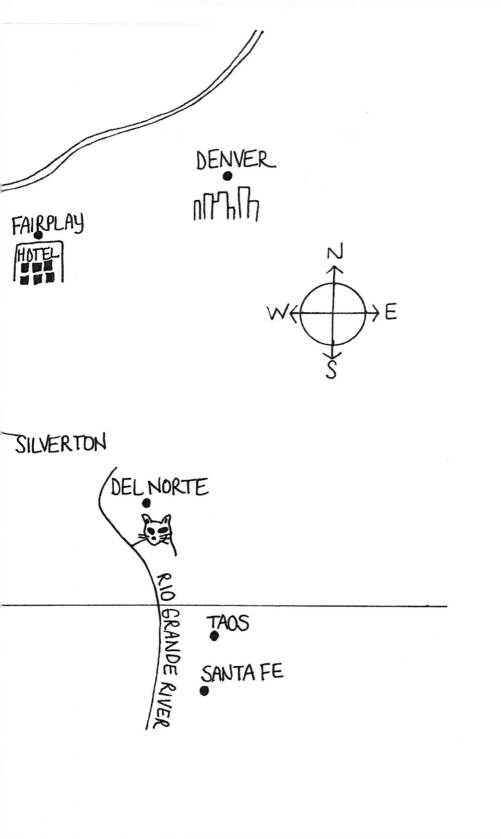

ONE

The Mighty San Miguel

C ooper waded knee deep into the gold streaked rushing water of the San Miguel River where, about twenty miles west of Telluride, Colorado, the giant brown trout had eluded tourists and their local fishing guides all summer. The dirty blonde tall twenty-six-year-old changed dry flies a half dozen times as he fished the pockets along the steep southern river bank, working upstream against the autumn flow of the headwaters but with no more luck than the tourists.

He paused, hypnotized by the soft, gold images of Aspen leaves in a quiet pool of deep water. A concave bend in an outcropping of bright red sandstone formed a broken eroding wall that dropped into the river from the mesa a thousand feet above him. Cooper's options were running low. He could quit dry fly fishing and wade across the river to a flat gray boulder bathed in late day sunlight. There he could reflect on his return to western Colorado. He could continue to dry fly fish the pool and hope that the twenty-inch brownie he was stalking would rise to the surface for a final snack before winter. Then Cooper's dinner plan would be solved.

If Cooper took a moment to rest on a riverside boulder, he had to think about the reality of running the vast family ranch after his altruistic service in the Peace Corps. Already the adventures in Fiji were migrating like late summer monarch butterflies from his memory. The laughter of the Fijian villagers was being replaced by the silence of his hard-eyed ranch hands in the harsh sun and wind of the Colorado Plateau. Cooper decided to fish.

Cooper could try catching the trout Cherokee Indian style, carefully cutting the eye out of the rainbow he already had in his handbraided creel and put it on a naked hook he carried for pond fishing on the ranch. No brown trout in the world could resist the trout's eye when the sunset turned it into a kaleidoscope of color on the crystal blue water.

Or, as a last resort, Cooper could try a fly-fishing trick he remembered from a trip to Gatlinburg Tennessee, his freshman year in college. The Smoky Mountain technique assumed the large brown trout was too lazy to rise on fall day near sunset. Using a lead sinker on his floating line would sink the dry fly to the bottom of the hole and the brown would eat it like a catfish.

Cooper chose the last option. The trout became his sole mission. He cranked in the floating fly line on his new reel. He waded across to the tabletop boulder to re-rig his Garcia bamboo fly rod, a tenth birthday gift from his grandfather.

The boulder's heat warmed Cooper through his rubber waders and khaki shorts. He checked his Royal Wulff dry fly and clipped two dull lead sinkers above it. He gunked the fly for good measure. The fly, hand tied by his grandfather, reminded him of his warning about fishing alone. Solo Colorado fly fisherman had been swept to their death in canyons when flash flood waters from the mesas above them roared through the narrow sandstone walled canyons. There was the story of renegade Comanche Indian drifter who ambushed, tortured and killed lone fishermen at the turn of the century. Cooper's great-grandfather whom Brigham Young had sent to the Paradox Valley to colonize and ranch it for the Mormon Church, always carried a pistol and saved the last bullet for himself. Cooper's grandfather had been expelled from the Church for refusing to deed back a portion of the YBarC to the Bishops after the ranch's loan was repaid to the Salt Lake City's Mormon controlled bank. Money, not multiple wives, was always at the root of a feud in the Church.

Cooper carried a pistol when he was fly fishing alone, a light weight .22 caliber Saturday Night Special with hollow point bullets tucked in a tan leather holster under his left armpit. At close range, it could blow a quarter size hole in a bear or man's head. He also carried a six-inch Toledo steel hunting knife in the long pocket of his tan fishing vest for hand to paw defense or to gut a trout. In his Jeep was a loaded short-barreled Winchester 30-30 rifle.

The soft roar of the river drowned out all but the loudest black ravens. After four hours, Cooper's heart and spirit had been purified. An ancient Hopi legend spoke of returning the earth's land to the winds of the universe, mocking the hollow achievements of the white man. Cooper believed the Indians were only mostly right because the half breed black baldy cows on his family's thirty-thousand-acre YBarC ranch had paid the bills for the last two decades.

As Cooper prepared to wade across the river he noted the flow was too low perhaps caused by a dry Indian summer, but maybe from use by the expanding Ajax Ski Company in nearby Telluride. Rumors were flying from Telluride's hard drinking miners about secret illegal water wells along the river by the ski area.

Cooper never drank a drop of the San Miguel's water because the hundred-year orgy of gold, silver and lead mining had turned the river into a toxic brew. Townsmen and ranchers had fought wars over water in the west since they settled it. Cooper had been taught from childhood that the ranch's water rights were more valuable than gold in the arid region. They were senior to every other deeded water right in the region and dating back to 1884.

Cooper's long legs were stiff after the long rest on the gray boulder so he waded carefully. He slipped occasionally as his rubber-soled waders searched for solid footing in the slippery riverbed. The fall water was now barely above his ankles as he approached the deep pool. One cast only. Ten feet from the edge of the quiet residence of the giant trout, Cooper raised the fly rod tip and whipped the gunked greasy fly into the pool's orange yellow surface. The fly sank a foot a second; not even his polarized sunglasses could penetrate the reflection of the aspen leaves and the perfect hues of the fading light on the river's surface. One second passed as Cooper prepared for that underwater touch so soft only an experienced fly fisherman would recognize it.

Suddenly, Cooper felt it, a soft touch he remembered from years ago on the nearby Delores River. With a quick lift of his right hand, the wet fly's Spanish steel hook set in the mouth of the largest trout Cooper had ever hooked in the shallow San Miguel.

Colors of the leaves, sandstone, the water and sunset blasted through Cooper's brain as the trout's battle for survival started. The big brown's vital organs would already be cancerous from years in the heavy metal tainted water, but he would fight to the end to die in his dark blue home.

TWO

The Big Trout

Cooper reeled expertly left-handed and the old bamboo rod doubled over itself, tip touching the water. The fish didn't rise from the cold bottom of the pool. A few seconds later, Cooper realized he had not caught the prize. He had snagged something very heavy and immobile, hidden in the shadows of the deep pool's sandstone bottom.

Cooper waded about ten feet upstream until he saw a discoloration below the surface as his foot searched for the pool's steep edge. He stopped on a sandy ledge. The San Miguel River had semi-quicksand pockets, which could sink him to his waist. Cooper remembered hearing that a dude fisherman from California had stepped into a river pool and sank chest deep into quicksand. Apparently, he didn't have a knife in his fishing vest pocket to cut himself free from his waders and float to the surface. He drowned, stuck in the quicksand when the narrow river rose in a sudden thunderstorm.

Cooper reached into the murky ruby sunset pool, following the invisible leader line down under the water's surface to find his precious Royal Wulff fly and identify the object it had snagged. Cooper was careful not to break the thin leader. Inch by inch his cold hand moved down as he kept the tension steady. The reel was stopped with his thumb pressure to protect the tapered bamboo tip of the rod. A second later his fingers hit a soggy bloated wool covered object. Cooper pulled his hand back fast, sensing danger. He let out two feet of line and stepped back from the edge of the pool. The surface of the river was turning dark blue, preventing him from seeing below the surface.

Cooper pulled his hunting knife from his fishing vest pocket. He was fifteen miles from a deputy sheriff's office and ten miles from a pay phone. Cooper edged closer and lowered his knife slowly into the pool, moving carefully to avoid severing the leader line. He flipped the knife blade to its dull side to poke the object.

The knife hit the firm surface of the underwater mystery and it stopped. He inched the knife blade left to right. The surface of the object seemed to deflate a little, like a heavy-duty rubber weather balloon; it felt thick.

Suddenly, a Juniper branch cracked above Cooper to his right on the high walled river bank. He froze, knife in his left hand under water, right hand on the bent fly rod, thumb on the reel. He looked up, his left ear cocked toward the ledge. A minute passed as Cooper waited, breathing yoga style silently through his nostrils, eyes riveted to the ledge ready to drop the reel and reach for the .22 pistol.

The vegetation on the ruby stone cliff was black-brown in the twilight. Cooper saw a large shape easing over the ledge just as a dying sun ray caught the pupil of a dangerous eye. Cooper had only seen this eye before on a remote part of the ranch in the head of a mature mountain lion. A mountain lion had recently killed a three-year-old in a newly subdivided ranch south of Telluride. His Swedish nanny had gone in for a pee at dusk while the parents were at a Fourth of July fireworks picnic in town. The boy had wandered off the sun porch through an unlocked screen door. Cooper's south Texas Mexican ninera would never have let a three-year-old Cooper out of sight at dusk on the remote ranch. The illuminated eye and head poked further over the red rock rim; a light brown paw edged over the sandstone. The hungry animal was a moment away from leaping onto Cooper's muscled neck and tearing out his jugular. Cooper had inadvertently stayed too long at its nocturnal watering hole.

Cooper reacted in a western second. He dropped the rod, reached his fishing vest pocket and pulled out the .22. He fired at the edge of the sandstone rim, spraying chips into the cat's eyes. He pulled his dripping knife out of the river with his left hand as his final line of defense if the cat leapt. The cat, momentarily blinded, backed away, which gave Cooper a second to step onto the mysterious object in the pool and onto a narrow ledge under the sandstone cliff. Cooper hoped the uninvited mountain lion would lose interest in him since it would have to high dive into the boulder-strewn shallows of the roaring river instead of onto Cooper.

A long minute passed then suddenly low brush crackled as the mountain lion retreated, probably deciding to hunt for a fat mule deer or a Telluride ski bum's dog in a fall campsite. The big cat's muffled paw sounds vanished when he cleared the rotting sandstone ledge. Cooper holstered the little pistol and sheaved the knife.

His blue eyes stared back at the dark, quiet pool of water below him, resolving to solve its mystery before he left. Cooper hoped his adventures with North American wildlife were over for the night.

Cooper's long fast step across the river pool had semi-confirmed his less obvious guess that there was a drowned, bloated calf body on the bottom, probably wedged tightly under the sandstone ledge he was standing on. It was his rancher's responsibility to pull the corpse out of the river. Cooper waded carefully around the pool back across the river, secured his bamboo rod and cut the leader line. Then he edged into the pool, reached under the flowing water with both hands to find a leg to pull the hapless animal free.

Cooper found the calf's limb, but it broke the surface of the water wearing blue jeans. A purple-bloated human foot emerged and Cooper almost vomited from the stink. He held onto the human leg, still attached to a human body that didn't float up. Cooper pulled out his hunting knife with his left hand and used it to probe the man's clothing, cutting it loose carefully until suddenly the body shifted in the current and the large torso floated to the surface. Cooper held onto the dead man's left leg while the fat, blue-white face, preserved in the icy river pool, broke the surface. The mystery solved itself.

In the now half-moonlit river he saw the dead face of a grade school classmate's father. Bill Daniels, the Montrose and San Miguel County district water engineer. He had been missing for two weeks and presumed lost while hunting bighorn sheep high on the north face of Mount Wilson. Hunting alone without a permit was a dangerous local custom left over from frontier days.

Many of the great-grandsons of the early ranchers, sheepherders and homesteaders still refused to be licensed to hunt. Their families had come west after the civil war to escape the U.S. government, which they hated, even as it closed in on them in the last half of the twentieth century. Bill Daniels had definitely not walked off a mountain trail in pursuit of a big set of horns and a good barbecue. He was floating in the dark blue river pool, kept from drifting downstream only by Cooper's tight grip on his blue jeaned leg.

This was a big story and it was going to shock Montrose and San Miguel counties to their frontier foundation, after Cooper delivered the corpse to the sheriff's substation in nearby Norwood.

THREE

Canned Foamy

A s Cooper sped back to the ranch along the deserted state highway near Norwood, he was guided by a bright moon-lit night. The bloated body of Bill Daniels had been water-logged, heavy, but well preserved. Cooper dragged it across the shallow river and onto the safety of the north bank by the cattle path and then secured his antique bamboo fly rod. He had seen a fallen cowboy on a neighboring ranch's round up, two dead miners at a Telluride mine head and attended funerals. But he had never handled a dead body.

Cooper was surprised when he tried to free Bill from the pool. He'd been lead weighted like a bass spinning lure on a light fishing rig. Cooper had viewed the entire corpse for the first time on the bank. Bill wore a wool plaid shirt, jeans and brown leather double stitched work boots. His belt was missing, which Cooper thought odd because Bill always wore a large, sterling silver NCAA rodeo championship buckle. He had competed for the Colorado School of Mines. No one Cooper knew would murder a man for his trophy belt, but the new ski area in Telluride was bringing in the biggest wave of outsiders since the 1890s gold and silver boom.

Cooper covered Bill's face with his fishing vest then walked the half mile back to his Jeep to drive it back up the narrow cow path. The short wheel base Jeep from American Motors was like an Indian pony and it could be driven about anywhere but straight up or down. Cooper carried his bamboo fly rod with the fly that he had recovered from Bill's pocket. He stepped adroitly around the cow patties left by the black baldies of the Star Ranch that grazed this stretch of the river on a BLM lease. They had been shipped back to southern New Mexico a week ago.

About a hundred yards from the Jeep, Cooper stopped dead in his tracks as he heard female giggling coming from a National Forest campsite up river. He shifted to an Indian style toe to heel walk in his clunky waders. Cooper wondered if the gigglers had seen his Jeep on their way into the campsite.

He approached undetected, stopping between two large cottonwoods. He peered into a Coleman lantern-lit scene reminiscent of a D.H. Lawrence painting in Taos' La Fonda Hotel. Stretched out on her back on the picnic table, buck naked from the waist down, was a good looking, twenty-year-old blonde with fading summer tanned legs. Her thighs were open, revealing her newly shaven smooth triangle. Her small vagina lips were still smeared with foamy shaving cream that glistened in the bright lantern light. Standing with her back to Cooper was a round-bottomed, flannel-shirted, black-haired woman. The woman held a disposable blue plastic razor in her right hand as she expertly stroked off the blonde's last small patch of golden pubic hair.

The black-haired woman picked up a hand towel from the picnic table and wiped the bare pussy clean of shaving cream. She stimulated the blonde as she worked. She tossed the towel onto the picnic table and climbed on top of her. They starting kissing and then the lithe blonde pulled her by the hand and they scrambled off the table into the two-person nylon tent. Two open backpacks were lying next to the picnic table with unused cooking gear on top. Cooper listened to a big city demonstration of girl on girl sex. The women must be from Telluride, he surmised. San Miguel County was changing. Cooper, grinning, knew the tent would be like a four-alarm fire scene when they heard his Jeep fire up in a couple minutes.

The unexpected sex play lightened his walk to the Jeep where he carefully stored the bamboo rod in its felt-lined hard leather case. He pulled off the waders and slipped into his Lee bootcut jeans and pulled on rough leather cowboy boots. Cooper flipped the key he had left in the ignition having anticipated a fast getaway from a twilight fishing bear.

He hit the headlight switch and the high twin light beam easily penetrated the downstream campsite. The partially nude blonde scampered from the tent, grabbing her hiking shorts from the picnic table. Cooper drove the Jeep down the trail and watched her pull on the shorts in the headlights. As he pulled to the edge of the campsite he leaned his cowboy hat clad head out the unzipped Jeep window and gave the women a hippie peace sign. Both women gave him the finger.

"You fucking bastard! Did you take our picture?"

Cooper couldn't lie to a blonde, so he yelled over the glasspacks, "I can't hear what you are saying!"

She shouted, "You fucking cowboy bastard! You watched us and probably took a photo."

He replied, "I can't hear you. Come a little closer."

The blonde approached warily as Cooper remembered Bill Daniels downstream and thought the women were a blessing sent by the angels to help him load the water-logged body. "Maybe, but if you want the negative I need a little help first."

The pretty blonde paused warily. "What kind of help? No sex Cowboy."

"Well, I hadn't thought of that. Do you do boys?"

She was pissed now. Her dark-haired friend exited the tent, glaring at Cooper.

The friend said, "You Colorado rednecks are all the same. Fuck you, dirt bag cowboy."

Cooper wasn't used to language like that from a man or woman so he was a little pissed off, his practical joke aside.

He led them on, "Well, little lady, if you want the negative film then you girls help me load some dead weight downriver. I have miles to go before I sleep."

The two women still misunderstood his intentions. They closed on the Jeep, whispering. The stronger dark-haired woman swung open the driver-side door, flailing her fists at Cooper's balls and horseman's thighs, which were mercifully protected by the black plastic steering wheel.

She yelled, "Sue, help me."

The blonde approached in hesitant steps but finally stepped onto the passenger side running board, gripped a soft top roof rod inside the door frame and diverted Cooper's attention until he realized the dark-haired woman had his balls in a rapidly tightening grip with her strong left hand. Cooper eyed an open Swiss Army knife's steel blade glinting in the moonlight in the blonde's hands.

"Time out," Cooper yelled as he reached over the dark-haired woman's arm into the glove box and pulled out the .22. "Drop your weapons please, ladies."

The woman with the pistol barrel near her forehead instantly pulled her hand off Cooper's balls and out of the Jeep's window. The blonde's hand froze with the knife point an inch from Cooper's tanned right cheek.

"War games are over ladies. Get your hiking boots on and jump in the Jeep."

"You can't kidnap us!" the blonde whispered angrily.

"You are not being kidnapped, only deputized. You get the film after the next stop down river a half mile where we pick up a drowned dead man," Cooper stated in a calm well-pitched voice.

After a slow sulking five mile an hour trip down the cow path, Cooper backed the Jeep up to Bill Daniels' body. The women gagged when they spied the bloated body with the fishing vest still over its face.

"Ladies, please leap out the door and help me load Bill Daniels' body so I can drive it to the deputy sheriff in Norwood before a bear discovers it. He has been underwater for two weeks."

The dark-haired girl protested, "You killed him. Are you going to kill us?"

"Found him in my favorite fall fishing hole. He was reported missing two weeks ago. He's the district water engineer."

"I read about him in the Telluride newspaper. They said he might have been lost hunting in the high country. How did he end up in the San Miguel?" the blonde asked.

"That, Sue, I believe your name might be, is the 64,000 dollar question."

The women waited to walk back to their campsite until after he wrote their names, addresses and phone numbers on a matchbook cover as witnesses. The blonde covertly added a peace symbol by hers.

Cooper said in parting, "See you in Telluride, I suspect. The deputy sheriff will call you tomorrow. Please be more prudent around highway Jeep access campsites."

He tossed them the negative film roll from his SLR camera he kept between the front seats and smiled easily. It had never been unspooled. The dark-haired woman gave him a furious look as the blonde smirked, chocking back a laugh.

The blonde might make it on the west's last frontier, Cooper thought. The roar of the glass pack muffler and the river drowned out the blonde's goodbye but Cooper saw her concealed wave in the red tail light glow as he accelerated slowly away. He laughed and pulled onto the state highway to deliver his silent passenger to the sheriff's substation in Norwood. The scent of the blonde named Sue lingered in the Jeep to remind Cooper to look her up in Telluride.

FOUR

Liz

Cooper turned onto the ranch in a flurry of dust and gravel. Winter was close and the first snow storm was near. Cooper's mother Liz would still be awake at the YBarC's headquarters house, reading a novel.

Liz was unique in both the world of women and ranch wives. At 60-years old Liz was still a beauty with an always suntanned lined face. Cooper's father had met her during a Denver livestock show where he played a rare indoor polo exhibition game in the rodeo arena. The Rocky Mountain farmers and ranchers gathered each January in Denver to buy, sell and parade championship livestock and then watch nightly rodeo and mule pulls to break their long, dull winters. Liz had been a department store model in Denver.

Cooper's father had gone to downtown Denver before the polo exhibition, to shop for his own mother's birthday present near the Brown Palace Hotel where his family had lodged in the same suite for five decades. It was one floor below the gold and silver mine owners' suites. The mine owners and their heirs had controlled Denver's business and its social scene since the 1860s. Ranchers had always been the meat suppliers to the mines in Colorado, unlike the neighboring states where cattlemen's associations controlled the state governments. Liz caught Cooper's father's eye on the second floor mezzanine as he charged an English leather handbag on his family's account. She'd been modeling an evening gown from Paris for a wealthy Denver matron.

Cooper's father was 35-years-old, six-foot-one, blonde and handsome. He cut a swath wherever he traveled in the southwest. He didn't much like ranching, but he loved polo and beautiful women equally. Unfortunately, most beautiful women, at the end of the depression, didn't want to move to an isolated high altitude ranch where even the cattle didn't spend the winter. Cooper's father walked over to Liz and gave her a ticket to the family's box for the polo exhibition.

Liz always said Cooper's father played his greatest game of polo that night and won her heart. He rode over to the arena side box after his team won the match and presented her with a dozen Pasadena long-stemmed red roses. He was mounted on his prize polo pony, Sugar Cube. Liz was flanked by Cooper's grandmother Susan and his grandfather Ted.

Liz teared up as old Sugar Cube licked her hand, probably trying to nibble a winter California rosebud. She fell in love with the whole family with most of Colorado society nodding in approval. Cooper's dad galloped over and accepted the sterling silver trophy for his team while the Denver Police Department's brass band played "Big Time Woman from Way Out West." It was a jazz hit of the era.

In Colorado, silver trophies were routine; the whole state did everything possible to prop up the price of silver in the grueling depression and keep the mines open.

Cooper's father and Liz went dancing in the art deco bar in the Oxford Railroad Hotel that night while Sugar Cube ate a half dozen rosebuds because Liz knew how to win a polo player horse's heart.

As Cooper approached the yellow-bricked Victorian two-story, he saw the light on in the parlor. His mother had taken to reading in that spot after Cooper's father died playing charity polo past his prime. Cooper was eight on the fatal Sunday afternoon, his father hooked his mallet into the opposing player's stirrup. The mallet jammed, breaking the other player's ankle. His horse stumbled, falling into Sugar Cube, and Cooper's father broke his neck in a high-speed fall. Cooper's father was barely breathing and completely paralyzed and unconscious when he reached the El Paso, Texas, General Hospital's emergency room.

No one had to say anything. Dr. Blacker conferred quietly with Liz and the priest. There weren't any legendary ten-goal polo playing quadriplegic ranchers in the west. Cooper's father in an iron lung, coma or no coma, was like Sugar Cube with three legs. Liz cried and held Cooper's father's head in her tear-stained lap while he silently chocked to death and the priest administered last rites. Dr. Blacker signed the death certificate - brain dead on arrival.

Cooper cut the engine and headlights in one motion as he parked the Jeep below the wrap-around porch. He leapt up the sandstone steps and walked into the California oak-floored entrance hall.

But a soft voice called from the library, not the parlor. "Cooper, you're home?"

"Yes, Liz. I went fishing down at father's old secret pool on the San Miguel and found a surprise."

"Well, come tell all."

"Soon as I get these dusty boots off my feet. I'm still not used to wearing them since I came back." Cooper sat on a blue hand-painted pine bench in the entry hallway and pulled off his cowboy boots.

The library and its polished oak floor gleamed in the lamp light. Liz was stretched out on a black Italian leather overstuffed couch. Three walls of built-in native pine shelves held four generations of books. A ladder ran on a bronze tract to reach the high shelves. The collection had been started by Cooper's great-grandfather who was taught to read by one of Brigham Young's wives.

Liz was reading a James Jones novella. Her red robe was partially covered by a hand-knit wool lap robe, which matched her nightgown.

12

"Well, you finally catch the great-great-grandson of that brown trout your father chased every fall?"

"No, but it's a real interesting fish story. You remember meeting Bill Daniels, I'm sure, at the Christmas masses in Montrose."

Liz went to church once a year, blizzards included.

"Yes, isn't he the water engineer who ran off with his secretary a couple weeks ago?"

Interesting how rumors mutated across two counties both the size of Rhode Island, Cooper mused.

"Well, he didn't run off with his secretary because I caught him alone in the deep pool under the red sandstone cliff."

She looked up from her open book; she shifted her long thin legs until her wool-socked feet peeked out from under the lap robe.

"He was drowned and lead-weighted in the bottom of the pool. I was trying an old Tennessee Smoky Mountain trick to catch the big brown when I hooked Bill after a mountain lion tried to jump me. I delivered his body to the deputy sheriff in Norwood a half hour ago."

Liz fingered the cover of the book and raised her eyelids slightly, "Bill Daniels checked the flow on our ranch's mother ditch from Lone Cone Mountain while you were in Fiji. He consulted for me, but he still worked at the Uravan uranium mill."

Cooper flopped into his father's overstuffed Italian leather arm chair. Liz always spoke of the ranch "ours" since both his father and grandfather died. But she only had a guardianship in the ranch until Cooper turned 30-years-old. Cooper had been home for two months after returning from boarding school, college, the Peace Corps in Fiji, backpacking around the Pacific and a year of agricultural school at the University of Hawaii. Already he knew ranch matters were rapidly coming to a head between him and his mother.

"Well, he'll be in the Norwood cemetery by Sunday without his silver rodeo buckle, which was missing when I found him."

"I'm going to La Jolla for a week, then to Dallas for Christmas shopping. You can ship the mother cows to Arizona winter pasture without me. When I come back I'm going to move into a house in Montrose." Liz began a conversation they both had avoided.

At least the first half of Liz's information was routine. After the ranch's Indian summer roundup, Liz always spent time in La Jolla's Valencia Hotel where she met Dr. Blacker, now a widower and her lover after Cooper's father's death. Cooper wondered why they had never married. Next, Liz would fly to Neiman Marcus as the ranch women had done for three generations.

The YBarC account was number 193, and it carried a permanent interest clause of three percent, net 180 days to allow the ranch's current year's calf sales to be collected. When Liz walked into the Dallas store, the aging clerks still almost saluted even though the Texas oil princesses had replaced western ranch wives in spending power if not prestige. Cooper knew this conversation was not about the beach trip or shopping. If Liz was moving to a rented house she had wanted to buy in Montrose, she was retiring from ranching.

"Cooper, dear son, the ranch is yours to run now that college and the Fiji Peace Corps adventure is over. I'm not waiting for you to marry before I exit. I am tired of bone cold winters out here and the ranch's problems."

Problem was not a word used lightly in Western Colorado ranching. Cooper's mind went on full alert.

"Cooper, I've been borrowing $45-55,000 a year to keep the ranch going since your grandfather died and it's accumulated. We owe about $600,000 now, which didn't seem like much when interest was three or four percent but since the Vietnam War, with inflation, it has risen to ten percent and the YBarC's lost big money the past year. Even with 2,000 mother cows I can't make ends meet with a $60,000 interest payment due each November."

Cooper had unwittingly signed a power of attorney on his eighteenth birthday after his grandfather's death that had given Liz the right to borrow and renew bank loans while he was in college and in the Peace Corps. His tab had just come due.

"You've done a good job holding this operation together. I'll meet with Sam Jr. at First National Bank next week and work out a payback plan. Meanwhile, I'll have Uncle Harvey draw up a quitclaim deed to terminate your life estate in the YBarC with a quarter share of annual profits paid to you until your death."

"That'll be fair, Cooper. I'll sign the legal papers before I leave. I borrowed the final $50,000 this spring for operating cash through the fall until the calves are sold. I'm taking $5,000 with me as usual for my trip. Things are more expensive in California and Dallas every year, plus I need furniture for the Montrose house."

"That's fine, Liz. Take furniture from here, too."

"Only my bedroom set, everything in this old house belongs here, not in Montrose."

Cooper rose, walked over and kissed his mother on her still soft but lined cheek, catching a salty tear on his lip as it made a wet trail. Liz had been dealt a strange hand in the wild, wild west and Cooper intended to make sure she was comfortable and loved until death. He would deal with the bank in Telluride, which had banked the YBarC since his great-grandfather started selling beef to the mines. He expected no problems from a bank that had known him since birth.

The YBarC carried the C for Cooper, his great-grandfather's name too, and the Y because it spanned two Colorado counties, San Miguel and Montrose. The ranch's house, land, cattle and senior water rights had always been good collateral and it had always paid off its loans and interest even during long drought periods. He planned to see Liz off for Southern California at the Grand Junction railroad station and then swing down to Telluride for a meeting at the bank.

Cooper also wanted to meet the blonde camper whose phone number he had on the matchbook cover in his shirt pocket. He wanted to check out Telluride after his long absence. Maybe part of the YBarC's future lay with the new Ajax Ski Company, although in his heart Cooper sensed they were oil and water. Cooper kissed Liz on the forehead and walked out of the library very alone for the first time in his young life.

FIVE

The Last Goodbye

On the drive to Grand Junction Liz silently said goodbye to the Y BarC and remembered her first visit to the ranch while Cooper drove. She had travelled across Tennessee Pass between Minturn and Leadville to Grand Junction in February. The pass was legendary in railroad circles as one of the steepest grades in the world with its track-busting winter blizzards and avalanches on the Continental Divide. Liz's trip became a nightmare when the passenger car in which she was riding derailed in a whiteout.

"I was thirty, but still a girl at heart, having never married because of my modeling jobs. My agent in Hollywood had placed me at various Southern California women's stores in between bit parts in MGM movies where his dad was a line producer for Louie B. Mayer. I was paid $300 a month by the Denver store and given a room at the Brown Palace Hotel."

Cooper had heard the story many times before but only recently wondered why Liz commanded $300 a month during the depression.

Liz continued, "I had no comprehension of what your father had roped me into. You know, I never returned to Denver or the eastern slope of the Rockies after that night in the frigid Pullman car."

It was true, Cooper thought to himself. Liz came to the ranch and never left, except to travel with her husband on the polo circuit and go to La Jolla and Dallas each fall with a stop in Salt Lake City, where Cooper knew she kept her secret 'cookie tin' bank account. His parents had been married in Montrose at the Presbyterian church that spring.

"Your father was the best athlete I ever watched in any sport, including Buster Crabbe who swam in a movie I appeared in as a woman lifeguard. On the polo field, cutting calves or fishing in a mountain stream, he was beauty in motion. He was a crack shot and we always had fresh game year-round. I don't think he would have really wanted to grow old. It would have bored him."

Cooper replied, still sad that his father had left him, "I remember flashes of Dad on Sugar Cube on the ranch's practice field. It was wonderful to watch him at full speed. I loved it when he galloped to the sideline and swept me up into his arms." Cooper fondly remembered the exciting danger of sitting against his father's chest. One arm held him while the other one swung the powerful mallet, hitting practice chukker after practice chukker at full speed. Cooper believed all boys should get to experience their father's youthful physical power, before it wilted, in a dangerous majestic ride across a polo field. Death held at bay by physical power only cements the warrior bond between child and male creator.

Liz, who never rambled before, continued, "Your father on a polo pony was one with the wind. The earth felt very young when Sugar Cube galloped down the field, your father's sun-bleached blonde hair flying in the wind. They were old spirits bound in sport and it was good they both died the same day on their field of honor."

Cooper realized for the first time that in Liz's memory, her husband and Sugar Cube had died instantly on the El Paso polo field. There had never been an ambulance ride to the hospital or a vet with a pistol. They simply went down together on the hard, dry, grass and never rose from the turf, like so many players and polo ponies before them. One man and one horse combined as a spiritual emissary of the wind god in a time when the earth was still young and free. They were practitioners, not theorists of sport - aggressive, never passive, brutally strong athletes, crafty and perfectly skilled players, never awkward. Both emotional and emotionless, tireless and exhausted, playful but ruthlessly competitive, they won at a game so fast and deadly it finally called in their markers for staying at the table too long. Or, as an eight-year-old Cooper had believed, they simply flew off the earth into the big sky that afternoon. Cooper hoped their spirit winds would never abandon the earth.

"You and I both held in his strong arms, knew his love and power at play with the spirits of the high Colorado Plateau," Liz said reading Cooper's thoughts.

Grand Junk Yard, as the ranchers referred to Grand Junction, Colorado, because of its railroad scrap yard, loomed into view as the Jeep crossed the muddy brown Colorado River. The mostly nondescript, rambling, hot and dusty western town existed because the Colorado River, once named the Grand River, and the Gunnison River met there. It was also the only major railroad stop between Denver and Salt Lake City.

Grand Junction seemed to be destined to be neither historically important in any era nor very prosperous. It had produced no national leaders, no famous scientists, no major companies and no artists of note - just real estate schemers who tried to inflate its cheap desert land with irrigation canals from the Colorado River and sell the nearby oil shale formations as the next cheap western oil patch. Recently, it had been semi-circled by ski areas at Aspen, Crested Butte and Telluride.

Cooper stopped the Jeep in front of the fading sandstone and yellow brick neo-Gothic railroad station at noon, which was ten minutes before Liz's departure to Salt Lake City. He guessed she would close her Zion National Bank account after her night's stay at the Hotel Utah and a meal in its dining room overlooking the Mormon Tabernacle. Cooper had heard that the conservative Mormon bankers of Salt Lake City made the Swiss bankers look like red-eyed gamblers.

Liz had never completely trusted the small town western Colorado bankers. She and

Cooper knew the family's near fatal bank story. In 1935, a few days before the Colorado State bank examiners arrived at the ranch's bank in Telluride, its president called his oldest and best customers, including Cooper's great-grandfather. The president asked them to come to the bank and withdraw their cash deposits in full. To hide his bad depression loans, he had borrowed money from a New York Bank under false pretenses to cover the large depositors' accounts when the bank failed. He went to prison but Cooper's great-grandfather was able to continue to operate the YBarC with the secured cash in the headquarters safe until the start of World War II when the Army started buying large quantities of beef.

Cooper waved goodbye to Liz as she looked down at him from the graying concrete platform with tears in her eyes. Then, he drove to a barbeque lunch across from the hospital where he had been born.

SIX

The Big Box Canyon

Telluride loomed at the end of its alpine box canyon. It was a dilapidated Victorian mining town built at the base of three aspen and evergreen laden peaks rising from the gravel river valley floor created by the headwaters of the San Miguel River. The river was created by its mother, Bridal Veil Falls, and its father, Ingram Falls, from the winter snowpack melting year-round on the slopes of the San Juan Mountain Range.

Ajax, the tallest of the majestic peaks, had governed Telluride since the San Juan Mountains were pushed up from an ocean floor eons ago. The town and its mines were a temporary pimple on the face of a natural beauty queen.

At Society Turn, Cooper drove past a crumbling coal loading dock that had once serviced the railroad locomotives that were the lifeline of this 100-year-old depressed gold and silver mining camp. Now Colorado had a new white gold, skiing.

Cooper passed a herd of black and white dairy cows on the valley floor as he drove into town. They were not the tough black baldies that grazed the YBarC six months each summer. The cartoonlike dairy cattle reminded Cooper of a tragic YBarC cow that had fallen off the north rim of the Grand Canyon one night in the late spring of 1951 and crushed a Wall Street heiress who was sleeping under the stars. The YBarC lost its winter BLM grazing on the North Rim because of a congressional investigation pushed by her husband's iconic firm but didn't lose the resulting lawsuit because the cow was in Federal Government airspace when it hit the National Park sandbar.

The heiress' husband had even called the owner of the Telluride National Bank to buy any YBarC loans at a two-hundred percent markup so he could call them and put the ranch out of business. Sam Sr., the owner and president, declined; the YBarC had paid off all its loans by the end of World War II.

Cooper slowed at the Telluride town limit sign that informed drivers of the 8,700 foot altitude. Turn of the century shingle-sided wood frame mining houses lined the wide state highway that also functioned as Colorado Avenue. The street was wide enough to turn around the twenty-mule team wagons that had brought the mine supplies and machinery to Telluride before the railroad reached there in the 1890s.

The winter-battered, steep-roofed houses faced each other like ragged union soldiers in a Confederate prison camp. Black coal smoke and white wood smoke poured from the crumbling red brick chimneys. Telluride still looked like its 1890s beginnings.

Blue smoke haze in the air signaled winter and its coming deep snow pack. The Spanish empire's explorers had stopped short of what was now the Silverton, Rico and Telluride gold and silver mining district. They camped in the town of Delores, Colorado, sixty miles south of Telluride. The mining district became the richest in the world from 1880 until the silver crash in 1902. The Spanish conquistadors had heard the legend of the golden cities in the Southwest and they seized large gold nuggets from the Ute Indians on the southern edge of the San Juan Mountains and the western flanks of the Sangre de Cristo Range in south central Colorado. They had governed southern Colorado as part of the province of New Spain (now New Mexico). They never discovered the location of the nugget's rich gold vein sources because they were hidden high in the rugged river valleys of the San Juan Mountain's Uncompahgre Forest. The secret trails into the mountains had been protected by the fierce Ute bands. If the Spanish had found the mother lodes then, Telluride would have been part of Spain and there might not have been a Mexican Revolution in 1822.

The sound of the Jeep echoed off the box canyon walls. The only new addition Cooper noted was a long double-chaired ski lift up the steep south wall. The chairs were eerily still in the late afternoon sun. The new lifts carried skiers into the sky like the old underground ones carried men into the mining tunnels. Cooper wondered who the new snow "miners" were. He knew there was a chance they would clash with the sprawling YBarC over control of the region's water rights and a vast chunk of its land.

The long closed red brick New Sheridan Hotel, with its faded painted work-jeans ad on its west side, was under renovation. Cooper pulled into a parking place in front of its bar, which had been open every day since the 1890s except during prohibition. The four o'clock shift of United Mine Workers gold and silver miners would soon be heading to it from the Newmont mine head and mill.

Some of the mine workers' families had worked the tunnels that honey-combed for 300 miles under the mountains and connected with Ouray, Colorado on the east face of Ajax since 1890. Cooper's boyhood impressions of the hardrock miners were that they drank heavily, were tough, poor-spoken men who lived half their lives in cramped, wet, cold underground tunnels in return for good paying union wages.

Still, most remained poor, never breaking the economic cycles of boom and bust between wars while they paid high rents and food costs in isolated lonely posts like Telluride. Their sons often dropped out of school by the eighth grade to work underground. The miners were trapped, it seemed to Cooper, like ancient bugs in fossilized amber. Their captors were the investment bankers, absentee owners, landlords and the company store. But, they drank good bourbon and ate prime YBarC steaks.

Cooper was relieved the New Sheridan Bar was empty except for a lean, graying blonde

Finn bartender in his starched cotton shirt and white apron. He stood silently behind the polished, hand carved mahogany bar with its shiny brass boot rail. The back bar mirrors reached to the tin-plated ceiling of Telluride's oldest working man's sanctuary.

The scarred Finn with a wandering glass eye did not look directly at Cooper when he asked, "What'll you have, mister?"

"A long neck Coors with a shot of Canadian reserve whiskey."

The Finn didn't move a face muscle as he turned to reach for the house's best whiskey. He silently watched Cooper in the bar mirror, a habit from the old days when men packed side arms. Cooper had the plastic handled .22 under his tan corduroy Western sports jacket which was a Christmas present from Liz. She had always dressed Cooper well and insisted he dress up for meetings.

The Finn turned, "Ice, mister?"

"Just a shot glass, thanks."

From a silver money clip Cooper peeled off a ten-dollar bill and laid it on the polished bar. Cooper tossed the shot down and it burned smoothly, throat to stomach, where it hit like a firecracker. Cooper chased the shot with the icy cold Coors as he heard Bob Dylan's "Nashville Skyline" cue up on a jukebox in front of a row of stained-glass panels that partitioned the paneled room at the end of the bar.

Sue, the picnic table blonde from the river bank, walked around the partition. Cooper had the matchbook cover in his shirt pocket; he had intended to call her from the bar's pay phone after the bank meeting. She was wearing crotch tight jeans, with a Pendleton shirt unbuttoned to her midriff. The profile of her braless, tanned round breasts was visible. The Finn looked away coldly. He clearly didn't like this woman in the Telluride boys club. She was trouble, to his old experienced eyes, potential dynamite if she lingered alone after the miners had a few shots and beers.

Sue recognized Cooper instantly and walked toward him. "So, Cowboy, you come to town to drink like the rest of us mortals."

"You bet, young ranchers are a big lonely hearts club."

She froze a pout in the corner of fine, full pink lips. Her shoulders sagged a bit, pushing her breasts against the thin, fine loomed wool.

"Name's Sue. I think you know that. I presume you can read phone numbers inside matchbook covers. You already know the best part of me," she teased.

The Finn shifted uneasily.

"Bet that matchbook's in your shirt pocket over your heart," she taunted.

She stopped a foot from Cooper as he, still partially facing the mirror, watched her image in it.

"You're in my town now, Cowboy, and times they are a changin'," she said, mocking Dylan's wail on the jukebox. "Pickup trucks are out, Cowboy, and hot tubs are in around here. Let's slow dance."

The Finn ducked under the bar and disappeared behind the stained glass partition.

Cooper turned and handed her the matchbook from his pocket. "Sue, here's the matchbook. What's it good for?"

Without hesitation, she tore its cover with her phone number off the row of cheap paper matches and tossed them on the bar. She creased the cover and unzipped her beltless jeans in one motion, revealing her hairless vee. She stuck the cover's edge into the top of her still hidden opening, shifted her weight, opened her thighs and closed her eyes. Then she withdrew the creased matchbook cover while she zipped up her jeans. She placed the tip of the matchbook cover against Cooper's left nostril. Her sweet perfume caught his inhale, her message delivered swiftly and effectively.

"Call me after your meeting at the bank, Cowboy." She stuffed the matchbook cover back into Cooper's shirt pocket, brushing his nipple deliberately with her finger tips.

"How'd you know that? You work at the bank?"

"No, Cowboy, but Sam Jr. said you were coming to Telluride today. We hot tubbed at Gary's last night. I thought, cowboy with a brown CJ5 Jeep and a big ranch coming to town must be you. So, in case you didn't call I thought I'd wait here. I like to ride horses."

"What about your girlfriend?"

"It was an experiment, Cowboy. Too much blow, too many mushrooms, Maui pot, and the woods. She finally broke my resistance. Girl's tongues aren't big enough for me, Cowboy, and I kind of like the effect that my smooth, shiny pussy has on a man."

Cooper took a swig.

"Finish your beer, Cowboy. It's five to four and Sam Jr. doesn't like to be kept waiting at quitting time."

"I'll wait by the phone. Sam likes short meetings. Everything is short about Sam," she laughed almost sadly. "Got a full name, Cowboy?"

The Finn shuffled from behind the partition and ducked under the bar.

Cooper replied, "Cooper Stuart. Ranch is the YBarC."

The Finn stared with tight lipped respect toward Cooper.

"Well, Cooper," she replied, "all I want is a cowboy with a hard dick and a string of horses. I'll bring the rest to the party."

The Finn hit a cash register key hard and its loud jangle announced the end of round one, at least in his barroom.

"Stay by the phone. Maybe I'll break a horse just for you at the ranch and then we'll party."

SEVEN

I Raise You and Call You

T he walk to the bank amazed Cooper. Colorado Avenue's store fronts were changing. Two doors east of the bar was a liquor store with $20 bottles of wine and a gray cat in the window. A few doors down was a ski shop with a window full of expensive plastic ski boots, nylon designer jackets, fiberglass skis and aluminum poles with plastic baskets. Cooper stared in awe. He had not skied since boarding school when he and a busload of classmates spent their March vacation at the Taos Ski Valley in Ernie Blake's legendary ski school. Cooper fondly remembered his metal seven-foot long Head skis, lace-up leather boots, bamboo poles with baskets, red gators, jeans, a surplus green Army jacket and a red bandana.

Ernie's ski school honcho Jean Mayer would run the twenty or so high school boys up and down Kachina Peak until they were butt sore and exhausted. Ernie, however, would not tell them where his infamous Martini Tree was located. Jean Mayer fed them French cooking every night in his Saint Bernard Inn where they stayed and drank red wine under the radar.

Ernie had come from the Swiss German alps and was determined to spend his life developing great skiers from the grandsons of gunslingers, ranchers, Confederate raiders, bootleggers, miners, loggers and gamblers.

Next to the bank was a real estate office with six new Polaroids of houses with typed descriptions and sale prices taped to its window. Cooper was shocked to read, that a one-story, dilapidated brick mining Victorian with a side yard going for $60,000 - owner will carry half. The house would have sold for $2,000 while Cooper was in the Peace Corps in 1970.

He wondered what the YBarC was worth now that the ski resort was open. The YBarC had historically acquired grazing land at $10 to $400 per acre depending on water rights, irrigated hay potential, fences, state and county road access. The ranch currently had 30,000 acres of deeded grazing land and 2,000 irrigated acres on the Lone Cone Ditch. It leased 25,000 BLM acres from the Federal Government in Northern Arizona for winter grazing.

The ranch controlled senior water rights which included Lone Cone Ditch shares, Delores River rights and San Miguel River water rights. The only other major water rights holders in San Miguel County were Newmont Mining and the town of Telluride. Liz had written to Cooper while he was in the Peace Corps that the Mountain and Southern Utes were trying to reclaim the ranch's Delores River water rights.

The ranch had five times the water rights it needed for a normal rainfall year but Cooper's great-grandfather and grandfather believed there were no normal rainfall years in the high Colorado Plateau region.

The Anasazi had simply walked away from their homes and vanished from the region seven hundred years ago during sustained drought. The YBarC had an Anasazi site on its northwest side in Norwood Canyon. The snow melt was the region's lifeline so the YBarC had hedged its water rights over the years. It had even borrowed in the depression to buy out failing 160-acre homesteads along the two rivers to consolidate its senior water rights.

Cooper knew that the YBarC's senior water rights could shut the town of Telluride's San Miguel River water off in dry years. The YBarC played cattle poker in the arid region but its ace in the hole was its large adjudicated water appropriation.

As Cooper walked to the bank he calculated that a three to five-year drought would wreck the new ski area. Then the gray cat in the liquor store would be drinking only Thunderbird wine like down and out Basque sheepherders.

Cooper walked through the glass doors of the ninety-year-old bank building. He noted churches still had heavy bronze and wooden doors while banks had modern glass doors which were easily smashed. The bank didn't even have a guard with a Smith and Wesson revolver in the lobby anymore. The old hand-painted steel vault door was wide open at 4:10 in the afternoon. Butch Cassidy and The Sundance Kid, would have loved the 1970s.

Margie, now white haired, looked up from her battered Frank Lloyd Wright deco desk in front of Sam Jr.'s door. The bank had probably acquired the desk in some forgotten mine owner's house foreclosure. Kentucky walnut paneling and mahogany teller's cages with polished brass bars reflected the light from converted Tiffany shaded gas lights. The tin ceiling was polished to perfection. Cooper noted the bank president's office no longer resided behind an oak door but had a double glass one, which allowed Sam Jr. to watch the three tellers and the lobby. Cooper assumed it was a new-fangled bank management practice but it provided no privacy for customer meetings.

"Why Cooper, I hardly recognize you, it's been so many years. You look like your granddaddy. It's like seeing a handsome ghost," Margie peeped.

A young tall dirty blonde ghost, Cooper thought, as he stopped in front of her desk.

"Sam Jr.'s ready to meet with you. In fact, you're late, Cooper," Margie said in a wary voice.

Cooper caught her coded warning. Cooper opened Sam's door and walked into the office he had last been in with his grandfather.

Sam Jr. had not turned out well physically. His father Sam Sr. had been a six-foot, silver-haired, courtly man, in a rugged western way. His grandfather had left the family bank to Sam Sr.'s eldest brother, and acquired four small-town banks for the other four sons. Sam

Sr. chose the failed Telluride bank because he believed the region's mines and ranches would boom if the United States entered World War II.

Sam Jr.'s mom was one of the town tragedies. His middle-aged father had married the eighteen-year-old Sara LaSalle the half-Mexican, half-Irish daughter of a Roma Saloon bartender. It was whispered locally her gigantic breasts and heart shaped bottom swept Sam Sr. off his feet. The quickly troubled marriage lasted ten years until Sara drank herself to death.

Sam Jr., nearing middle age, had inherited his mother's genes. He was overweight, with thin lips, with a vacant too-round face, dull blue eyes and slicked-back black hair. He wore a white Brooks Brothers dress shirt, gray suspenders, and a bow tie, which looked odd in the Southwest.

Cooper took the offensive, "Sam Jr., it's been seven years since I've been in Telluride. I've seen some of the world since then. Let's catch-up."

"Well, Cooper, you've got mixed reviews in the county. A lot of folks are still angry you didn't join up for Vietnam. They don't understand this Peace Corps deal - not even the Catholics here in town that voted for that asshole Irish bootlegger's kid, Jack Kennedy."

Cooper knew his decision to stay out of Vietnam was unpopular, but the YBarC had never run a popularity contest.

"Sit down, Cooper. You want some coffee or a Coke? Margie will get it for you."

"I'm fine, thanks. Let's get down to business if you are short of time. Liz is quit-claiming her guardianship and therefore life estate in the ranch to me," Cooper begun. "Liz is moving to Montrose. She says she's been borrowing from you regularly, interest only paid the last few years."

"That's true. The YBarC is up to $610,000 at prime plus one, which is ten percent per annum. You've got $61,000 in interest due the week after you ship calves with only $42,000 on hand in the bank in 90-day CD's and your checking account."

"Well I'll need interest only this year and probably four years more to pay the principal down," Cooper stated. "I need time to reverse the negative cash flow. There are too many hands who are paid too much, living too well and probably stealing some, too. I need to improve the fences and add new rolling stock."

"Cooper, I'm going to be frank. You don't have five years. I've been too lenient with Liz and the state bank auditors are on my ass. The bank's got too much of its loan capital in the YBarC and the mine is in trouble again and will probably close by the end of the decade."

Cooper sat silently in shock. The bank had never called a YBarC note.

Sam continued, "Business is changing in Telluride, Cooper. Skiing is our new business and it's going to boom. Mining is busted again. The bank needs its loan capital for the local real estate market to help develop a hotel rooms, restaurants and new retail for the ski area, not feed mother cows and produce calves."

"The ski area needs water; the YBarC, the town, and the mine own most of it. The YBarC has all the water the Ajax Ski Company needs to make snow during drought years and flush

15,000 toilets by the end of the century six times a day. The Ajax Ski Company also wants your land for future thirty-five-acre ranchettes for rich bored city people who want to experience the west while they ski and hike. It's a perfect deal, Cooper. I'm going to broker it for you."

"The YBarC is not for sale!" a shocked Cooper shouted.

"Cooper, no one's run the ranch since your grandfather's death. You're out of the loop. The deal's fair, Cooper. Lonnie Halstrom Jr., whose father owns the Ajax Ski Company, will buy the YBarC for a million dollars, 50-50 cash and Ajax Ski Corporation stock plus pay off your loan and interest at closing. You keep your aging 2,000 mother cows, the rolling stock, horses, your Arizona BLM leases and the headquarters house on its section of land. You can start a new ranch or cash out and clip coupons and chase Arizona ski bunnies. The stock is preferred with a six percent annual dividend. I wish I could charge you a commission on this deal, Cooper, but I can't by law."

He smiled, his thin unpleasant lips continuing, "Margie has the paper work. Take it home, have the notary in Norwood witness your signatures on the contract. Bring it back to me by this time next week and the deal is closed."

"I will have a cashier's check for $500,000 dollars and the preferred stock certificates, which you can put in your lock box here. Lonnie Jr. will be here for the closing."

Cooper knew Lonnie Jr.'s father was an ex-bootlegger from Cortez who now owned a uranium mill at Naturita, which had long been rumored to be polluting the San Miguel River west of the YBarC holdings. He wanted no part of the family.

"Keep your paperwork, Sam. You do not own or speak for the YBarC."

"Hear me, Cooper, the YBarC will be sold on the courthouse steps unless you have $61,000 in interest and $610,000 in principle one month from today when the state banking regulations say it's due. Call your hotshot attorney uncle over in Fairplay and have him review the contract and your loan documents. The YBarC's dance is over in San Miguel County. And Cowboy," he paused with rage visible on his face. "Stay away from Sue girlie. She is my private pussie cat."

He promptly buzzed Margie and told her to bring Cooper the paperwork.

Margie opened the door with a stricken look on her face and handed Cooper a manila file folder. Cooper took it without a word, and turned on his dress boot heels and tore it in four equal pieces, which he threw on Sam Jr.'s desk. Tears formed in the corner of Cooper's eyes as he walked out of the office. The YBarC was his family's home and way of life. He would defend it until death.

Sam Jr. screamed, "You fucking ranch brat. I'll screw you and the YBarC for this."

"I'll call my Uncle Harvey who is the ranch's attorney," Cooper said over his shoulder. "I am sure he can handle the this matter. He knows the Colorado State banking. I have to boogie. I have a hot tub date with Sue."

Cooper felt his anger retreat and his strength build with each step he took toward the

New Sheridan. The last light from the west played with a low cloudbank setting off a spectacular sunset, which turned the gray granite canyon wall into soft pink - a disarmingly peaceful color. The golden Aspen's shimmered on the canyon walls. The southwestern breeze brought in the chill of gunmen long dead as smoke curled from a hundred brick chimneys.

EIGHT

Early Show

The roar of the five o'clock crowd in the New Sheridan Bar boomed onto Colorado Avenue when Cooper pulled open the heavy hardwood-paneled double glass doors. Fifty or so wan-faced miners and union pensioners were drinking up their weekly wages and monthly allotments at the bar. Sitting around the tables opposite the bar in the battered Captain's chairs were a few young, suntanned carpenters, returning ski town workers, and a couple of LA custom western-wear, duded-up, mustached, tanned twentysomethings with hundred dollar bills openly displayed under empty drink glasses. A New England Ivy League trust funder in a button down blue Gant shirt and khakis with a Brahmin face looked as out of place as a Norman Rockwell painting.

Johnny Cash blared on the juke box with some very tight Nashville studio musicians. Cooper eased up to the end of the bar and looked up into high tilted mirror located above the back bar's mirror. It had been mounted there to protect the drinker's backs in the rough and tumble boom days of the early 1890s when claim jumpers and hired gunmen shot or knifed miners for their gold and silver claims in the mountains around Telluride. Cooper was startled by a hard tap on his blind side left shoulder and reflexively started to reach for his .22 pistol under his jacket.

"Must be the genuine Cooper Stuart. You look jest like yer granddaddy."

"You're dead, Hardrock."

"Then you are part Blue Bob Thompson the YBarC's greatest gun hand, by God." And the stout eighty-five-year-old hardrock miner laughed in a gravelly voice because he had chewed too much tobacco and drank too many shots.

Hardrock, who started delivering the Telluride Times to the New Sheridan Bar at age five, was one of the miners Cooper's grandfather had befriended because he bought beef for the Tomboy Mining Camp above Telluride and he provided a listening post for the ranch among the miners. Hardrock had also sold the Stuart's "lunch pail" gold nuggets for cash during the depression, which the miners smuggled past the owner's security guards during their shift changes. Cooper noted Liz had neglected to mention if the gold nuggets still existed and he made a mental note ask her. He knew they were not kept in the bank's lockbox.

"Hardrock, I thought you might be sleeping in Boot Hill by now next to Blue Bob Thompson."

"Blue Bob sure cleaned them no count drunken square chested Basque sheepmen off Wilson Mesa for your great-granddaddy. Son, I know you are not a coward for not fighting in Vietnam - not a dime of hard rock gold and silver to be had there, not even a cow pasture just rice paddies. Only them Chinamen that build the Hangin' Flume on the Delores River ate that stuff with their opium."

Cooper looked up at black haired mustached ski bum bartender who had joined the Finn, "Two shots and two long neck Coors."

"Vodka shots?"

"Canadian reserve whiskey," Cooper said as he placed two twenty dollar bills on the polished bar.

Cooper turned back to Hardrock and fished, "Been gone almost ten years and things sure changed around here, I suspect."

"Cooper this ski area's something, by God. My niece, Ella, just sold her three-bedroom brick Victorian house up Oak Street for $30,000. Three years ago, you couldn't have sold it for back taxes. Cash at closing, bundles of one hundred bills. Buyer some dark Spanish speaker from Miami, Florida, with a real Swedish blonde wife. I was weaned on a young Swedish whore on the southside by my daddy at fourteen the year I went underground."

Cooper thought to himself that miners marked their lives by four events. Their first whore, their first trip underground for pay with a lunch pail and a headlamp, their first son destined to follow them into the tunnels, and that flash before the fatal blast that injured them or killed a fellow miner.

"You going to sell out too, Hardrock."

"Can't Cooper. Too blind to follow a path to the New Sheridan from another house, plus I got a southside block with no neighbors since the 1944 fire. But I sure would like to have one of them Swedish girls one more time before I die. Dem damn Ajax Ski Company owners closed the last house on the southside and chased all three whores out of town."

Cooper made another mental note to help his family friend.

"The Ajax Ski Company is trying to run everything in town Cooper, maybe the county, I hear. New town council fired the long time marshal. Brought in some kid looks like a hippie who wouldn't know where a gambler kept his Derringer hid. Sheriff can't help you much in town limits. You watch your back. They put Jerry "The Swede", the best dynamite man in the mine, in jail last night for jest throwin' a punch in here after drinking twelve beers and twelve shots after his shift and he didn't even blow nothin' up. Mining company can't even help. Bad for the town's image. They say skiers don't like barroom brawls. They spend a hundred dollars a day to ski and stay here and don't even get no local pussy for that. Go figure Cooper."

"Where is the big cash money I see on the tables coming from, Hardrock?"

Hardrock replied in an almost too hard to hear whisper, "I ain't seen so many hundred dollar bills in this bar since prohibition when the bootleggers drank here after midnight. Half of them roll up because they say them fancy western big hat no cattle dudes over there selling opium jest like the Chinamen did at their laundry. Only dis opium you snort not smoke. One hundred dollars a gram thay say. Golds only a hundred an ounce posted price."

"Bingo!" popped out of Cooper's mouth before he could stop himself. Cocaine had replaced Chinese whorehouse opium in Telluride. Cooper had read about a big bust in Aspen. History always repeated itself.

"Thanks Hardrock. I just have these ol' twenties…they won't impress anyone, especially that long-legged blonde with them dudes at the window table."

"Cooper, you get two of them blondies and we will turn back the clock to the ol' days. We'll dance them on Saturday night 'til their panties is all wet then fuck them 'til the church bell calls us on Sunday morn."

Cooper knew Hardrock believed he'd been kept safe in the mines due to his never having missed mass at the Catholic Church and never marrying.

"Hardrock, I have to make a payphone call," Cooper said as he glanced at his watch and saw it was already 5:30. "You hold down the bar for me and if I don't make it back by last call, cash us out here with these twenties."

Cooper walked across the narrow barroom and pushed open a door that connected to the hotel lobby and the bathrooms. He pulled the match book cover out of his pocket and dialed Sue's number into the aging black payphone. It rang twice.

"Hello Cooper. Sam said not to talk to you but he had to go home for dinner. Hot tub and drinks here. Pick up a fifth of Russian vodka. I'm on upper North Oak Street, in the only freshly painted white Victorian. Hot tub water's 105 degrees and I'm 115, cowboy. Sam Jr. gets hand jobs, but you like the real thing, I bet. 'Bye."

The phone went dead as a constant flow of men and women in the narrow hallway jostled Cooper as they entered and exited the bathrooms.

Ten minutes later Sue answered his knock wearing a breast-to-floor length beach towel with a Scottsdale hotel logo. She led him silently by the hand straight to the glass enclosed hot tub room through three expensive antique-filled rooms. The steamed-up glass enclosure was filled with bright green tropical potted plants.

Sue dropped the blue beach towel at the edge of the sunken hot tub.

She stepped into the steaming mist, firm buttocks disappearing as she sank under the bubbling water and said, "Cowboy - or Cooper, I should say. Disrobe and come in. No swimsuit or underwear needed in Telluride."

"Okay, your party, your rules." He undressed and climbed into the soothing hot swirling water.

"You smoke pot, Cooper?" She pulled a half-smoked joint from the hot tub's redwood deck, lit it with a lighter and took a toke.

"Yes, even cowboys smoke pot nowadays." He took it from her dry hand and enjoyed a long hit, his first since Fiji.

The pot was smooth and expensive. It both relaxed and sexually aroused Cooper. He had another hit and passed it back to Sue.

"It's for great sex, Cowboy. I have a dozen kinds, but for you, tonight, it's special Maui."

"Why me? Why now?"

"Because I'm bored, Cowboy, and I'm horny and you are interesting. Gary, my ex-playmate and owner of the house, has been gone a month on business," she replied.

Cooper felt her breasts float into his chest as she perched, legs spread apart, on his rider's thighs.

"Not in here, Cowboy. Knocks me out early if I fuck in the hot water," and she stroked his dick. "I bet you have not had a girl out on the big ranch in a long time."

Sue scooted over the slick side of the hot tub and the lean but well-muscled Cooper followed. She stretched out her beach towel onto some oversized cushions on the deck and rolled over onto her back with her knees bent. Cooper eyes worked down from her blue eyes and high cheekbones to her full breasts to her newly shaved triangle ending on her open firm thighs. The hot tub jets cycled off as music from a San Francisco rock band played from small overhead stereo speakers.

Cooper stood over her, admiring her perfect, tan, lithe young body. Sue reached under the side of the cushions and produced a glass vial with a black top with white powder inside. Cooper was puzzled.

Sue caught his look. "This is cocaine, Cowboy. Ever have it?"

"No, heard rumors that our Mexican winter hands in Arizona use it on big occasions."

"It's great for sex. It needs you and you need it tonight. Roll a hundred if you have one."

Cooper fished a fifty out of his jeans pocket and rolled it up. Sue dried her triangle off with the edge of the beach towel, opened the vial and spread two thin lines of fine white powder along the edge of her now dry smooth vagina lips.

"Snort the lines with the rolled up fifty, Cooper and then lick me clean." She purred. She relaxed, arms above head, back arched slightly, the petite vial still in her left hand.

Cooper knelt and easily snorted the white line on the left lip of her pink opening, breathing in her sweet scent. The fine white powder hit his brain like a rifle bullet. His pulse quickened as his dick seemed to enlarge and harden simultaneously.

He snorted the second line, dropped the rolled bill between Sue's thighs as his tongue hit the white power on her lips and then her clit. Cooper's lips and gums went numb as he licked her pink opening and his brain revved into sensual sensory mode.

Sue snorted the last of the white powder into her left nostril and tossed the vial onto the deck.

"Take me now and take me deep, Cowboy." And she arched her pelvis into the air, hips raised, weight on her elbows and shoulders, breasts stretched firm across her chest, nipples taut.

Cooper entered her in an easy motion. His thoughts and common sense had been erased by the alcohol, pot and coke pulsing through his brain.

The effect was erotic as his penis parted her tight, wet opening that contracted with each deep hard thrust. Their touch was magnetic and intense as the cocaine dislocated real time.

Sue seemed wetter, hotter, tighter, deeper than his memory of other women. His thrust seemed more rhythmic and powerful with the aid of the white powder. There was no urgency to come - just ride the wild Telluride woman. They came together twenty minutes later, Sue's legs pinned by Cooper's arms, with four deep thrusts that seemed to end at the edge of her lungs. He exploded into her as she orgasmed. Sue laughed and cried simultaneously as she teased the skin on his hips with her fingernails. Her orgasm ended like a gunshot.

"Great orgasm, Cowboy," she smiled. "The white powder is always magic the first time. Wish I could get back there again. We need another half gram. Stay here, I'll take the fifty and run down to Jack's house. Gary locks his up in the safe when I'm housesitting. Doesn't want to kill me, he says. Be back in five."

She struggled free of Cooper's arms, which still pinned her and rolled out from under him, her hard nipples raking his wet chest. Cooper languished in near bliss, her sexuality still pulsing thru his addicted body. It would be a long perfect night.

Hardrock was right, the new opium had returned to Telluride.

NINE

The Morning After

Cooper woke up at first light in the solar greenhouse hot tub room. He slowly pieced together the night's events in his still buzzing mind. He had slept only two hours.

Sue, the coke angel, slept face down on her stomach with her head buried under a large down pillow. Rays of sun accented her nude bottom in the cool morning mountain air. An empty glass vial with its missing black plastic cap lay on the floor near her blonde head. Cooper lay on his long back covered by a Navajo blanket. He surveyed the clothing strewn around the hot tub as mist dripped from the glass panels in the early light.

Cooper silently rolled up onto his feet, his eyes following the beautiful curve of Sue's strong back, her round firm hips and tanned athletic legs. He could still smell her sweet scent as he tried to regulate his breath, yoga style, to control his searing hangover. Cooper tried to dress quietly but stumbled against the oversize cushion as he pulled his jeans on to hide his rapidly hardening dick.

Sue rolled over and opened her blue eyes. "Don't wake me up so early cowboy unless you want to play."

She pulled her knees up against her flat stomach. Her breasts flattened against her chest.

"Got to return to the ranch and get the round up organized."

"You, Cowboy, have to pay Sam Jr. in a month or you're on the street. But Sam can make you big rich."

"Sam tell you that?"

"Sam has a sloppy mouth after a line of blow. No secrets in the big ditch, Cowboy, the canyon walls have eyes and ears."

Cooper angrily made a point. He bent over, grasped her thin ankles with his right hand and pushed her knees against her flattened breasts. "Don't discuss the YBarC bank business around town."

"I understand, but I can't stop Sam's mouth. I can help you. Gary's developing a liftside condo project and he needs one more investor. Sam turned him down but I can introduce you to Gary. There's money to made, according to Gary. That would help your ranch and fuck Sam because he is hoping Gary will lose his option on the lot so he and his pals can buy the site."

33

Cooper blinked but replied coolly, "YBarC's in the Norwood phone book. Call me and I'll drive over to meet with Gary."

"Can do. Now release me from cowboy bondage and lick my very wet clit and have a breakfast snack before you bust your zipper."

Cooper released his grip on Sue's ankles and started to retreat but she rolled to her knees and pulled his beltless jeans down in a quick motion. His dick was in her mouth before he could utter a protest. Early breakfast at the Iron Ladle would have to wait.

A half hour later Cooper approached his Jeep on a deserted Colorado Avenue and it had a parking ticket under its wiper. Cooper didn't even know Telluride had parking tickets. He tossed it into the gutter with a belly laugh.

Over his shoulder he heard, "You drop something buddy?"

He turned to face the hippie looking town marshal. "October first starts snow removal season and your Jeep could have been towed to the impound lot if it snowed last night. See the sign up the street?"

Cooper stepped toward his Jeep and opened the door as the marshal reached down, picked up the ticket and reattached it to the windshield under the wiper.

"Nightshift says you were at Sue's in the hot tub room all night probably doing drugs. We patrol the alleys these days to look after the second homes," he said proudly.

Cooper was surprised for a second time as his empty stomach rumbled.

"We don't take kindly to peeping Toms in the west, Tin Badge," and he slammed the Jeep door shut and revved the engine.

"You watch your tongue, Cowboy. Finn bartender told me who you are. Miners and cowboys done busting-up this town. You going to take my ticket off your windshield."

Cooper couldn't remember a law requiring him to remove the ticket, nor could he remember the YBarC ever paying a parking ticket. So, he gunned the Jeep out of the parking place, its off-road tires creating a cloud of dust as he sped toward the ranch. The ticket flapped furiously in the wind before it flew over a cliff as the Jeep sped down Keystone Hill.

TEN

The New Deal

A s cocktails were served in the corner booth of Adrianna's Spanish Bistro. Gary introduced himself to Cooper. Sue sipped a Russian vodka martini, a faint coke ring visible
in her left nostril after a trip to the ladies' room.

"Name's Gary Pecos, like the river where sweet melons grow in Texas. My family's from
there by way of Houston since World War II - some oil business, but melons, too. I have business in Phoenix now."

One thing Cooper knew at first sight, the pock-marked Gary wasn't an oil man. His
family might have worked in a refinery in Houston but they did not own oil production. If
Gary had Texas oil dollars he would not be pitching Cooper the condo deal.

Cooper politely probed, "Enjoyed your hospitality in absentia."

Gary bit, "You're always welcome at the hot tub. After we finish up dinner and I pitch
the condo deal, we'll initial a reservation contract in the hot tub room with Sue and our
waitress Jenny as witnesses, so to speak."

The smell of olive oil and garlic filled Cooper's nostrils. The twenty white laced-cov-
ered tables and half dozen booths were in the old ballroom of the New Sheridan Hotel where
Taos school oil paintings and New Mexico religious art decorated the walls.

The hotel ballroom had been closed Cooper's entire adult life. Local legend had it that
big mining deals of the 1890s had been completed in the old leather booths with pull curtains. During Prohibition, mining camp whores supposedly gave the bootleggers and their
prized customers sexual favors behind closed curtains. There hadn't been Spanish food near
Telluride since the Conquistadors gave up looking for gold and silver.

"Adrianna darling, you look beautiful. Meet Cooper Stuart, owner of the YBarC," Gary
said to a stunning Spanish woman walking by.

Cooper noted the woman's brown black pupils locked on him like fighter plane radar.
Adrianna was beautiful and in her twenties. Her black straight hair flowed to her small waist,
which widened into round firm hips that balanced her large full breasts. Her oval eyes were
home to marble-sized pupils, separated by a Roman nose. A Roman Legion commander
must have made love to her Spanish mother 2,000 years ago to produce her cheekbones.

Cooper involuntarily mentally undressed her. Their eyes remained locked. Her breasts would be tipped with half-dollar sized dark brown nipples. Her olive body would be soft-skinned, covering muscles of steel, with her thick black pubic hair making an erotic triangular bed. Her pure Latin blood was cool now, but in bed it would sear a man's spirit when he drank from the ancient fountain.

"Please, gentlemen, rest in my cantina. Eat, be well, talk, as winter nears. Smell the pinon fire and drink my Spanish Rioja wine."

"Perfecto," Cooper uncoolly blurted out.

"This is Jenny, your waitress for the evening." A tall thin woman with long red hair braided to her waist appeared at Adrianna's side.

"I will select your dishes and wine tonight and join you for the main course, if I may. Jenny will take your cocktail orders."

Adrianna vanished as Gary ordered, "A pitcher of Martinis for the table and you at my hot tub at eleven."

Jenny blushed and turned toward the bar. Sue giggled.

Gary continued, "Adrianna opened the Bistro last ski season. The ballroom had been locked up for years."

"The last Mule Skinners Ball was here in the early fifties, the night Billy Joe Smith, the town druggist, shot Matt James, a mine foreman, in the forehead on the dance floor at midnight, killing him," Cooper said.

"Adrianna never told me that story," Gary asserted.

"Not much of a story. Billy Joe Smith saw Matt James in the back seat of his 1951 Chevy Coupe with his wife Helen when he stepped out for a nip in the alley. Her skirt was above her waist and her panties were on the steering wheel. The YBarC still gets a finger painted Christmas card from Billy each year sent from the Salida State prison. He was the family druggist."

"Well that's a great tale, Cooper. You'll have to tell Adrianna yourself. Sue said you might be interested in my condo deal and getting Sam Jr. off all our asses, including Sue's," he paused as Sue frowned.

"I know cattle deals and water deals," Cooper laughed, "but not condo development deals. So, fill me in on the essentials."

Jenny reappeared dressed in a calf length tight light wool skirt for her dinner shift. She served cocktails as Gary flirted with her and Sue pretended she didn't exist.

As her bottom bobbed away from the booth Gary started the pitch, "Deal is simple, partner. The land is $15 a square foot and we build for $75 a square foot and sell for $180 a square foot doubling our money, less real estate commissions which are a necessary evil. The project is for 50 two-bedroom condos, so that's a four million profit. My Phoenix bank makes us a four million dollar construction loan and I sell ten shares for $50,000 and I buy half of them. And with the five investors we all co-guarantee the note which is $400,000 per share. At the end of the rainbow, which is six months after completion max in this market, you make $200,000 per share easy money. There's no inventory of condos in Telluride yet, so we control the market."

Cooper ran the numbers in his head. His grandfather had warned him to walk away from any deal where the principal called him partner. He always said "partners were for dancin'."

Two shares cost Cooper $100,000 and produced a net profit of $300,000, which added to three years of calf sales would rid the ranch of Sam Jr.'s bank forever. He needed his Uncle Harvey, one of the state's leading attorneys, to rope and tie down the bank. Cooper figured even if he could buy only one share it would start him toward his goal of paying off the loan.

Cooper asked, "How many shares left in the deal?"

"Two shares, partner."

"I'm in for one after my family attorney reviews the paperwork. Maybe a second in January after the final calf payment."

"Well, partner, you sign the reservation agreement in the hot tub room after dinner and we pop champagne with Sue and Jenny. I supply and buy. Sue celebrates her finder's fee. You have four weeks to pay up or the deal moves on."

Cooper wondered what Jenny would look like in the hot tub.

"Works for me," Cooper replied smiling at Sue.

Adrianna arrived with a blushing Jenny carrying the tray with their main course. Cooper wondered if Jenny had read his mind.

"Senors and Senoritas, the first course of lamb with Yukon gold potatoes is accompanied by Spanish Rioja."

The Castilian Spanish rolled off her deliciously ruby red lips as she deliberately brushed Cooper's right shoulder with her breasts and Sue frowned, downing her martini. Adrianne sat down next to Cooper across from Sue. Her left hand lightly brushed Cooper's hard mid-thigh as Jenny served the first course.

"Adrianna, Cooper took one share, maybe a second, so I guess your dad will be disappointed," Gary reported.

"He will and he won't, Gary. His gold mine at Redvale is struggling now that Vietnam is over. There are layoffs. My family has invested in nothing but gold and silver for five hundred years. My father has a saying, 'The sun melts the spring snow each year, but a man's desire for gold never melts.' And you, Cooper, you like snow or gold?" She subtly thrust her breasts against her lace blouse so her firm dark nipples formed a translucent outline.

"Snow, Adrianna," Cooper replied transfixed.

"Cattle can't drink or eat gold."

Adrianna's dark brown eyes narrowed, her smile taut as she absorbed Cooper's reply. Her delicate fingers reflexively reached up to touch her gold necklace, her 500-year-old link with Spain. She instinctively knew the ranchero was long in water rights in the arid southwest but short in vaulted gold. Cooper and Adrianna were an old world matchmakers dream. The equal parts of old gold veins and deeded water rights.

Adrianna raised her wine glass and toasted, "Then to snow and gold."

Two hours later Cooper scrambled out of his dusty cowboy boots, as Sue yelled, "Jump in the hot tub my Colorado cowboy. Get wet. Get high."

Cooper joined the party with a big splash. He had signed the condo investment reservation agreement and then secured the package of investment documents in the Jeep. He planned to mail them to Uncle Harvey for review.

Sue carefully picked up the black-topped vial on the edge of the hot tub, along with a tiny antique nose spoon. She expertly filled the shiny spoon with coke and held it up to Cooper's left nostril and he snorted it as she pinched his right nostril closed. Then Sue tooted his other nostril. It hit Cooper's brain instantly and his dick stirred under the bubbling water.

Jenny watched Sue casually as her breasts floated on the swirling water's surface.

Suddenly, Jenny stood up and scooted her bottom onto the varnished deck that ringed the tub, revealing her wet, red-haired triangle. "Too hot, Gary."

Her red-nippled breasts pointed straight out over the tub like German Bratwurst sausages. Cooper stared at her erotic breasts. Sue's hand found Cooper's balls under water and lightly squeezed a message.

"Want to feel them, Cooper?" Jenny smirked and jumped back into the hot tub facing a shocked Cooper. "Eighth wonders of the world, Cowboy. That's if Sue girl here ever lets go of your balls," she giggled.

Sue's free right hand came out of the water and slapped the air full force, narrowly missing Jenny's protruding breasts.

"Girls, girls," Gary said hooting, "this is the 1970s, let's not get excited about our anatomies. Jenny has something special. No use to pretend they ain't here and they aren't fun, right Cooper?"

Sue's grip loosened, but she was red-faced angry so Cooper demurred. "Gary, it's your hot tub, your house rules but I'm sticking with Sue."

Jenny frowned and turned her bare round bottom toward Cooper's face and sat down on Gary's thighs under the bubbling water. Gary's right hand disappeared below the hot water's surface and positioned her for entry.

Sue had enough of Gary's vulgar act. She stood straight up, pulled Cooper out of the hot tub and gathered their clothes. She led him out of the steamy hot tub room, slamming its teak door and bolt locking it. Teary eyed, she toweled Cooper and herself off in the hallway. The coke, vodka and Spanish red wine paralyzed Cooper logic. They dressed in silence. Cooper was unable to take his eyes off Sue until her last western button snapped closed.

"Take me out of Gary's house, Cooper. Fast!"

Gary yelled then pounded on the slide bolted teak door, "Sue! Cooper! The celebration's not over yet. Champagne still in the beer cooler in the kitchen. Don't make us walk around the house to get it. It's twenty degrees outside."

Sue ignored him, silently leading Cooper out the front door onto Oak Street then locking the door behind them. Cooper laughed, realizing if Gary didn't have his key he'd be spending the night with Jenny in the hot tub room.

"Let's go to the Johnstone Inn on West Colorado. It's just been renovated. Used to be a miner's boarding house," Sue whispered.

"Perfect idea, Sue. Just you and me." Sue honestly smiled for the first time in four hours.

ELEVEN

Amigos

C ooper drove east over Engineer Pass, a summer only four-wheel-drive road lit-
tered with closed crumbling mines. He was headed toward Lake City to meet Jesse
Valesquez, a boarding school friend. They planned to play some poker and then go mountain
lion hunting for two days. An old cat had started hunting local dogs and calves near Lake
City, which meant children were next. Colorado State Wildlife had issued a permit to a local
outfitter who was a friend of Cooper and Jesse's to kill the dangerous cat. The western sun's
orange glow filled Cooper's rearview mirror, but after the night at the inn with Sue, his eyes
begged for a nap.

Cooper drove past more aging gold and silver mine structures on the flats by the swiftly
flowing river. Jesse's family had owned the sawmill in nearby Del Norte since the 1890s
when the railroad pushed through to the goldfields of the southern San Juan Mountains.
They also owned the boarded-up Spanish-style railroad hotel in Delores.

Cooper had seen Jesse only once since boarding school but his family's sawmill had
supplied the YBarC with fence posts for the past forty years. The ranch was one of its major
fence post customers. Cooper planned to place the largest order for fence posts in YBarC
history so he could start rebuilding the ranch's two hundred plus miles of battered corral,
cross and range fences. But he needed credit from the saw mill for the order. He would start
after roundup and stop at the first hard freeze, then start again in April. It was phase one of
his game plan to make the YBarC profitable again to keep it out of the bank's hands.

Cooper passed a tall abandoned brick chimney, the remnant of a turn of the century
limestone mill, which marked the entrance to Lake City's summer cabins and its few hard
scrapple ranches. He looked forward to hunting with Jesse, who was descended from the
third governor of New Spain. His family's original timber concession had been granted by
the King of Spain for his relative's service to the impoverished province, which became New
Mexico.

After unpacking in his cabin, Cooper sat at the hand carved oak bar near a roaring pinion fire at the San Luis Inn. The historic inn was on the headwaters of the Rio Grande where
wealthy Texas fly fisherman resided in the summer. Lake City depended on its legendary fly

fishing and elk hunting now that its mines had played out. Cooper had always stayed here with his grandfather. A secret stairwell from behind the bar of the log hotel led downstairs to a prohibition speakeasy and casino. In the fall hunting season the casino hosted nightly $100 dollar limit poker games. Cooper's father had been a Lake City regular after roundup. It was rumored he won $10,000 in a poker game and that on one occasion he lost two of his prize polo ponies to an independent oilman out of Tulsa.

Cooper's attention was broken as a worn but pretty brunette sat down on a bar stool and ordered bourbon with coke. Lake City had some amateur hookers who supplemented their meager incomes with $100 a night flings with the oilmen hunters in the fall. Cooper sipped Canadian reserve whiskey on ice and listened to Hank Williams on the jukebox. He stared at a collection of black and white silver print photos of depression era fly fisherman rumored to have been photographed by Ansel Adams during his WPA days. The photo Cooper was staring at was his grandfather taken in the 1930s.

Cooper's eyes shifted to a fading oil painting of the shootout between the infamous northern New Mexico pistolero, Griego and the ex-confederate gunslinger Clay Allison in the Cimarron Hotel barroom. Griego who often crossed the border to end land and water disputes died at a bar table.

"You fucking gringo, your mother cows are eating every hippie's marijuana patch in the San Juan Mountain National Forest. That's why your cows are high all summer and the hippies want your grazing leases cancelled. De hippies they come and buy corner posts and fence posts for their plots to run wire around dem plants. Four named Henry Thoreau and one named Bobby Seale, dey been to the sawmill this summer. We are making a fortune off the Aspen and Telluride hippies." Jesse belly-laughed, slapping Cooper on the back and almost knocked him off the bar stool.

Jesse was 5'6" and 250 pounds with a 54-inch chest, and legs like cast iron fireplugs. His Conquistador ancestors wore heavy Spanish armor on horseback during their ride from Mexico City to Santa Fe in 1600. They pillaged the pueblos and murdered the Indios in the name of Jesus Christ, the Pope and the Spanish King and Queen.

Their surviving families had worked gold, silver, timber, sheep, horses and cattle from Taos to the Sea of Cortez. They had lost their landed empire to the norteamericanos after the Alamo. Jesse was the guy you wanted at your back in an Albuquerque bar fight. He had been an all-state high school football guard as well as the state heavyweight wrestling champion. Jesse didn't attend college because his dad needed an assistant manager at the sawmill after his uncle died.

"You log head, sit down and have a drink or two or three. Then let's eat some dinner. Make sure the YBarC gets a commission on every fence post you sell to those Telluride pot farming and mushroom picking hippies. It's YBarC cow piles that fertilize their plants."

Jesse ordered a double Spanish gin martini from the ancient bartender.

"Salute, Cooper, to the lion hunt and the first YBarC fence post deal since your

41

grandfather died. I have the contract with me, we just have to fill in blanks for quantity and payment terms. The ranch's credit is still good with the mill but dem hippies and log cabin builders are cash and carry."

"That takes care of business. Fill in fifty miles of new fence posts and corner posts half due after fall calf sales, January one, and half carried at three percent interest month to month. Delivery split yesterday and March 15."

"Bueno, amigo. We'll light the boiler fire and spin the saw blades after the hunt. A truck-load will roll every day until the November hard freeze."

"Then ribeyes on the YBarC and Mr. Henry's Spanish brandy with dessert."

They adjourned to the lantern lit dining room to discuss the hunt. After ribeyes with fresh baked San Luis Valley russets, Cooper and Jesse chased espresso with Spanish brandy. They walked back to their cabins to check and clean their lion hunt guns. The nightly poker game had not materialized but the brunette had disappeared from the bar.

"Bob White still the Marine sergeant Korean War silver-cross by-the-book hunting guide?" Cooper asked.

"You bet, his son Andy's already an all-state half-back at Alamosa High."

"So he's stripping and cleaning his Browning 7mm magnum as we walk."

"You can take that to the bank, Cooper."

Cooper opened the door to his cabin and unpacked his rifle and cleaning kit.

TWELVE

The Hunt

The horses galloped at speed on a narrow rocky dirt trail. Bob was leading, followed by Jesse with Cooper riding drag. Each rider was spaced about twenty yards apart to minimize the trail's fine dust. A mini drought had dried out the San Juan National Forest. Cooper wore a faded red bandana that covered his mouth and nostrils. The Aspen were almost leafless except in one extreme south-facing grove where renegade gold-yellow leaves still shimmered in the fall light.

Cooper, Bob, and Jesse were on a mission. Jesse rode straight-backed ahead of Cooper in the style of a townsman as he bounced too high in the saddle. Each horse had a hand-tooled Spanish saddle from the Russell tack shop in Chama, New Mexico, and oversize saddlebags. Blue Australian oilskin dusters and bedrolls were tied off behind each saddle. Bob's saddle had a three-man nylon tent tied to it in case of a snowstorm; otherwise, the party planned to sleep under the stars in their bedrolls. Five miles into the fifteen-mile ride the last vestiges of civilization disappeared in thickening ponderosa pine and blue spruce forests.

Cooper rode up alongside Jesse, "Sure nice to be riding with no ranch work at the end of the trail."

Telluride National Bank had faded from Cooper's mind. The rhythm of his horse produced a near meditative state broken only when his Browning rifle stock slapped his thigh, reminding him of the group's deadly purpose.

Suddenly the lead horse broke tree line as the trio rode onto a narrow rocky trail that switched back up five hundred yards. Bob slowed the lead horse to a walk. All the horses struggled to retain their footing. Trail dust disappeared as the riders closed to ten yards apart to keep just enough space to dodge a horse and rider that lost their footing. It was a 500 foot plunge off the steep left side of the cirque. Cooper enjoyed the breathtaking view of the alpine valley below as he rode toward the high pass. He could still see Lake City nestled in pine and spruce trees below.

The slow pace allowed Bob to speak for the first time in an hour. "You boys okay back there? Watch your cinches up here. Don't want you to roll over into heaven."

Cooper knew his saddle had been double cinched before he left Lake City but silently wondered about Jesse's. "Real pretty up here. A person can get spoiled fast in this high country."

"Beautiful but bumpy," Jesse cut in. "Next time we hunt let's Jeep and walk. My ass is too fat for this saddle."

"These boys are a little bumpy in low four-wheel drive but they never took a fall up here yet," Bob laughed. "They're as good as Grand Canyon mules."

Colorado mountain humor, Cooper mused. He glanced over his shoulder at Jesse who tightened his thighs against his horse's flanks. A bald eagle rose from her nest in a granite outcropping a hundred feet above Cooper and started a slow spiral into a morning thermal, which was too weak to push her massive body into the cooler air above her. Cooper observed the giant bird's feathers, which were ragged from a summer of diving at high speed to catch deer mice, rattle snakes, marmots, rabbits, and squirrels for her eagle chicks. Eagles were still wild and free in Colorado but Cooper silently wondered how they would adapt to industrial strength tourism.

Three hours later, after a tortured 2,000 foot ride down the south side of the ridgeline the hunters reached an almost completely dry streambed. They dismounted and tied their horses to a blue spruce burnt from lightning. Its gray blue pallor made it a natural sculpture in the extreme alpine landscape.

Toward Pagosa Springs Cooper could see giant groves of golden Aspen in southern Colorado and northern New Mexico. Their gold streaks painted rivers through the pine forests. Bob disappeared to scout. Cooper and Jesse took a one-eye siesta on their bedrolls. Their hats shaded their heads from the bright midday sun. Cooper drifted off, his left ear listening for a horse whinny alert. An hour later, while Cooper dreamed about surfing away from Sam Jr. in Fiji and leaving him on a shark infested reef break, suddenly, one of the horses sounded an alarm. Cooper startled awake. Bob silently emerged from a thick grove of pine trees fifty yards downstream. He cradled his Marlin 306 in his right hand and when he reached Cooper, he leaned the rifle against a gray rotting stump while Jesse snored loudly on his bedroll.

"The old lion drinks about a half mile downstream. There are fresh paw prints and scat from just before dawn. Sundown's about six, so let's eat a bite and set an ambush about four o'clock. Maybe we'll get lucky our first day out," Bob reported.

"Nothing else is going to happen here but a long cold night's sleep under the stars, so let's do it," Cooper replied.

Jesse, lying on his double-wide butt, interjected, "I'm all in boys."

After a snack of Wisconsin cheddar, crackers, sardines in mustard and cookies chased with canteen water, Cooper and Jesse loaded their rifles. Then they put on their orange hunting baseball hats and followed Bob down the rocky creek bed leaving the horses tethered. Their saddlebags were hoisted over a tree limb in case a bear wondered into the campsite. The walk was slow. The creek snaked its way down the head wall eventually emptying into the pristine icy blue lake.

44

The party stopped silently after Bob's hand signal. "Cooper, you take the pool where he drinks for the kill shot. Jesse, you drop below it for the upstream approach shot. I'll cover you boys from a high point. Most likely he'll come upstream from a warm sleeping hole below us if he shows tonight. He might go low, though, to track mule deer now that the cattle are down below for shipping."

It was an hour before dusk as Cooper and Jesse started working their way along tree line downstream. Jesse carried his heavy Spanish hunting rifle. He had a .357 magnum pistol holstered on his waist. Cooper carried a bolt-action Browning 7mm rifle plus his hunting knife. Bob had a high-powered scope on his bolt-action Marlin 306 for the critical fatal shot. He hiked up to cover Cooper and Jesse from the flat top of a large boulder, white hunter style. Each step Cooper advanced toward the ambush point was deliberately quiet.

Cooper stopped above the rocky creek bottom in a blue Spruce grove directly above the lion's drinking pool. He dropped behind a low granite boulder that gave him a clear sight line to the pool. Jesse kept ambling downstream a little too carelessly, Cooper thought, but he was a big man who was carrying a cannon. The sunlight was disappearing quickly as the gray shadows lengthened and the temperature cascaded. It was already below freezing at 11,000 feet and Cooper's shooting hand was numbing under his light deerskin gloves. He stuffed his right hand into his waxed cotton Scottish jacket's pocket to warm it. Then he began to scope his potential kill shot if the old lion was lazy and walked carelessly to his watering hole.

Suddenly Cooper heard a terrifying human scream downstream as he expertly swung his rifle toward it. He sighted in on the edge of the tree line where Jesse should have been. But he was not there. He panned his sight downhill. The mountain lion's large mouth was wrapped around Jesse's neck. The cat had knocked Jesse into the dry streambed and his rifle out of his hands. Cooper heard Bob's Browning rifle fire simultaneously with his retort.

The big cat rolled, his teeth tearing Jessie's artery from his thickly muscled neck. Jesse's right hand futilely struggled to free the .357 Magnum pistol from its holster. Jesse's backward roll had pinned his left arm under his back. The mountain lion, bleeding from his heart, loosened his jaw.

Bob and Cooper both fired a second round into the mountain lion's head, their bolt action rifles snapping in unison as Jesse's powerful right hand flailed at the massive male lion's shoulder. Jesse's fist opened limply as blood spurted from the artery in his neck. The old mountain lion's jaw unclenched in slow motion and it rolled off Jesse like a raindrop dripping off the tip of a pine bough. The massive cat lay stone dead.

Cooper ran at full speed. His rifle felt like a toothpick in his hand. He heard Bob, Marine trained, quietly moving behind him, still on battle alert. Cooper's lungs burned and he guessed the old cat had probably been looking for an ascending hiker or elk hunter, when by cosmic coincidence, he discovered Jesse.

Cooper's heart pounded and his lungs heaved in thin air as he reached Jesse. Bob's

45

vast wilderness experience had been KO'ed by the cat's route change. When Bob reached Cooper neither Jesse nor the mountain lion were moving. Bob fired a coup de grace bullet into the big cat's small brain. Cooper knelt warily and in a lightning smooth knife thrust cut the mountain lion's throat. Jesse's eyes seemed to flicker once, trying to see his assassin. The cat's assault froze Jesse's right hand grotesquely into a fist.

Cooper and Bob quietly administered Jesse his last rites with a blessing consisting of the sign of the cross plus a few of Cooper's boarding school Latin words. Bob expressed no emotion or anger. Jesse had been killed on his watch, but like Cooper, he had known the danger of hunting a calf killing aging mountain lion. Jesse also had long ignored Bob's advice against hunting with heavy antique Spanish guns and pistols instead of modern weapons.

The light was disappearing when Cooper stared over the mountain range toward Del Norte where Jesse's children would be playing in their yard. The kid talk would be happy on a late fall afternoon while their mother prepared dinner and their grandmother watched over them. They would sleep one more night before their reality was altered forever. A single hot and salty tear formed in Cooper's right eye, acting as a prism for the orange rays of the great fireball as it dropped behind the San Juans.

Bob cut the cat's head off with a dozen powerful strokes of his long knife. He hoisted the cat's head into the twilight sky on a sharpened pine pole over the death site. Then he stuck the other end of the pine pole into the hard, rocky soil with a fierce thrust and a roar from the center of his being. Next, he cut cat's heart out, Indian style, and blessed the cat's spirit. Cooper prepared Jesse's body so they could pack it out at first light, while Bob skinned the mountain lion. Its pelt was evidence for the Lake City inquest. Cooper completed his task as the stars provided him light. He felt Jesse's spirit fly into the brisk autumn air and he knew Jesse would visit his children in their dreams tonight before he departed Del Norte for heaven.

THIRTEEN
The Funeral at Del Norte

Cooper sat alone in the adobe Catholic Church at midnight, staring at the open mahogany coffin. The faces of Jesse's children flickered in hundreds of handmade white beeswax candles. A hand carved Virgin Mary, paint fading on her 300-year-old wood, stared down at Jesse with tears in her eyes. The spirits of a thousand Spanish parishioners who had lain in state in the small church paid their respects. A bevy of angels dressed in black embroidered lace dresses and veils formed a choir. A carved wooden half Pueblo Indian, half Spanish priest hovered above the brightly painted altar, a Ute arrow piercing his brown woven robe belted with ancient hemp. Earlier, the elderly Bishop of Santa Fe had blessed Jesse as Cooper watched the priest's solid gold cross perform a Latin ritual lilted by his Castilian Spanish accent.

The spirit mourners passed the coffin, stuffing dollar bills in a faded blue wooden box to the right of the altar. Other mourning spirits brought wild flowers that they dropped into Jesse's open casket.

Earlier in the evening Cooper had watched wave after wave of Jesse's relatives and friends silently and tearfully pay their tribute. When the spirits quieted, Cooper saw an old man appear by the coffin and start to play his Spanish four-string guitar. The ancient Spanish songs filled the cold air of the frontier church. The Castilian words were so pure., Cooper could translate most of the lyrics while his college Spanish lessons floated through his conscious mind. He remembered Jesse's grandmother had once spent a winter being interviewed by a scholar from Madrid who had come to New Mexico's northern Sangre de Cristo Mountains to preserve the Spanish dialect and accent long since lost in Spain, but perfectly preserved in the isolated villages of the New World. The 400-year-old ballads lilted into the sanctuary as they comforted Jesse's spirit. He had listened to them since birth, as had his children, who were being sung to sleep by their ninety-year-old grandmother as they grieved. She would preserve the legend of their father in folk song.

At 1:00 a.m. but without a signal, the balladeer stopped singing and swung his frayed wool guitar strap over his thick shoulder and departed by the priest's door. The silence was immediately broken by a thud as the heavy wooden door opened. Cooper's head turned as the first Pentatente mourner, wearing only burlap shorts, crawled into the sanctuary his scarred knees leaving blood stained streaks on the rough-hewn pine floor. Cooper gasped. He remembered Jesse's grandfather had been a member of this obscure Catholic sect. This secret cult, banned by the Vatican, believed if its members inflicted the pain of Christ's suffering upon themselves, they would be saved. Even in the more tolerant, predominantly Catholic state of New Mexico, the members kept their religious practices away from public view except at Easter. A line of four men, ranging in age from mid-twenties to seventy, crawled down the aisle flagellating each other with small rawhide whips, mumbling prayers in an ancient Spanish rhythm oblivious to Cooper's presence. They left a blood-spattered trail as they halted in front of the Virgin Mary by the altar.

Cooper breathed so silently he could have been pronounced dead by the county coroner. Suddenly, the vaporous angels reappeared over Jesse's coffin, providing a shield. The man on Cooper's left produced an old hammer with a thin head, and a hand-forged nail from his hemp rope waistband; with one quick strike, he drove the nail through his hand into the open casket's wooden side. Blood oozed from the palm wound as the other men chanted a prayer in Spanish. Cooper watched in awe. As suddenly as they had appeared, without even a glance at Cooper, the four men departed through the priest's door.

Cooper hypnotized, gazed at the dark red nail hole in the side of the casket. He wondered why Bob White had assigned Jesse to point instead of him.

The sanctuary door opened behind him again. He heard the night wind rush in as cold air licked his neck. A woman draped in layers of expensive antique black Spanish lace with a thick black veil on a pillbox hat, walked down the aisle. She cradled a small solid gold antique cross in her right hand and dropped rose petals with her left. As the mysterious woman passed him, Cooper recognized Adrianna. She stepped onto the altar's platform and relit one candle with another that trailed hot candle wax across the bronze rim of the casket. She turned, revealing only the dark outline of her round brown eyes through the veil and in a muffled voice said, "Come Cooper. Stand by me so you may bid good-bye to Jesse, my godfather's son."

Cooper hypnotically stepped onto the altar with a thud. The sound of his boots echoed as they hit the dry pine flooring. Adrianna reached down into the casket and opened Jesse's closed eyelids as she waved the golden cross over his stark white face. She spoke ancient Spanish words so chilling they reminded Cooper of the war chants of the old Fijian women. After two minutes of chanting, Adrianna pulled a mica vile of murky black liquid from her ample cleavage. She gently parted Jesse's blue lips and poured the potion into his open mouth in the flickering light. Jesse spoke, "Adrianna, you have finally come to me." Cooper froze motionless and mute.

She replied, "The word of your death after the attack by the Ute war chief in the form of the old mountain lion reached me on the wind."

"Please bring my wife to me so I may bid her farewell and see my unborn child."

"She is walking in the night wind to the church as you speak. You will have until the east sun rises over the Sangre de Cristo Mountains to be with her. Cooper, you may speak to Jesse."

"Jesse, I wish Bob had assigned me your place on point downstream. The old mountain lion surprised us with his route from the outcropping above you."

"Cooper," Jesse replied. "Life is not yours or Bob's to grant or take. The Ute spirit warrior in the form of a lion was sent by the mountain gods to settle some ancient score. My family has been in this conquered land four hundred years with many markers owed to the gods. We have fought, murdered and enslaved many Utes and not always in battle. You could not have changed my destiny nor can I change yours.

"Walk this beautiful land without guilt like Bob White who is a rare Anglo who understands these things. I ask only that you watch over Brenda and the children with my old uncle and my brother. The time is coming soon when they can cut no more trees. Help my children into the future world since I can no longer guide them."

Cooper answered, "I will always watch over them as long as I ride the ranges of the Southwest, but the wind of change is blowing hard in all our faces."

Adrianna spoke, "Evil is again returning to this land as new conquistadors come to rape and sell its virgin beauty."

Jesse spoke again, "Cooper, Adrianna is a powerful guide and if your hearts merge my spirit will smile on the blessing. Your strength and purpose, merged with her ancient spirit knowledge, can blend to crush the evil in the wind."

Before Cooper could speak again the heavy church door opened and a mysterious warm night wind filled the sanctuary as Brenda walked down the aisle veiled in black lace. She stepped light-footed up to the coffin and stood on Adrianna's right side. She lifted her veil and smiled as she touched Jesse's cheek with her gold wedding band.

Adrianna touched Cooper's shoulder gently and silently signaled their departure. Brenda opened her black cotton dress to reveal her round plump stomach. When Cooper stopped at the door and turned his head for a last farewell to his fallen courageous friend, he observed Brenda's young bride-like face. His eyes shifted to the trail of wilting red rose buds and back to her smiling tender eyes as she spoke Spanish in soft tones to Jesse. Adrianna pushed open the church doors and gently guided Cooper toward the sleeping village. The half-moon lit a path. In the starry sky, he saw a fast moving cloud in the form of an ancient battle horse. It quickly covered the half-moon and Cooper's eyes refocused on the darkened church. When he looked away Adrianna had vanished. He was very alone.

FOURTEEN

The Grand Jury

Cooper looked at his Swiss mountaineering wristwatch as he climbed the steps of the Montrose County Courthouse. The district attorney had seated a grand jury in the investigation of Bill Daniels' death. It was eleven o'clock on a gray fall day, the same hour Jesse's coffin was to be lowered into a cold grave in the church cemetery at Del Norte. A thousand mourners had come from the San Luis Valley.

But Cooper was at the courthouse because Bill Daniels' body had presented the ambitious young district attorney a headline grabbing case.

When Cooper reached the top step of the courthouse a tall thin man in a wrinkled wool plaid sport said, "Cooper Stuart, I'm Andy Deloach from the Rocky Mountain News."

"How'd you know me?"

"Same long stride as your uncle when he was in the State Senate. Mind if I ask you a few questions about the Daniels' case?" Cooper paused a yard short of the double doors. "Normally yes, but today no. This publicity-hound DA compelled me to testify this morning. I should be in Del Norte at a friend's funeral."

"Sorry about Jesse Velázquez, I was in Del Norte for his inquest," the reporter replied. "I cover the southern part of the state for the paper. A water engineer is dead and water has always been very political on the western slope of Colorado. Boys at the Cattleman's Cafe say you pulled the corpse out, and other than that nobody knows anything but the victim."

"Well, I'm no witness. Just an unlucky angler."

"Sheriff's report says the body was weighted," the Denver reporter probed.

"It was for sure," replied Cooper with a frown.

"Bill have any enemies you know of?" asked the reporter leading Cooper gently as he scribbled on his note pad.

"Any person who appropriates water is always going to have enemies in a dry region. But I've been away too long to know the latest sandbox fights. District water court records are public and a person could do a little reading."

"Boys around here say only the YBarC, the Lone Cone Ditch, the ditch at Nucla, the

Idarado mine at Telluride, and the Town of Telluride have any senior water rights worth anything." Cooper looked at the reporter and he went stone-faced rancher silent.

"Well, my best to your uncle in Fairplay when you see him. He was a fine lawmaker," Andy almost whispered.

Just then the door opened and a heavy-set blonde woman Cooper recognized from grammar school approached him. "Cooper good to see you. Sorry it's under such terrible circumstances. Jesse's family supplied my father's lumberyard for years. This new prosecutor is a tough hombre. No one could back him off calling you today. We're ready now; please follow me before he sends a bailiff out here to get you."

Cooper frowned. Jane Soapstone used to be a skinny, freckled, pony-tailed barrel racer who now lived in this woman's body.

They passed a hippie couple coming out of the main courtroom and Jane sneered when they were out of hearing range. "Dope smoking hippie scum from Telluride. A ranger caught them smoking pot and doing it butt naked at Woods Lake in broad daylight. Claims they offered to turn him on if he didn't arrest them. Maybe even all three had a little 'free love' together in their camp tent."

"That's quite a tale," whistled Cooper with a feigned look of astonishment. "I hear the skiers are spending hard cash in Montrose."

"That's true enough. Dad had his best year since the end of the uranium boom with all that building over in the east end of San Miguel County." She added, "Better accounts than the ranchers who only clear their balances once a year at best."

Cooper deduced the Montrose shopkeepers would sell the ranchers, miners and farmers out in a country second for resort construction customers with hard cash and second homeowners with credit cards.

He followed Jane into the grand jury room. The prosecutor's voice barked as Cooper scanned the room for a familiar face, but he found no one.

"You want a lawyer present, Mr. Stuart?"

"No sir," retorted Cooper slowly, not used to being addressed by his last name on his home turf.

"Well swear him in," the prosecutor commanded, adding,

"Everything you say is under oath, the whole truth and nothing but the truth."

Cooper took the oath, which was administered by Jane who bit her lip to keep from giggling as her cheeks flushed.

Cooper gauged the jury members as he walked to the witness stand and took a seat in a hard-bottomed chair. The members were housewives, retired men and disabled veterans. All of them were white Anglos, so apparently, no Blacks, Hispanics or Native Americans were available for grand jury duty in Montrose County. The gray headed Judge, whom Cooper now vaguely recognized as a friend of Liz's, called the proceeding to order.

The DA who introduced himself as Joe Bevins said, "Welcome, Cooper, if I may call you that. I appreciate you coming from Del Norte this morning to accommodate the grand jury. Jesse Velázquez was a good citizen of the great state of Colorado by the newspaper account."

Cooper, astounded at the boldness of the lie, tersely replied, "You may of course call me Cooper but I believe sir I am here this morning instead of at my friend's funeral to accommodate the five o'clock TV news crew from Grand Junction and the morning edition of the Denver newspapers."

Joe asked abruptly, "Cooper, what activity were you engaged in on the late afternoon of September 10 and what was your approximate location?"

Cooper answered, "Fly fishing on the upper San Miguel for the big brown and fighting off a nosy mountain lion. The spot's near Ed Jerkins place but it's secret." The jury members laughed but Joe didn't even crack a smile.

"Did you see or hear anything unusual in that part of the river on that day?" A scowl on his youthful face was rimmed with blow-dried red hair.

Cooper smirked as he remembered Sue half nude giggling on the picnic table but continued in a serious voice as he recounted the events. "He was weighted on the pool's sandy bottom but the river, which seemed too low even for early fall, was only a foot or so over the body."

Joe asked, "Anything unusual about his appearance except he was dead?"

"Yes. His championship silver rodeo belt buckle was missing. He always wore it…was famous for it," Cooper asserted.

"You or the young ladies that helped move his body to Norwood take the belt or lose it moving him?" he asked curtly.

"I don't wear silver rodeo belt buckles. We're ranchers at the YBarC, not entertainers," Cooper deadpanned, having read in the Montrose newspaper that Joe's father had been a pro circuit rodeo clown.

"What else happened that evening Cooper?" Fire spat from Joe's mouth.

"Loaded the body into my Jeep. Two women from Telluride helped me who were camping by the picnic table," Cooper said omitting the details of their activities. "Drove the body to the San Miguel County sheriff's substation in Norwood. I helped the deputy unload it and then gave him a report."

"The YBarC have any pending water issues or disputes that Bill Daniels' was reviewing or consulting on?" the prosecutor asked.

"In the past, yes, but currently no."

"The YBarC have any water legal problems to the best of your knowledge, Cooper?"

The naiveté of the question struck Cooper like the big cat pouncing on Jesse. "No. The YBarC owns fifty percent of the San Miguel River water rights plus twenty percent of the Delores River water rights south of Naturita, Colorado and a 1,000 Gurley Reservoir water shares for irrigating hay over at Norwood, most bought since 1937. And they are all are senior water rights, adjudicated and deeded."

Some members on the jury gasped at the first public disclosure of the extent of the YBarC water holdings in memory. The prosecutor's face turned so white he looked like a Ute arrow had been shot through his heart.

His lack of homework was apparent to the entire room. He almost mumbled, "You're dismissed Cooper. The proceeding here is secret and I implore you not to discuss the murder with the press until we can arrest a suspect and for your own safety since you are the only material witness at this point in the ongoing investigation."

FIFTEEN

White Water

C ooper sat in his Jeep in the midafternoon sun with the engine idling after the grand jury hearing. He was waiting for Adrianna who had asked him over for a predawn breakfast before they left Del Norte to go on a Moab, Utah rafting trip together. She had won it at a Telluride Volunteer Fireman's fundraiser. He parked in front of a weather-beaten asbestos shingled building that functioned as Telluride's Chrysler dealership. A half completed windowless motel flanked the derelict building's showroom that had two shockingly misplaced Chrysler 300 Convertibles in its window. The gray-haired lady who owned the dealership and was its chief mechanic peered out as she shuffled past the showroom windows. She waved to Cooper, whom she had known from childhood.

Liz's one luxury had been a new Chrysler 300 convertible every four years. Cooper had seen his stern grandfather chuckle on many occasions when Liz hurled her car full speed down the main ranch road with the top down, cattle trucks and pickups following her in the dust. Cooper always elected to ride with Liz on their winter trip to check the YBarC herd in Arizona. Liz drove like an Indy racer and was well known by the Arizona Highway Patrol, which happily accepted an annual $100 donation to its widows' fund in an exchange for a rear window sticker.

Cooper fondly remembered the soft warm desert air in his face as they drove the empty state highway through the crumbling monuments of the Navajo's Valley of the Gods. He imagined them to be giant abandoned space cities and the red hues haunted his dreams for days after each trip to Arizona.

A voice startled Cooper from his memories. "Cooper, dear, boy haven't seen you and Liz in a coon's age."

Cooper answered politely, "Martha, the chores at the ranch keep us plenty busy, especially with roundup near."

She frowned, "Liz coming in for a new model convertible after roundup? Her old 300's going on six winters…longest she's ever kept one."

Cooper paused as he considered his answer, not wanting to confirm any financial rumors about the ranch. He replied matter-of-factly, "Maybe after we get a calf count if the mountain lions are good boys this summer, there could be a new model convertible in her future."

"How's your foreman, Polecat? He still ramrodding the operation jest like his daddy?" she asked, still probing. "Bet he'd like a new Dodge pickup to replace that beat-up one I see drive by here to Montrose."

"You know that Ford F150s have a twenty-year warranty and it has five years to run," Cooper joked.

Cooper knew the YBarC's rolling stock was held together with bailing wire and welding torches. But he didn't want to discuss it publicly. He heard a motor as a vehicle turned off the highway, crunching gravel as it pulled up behind him. Martha inadvertently blocked its route to his driver's side window.

Cooper saw Adrianna at its wheel, a smile on her face as she cut her engine and rolled down her window. She asked, "Where do I leave my Wagoneer, Cooper?"

Cooper leaned out his window, glad to be rescued, "Martha here's the owner so she can tell you." Cooper said, looking Martha directly in the eye and deliberately not introducing Adrianna.

"Park it over there by them unfinished motel rooms." She turned and walked away a little miffed while Adrianna parked. Cooper wished the motel was operating because he needed a nap before the three-hour drive to Utah through the warm desert. But the languid Colorado River, which flowed past Moab, beckoned for the half-day raft trip. They were driving Cooper's less comfortable Jeep so they could off road in the rugged canyon paradise.

Cooper had an old pea green army blanket in the Jeep with his Peace Corps duffel bag that contained two days of Levi jeans, white cotton western shirts, underwear and a swimsuit. His hunting gear and rifle were still in the Jeep.

Adrianna walked toward the Jeep carrying a black leather overnight bag slung over her shoulder dressed more for a weekend in the countryside near Madrid than for visit to a depressed southern Utah uranium-mining town.

Adrianna tossed her overnight luggage in the packed rear compartment where it landed with a heavy thump. She climbed into the Jeep in an easy motion. Her heavy cotton skirt parted, revealing her black satin panties for a quick second. Her large nipples pressed against the loose weave of a baby blue Portuguese fisherman's sweater. She wore handmade brown leather Spanish boots with inlaid purple mountain wild flowers. A blue Chinese silk scarf, rolled into a headband, surrounded her black hair. She settled into passenger seat and her brown thighs rippled under her skirt as she tossed her hair over her shoulder.

"Cooper, how did you manage to arrive first?"

Cooper eyes were locked on her thighs. "The DA didn't like my answers much, so he dismissed me early."

"Who's the old lady with grease under her fingers?" she asked again as she pulled her skirt toward her knees.

"Figured you knew about her. She owns this car dealership, if you can call it that. My mom's an old customer."

Adrianna smiled, "Let's get on the road if you can take your eyes off my thighs. I promise you can see them on the raft trip cowboy."

She opened her mouth slightly as her tongue wet her red lips with an easy glide. She sat saddle straight with her head against the high seat back, causing her nipples to stretch the light wool sweater. Her thin long neck turned her beautiful face inches from Coopers. Her warm breath caressed Cooper's cheek as her tongue darted, splashing her words with a barely detectable soft feminine Castilian accent.

"There is an old Spanish proverb for travelers that says the road is like a river, which eventually tumbles over a waterfall. There it forms a cool azure pool by an inn where the traveler can abandon his or her dusty clothes and refresh with a bath. The traveler is granted one fantasy by the God of the waterfall that feeds the pool. The fantasy will only last the night until the sun rises again. Let's travel our river road quickly so our night in the inn's pool is long."

Cooper gunned the Jeep spewing a cloud of dust and gravel behind it. The first hour went quickly as Cooper killed the drive time with snippets of local history while Adrianna's eyes drank in the breathtaking Colorado Plateau landscape broken by gold streaked ranges, deep red sandstone walled canyons and green hay pastures ready for their second cutting. The mountain range's bald granite peaks were already dusted with fresh snow. The air was so clear they could see Little Cone, Lone Cone, the La Sals, and even the Blue Mountains to the extreme west in the hazy distance.

Cooper had explained the ownership of water shares in the Gurley ditch as they drove through Norwood and Redvale's small ranches. "These ranches grow hay for winter feed while their cattle summer graze in the high country on leased state or federal grass."

He pointed to a branch of the ditch that led to a portion of the YBarC hay fields. "So each April, the water is allocated by the number of shares the ranch owns based on the winter snow pack in the Beaver Creek basin which drains Little Cone and Lone Cone Mountain. The ditch rider then allocates the water to the various hay fields when it's requested by the rancher."

"Interesting Cooper," she replied. "Guess in a dry summer a ranch's real wealth is its water and its cow-calf pairs."

Smart woman, Cooper thought. "Bulls eye. You can always feed cattle if you have water to grow hay but it will break an operation in a long drought if it has to buy hay on the open market."

The final sixty miles to Moab was Hole-in-the-Wall Gang country. The Jeep rolled to a stop in front of the historic Bedrock frontier store.

"How about a cold sarsaparilla before my tongue shrivels up?" she asked as her hand opened the Jeep door.

"Race you to the cooler; loser pays," Cooper challenged and he snapped open his door.

The warm Paradox Valley afternoon air teased his face as Adrianna skipped up the crumbling concrete steps before Cooper could exit the Jeep. Her skirt outlined her ample round hips as she bounded onto the porch of the store. Cooper's eyes drank in her soft curves like a man in the desert without water. He followed her through the tired screen door into a general store unchanged from the turn of the century.

"Hello, Cooper. Haven't seen you since before them idiots in Washington put them boys on the moon with a go cart and a cheap home movie camera," boomed Larry Clark, the owner of the store and the best elk hunter in southeastern Utah.

"Well, Antler Head, I haven't been in these parts for a long spell," replied Cooper. "You still the Utah record holder for a bull elk?"

Larry's eyes followed Adrianna's breasts as she bent over the cooler to fish for a root beer. "Ten points, ain't nobody going to break that record anytime soon, still got the best pair of Mormon eyes southwest of Salt Lake."

Adrianna, sarsaparilla root beer now in hand, teased Larry with her taut full breasts and smiled, "I'm ready for an introduction now, Cooper, if he takes his eyes off my chest and saves them until elk are fair game."

Cooper jumped in as Larry turned beet red, "Adrianna, Telluride restaurateur supreme, meet Larry Clark, Mormon Bishop of Paradox Valley, storekeeper, and rumored to be husband of three beautiful women in three states. So, you stand clear of him or you might fall for his charm and be number four."

Larry let out a belly laugh and said, "Not the 1870s anymore, Cooper, not even a Bishop can have more than one wife at a time. The state tells the church what to do just about like it does everyone else, except the big ranchers like you. A capital city girl health inspector even came down here and wrote me up for selling wild elk steaks out of the ice cream freezer. Can you believe that happened in this county where a person would rather have a good elk steak any day than ice cream? I just told her she could take all the ice cream over to the grade school and there wouldn't be a problem. I don't want no Salt Lake City ice cream polluting my elk steaks either."

Cooper and Adrianna laughed.

"Well, I'm happy to meet you, Bishop. You have any information on Cooper here I need to know?"

"Not up to date, but you be good to him. He's a shy ranch boy. I only wish he'd come back to the Mormon flock like his great-grandfather." His voice was serious now as he realized Adrianna was probably a good Catholic.

Adrianna started to place a dollar bill on the counter but Larry caught her hand gently in midair. "Not necessary ma'am, Cooper's family has the oldest account here. It dates to 1893."

As the screen door closed Larry said, "Watch your fence lines, Cooper. No one's been riding them since you left for your high schooling in New Mexico."

"What does he mean by that, Cooper?" Adrianna asked as she opened the Jeep door.

"Same as your kitchen's freezer - leave it unlocked too long and things will walk. At the YBarC they can weigh a thousand pounds a head. Guess one of my cowhands has been selling the Bishop beef he doesn't own."

"What are you going to do about it?" A small frown crossed Adrianna's lips.

"Nothing today but plenty when I return to the ranch. Let's get on the road before I lose control and kiss you here."

"Find a back road after we pull out of here. I love this valley. I want to make love to you the first time under the blue-sky near this river, not in some motel. We need to renew our strength together." Adrianna spoke so softly that Cooper was hypnotized.

The glass pack mufflers rumbled their deep-throated song as Cooper slowed the Jeep at the top of a mesa that overlooked the Paradox Valley. He turned down a dirt track and after a mile pulled to a stop in front of a roofless log cabin. It was shaded by a grove of cottonwood trees at the mouth of a running spring. "This is where my great-grandfather headquartered with his cowhands from 1885 until spring of 1894 when he oversaw the La Sal Land and Cattle Company."

"Beautiful. Like living near the Grand Canyon without the tourists," replied Adrianna. She opened her door and ran to the spring where she knelt and scooped the fresh water into her mouth with her hands.

Before Cooper reached her with the battered green army blanket, she pulled her sweater over her head in an easy motion. Then she unsnapped her white satin bra, letting her full olive brown breasts flow onto her chest. Cooper stopped beside her. He dropped the blanket behind him as she unbuttoned her skirt, letting it slide slowly over her full thighs, revealing the outline of her triangle under her black satin panties.

She spoke in a soft voice. "If you wish to enter my very old spirit freely in this chapel of your family, join with me. Enjoy the female beauty of this harsh land you ride so freely. With me you will find the female center and love you need so much now. You will find the energy for your long fight for your ranchero. We have the savvy to save it together."

Cooper paused in the shade of the ancient cottonwood trees hearing only the faint gurgle of the spring and the whisper of the west wind. He thought for a long moment about Adrianna's brave offer. It brought more to the table than immediate sexual conquest and gratification. This was not a Telluride resort hot tub and coke tryst. Making love to Adrianna opened a door that would not close easily. It would be like passing through a ranch gate with no return.

Five hundred years in the Spanish New World had made her spirit a force that his Anglo family had no knowledge of or intimate interaction with in marriage. Somewhere deep in his subconscious an ancient voice from perhaps another incarnation told him to accept her offer. Cooper dropped his jeans with a snap of his silver buckled belt. Then he pulled the black satin panties down to Adrianna's boot tops and she stepped out of them as he knelt. His eyes and then his tongue met her pink-rimmed opening. Cooper tasted the juice of Spanish Rome.

After a long minute Adrianna gently pulled Cooper to his feet and stroked him gently as the warm afternoon desert air rustled the trees. Her heavy breasts rested against his chest. Her nipples excited his taut muscles, their heat piercing his thin white cotton cowboy shirt. His finger found her clit that hardened to his touch. Their tongues danced with each other as their lips touched like Aspen leaves in the wind. She pulled Cooper into her while they both stood. Her sweet liquid flowed like water from a secret Ute hot spring. She wrapped her strong thighs around him as he lifted her open hips with his strong hands. She throbbed with pleasure, wild like the San Juan Mountains.

Cooper carried Adrianna backward a half dozen steps and rested her strong back softly against a cottonwood tree. With each deep thrust he felt her orgasm again and again. Their spirits united and flew free together in the vast clear sky of the west. Her breathing was heavy. Her hot juices flowed over his thighs until he was lost in her ecstasy and the vast silence of the landscape as he orgasmed. For their long moment, the rustling cottonwoods provided a musical score for their journey.

SIXTEEN
Paradox

The fan slowly rotated slowly on the graying white ceiling of the suite at the Whitewater Inn in Moab as Adrianna's kiss woke Cooper from a light sleep. A long turquoise and silver necklace circled her breasts as they rose and fell with her breath. Cooper rolled over and fingered the tiny gold ring that pierced the upper apex of Adrianna's vaginal lips. It had surprised him when he discovered it.

"It is the sign of the cult of witches I belong to from the old country that dates to Roman Spain. It was implanted when I was six by an old woman in northern New Mexico. The mistress of my cult was removed from Jerusalem by a Roman legion commander and given as a slave to Seneca. Its members came to control the gold mine owners who worked for the King of Spain. The cult followed the miners to New Spain."

As Cooper released the soft gold ring, Adrianna's pink flesh closed around its nestled hiding place in her black pubic hair. "Do you have this ring implanted for life like some bulls do?"

"No. Only until I bear a daughter, then she has it implanted in the same spot. My power passes to my first daughter only." Her fingers stroked the ring gently.

"And no daughter, what then?" Cooper asked.

"That won't happen," replied Adrianna with finality.

"And your Doctor's thoughts on this?" Cooper probed, as he looked deep into her coal black eyes.

"A quaint Spanish mountain custom if we are examined or give birth without a Spanish midwife."

"And revealing the secret to me out of wedlock?" Cooper's twenty-six-year-old mind was very curious.

"You won't reveal my secret Cooper or I wouldn't have made love with you. Besides, you already enjoy the erotic pleasure the ring gives you in certain positions of our lovemaking. Cooper, if you reveal the existence of my ring its curse will make you impotent. To remove the ring from a cult member even by accident brings a curse that causes a horrible death."

"Can you prove that?" Cooper challenged.

"Will I have to?" she answered darkly.

After the briefest consideration Cooper answered, "No ma'am. Liz strongly cautioned me about talking about my sexual encounters," adding, "a curse definitely seals this cowboy's lips."

Adrianna smiled as he stared at her in awe. Neither his boarding school nor college education had covered sex with Spanish witches.

Breakfast was at the Uranium Cafe. Cooper talked to Adrianna between bites of hash browns, fried eggs and smoked pork sausage.

"The uranium mining boom is dying a slow tortured death and Moab is its heart. Making electricity with uranium is like boiling water with an atomic blast. There's plenty of western coal, gas, hydro, wind and sun to make all the electricity for everyone if folks would stop wasting it in the big cities. Plus, Vietnam proved we will never drop an A bomb again."

"So next time we come back, will there be tumbleweed in the streets?"

"Probably not. The Mormons who run the county government are a resilient group. Moab's the back door to Monument Valley and the front door to Arches National Park so the tourists will drive through here every summer like clockwork. If anyone can find a use for the maze of desert canyons around here, the Mormons will."

"My cousin rides his Bultaco DT175 trail riding motorbike in the mountains around Leadville. He would love to ride these rim rock canyons," Adrianna suggested.

"Let's go meet our guide. Horses, jeeps and rafts are my choice of transportation until they can beam me around Buck Rogers-style."

Adrianna laughed. Cooper paid the check at the counter near the dull aluminum door with a cracked upper glass panel. Adrianna had eaten little of her breakfast but he figured it didn't meet her standards.

The Jeep whined in high gear as Cooper drove away from Moab and Adrianna dozed in the passenger seat. Her tanned thighs blazed against the tan khaki hiking shorts she had worn on the river. The trip had been an autumn sun-splashed afternoon.

Adrianna breathed lightly, her full ruby lips rimmed her mouth in a seductive repose. Cooper's mind was still a little bleary from the mushrooms the guide had shared with them during a lunch stop on a pristinely white sand bar. While the guide prepared a picnic lunch, Cooper and Adrianna had walked around the bend out of sight. They had stripped and taken a cold but exhilarating swim. Then they had made love quietly on the sand bar's edge. Sex with Adrianna high on mushrooms had been exotic; and her sensuality still lingered in Cooper's thoughts.

Cooper remembered a boyhood story about Ute warriors who captured pioneer women on the Colorado Plateau and took them to their warm campsites along the Colorado River, where they raped them. Some women, rather than submit to the sexual abuse, had jumped into the Colorado's raging waters and been swept to their deaths in the rapids. The old-time river rats around Moab said these spirits haunted the sandbars, which was their purgatory for taking their own lives. Cooper didn't know if the pioneer stories were true but he did know the Utes had picked a magic place to winter.

Adrianna awoke when Cooper down shifted. The state highway dropped into a series of slow switchbacks that produced stunning views of the Paradox Valley and its ranches with freshly cut irrigated hay circles. The Jeep's soft-top had been off since the turn at La Sal and the dry mesa wind felt refreshing in Cooper's face. The sun was setting in the side view mirror over the La Sal mountain range.

The Jeep was a thousand feet above Paradox Valley on a narrow switchback when an explosion shattered its windshield, showering him and Adrianna with safety glass. The bullet nicked Cooper's left ear and embedded in the duffel bag with a thud; Adrianna screamed and instinctively grabbed Cooper's right arm. He swerved the Jeep as he shoved Adrianna hard to the floorboard.

The visit by the river spirits had been an omen, Cooper thought as the second shot hit his seat's steel bracket from behind.

Cooper shouted above the roar of the muffler, "Crossfire. Keep your head under the dash. A shooter is behind us in the rocks and the other one is below us on the switchback turn. We have to get past him."

Cooper downshifted into second gear slowed the Jeep inches from a 1,000 foot drop. The off-road tire spun violently, fighting for traction on the soft shoulder. A third high-powered bullet thundered from below them and destroyed the thin rearview mirror. Then a fourth bullet fired from overhead pinged behind the gearshift lever as Cooper steered back to the centerline. Cooper thought his best chance was to take out the downhill gunner and shoot back uphill at the other two with his hunting rifle.

"My rifle is on the back floor behind the duffel bag. Jump between the seats and hand it to me when I hit the brakes. Stay low."

Cooper down shifted into first gear, steered the Jeep down the highway's yellow centerline straight toward the apex of the switchback where the downhill gunner laid sniper style behind low sagebrush. The sniper's face froze as he saw the Jeep accelerating straight toward his head. A shot hit Cooper's right rear tire as he shoved Adrianna through the gap between the seats. He pulled his lightweight .22 from the Jeep's glove box and fired a covering shot through the empty windshield frame. He steered with his left hand as he fought to control the Jeep's downhill acceleration while its right rear tire deflated.

Cooper heard another shot rip through his left rear tire. Cooper's steel bumper hit the downhill gunner in the forehead as he rose to fire point blank at Cooper. His teetering shot ripped through Adrianna's empty high backed seat and ricocheted into her left hip. She screamed in pain, losing her grip on the rifle. Blood gushed from the shooter's smashed forehead wound and he rolled to a slow motion stop at the edge of a sheer cliff.

Cooper hit the brakes hard and tried to steer toward a sandy runaway truck ramp. The

Jeep went into an uncontrolled death slide. Adrianna, wounded and bleeding, struggled to hand Cooper the rifle as the Jeep lunged downhill, its back tires smoking. A shot rang out from uphill again as the Jeep finally stopped in the deep sand runaway truck ramp and the wounded gunner's bloody head reappeared in the rearview mirror.

Another bullet from uphill lodged in its tailgate. Cooper shouted at Adrianna who now had the Browning rifle in her hand.

"Hang onto the roll bar when I shift into reverse."

A rooster tail of sand spewed into the air blocking the gunmen's sight lines. The Jeep rolled in slow motion onto its side as Cooper and Adrianna jumped onto the sandy runaway truck ramp. The wounded gunman fired a last desperate shot into the sky as he fell backward mortally wounded. Cooper hit the sand on his knees and his jeans saved skin as his arms shielded his face. His .22 pistol skidded away as he rolled toward Adrianna. An automatic rifle opened fire. He reached a stunned, blood-streaked Adrianna whose eyelids blinked in disbelief. She clung to the rifle in shock. Cooper yanked it away from her. Then Cooper grabbed Adrianna's hand and pulled her behind the Jeep as a hail of bullets hit it.

"Follow me around the blind curve to that big red sandstone boulder. That gets us out of their line of fire. The gas tank will blow for sure. Deep breath, center or we are gone from the earth," Cooper calmly ordered.

Cooper carried the rifle in his left hand and he led Adrianna with his right. He darted downhill toward the safety of a large boulder. Bullets pinged behind them. The gunfire stopped as they reached the cover of the monument-size boulder. Cooper checked the rifle's magazine; it still had six bullets. Cooper could not shoot uphill because he could not risk exposing himself. He heard steel soled boots walking on the highway toward the runaway truck ramp.

Cooper held his hand across Adrianna's mouth as she silently cried from fright and pain. A pickup truck stopped and Cooper heard a thud as a body was loaded into its cargo bay. Then he heard boot steps start downhill and he levered a bullet into the empty chamber to face the gunman. Suddenly he heard the whine of a second pickup truck pulling a rattling cattle trailer coming uphill toward them only one switchback below. The boot steps turned back uphill and a door slammed. The pickup U-turned and it accelerated uphill.

Cooper eased out from behind the boulder, hoping to get a license plate number but all he saw uphill at dusk was a late model navy blue Chevy pickup with an Arizona license plate disappearing around the switchback. He turned and saw Jed McBean, foreman of the URR Ranch driving uphill toward them. Cooper stepped onto the pavement to flag down Jed. Cooper smiled to himself, now sure he had survived the worst ambush near Paradox since cattle rustling days of the 1890s. But he needed medical help for Adrianna, immediately.

He saw Jeb's Winchester on its mount in his pickup. Cooper knew he would need more than a second rifle during the coming days. Someone had just tried to take title to the Y Bar C the old-fashioned frontier way.

SEVENTEEN

The Rescue

Jeb McBean stepped onto the state highway with a 44 magnum pistol in his right hand. His sunglasses and weathered Stetson hid his eyes. He was clean-shaven and spoke in a drawl as he stared at the overturned bullet-riddled Jeep.

"You okay, son? One of them shell shocked drunken west-end Vietnam vets shoot up your Jeep? Bunch of them been talking mean against you since your return home."

"Not unless they hired someone from Arizona in a new blue pickup to do the shooting. I need your help. Adrianna is behind the boulder. She's bleeding from a hip wound. Please call down to the URR's headquarters on your CB radio. Have them call Doc Williams over in Montrose. He can fly over and land on the ranch's airstrip."

"I'll tend to it right away, Cooper. Got a cowboy line rider's first aid kit in my door compartment. Good thing I was checking a fence break; a bunch of steers loose."

Adrianna limped from behind the boulder, her blood soaked khaki shorts. "It's a flesh wound, Cooper. It bleeds worse than it hurts. Do you have a first aid kit?"

"Jeb has one. As soon as he calls in for help I'll fix you up Boy Scout style."

"Fine," replied Adrianna, still pale. "But keep your hands on my hip when you patch me up."

Cooper bandaged Adrianna's hip discreetly behind the boulder and brought her a clean change of clothes from the Jeep. While she sponged off the dried blood with alcohol and dressed, Cooper and Jeb winched the overturned Jeep with its two rear flat tires back onto its four wheels on the sandy runaway truck ramp. Cooper turned the ignition key to test the engine. It fired to life with a roar and Cooper feathered it. Jeb transferred their scattered belongings to his truck bed and covered them with a tattered canvas tarp. Cooper helped Adrianna into the cab so he could ride shotgun stagecoach style.

Jeb said, "Doc is in the air by now. We all better hightail it down to the ranch headquarters. Cooper, I'll send a couple hands up to tow the Jeep down. We can loan you a couple of used tires. The ranch mechanic can fix it good enough tomorrow to get you back to the YBarC."

"Tomorrow, after Doc patches up Adrianna," Cooper asked,

"can you saddle us a couple of horses and spot us two days of grub? We're going to hide out up at the abandoned mine cabin west of the ranch until things cool off. Give the Utah state patrol time to look for the gunmen and make sure they don't double back to the YBarC on county roads. My hands can secure the ranch."

"Consider it done, Cooper, but you keep my rifle handy until we clear the ranch gate in case they make another try on our way down," replied Jeb. "And just one question? How are you and your cowhands going to secure the YBarC without any gunslingers?"

"Good point. It's the second time this month I wished it was my great-grandfather's era and I could send Blue Bob Thompson and his boys out to settle the score."

"Never been anybody tougher than your great-grandfather and Blue Bob Thompson except maybe them conquistadors. Ma'am, your family involved in that New Mexico pueblo uprising thing?"

Adrianna measured Jeb and her response that she knew would forever mark her among the old-time cattlemen.

She answered him with hell in her ice-cold words, "In 1702 my family crossed the Rio Grande at El Paso del Norte and crushed the Pueblo Indio rebellion against the King of Spain and the Catholic Church. It is said a relative drank the blood in Holy Communion of the Pueblo Indian leader Po'pay who tortured and massacred the priests. He had them beheaded, and the Spanish soldier's spears rendered their wives and daughter's wombs barren so no more Antichrist children could be born in the leader's pueblo. His men chopped off the right hands and feet of the male Pueblo warriors who had rebelled against the crown. He became a great and feared hero in New Spain and when he rode past Pueblo Indians with silver crosses around their necks they fell on the earth and snow to beg for their lives."

A chill passed through Cooper's heart. An alliance with Adrianna would produce a union of two ruthless energy fields that had ruled without mercy in the southwest. Maybe she was Cooper's modern day Blue Bob Thompson, he silently thought. Cooper was now sure he could kill to save the YBarC. He had done it once in self-defense today. Adrianna had bravely fought wounded at his side with no panic in her actions. Maybe ancient spirits were reappearing to protect the ranch, but what Cooper really wondered was why it had to be on his watch.

Doc William's attended to Adrianna's wound with Jeb's wife, Anita's help while Cooper talked to a Utah state patrolman and a Montrose County, Colorado deputy sheriff.

Cooper repeated their conclusion, "You're technically correct that the attack occurred a few feet over the Utah line but to me it's a Colorado matter because that is where the YBarC is located. I want Colorado lawmen on this case, too."

"Not going to work that way, son," replied the chubby cheeked Utah state patrolman. "Wish it did but the law says we have jurisdiction. We can't even prove you killed one of them until we find a body. We have an all-points bulletin out four corners wide, plus on the Navajo reservation, for a blue Chevy late model pickup truck with three men, one possibly a white male wounded or dead."

The deputy sheriff added, "Sheriff thinks it might have been some liquored up Vietnam burnouts try'n to scare you and it got out of control. There is a river of red blood near the Jeep that ran ten feet in the dust downhill, I reckoned you killed him with blood loss like that. No hospital report from Moab or Monticello has been called in yet. I reckoned it was self-defense on your part judging from the scene and you got the only witness. But at the end of the day Utah has the lead in the case."

The Utah state patrolman cut him off, "A Utah inquest will decide if it was self-defense if we find a body. All we have now is his story, a shot up Jeep and his Mexican girl's wound." Then he looked toward the closed bedroom door where Adrianna was being treated, disapproval in his eyes.

Cooper took a beat and replied, "These weren't drunk townies on a patriotic mission. But the sheriff will know for sure in a couple days if anyone turns up missing."

Cooper addressed the Utah patrolman directly, "Adrianna's Spanish family been in the southwest almost 400 years. She will testify real fine in court if necessary. You let your superiors in Salt Lake City know I'm Mormon blood on my great-grandfather's side even though I don't practice or tithe. I expect a reasonable effort on their part to apprehend the ambushers. That was a yellow way to attack a man and a woman."

The state patrolman turned a little red at the collar. "I'll pass along your message. The Montrose County sheriff's offices will keep you informed, good evening. Please vacation in Colorado next time." He walked away without even checking on Adrianna's condition.

Cooper barely held his tongue, but he knew he needed the Utah State Police.

Doc emerged from the bedroom, a smile on his old sagging cracked face. "She's all right, Cooper. The bullet only creased that young firm hip. Got it out easy, cleaned up with iodine and stitched the hole up good. Gave her a tetanus shot for good measure. I want her to rest here tonight even though she's strong as a bison. I gave her painkiller pills. My guess is I got a baby to deliver tomorrow so I'll bunk in the guest bedroom and fly out at first light. You take good care of Liz, too."

"She's in California. Thanks for patching up Adrianna. Bet you'll get the dinner of the century next time you come over to Telluride," Cooper added.

Doc disappeared down a hallway.

The deputy sheriff said in a low voice after Doc was out of earshot, "Jeb and I will set up a watch tonight to be on the safe side. But off the record, I believe those boys are burying a body in the Arizona desert just south of the Utah line and burning the blue pickup and it's probably stolen license plates tonight. Personally, I think someone's trying to even an old score with the Y Bar C."

Cooper didn't reply. He disappeared into Adrianna's room, where she was already asleep from a sedative. Anita silently exited with a nod to Cooper. He stood silently and watched Adrianna sleep. He was thankful the new range war had not taken her young life.

EIGHTEEN

Aztec Treasure

It was an hour after first light when Cooper led Adrianna on a paint horse up the steep rocky trail toward the URR Ranch line shack number six, which was the old mine's cabin. Adrianna rode uncomfortably. Her wound was double bandaged but the pain showed in her eyes. Cooper and Jeb had trailered the horses to within an hour's ride of the pine shack to save Adrianna saddle time. But Cooper knew it would be a slow hour until they reached their hideout.

"Doc said your Spanish genes protected your hip bone or you would be in Montrose at the hospital today," Cooper teased.

Adrianna retorted, "Am I to believe the Conquistadors' butts, not their armor, saved them from the Indian's arrows? Is this the cowboy Cooper and Doc Montrose's theory of how we won the new world?"

Then she added for effect, "Doc analyze any of my other body parts for you?"

Cooper blushed and quickly offered her a peace sign. They reached 10,000 feet and a dry brown empty summer pasture. The cattle had recently been moved down to lower elevations. The sound of the horse hoofs struck the rocky trail as the dilapidated log line shack finally came into view.

Adrianna and Cooper tied their horses up to a porch post. The old miner's cabin was furnished with only a wood stove, pine cupboard, a double mattress on an old-fashioned exposed steel spring bed for their sleeping bags and a hand-hewn pine bench table with three chairs. The air was brisk as the Indian summer sun began to warm the frosted meadow grass. Cooper snapped five rounds into the chamber of a URR Ranch Winchester 30-30 repeating saddle rifle and left the safety off. Adrianna unpacked their saddlebags while Cooper built a fire in the open-hearth wood stove. He opened the cabin's south facing wood shutters. Adrianna warmed her hands over the black cast iron stove.

"Nice hotel Cooper. Hope they're not overcharging you."

"It'll grow on you. We have a view all the way to Telluride with no tourist station wagons to junk it up."

"That's very cool but what activities do you have planned while we hide out? I'll get big red blisters on my knees if you plan a day and night of solid lovemaking now that I'm your total prisoner," she said with a hearty laugh.

"Tour of the Ghost Mountains by horseback. That's what the old-timers call the La Sals. Ute Indian legends speak of a ghost mine where the Aztec's high priests buried solid gold gods. One of my great-grandfather's cowboys claimed he found a small cave with an Aztec inscribed quartz rock covering the entrance."

"You're just telling me ghost stories to get me in bed with you. It's working," Adrianna challenged as her brown eyes widened.

"You wish," Cooper teased. "The cowboy pushed the rock off the entrance and climbed down an ancient pine wooden ladder twenty feet into the tunnel. He found a short pigmy skeleton with a solid gold bracelet on its right wrist. He pulled a Macaw parrot feather from its headdress. It spooked him so much he scrambled up the rotted ladder forgetting to take the bracelet."

Adrianna's eyes hardened. She involuntary thrust her ample breasts forward. "Tell me more."

"Two rungs from the top the cowboy swore that the quartz rock cover started to vibrate as if controlled by an invisible force. Then it began to mysteriously slide closed. The cowboy managed to get his rifle butt between the edge of the opening and the quartz rock or he said he might have been entombed."

"So why wasn't this information presented to the proper authorities?" she pressed.

"These old-time Mormons hated the government and distrusted the Anglo Christian settlers. They were all part-time gold hunters who didn't mind looting Indian graves to make a dollar. A pristine Anasazi pot paid for a week in Salt Lake City. A heavy early snowstorm kept the cowboy from returning until the next summer but when he did he couldn't find the quartz rock cover again. He guessed avalanche debris covered the tunnel's entrance but he searched for it in vain every year until his death. He finally told my great-grandfather his story as he was dying after being gored by a renegade longhorn bull in 1918. The feather is in the ranch house safe."

"So why didn't your great-grandfather hunt for the entrance or alert the authorities?"

"He didn't like the Feds either and he considered treasure hunting and prospecting a fool's game. Cheaper to buy a claim than look for one, he told my grandfather. Best he could figure, the tunnel, if it's still here or ever existed, is near this line shack to the northwest."

"So our activity for the day is to find the lost Aztec treasure, which is hidden in the ghost mine." Adrianna replied with a smirk. "That would solve your cash flow problem nicely."

"Plus an old Bambi for a dinner stew and a new doeskin skirt for you. They're no game rangers up here this time of year. It's too far from a cafe with hot coffee."

"You're a bad boy, just like my brothers. I love fresh killed venison. I'll watch for the quartz cover while you track. I want to bead a new deerskin jacket for the Christmas season."

"Done deal," Cooper replied. "Polecat, the YBarC foreman, is the best tanner on the western slope. You're dead right that a little Aztec treasure would sure help the YBarC."

"Treasure split is fifty-fifty," she demanded.

"Twenty-five, seventy-five," replied Cooper, "It's my information. You're only half the eyes."

"Tough deal, Cooper, but that's why your family owns the YBarC. I'm in, but remember two eyes and a nose for gold. Yours are for water. My little ring vibrates when I find gold," Adrianna only half teased as she picked up her woolen jacket off the bed.

After cowboy coffee boiled in a frying pan and eggs over easy, bacon and biscuits, Cooper and Adrianna mounted the still saddled horses. They rode northwest into a high yellow Aspen lined bowl in search of fresh game and hidden gold. Midway up the autumn colored bowl, they began to crisscross it to pick up deer or elk tracks. Adrianna was intensely searched for signs of gold while Cooper searched for fresh mule deer droppings.

Aspen groves, Cooper knew from his boyhood studies, grew on unstable soils until the Ponderosa pines eventually replaced them. This grove could have regenerated after an avalanche in 1906 that corroborated the cowhand's deathbed story.

After an hour of the slow crisscrossing Cooper reported, "No deer. They're below us, and no gold. Let's ride back to the cabin. Your bottom has to be raw again by now."

"Not yet," Adrianna replied. "I see the light waves gold emits near the top that narrow arroyo, or gulch as you would call it."

She pointed to the upper northeast portion of the bowl, which had just come into view at tree line. Cooper looked up and saw a cluster of Aspens below the Ponderosa pines. As they rode toward the draw, the horses fought for footing on the steep rocky soil. Cooper saw spring avalanche debris at the base of the pines. As his eyes scanned, he heard Adrianna whoop with joy.

"Cooper, look at the top left of the gulch in that small rockslide. There's the edge of a large exposed quartz rock. Let's dismount so we don't start a slide. I'm a mine owner's daughter. This gulch is very unstable."

"Let's drop down on it from the pines above it then. They're on stable soil. If that old tunnel is in the neck of the draw one of us could plunge into it," he asserted.

They tethered their tired horses where they could drink from a trickle of glacial water in the stream. They worked their way along the edge of the pines on hard ground until they were above the protruding exposed edge of the mud streaked quartz rock. Then they dropped down onto it one step at a time until they both reached it.

Adrianna knelt and brushed dirt off it. Cooper watched as the top of a battered semi-circle emerged revealing a hieroglyphic lettered word.

Adrianna said with authority, "It's Aztec lettering. My uncle had it on the granite rocks above the entrance of his oldest gold mine in central Mexico. The tunnel entrance is under this avalanche debris, probably just above the tree line so the Aztec priests could mark it by the sun's position for return some future year after Cortez and the Spanish were defeated. Except Cortez destroyed their empire and the Spanish never left Mexico City so the high priests died in hiding with their secret or were killed by the Navajos or Utes on the way back."

"So how and why did the skeleton remain at the bottom of the ladder?" Cooper asked.

"My family found one in 1657 in a mine near Mexico City with an empty bag of what probably had been dried fruit and clay pots of water. I suspect your cowboy saw a clay pot too. The skeleton was a priest initiate who was left behind to guard the treasure in life or death until the high priests returned. His spirit will still be dangerous to anyone who unseals the mine who is not Aztec. The priests had supernatural powers," Adrianna said cautiously.

"We'll need picks and shovels and probably backhoe to uncover the buried entrance so we need to mark it until we can return."

"We also need a couple trusted men and pine posts to shore up the tunnel mouth if we find it. Will red satin do the job?" she joked.

"Perfect material, better and brighter than surveyor's tape."

With a laugh Adrianna pulled up her skirt. "Pull my panties off Cooper and cut them into four strips. Let's mark each corner with a tripod of rocks and a red satin strip on a pine branch stake."

Cooper pulled her red satin panties down to her ankles, her riding skirt falling back into place as he caught a momentary glimpse of her silky black triangle. She stepped out of the panties and he cut the strong red material into four perfect strips with a pocketknife.

She smiled, "That view make you horny, Cooper. Gold arouses me when I feel its presence. I'm going to bend over with my hands on the quartz rock. Enter me from behind carefully so you don't pull the stitches out. I want to make love on this holy spot and absorb its power both good and evil. Then we'll stake our claim."

Cooper whistled to himself, happy they had spotted the quartz rock instead of fresh deer tracks. Adrianna positioned herself with only her denim riding skirt covering her bottom as he unbuckled. He was eager to give all for Spain and Aztec gold. He reached for the hem of the faded denim skirt and lifted it up over her hips as a puffy white cloud slowly passed over them, showering refracted light rays onto Adrianna's smooth skin.

Her open olive lips shimmered in the sunlight. She moaned as he entered her with his hands braced around her waist and they moved gracefully together in the warm afternoon sunlight toward a magic union men and women have enjoyed in the west's vast landscape for centuries.

NINETEEN

Saddle Time

Cooper rode his favorite quarter horse, Buckaroo, at a gallop as the YBarC's Victorian house faded from view. While he had been returning from the hideout there had been a suspicious cattle breakout from the fall holding pasture north of the house. Polecat had left Cooper a note that someone had cut a critical boundary fence line. Two hundred and fifty of the ranch's 2,000 mother cows were wandering unchaperoned toward Norwood when last sighted. Polecat and his hands had been watching the headquarters in case the shooters doubled back but someone had gotten under the radar. Cooper was anxious to ship the mother cows to the Arizona winter range now that their calves had been sold.

Cooper's tarnished silver spurs had belonged to his Grandfather. He had a forty-foot length of worn rawhide rope for the roundup of the escapees. He rode his quarter horse in an easy gait. But Buckaroo snorted and cut left without warning. Cooper went on red alert. His eyes caught a momentary glimpse of a gray green prairie rattlesnake. The snake coiled to strike Buckaroo's left rear shin. Cooper spurred the range savvy horse into a backing spin and drew his single action Colt 45. The snake's head froze. Cooper fired a single shot and the flat head split in half with venom dripping from its fangs as the body contracted in spiral spasms. Its decision to confront a superior unidentified force had proved fatal. The snake's confronting overwhelming power raced through Cooper's brain as an omen for his own fate.

Two cowboys galloped into view with their Winchester rifles drawn. They sighted their rifles on Cooper until they identified him and Buckaroo at fifty yards. They both whooped when they saw the dead rattlesnake. Fifteen minutes later the trio of riders closed in on a dust cloud. Cooper saw Polecat and two hands struggling to herd the two hundred and fifty escaped cows. Polecat was riding point with Elbow Williams, the ranch's top hand, on flank. Pete, an autumn hire, rode drag. Cooper signaled Jesse and Ben to take the swing positions to reshape the ragged formation. The mother cows had agitated looks on their black and white faces; they clearly were not happy about being recaptured a few days after their calves had been shipped.

Cooper rode quickly to point and reined Buckaroo to a walk beside Polecat. "Where'd you find the cattle?"

"Down at the duck hunt'n pond drinking sweet water on Naturita Creek. I count two hundred seven only. Still got forty missing but I reckoned they already hightailed it back to the ranch."

Cooper considered his choice of words. "See any cattle truck tracks near the break or on the county road shoulder?" He almost whispered so he didn't spook the cattle.

Polecat, who spoke his own brand of English especially when he wanted to cover his ass, replied, "Cooper them other cows probably down further on the crick if they didn't head for home. That black mama ear tagged number 82 is a herd quitter and she might have detoured them young cows off toward pond 16. Didn't see no big rig tracks anywhere but my eyes ain't what they used to be."

Cooper knew Polecat still could drop a bull elk at a quarter mile. So, there were no cattle truck tracks, only a desire by Polecat to skip extra saddle time at age 67.

Cooper drifted left in a wide easy circle; Ben, at the middle of the long thin column, pulled his blue bandana up over his nose to cut the choking dust.

Cooper said, "No point in scouting then. We'll pick them up when we reach pond 16. They won't break up before dark unless something spooks them. Let's keep the herd moving or they'll miss the train to Arizona Friday."

Cooper briefed Pete on his plan as they rode in a quick gallop toward pond 16 and the suspected cow hideout. He intended to cull the lead cow for winter freezer beef.

A hundred yards from the pond Cooper and Pete rode out of an almost bare Aspen grove like silent knights of the west. They saw the mostly two and three-year-old mother cows grazing around the nearly dry pond while number 82 eyed a depleted salt lick. Both riders split and circled south to prevent a herd break away. Neither Cooper nor Pete wanted to spend a windy cold fall night rounding up strays until sunrise.

Number 82-eyed Pete. She knew the game too well and the other girls started to bray. Cooper knew a wrong move could stampede them south any second behind their leader and trample Pete and his horse in the melee. Many a cowboy's dreams had died after being trampled by a spooked herd.

It was the moment of truth for Pete because Cooper could not reach him in time to help. Number 82 made yet another break for freedom, perhaps sensing she was going to be culled from the herd after a barren summer. Pete reached for his rope as he wheeled his horse into a near perfect position. With his hand forming a perfect loop in the lariat, he charged after the thundering cow while the herd watched; tramping their hooves, ready to stampede.

Pete prepared to execute the aggressive but effective version of the head loop as he caught the cow from behind. He dropped his looped rope over number 82's horns as Cooper moved Buckaroo between Pete and the herd. Pete's rope looped her horns and he yanked the slack from the loop. Next, in an easy, all-pro cowboy motion he flipped the rope over the cow's flank while spurring his quarter horse to full speed parallel to the cow. Buckaroo and

Cooper silently held their position, daring the herd to stampede. With a precision motion Pete turned the quarter horse to a forty-five degree southeast angle away from the renegade cow's path. Cooper watched Pete with one eye and held the herd in check with the other one. Pete's rope twisted the cow's head back and lifted her hind legs as he flipped her. The cow's direction reversed in a violent corkscrew somersault across the mesa grass. She would never bolt again.

The other forty-two cows brayed in disapproval but remained frozen behind Cooper. Thirty seconds later number 82 rose majestically to a standing position. She was uninjured but dazed as she drifted back to the security of the herd. Cooper had only seen this rarely used roping technique a few times in his young life because no hand or rancher wanted to risk injury to an animal. He knew Pete had made the right decision.

When number 82 rejoined the herd, Cooper lowered his alert status one level but did not move or speak. He heard the main herd braying and moving in the distance. Cowboying again made Cooper feel good but the ranch's financial problems drifted back to the edge of his thoughts as Polecat came into view with the dust cloud of the herd behind him. Also nagging at Cooper's thoughts was the ambush, the cut barbwire fence and his grandfather's advice that idle time in town produced immoral behavior.

Cooper returned to the ranch headquarters at five in the morning. The north wind had been in their faces all night, slowing the herd. He woke Liz when he called her in Dallas. He cautioned her to stay close to her hotel or in Neiman Marcus' private rooms until she returned to the ranch. Cooper slept fitfully for three hours and then rejoined the hands as they prepared the herd for truck shipment to Grand Junction to meet the railroad cattle cars.

It had been a long tough day for the ranch's hands. The cows were counted and positioned near the loading pens by dark. A two-day job had been accomplished in a day.

At daybreak Cooper oversaw the loading of the cattle as they walked up the log and plank loading-chute his grandfather had built. During the depression, his grandfather had been a mini WPA for the county. He spent the ranch's meager profits on capital improvements so proud men could feed their families.

One by one the twenty trucks backed their cattle trailers up to the perfectly maintained corral with its short Ponderosa loading chute. Ted and Elbow, with the ranch's two Blue Healer dogs, worked the cattle in the loading corral. The other hands under Polecat's eyes moved the cattle from the holding corrals as truck after truck loaded and formed a caravan in the ranch's two-mile driveway.

Cooper oversaw the operation, evaluating each mother cow on a chart Polecat had prepared as Pete quietly called out ear tag numbers. Cooper's concurrence with a Polecat penciled "x" meant Winter auction for a retiring mother cow and a job for one of the ranch's best two hundred and fifty female heifers that would be loaded last. The 757 steers had already been sold and trucked to Nebraska feed lots. But the remaining 527 prized YBarC heifers had been sold to other ranches in the need of young mother cows.

The last of the cattle moved peacefully up the planks into the tightly packed double-decked cattle trailers. The caravan would take three hours to drive to Grand Junction via Gateway. Cooper planned to lead it in his overhauled Jeep. Polecat, with two top hands, would drive a pickup behind the caravan and then travel by rail to northern Arizona. Their pickup would be rolled onto a flat car with its loaded six-horse trailer. Six top quarter horses spent the winter on warm range while the remainder of the remuda ate hay in cramped stalls or in the cold corrals near the headquarters. The YBarC kept its top hands on the payroll year-round. Cooper refused to hire cheap seasonal illegal Mexican hands. Ranch policy was able-bodied local men hired full time and seasonally in summer when extra help was needed.

Polecat checked the last sealed door of a cattle trailer as he had since 1933. At exactly noon and precisely on schedule the twenty White Motor Company tractor-trailers shattered the tranquility of the autumn day as wind driven corn snow began to pelt the idling caravan. The chrome stack pipes belched blue-black diesel smoke into the pristine mountain air under a low dark sky. Cooper knew their route would take the caravan past Lonnie Sr.'s uranium processing mill. Cooper and Liz suspected the YBarC's extreme western sections had uranium reserves but his grandfather refused to allow prospectors or federal geologists on the ranch, the cold war notwithstanding.

Cooper climbed into the Jeep's driver seat with Pete riding shotgun. Cooper didn't need to walkie-talkie Polecat because the routine had been well rehearsed over the years. He gunned his battered Jeep's powerful engine and signaled the lead cattle truck to move out. The convoy rolled slowly forward as the cattle brayed nervously and cold corn snow pelted Cooper in the face before he could zip the plastic window closed. He wished he was going to warm Arizona for the winter but he knew his fate was tied to Telluride.

The trucks thundered past the infamous hanging wood flume that overlooked the spectacular red rock Delores River Canyon. The 10-mile-long gold mining flume had cost almost $2 million at the turn of the century and had been considered an engineering marvel, suspended over the red sandstone cliff of the north canyon wall a thousand feet above the Delores River. Many lives were lost building the flume and like the Union Pacific railroad much of its labor was brought from China. After only two years of operation the hanging flume was damaged by a spring flood and, coupled with the silver crash of 1902, it was never repaired.

The Jeep cruised along the languid but always muddy lower Delores River. It was rumored to be mildly radioactive from the leaking pollution of Atomic Energy Agency's mill and Lonnie Sr.'s operation. Cooper spotted a jackknifed pickup truck with a four-horse trailer blocking the two-lane blacktop highway. Cooper signaled the already slowing lead truck behind him as he began to brake, hoping the twenty trucks behind the Jeep could stop without accident. After an uncertain moment Cooper's Jeep braked to a stop twenty-five feet away from the late model white Ford pickup.

He said to Pete, "Get the Winchesters quick from the back compartment."

Before Pete could reach the two loaded Winchesters, a bullet shattered the windshield. Cooper dove out the driver's side door onto the unforgiving pavement and ripped his wool shirt when he hit. He had managed to grab the walkie-talkie that was lying behind the gearshift rod but realized he had stupidly worn no sidearm.

Cooper yelled at Pete, "Roll over your seat and out the tailgate with the rifles or we're goners. Polecat's twenty trucks back with our only real help."

Another bullet pinged on the white line near Cooper. He hit the talk button on his walkie-talkie as he rolled under the Jeep.

"Polecat we're under attack by armed rustlers up here. You boys move up through the trucks on foot with your Winchester's. Leave somebody in drag position in case they hit from the rear out of Blue Creek."

"Roger, Cooper, we're half way to you already. Ted and I'll protect the cattle. Most drivers got pistols in their cabs. Keep your heads low 'til you hear our covering fire."

Pete crawled under the Jeep and handed Cooper a Winchester. The Jeep was bumped hard, forcing them to roll together under its drive shaft. Neither Cooper nor Pete could sight a shot as bullets continued to probe the pavement around the Jeep. Then Cooper heard the truck behind them pull around the Jeep, followed by a second cattle truck as they shifted to low second gear for acceleration. The Jeep vibrated as the cattle trailers passed it. A voice warned the two lead cattle truck drivers to lay face down on the pavement or their heads would be splattered like road kill.

Cooper gambled and rolled out from under the driver's side only to see the taillights of the second trailer moving past the Jeep. He couldn't fire at the trailer's tires because it might jackknife and injure the mother cows. They were being hijacked in broad daylight to his total astonishment.

A second later he heard Polecat yell, "Cooper and Pete, you all okay up there."

Cooper responded, "Yes, but the rustlers have two truckloads of our cows. Get your truck to the front of the convoy so we can chase them."

"No way to do that easily, Cooper. Got partially jackknifed cattle trailers for a good quarter of a mile in a too tight canyon. They'll hightail across the Utah line and hide them cattle in some remote canyon before we git this tangle of trucks ready to roll again. Only payphones twenty miles up at Gateway."

"Damn it!" Cooper saw Pete scramble to his feet unhurt next to the disabled Jeep with its two shot out front tires. "They just drove away with two hundred prime Y Bar C mother cows worth $50,000."

"First time the Y Bar C been big time rustled since my daddy was a hand," replied Polecat, coldly insinuating with his calculated inflection Cooper's return to the ranch had brought havoc.

Cooper perceived the disapproval but he ignored it, "Well get something rolling so I can get to the cafe in Gateway and call the highway patrol and the Union Pacific."

He walked quickly away from Polecat to avoid his urge to coldcock him. He needed him to move the herd to Arizona while he hunted down the rustlers. He wanted to hang them from a high cottonwood limb. It was total warfare on the YBarC and law was suspended on the range in Cooper's roiling young mind

TWENTY

The Straw Boss

The repaired Jeep whined in high four-wheel drive, as Cooper drove west on Colorado 145 toward Telluride. He drove the dead end spur from Society Turn into the majestic box canyon. Ajax Peak was already snowcapped from a two-day November snowstorm, which hit as the YBarC cattle left the Grand Junction rail yards. The state brand inspector's required paperwork for the rustled cattle had ruined Cooper's annual duck hunting trip. Cooper was relieved because he had recently learned that wild ducks mated for life and he felt guilty hunting them for sport. Polecat had confirmed that the cattle had been unloaded at the Arizona BLM grazing allotment.

Cooper enjoyed the breathtaking snow-flocked, tree-rimmed steep canyon walls that surrounded the Victorian mining town. The bright morning sun had already melted a track into the snowpacked highway and the Jeep's studded winter tires sang their metallic song. The storm had ended Indian summer, but its real beauty was its snowmelt water for the YBarC's range land.

Cooper slowed the rocketing Jeep when he passed Sundance Auto Repair and the adjacent empty wetlands, which were the mining company's tailings reserve that buffered Telluride on its western boundary. He drove straight to Gary's for an update on the condo deal before a surprise visit to Sam Jr. He hoped Sue was not at Gary's because he planned to see Adrianna in the evening. He passed the dilapidated red brick Opera House that was now showing art films and hosting a Labor Day film festival.

Cooper parked in front of Gary's perfectly restored Victorian. He knocked on the door but no one answered so he rang the buzzer. A minute later the door opened and Cooper was startled to be face to face with Sue. She was wearing a green plaid flannel shorty nightgown with black mesh tights that disappeared into deerskin Indian moccasins. Before Cooper could say anything, she said with a low gravely draw, "Cowboy, Gary's not here and neither am I."

Cooper winced, "Not very friendly today, are you?"

"Not since you took up with that wetback tortilla bitch. Guess blonde pussy is too sweet for your redneck roundups."

Cooper was not happy with her racially tinged choice of words.

He retreated a step and said, "Please tell Gary that I'm staying in Telluride off and on for the winter. He can contact me at the inn. I want to review the plans for the condo project as soon as possible."

Sue caught Cooper's involuntary glance toward her tights where they met her nightgown. "Yeah, it's real golden hair peeking out, Cowboy. Bet you remember it drips with sweet honey for the right bee, but you turned wasp. Gary will be back in two weeks from Mexico City. You can tell him yourself if you're still around," she added with malice.

"He have a phone number down there?" Cooper asked angrily. "Gary left town without phoning me an update."

Sue ignored his question, continuing her assault, "Sam Jr. said you are a paper cowboy tomorrow. I bet it all goes up your nose chasing that big-assed bitch around town. At least Sam Jr. knows the difference between a real woman and a Mexican whore."

Cooper reflexivity raised his hand to slap Sue across the mouth but she slammed the door in his face, narrowly missing his nose as he stepped toward her. He heard the dead bolt snap as he grabbed futilely for the doorknob.

Sue taunted through the solid door, "No blow for poor cowboy Cooper before banker Sam Jr. repos his horse."

Cooper stepped back onto the snowy flagstone walk to regroup his scrambled thoughts. He heard Sue's footsteps disappear into the house. He was surprised at the depth of emotion in Sue's voice over his abandonment of her for Adrianna. He had mistaken her for the town's mindless hot tub party girl. After his meeting with Sam Jr., he needed to think about her reaction as well as Gary's trip that would delay the construction start of the condos.

Suddenly the bedroom window above him opened and a double vial of coke plunged into the snow beside Cooper.

"Forgot - a present from Gary until his return. He'll spank me if he finds out I didn't give it to you."

Sue glared down at Cooper as one of her perfect breasts flopped out of her low-cut nightgown. "Dream about them Cooper. Even Gary can't make me fuck you again."

She retreated from view and the window slammed shut. Cooper picked up the full white vile and angrily twisted open the small plastic black top and filled it with coke. The blast hit his brain like wind driven snow on the range. He turned to walk to the bank, determined to confront Sam Jr. and save the YBarC but he felt Sue's tear filled eyes pierce his heart. He turned and saw her silently crying behind the window. He knew in his heart he owed her an explanation but it would have to wait.

Cooper walked directly into Sam Jr.'s office without an invitation. A teller ducked out to avoid the confrontation. Sam Jr.'s pale blue eyes drew a bead on Cooper.

"Howdy, Cooper, ready to sign a new set of papers for me?" He did not offer a chair.

"No, but here is your interest only check and a loan rollover letter drafted by my uncle."

He replied coolly, "This bullshit won't stand up in a court of law in the State of Colorado today. It is not 1890 in Telluride, Cooper. This is a state chartered bank not a federal bank so I don't have to fuck around with that liberal Democratic judge that Kennedy appointed in Denver. State judges apply the law the way the Colorado State Bank Association attorneys wrote it. Your uncle was a state legislator and he knows the score unless he's getting senile."

Cooper had had enough of Sam Jr. and the coke only shortened the fuse. "The ranch is not for sale now or ever in my lifetime."

"Cooper, you are being a jerk just like your morphine addicted daddy was, only he had his daddy to protect him and you have no one. You better take this offer right now, son, and I'll tear up this no count letter," Sam shot back harshly.

Cooper had heard the rumors about his father's addiction. He had used morphine to kill the pain from too many polo injuries rather than retire from the game.

Cooper lost his temper anyway and challenged Sam Jr. without hesitation, "Don't insult my dead father or we settle this on Colorado Avenue, barefisted, you fucking townie."

"This isn't the old west anymore, Cooper. You touch me and the marshal will lock you in jail, you son of a bitch," Sam retorted with fire his eyes. "Final offer from Lonnie Jr. is one million cash with a two-week closing after a survey and no Ajax Ski Corporation stock. You still keep the cows, Arizona federal grazing lease and your family's homestead house with 160-acres. That should keep you in women and coke for life if you invest in tax-free municipal bonds. Triple A only, of course."

Cooper had cooled off some so he played the hole card his uncle had suggested to flush out Lonnie Jr.'s real intentions.

"If it's subdivision land the Ajax Ski Company needs, I'll sell him the two Wilson Mesa sections with their Fall Creek water rights. That's 1,280-acres to subdivide with six cubic feet a second of senior water rights. It's twenty minutes from the base."

"Not enough Cooper. Lonnie wants all the YBarC water rights in both counties to grow the Ajax Ski Company's base village, subdivisions and make snow. Your ranch land is bonus for future growth." Cooper shook his head. Their intention was crystal clear.

Sam Jr. continued, "Two weeks, Cooper, and you retire to hot tub heaven with Sue and no more saddle blisters on your butt. Some reason she really likes you, Cooper. I didn't know the girl had a heart until you showed up in town."

"No deal," Cooper tried to be polite but clear. "It's my ranch now and two weeks won't change my mind."

"It will," asserted Sam Jr. "I'm going to call Lonnie Jr. now on this brand-new speaker phone so you can go straight up and see him before lunch."

Sam dialed four numbers and a female voice answered, "Ajax Ski Company, Lonnie Jr.'s office. Whom may I say is calling, please?"

"It's Sam Jr. at the bank. Cooper Stuart's in my office right now regarding the YBarC sale."

"Send him right up. Lonnie wants to talk to him and personally explain the deal in business terms, not banker's terms."

The line went dead, leaving Sam looking miffed.

"That ol' girl went to school with me and Lonnie at CU. He used to bang her in a friend's family's hunting lodge up near Ward. Now she's putting on airs since she's the gatekeeper up at the Ajax Ski Company headquarters."

Cooper turned and walked out of Sam's office without saying goodbye. He was $60,000 poorer from paying the interest on the bank note but he still owned the YBarC less the rustled cows.

As Cooper drove up to Lonnie Jr.'s office, he remembered his grandfather's warning story that Lonnie Sr. had been an unsavory small-time bootlegger on the Navajo Reservation in the 1930s. According to gossip, he had parlayed his illegal untaxed profits into a small fortune by investing in small gas and oil wells near Cortez, which he and a silent Midland Texas partner consolidated into a regional producer with pipeline interests. When the uranium boom hit western San Miguel and Montrose counties, Lonnie Sr. and his partner were able to secure the non-union subcontracts at Uravan mill that put them into the big time. He crossed swords with Cooper's grandfather when he wanted to lease a remote canyon on the ranch to dump radioactive tailings. Cooper remembered his grandfather had turned down the deal because he feared Lonnie Sr. was trying to circumvent the law.

A small time neighboring rancher provided the dumpsite and retired to Tucson five years later. Cooper suddenly realized there had been conflict between Bill Daniels and Lonnie Sr. He remembered that Lonnie Sr.'s company had bought the leased ranch after rumors flew countywide that Bill had found high levels of radioactivity in a well near the tailings site.

Lonnie Jr.'s only success to date had been as a college ski racer, followed by a lot of last place finishes on the Pro Ski Tour in the Spider Sabich era. Lonnie had the last laugh, Cooper mused, since his daddy bought him a ski area while most of the other pro racers were lucky to own a ski shop. Only one thing didn't make sense to Cooper about the rumors. Maybe this meeting would reveal the answer.

The expensive chrome furniture looked out of place in Telluride.

"You must be Cooper. I'm Ellen. Lonnie is expecting you." Ellen stood up from behind her spotless desk, revealing an athletic figure and an expensive blonde dye job, which framed a television soap star's face. Cooper followed her into Lonnie Jr.'s open office door noting her skier's hips under a red wool plaid skirt. Lonnie Jr. rose from behind his polished glass and chrome desk that reflected the noon sun and made Cooper wish he had kept his sunglasses on. His boots heels rang richly on the gleaming Italian marble floor as Lonnie Jr. extended a well-manicured hand.

His expensive brown Italian leather chair was from a Neiman Marcus Christmas catalog.

Lonnie was rugged, good looking, six feet in height and well-tanned. He had jet-black hair and a too broad nose that probably indicated reservation blood in the family tree. He had the powerful thighs of a ski racer under his gray flannel trousers but a lean upper body under a cotton shirt.

He smiled and barked, "Sit down, Cooper. I have wanted to meet you ever since Sam Jr. told me about the YBarC. Maybe we should have discussed the deal before Sam got involved but he insisted he advised your family so I deferred, being the new kid in town. May Ellen get you some coffee or we always have coke in the classic green bottle here," and he laughed at his inside joke.

"No thanks," replied Cooper still buzzing a little from the real thing. He sat in the proffered Hollywood-style steel framed and black leather director's chair.

"Buzz me if you boys need anything." Ellen exited a little too casually, Cooper noted.

"Well, Sam tells me you're holding out for more loot like any good businessman, Cooper, even if you are new at the helm. Nothing wrong with that, my daddy would say," he added.

"Not really," countered Cooper. "I just like ranching the YBarC like my father and grandfather and great-grandfather. It will be even more fun now that I can ski in Telluride."

"Hadn't heard you were a skier," Lonnie Jr. said a little surprised.

"Learned at Taos," Cooper replied.

"So did I," replied Lonnie Jr. "Taos Ski Area was my first choice to buy but Ernie Blake wouldn't sell. It's closer to our Dallas headquarters."

Cooper silently guessed Lonnie Jr. would rather be in Dallas wheeling and dealing in gas and oil circles instead of in Telluride operating a startup ski area.

"I'll have Ellen fix you up with a season pass." He barked the order for the pass into the intercom, and then he looked Cooper straight in the eye and said, "Well, Cooper how about 1.5 million dollars. All cash. We still assume the debt. That's half a million for driving up here today."

Then his eyes turned stone cold on a dime. "Hear someone took a pot shot at you and helped themselves to some cattle. I hear a lot of folks around here are still upset about your family's land acquisition tactics. Also, I hear skipping Vietnam has not helped you around Norwood or Montrose. Maybe it's a good time to cash in here and buy a big ranch somewhere else if you want to work instead of clip coupons."

"Well, ranching is in my blood and I don't know anything about being an idle trust-funder."

"Think about our final offer for a couple weeks. I want your land and frankly need it for expansion and to keep the real estate sharks from New York and California off my flanks. It's a fair all-cash-at-closing offer."

Cooper realized he never mentioned the ranch's water rights. Lonnie stood up, signaling the meeting was over before Cooper could reply.

He added, "Got a lunch with a fairy from some television show in Hollywood. He and his boyfriend want to pay too much for a lot at the base of chair lift for a hideaway. At least Ellen says they don't fuck little girls like that perverted European director. Hope the film festival doesn't drag too many perverts to Telluride."

"Well top dollar for elk pasture is good business, I guess," replied Cooper as Ellen walked into the office.

"Here's your season gold pass. Good for ten percent off at the restaurant, too. Food will be better this year since Lonnie booted the local steak burner and hired a Swiss chef." Ellen's eyes racked Cooper.

Cooper followed Ellen out of Lonnie's office, closing the door. "If you need someone to show you around the mountain this winter I'm off Saturday through Monday. Lonnie and I both ski raced for CU."

"Thanks. I may take you up on your generous offer since I haven't skied this mountain. In fact, I haven't skied since boarding school."

"Well, call me then and I'll make sure you get the right equipment and our top instructor," she replied, as she turned toward Cooper. Her firm breasts were accented under a light wool pink sweater.

Cooper made a quick exit, but he made a mental note to call Ellen when ski season started unless Lonnie Jr. revoked his pass.

TWENTY-ONE

The Real Deal

T he whine of the ski lift motor broke the silence of the morning before Thanksgiving. Cooper stood in a long cold line at 8:45 and waited for his first tracks of the season. In front of him in the unruly line were a motley group of skiers, ski bums, mountain hippies, shopkeepers, cocaine dealers, real estate agents, resort hustlers, waitresses, trust funders, ski racers and a new group of athletic mountain town women. Season passes dangled from almost every skier's neck. Clothing was mostly from the town's free box where the few affluent townies or departing seasonal workers left their cast-off clothing. Duct tape held together ripped ski pants, soiled jackets, broken goggle frames and beat up plastic ski boots. The only item the crowd seemed to spend big dollars on were skis. Cooper noted the people in line with him selected their skis as seriously as cowboys bought their cutting horses.

Cooper was embarrassed to look like the drug dealers who were attired in clothing purchased from Telluride's newest ski shop. Cooper had invested in an expensive well-designed nylon ski jacket and a warm Italian knit sweater but he still wore blue jeans with red gaiters. Until he learned more about the new ski equipment he had decided to rent demo skis, boots and poles. French plastic sunglasses seemed to be in vogue, accented with bandana headbands. Cooper wore a blue bandana with metal-rimmed sunglasses with his goggles turned against the back of his strong neck. The air temperature was only twelve degrees but the sun was bright. A few tourists with day or weekly passes stuck on triangle wire clips seemed to have invaded the noisy local scene. Everyone in line seemed to know everyone else; clouds of marijuana smoke wafted through the cold air and joints were passed openly from friend to friend.

Cooper was almost trampled when a red haired, freckled faced lift attendant wearing a Dodgers baseball cap lifted the red nylon rope between the crowd and the chair lift. Five minutes later, Cooper was swept safely into the air by the lift for the first time in almost a decade.

Cooper mentally reviewed the meeting he had scheduled with Gary, who'd finally returned to Telluride after a six-week absence. Cooper became angry every time he walked past the silent construction site with its red-ribboned survey stakes the only hint of activity.

Gary had only returned to Telluride after Cooper's uncle froze Gary's first payment of $50,000 that Liz had loaned Cooper. Sue had called Cooper to set up the mountaintop lunch and he had noted stress bordering on panic in her voice. He suspected Gary had learned she had not been baby-sitting Cooper in his absence and Sue was in major trouble with her boss. Cooper and Sue had not spoken since she slammed the door in his face.

As the lift neared the ridge top, Cooper reflected on his approach to the meeting. He could not be too confrontational because he needed the profits to help save the YBarC. Two weeks after his meeting with Lonnie Jr., Cooper had again refused his final offer. A day later a demand letter had been hand delivered to Pete, the winter hand, at the ranch. It demanded the full payment of the $600,000 the ranch owed plus all interest due in thirty days or foreclosure proceedings would began. Sam and Lonnie were sandwiching Cooper. There was nothing he could do except pay off the bank or have his uncle fight them in court to buy time.

Mount Wilson, Colorado's second highest peak, came into Cooper's view as prepared to ski off the lift. Cooper held his poles in his gloved hands. Rocketed off the chairlift, his skis met the slippery snow. He wobbled, lost his balance and fell to his left into the cold groomed snow. He landed on his left hip with a swishing sound as the silent ski bum who had ridden the lift with him gracefully skated away at high speed.

The lift motor slowed while Cooper awkwardly tried to stand on his skis again.

Distress was turning to panic as Cooper heard a confident voice, "You must be Cooper. I'm Brady Fox, your ski instructor that Ellen arranged. You're on time, which is rare around the Big Ditch. Grab my hand; it's more fun to ski than to grovel in the snow in an unloading zone."

He reached down and with a linebacker's pull yanked Cooper up and stabilized him with a forearm across Cooper's chest.

"Thanks," Cooper said. "I owe you one."

"Clients who take a decade off from skiing are naturally dazed by the rapidly changing equipment revolution. In a couple of hours, you'll be begging me to quit making you practice your turns."

Cooper liked Brady's easy confident manner and forgot his embarrassing dismount.

"Ellen said you played polo in boarding school. From what I hear about western polo, skiing will be the same big fast action when we hit the steeps. Until then, we practice on runs groomed for Sunday golfers."

"So where do we start?" Cooper asked as the ranch's financial problems vanquished.

"Eyes right, Cowboy. They call this run 'Angel Food Cake.' We start with a warm-up run down the center just like Gary Player drives a golf ball. First, I need fifteen dollars for the first two hours. I'll turn the meter off then if I can bring my girlfriend Kara out to your ranch for a ride. We can't afford to keep a horse on the Ajax Ski Company's wages," he explained with youthful hope in his voice.

"Done deal," replied Cooper. "I have a dozen quarter horses that need winter exercise. You're both welcome to keep them from getting fat."

The young ski instructor smiled as if he had struck gold.

"Follow me and start in a snowplow. See you at the bottom. Stay in my tracks like you're tracking an elk."

"That's too easy," replied Cooper. "Bagged a six-point bull on the ranch last week." And he followed Brady down the novice run, his ski legs already returning.

Three hours later Cooper sat in the lodge restaurant across from Gary who had a reduced set of blueprints spread out on the table between him.

"Trust me, Cooper, here are the final blueprints fresh from Taylor Construction in Phoenix. I had to spend two extra weeks with our rich investor from Mexico City. Things go slowly down there. Anyway, HARC, which protects Telluride's historic zoning code, made Taylor revise everything anyway. These plans will finally clear HARC tonight. I guarantee it and we can get a spring construction start date."

"So who's the Mexican money? I didn't know they skied."

"Friends of friends in Phoenix. They own meatpacking plants in Mexico City. They pay workers a dollar a day and invest some of their pesos in the USA as a hedge. They own a ski house at Vail where several other Mexican government and big business families have bought places. Down there, government and business are one and the same. One payoff satisfies all."

"Sounds shady to me but they're your investors," replied Cooper. "Mexican buyers pay cash up front for YBarC cattle. Is the Mexican money in the Bank?"

"It is."

"I will have my uncle release the fifty thousand for one share only, wave our option on the second one. I need you to move earth. Ranch needs the profit yesterday."

"Soon as the zoning is in place and I sell the last share. No more than a month."

Cooper spent Thanksgiving Day with Liz at the ranch. She supervised the serving of her traditional dinner that included oyster dressing, prime YBarC rib eye steaks, elk steaks, wild turkey, rolls, pumpkin pie, and reserve New Mexico red wine. Uncle Harvey flew his twin-engine plane from Fairplay to Montrose and drove over since Norwood's grass landing strip could not accommodate it. Several of Cooper's distant relatives and various friends of Liz attended the feast. Adrianna had been invited but could not leave her restaurant on the first big holiday weekend of the ski season. The YBarC's financial problems were not known in the extended family beyond his uncle so the lunch had been a pleasant interlude.

After the guests departed, Liz, Uncle Harvey, and Cooper retired to the parlor.

Cooper opened the conversation, "Sam Jr. is not going to back off unless Lonnie Jr. calls it quits. The offer is still 1.5 million cash and I keep the cows, headquarters section and the Arizona BLM lease. Also, Lonnie assumes the loan and any back interest."

"Well that's a fat offer in today's ranch market with low beef cycle prices if you want to sell out. I never liked the original cash and stock deal. I don't ever advise being a minority stock holder in a private family corporation," Uncle Harvey stated. "What is the ranch's cash position?"

"Not pretty." Cooper tried to soften his tone with Liz in the room. "Interest paid through the end of third quarter with a $600,000 loan balance, but most ranch business accounts ninety days or more."

"What's your receivable position?" asked Harvey. Liz listened with her thin-lipped mouth in a pout.

"The second calf payment comes due in January, but the annual fixed ranch overhead and the clearing of the critical overdue accounts plus paying quarterly bank interest again in January, will exhaust it. Sam Jr. won't clear overdrafts either. The ranch bounced a truck repair check for the first time in its history last week. There's no way to pay much of the principal until next fall except with the insurance claim on the rustled cattle, if we don't find them. That will take six months at least before the state police and the Brand Inspector declare them officially unrecoverable."

Liz looked distressed. Uncle Harvey cleared his throat. His tenor voice still boomed strong at 71, his looks distinguished by his silver gray hair. Cooper always thought of him as William Jennings Bryan.

"Well, Cooper, they have you between a rock and a hard place. They're about to roll the rock down onto your head. The YBarC is cash poor until you build it back to its old production levels. Beef prices are in a down cycle now that the war in Vietnam is winding up. That means we liquidate some of the herd and sell some ranch land over the next five years to make a small profit. The bank's safe should have been full of YBarC cash coming out of this war."

Liz looked away as anguish gripped her fragile doll like face. Uncle Harvey's reprimand had hit its target but she still remained silent.

Cooper said, "I can still turn the YBarC around with high calving rates, new fences, and tight-fisted management. I want to ranch. It's my life's work. I can't allow the ranch to be cut up into ranchettes and the water rights used to make snow and build a second home city."

Liz remained silent, her guilt overwhelming.

"I can get you eight months breathing room. Maybe a year when I call in a judicial favor or two from the day they serve you the foreclosure papers. I helped rewrite the state bank laws and they favor the bank owners. After that the marshals arrive to seize the ranch unless you can pay off the note."

"Can you help me find new financing?"

"Of course, but friendly terms are hard to find these days. Mining has been the big economy. There's nothing to replace its high paying jobs and big profits. The new resort job dollars got no mule kick. The ski towns will be like the mining towns before the unions came to Colorado. Lots of poor workers with a few owners riding high in the saddle."

Liz spoke for the first time, her voice armed with a mother's emotion. "Harvey what are you really saying to Cooper?"

He paused, "They mean to play rough with Cooper if he doesn't sell out. Big real estate is taking over the state's ski industry fast. It's already happening at Vail and Aspen. More profits to be made selling a dude a vacation home lot than a ride on a ski lift and a beer. Cooper has the water and land they need for a fifty-year high profit ride."

Tears formed in the corners of Liz's eyes.

"The score's one probably dead for the out of town team and none for the YBarC. Screw them," Cooper sharply responded.

"Lonnie Sr. may send hired killers that work for the Houston oil boys next time not retired Phoenix mob hustlers or Nevada casino kitchen rustlers. Gunmen have always been able to find work in the west," continued Uncle Harvey. "You choose to fight them, then you have to be smart, not a polo circuit tough guy like your father. So you either plea-bargain out, Cooper, or be prepared to fight an old-time range war. There's no middle ground."

Liz exploded into tears knowing that her stewardship of the ranch had helped paint Cooper into a corner.

But Cooper calmly said, "My marriage contract with the YBarC is until death do us part."

"Well, son, then load your best repeating rifles. I'll handle the legal for you and look for a sweetheart loan in Denver or a not so sweetheart Mormon loan out of Salt Lake City. Liz here ought to move to Montrose quick as possible to stay out of the crossfire."

Cooper spoke softly to calm Liz. He knew Uncle Harvey had never approved of her operating the ranch as Cooper's guardian. He believed that he should have overseen the operation after Cooper's grandfather died. "Liz, I know this is a hard discussion for you so please let me and Uncle Harvey finish it alone. It's not your fault the Vietnam War delayed my return home. You start the move to Montrose Monday."

Liz regained some composure, "That will be fine, Cooper. I'll fix Harvey some fresh coffee in a thermos for his drive to Montrose airport." She exited gracefully.

Harvey watched the leaded glass parlor door slide close.

"Liz is still the best-looking woman in Western Colorado, but she has left you with a bad hand, no chips and no insurance for the rustled cattle, Cooper. I'll fly to Denver midweek to look for some refinancing. Some of the business boys up there still owe me a favor from my days in the legislature. Maybe one of them can help. I have to get to Montrose before they close the airport and I have to sleep in my plane."

"Thanks, Uncle Harvey. I'll be in Telluride most of the week at the Johnstone Inn. Pete will help Liz move to Montrose. I carry a pistol or a rifle everywhere now." His voice was devoid of emotion and his eyes were like lasers. This might be the last Thanksgiving he ever spent in this home that had stood as a fortress on Wright's Mesa for almost eighty years.

The Jeep high beams searched for mule deer as Cooper drove toward Telluride. A few lights were on in the roadside town of Placerville. He had promised Adrianna he would have New Mexico pumpkin pie and Cognac with her at the restaurant. Telluride would be bustling on the first holiday night of the ski season in high contrast to the deserted snowy mesas that surrounded it. Cooper pressed the accelerator, confident the sheriff and his deputies were all at home for dinner; he wanted to see Adrianna.

Fifteen minutes later he was with Adrianna in her small office behind the kitchen. Their tongues tangoed. His eyes saw the four neat lines of coke on the glass top of her desk next to two half full snifters of hot brandy. His gloved hands found her hips under her skirt. Cooper was surprised she wasn't wearing her trademark satin panties.

She pulled Cooper's hands away as her skirt fell back into place like a curtain in a movie theater and said softly, "Do the coke now. Sip brandy. Think about me and eat the pumpkin pie. It is magic because the mushrooms from a secret Pueblo cave are mixed with the filling. They are only edible this week each year after winter makes their roots sleep."

She turned and disappeared back into the din of the kitchen. Cooper looked forward to Thanksgiving night in a canopied bed with Adrianna with a log fire roaring in her bedroom with hallucinogenic sex and mystical visions dripping in gold.

TWENTY-TWO
The Jack Dempsey Ordnance

Cooper sat facing an empty desk while the Ajax Ski Company and bank board of directors illegally met with Sam. They had called a special meeting to decide the fate of the YBarC but had refused to include Cooper. He was tipped about the secret meeting by Brady's girlfriend Kara who worked as a receptionist and secretary for the Ajax Ski Company. She had heard office gossip that the long-range plan called for clustered satellite second home villages and ranchette subdivisions that stretched forty miles west to Redvale, Colorado on the region's undeveloped ranching mesas. It also called for over a thousand acres of snowmaking for the Ajax Ski Company to insure Christmas/New Year's week skiing.

YBarC water rights would be piped to the new developments or swapped for aquifer well water draws along the river valley at key locations, including Telluride. The projected peak Holiday population was 30,000 people living and vacationing part-time in an arid county that now has 1857 scattered citizens.

The Ajax Ski Company also planned to have the State of Colorado build a four-lane highway from Interstate 70 at Grand Junction south to Telluride. Also on the short term drawing board was an FAA funded county airport as close to Telluride as feasible. The only scheduled vote on the scheme apparently was in the bank boardroom. Polecat was fond of saying, the tail planned to wag the dog until it killed it.

Suddenly the oak doors between the boardroom and Sam Jr.'s office burst open. Sam's presence saturated the room. Following in lockstep was Jesse Smith, the bank's new attorney, who recently arrived from his father's law firm in Phoenix. He was the first new attorney to open a law office in Telluride since the World War II Two mining boom. His main mission, according to rumors, was to scout opportunities for Phoenix investment money. Lonnie Jr. was absent but Cooper knew he was the real puppet master.

A frowning Sam Jr. sat down behind his spotlessly clean desk while Jesse sat down in an empty chair next to Cooper. Jesse was dressed in an expensive dark blue suit that made him look more important than his current station in life. At 28-years old he was in perfect shape from years of karate practice. Jesse coached a free karate clinic every Thursday night at the high school gym. His black hair and rugged good looks fit the ski town scene.

Sam opened the meeting, "Cooper, meet Jesse Smith. He'll outline the bank board's final position."

Jesse spoke, "The board voted 5-0 to foreclose on the YBarC if the principal and any interest due are not paid in full by January 2. The board believes the ranch's cash flow is insufficient to meet future principal and interest payments and operating expenses. The board also believes you do not have the experience to operate the ranch and reverse its poor financial condition in a timely manner. Finally, the board was outraged at the rustling of two hundred mother cows that it believes was caused by your carelessness. Your cattle are pledged assets to this bank and we will not allow you to dissipate them before you pay us off in full. Finally, your loan documents require a daily $20,000 minimum balance in the ranch's account which neither you nor your mother acting as your guardian, have met for years."

Cooper listened to Jesse's canned legal speech feeling the noose tighten around his neck. His anger was unchecked by the naked attempt of the newcomer to legally justify the theft of the YBarC for Sam and Lonnie. "All that just spells rat fuck, Sam. You and your new mouth piece stay off the YBarC or I will have you shot for trespassing."

"Cut the cowboy act, Cooper. This ski town doesn't need you. The bank board took your character into consideration. The last two generations at the YBarC are substandard," retorted Sam.

Cooper exploded. He dove across Sam Jr.'s desk and hit him in the mouth with a round-house right hand punch. The punch flattened Sam's thin lips against his front teeth and chipped a tooth. Sam slumped over his desk, out cold. Cooper slid off the desk and retreated toward the bank lobby.

Jesse shouted coldly, "You, Fuckup, are going to jail for this." He stood up, his hands ready to karate chop Cooper.

Cooper stepped through Sam Jr.'s open glass office door and slammed it shut just as Jesse karate chopped where Cooper's neck had been. The door shattered into a hundred pieces in a loud cracking sound that vibrated throughout out the bank.

Cooper pushed through the bank's front door and climbed into his Jeep. It was time to skip Telluride because the marshal's office would arrest him if Sam Jr. filed charges. He crossed the town limit in record time and headed to the ranch house.

Cooper mused that America had a long history of accusing principled people of holding up progress if money was the main game. Greed had returned to the tattered queen of the mining towns. History repeated itself every hundred years and Telluride was right on schedule. This time it was guided by a secret Ajax Ski Company resort master plan instead of an oligopoly of union hating and claim jumping mine owners. The only thing Cooper wondered was what would eventually cause the bust this time.

Cooper whistled Silent Night as he pulled into Liz's driveway in Montrose. Christmas Day was a shadow of its bygone version. Liz lived in a freshly painted white brick two-bedroom house. The Montrose landscape was a dull winter hued brown since no fresh snow had fallen. Only a vanload of holiday skiers being transported to Telluride indicated major change was in the region's wintry air. The joyous skiers were oblivious to the little western town on the edge of the Colorado plateau.

After Christmas lunch, Cooper briefed Liz on the ranch.

"Uncle Harvey is hunting bridge money and holding the bank off legally. I am using the new artificial insemination technique for the herd. It'll probably calve at ninety-five percent this spring. That will produce the same amount of calves we had with 200 more mother cows last year."

Before he could continue Liz pleaded, "You are ranch royalty, Cooper, not a reservation bootlegger's son. Lonnie Sr. hated your father for his big ranch, easy way with women, and blonde good looks. He has always wanted to be king on the hill in Western Colorado. You and the YBarC are all that remain in his way. He'll call the shots from now on, not his son."

Cooper silently realized for the first time that the broad swath his father had cut through the region had affected everyone in his generation. There were more people than he had guessed lying in the bushes waiting for a back shot. Add that to the sins of his grandfather and great-grandfather and he probably had other hidden enemies circling him like the ghosts that used to live under his boyhood bed.

Cooper drove slowly in a blinding blizzard, his powerful Jeep plowing through the rapidly accumulating snow. He had a midnight Christmas dinner date at Adrianna's restaurant with her and a few of their town friends. Polecat had expressed no opinion when Cooper told him there would be no YBarC Christmas bonuses for the first time since the silver crash. That was the final budget cut in a series of actions, which included the elimination of overtime pay, a moratorium on new equipment purchases, and even a requirement that the hands pay for the repair of their personally owned saddles as well as purchase their work clothes. Cooper had hoped Polecat understood but he would have liked a little vocal support for his hard decisions to ration the ranch's vanishing cash.

Cooper wondered if Polecat approved of the time he had been spending in Telluride. He wondered if word had reached the ranching community about his time on skis, instead of on horseback. He knew Polecat would disapprove of his relationship with Adrianna. The line between Anglo and Spanish culture was still rigid in western Colorado's ranching community and he had carelessly crossed it.

Without warning, the Jeep went into an uncontrolled skid and Cooper downshifted carefully to let the big engine's compression brake the Jeep in the deep snow. Unable to steer he skidded across the oncoming empty lane near some newly erected cookie cutter condos and finally came to a stop in a snow bank. Cooper figured his mechanic had probably missed a damaged tie rod after one of the Jeep's ambush accidents. Like most mechanical parts, it broke in the worst weather conditions at a late hour. He would call the Sun Dance mechanic in the morning to pick it up and tow it across the road to his ramshackle garage.

He slipped into his oilcloth ranch slicker to protect himself and his new aviator jacket from the blizzard. He pulled his .22 pistol with its cheap silencer from the glove compartment for a stop he had planned before he reached Adrianna's late dinner party. Then he stepped into the teeth of the snowstorm and started to walk slowly toward town hoping to hitch a ride.

An hour later after a stop at the inn to warm up, Cooper looked up at Lonnie Jr.'s new house. Lonnie's Dallas wife had built it into the steep north canyon wall because she didn't like old Victorian houses with bad views. A steel shark net imported from Australia was suspended behind it to protect the house from rocks and boulders that regularly rolled down the south facing slide zone above it. Cooper had a Kara tip that the family was in Dallas for the holidays visiting Lonnie Sr.

He pulled the silencer from his slicker pocket and snapped it onto the pistol carefully. Then he sighted Lonnie Jr.'s lit Christmas tree and began to fire, stopping only to reload once. When he finished shooting, Cooper had demolished the Christmas tree and the entire two-story thermal pained glass front of Lonnie Jr.'s new home. Cooper knew the water pipes would freeze as he unscrewed the hot silencer with a gloved hand, cooled it in the snow and slid it carefully in his pocket. He put the pistol in the inside slicker pocket. He briskly walked the four blocks through alleys to Adrianna's bistro, encountering no one.

Cooper eased himself through the unlocked kitchen door to the Bistro. He could hear laughter in the dining room but the spotless stainless steel kitchen was empty. He slipped into Adrianna's office and hid the pistol and silencer behind her safe. He hung up the soaked slicker and cowboy hat on a rack. He poured himself a long drink from a reserve bottle of Spanish brandy Adrianna kept on her desk. He checked his bomber jacket pocket for the tiny wrapped box he had brought from the YBarC. He found it still nestled there, protecting an antique turquoise Hopi ring that had been part of his Grandmother's collection. She had bought it after her marriage from a Hopi Medicine Man who claimed it insured spiritual purity. Cooper had always liked its smooth cool surface that seemed to connect him to a vein of ancient Hopi spirits when he rubbed it with his fingertips. Once as a child he had rubbed it against his forehead and the stone turned light silver blue like the big western Colorado sky. Cooper hoped Adrianna would like it.

Twenty guests sat at a long table with Adrianna at its head, an empty seat to her right. The aroma of fine Spanish wine and food overwhelmed the room. Everyone welcomed Cooper as Adrianna rose and kissed him on the cheek as he sat down facing Gary, who was sitting next to Sue. Brady and his girlfriend Kara shouted a Christmas salutation from the other end of the table; guests ate and drank with gusto. Cooper recognized a Hollywood actor who frequented the Bistro when in Telluride and several of Adrianna's regulars from other points on the compass completed the party. The holiday season brought Telluride an electric mix of wealthy ski types who helped fill the local cash registers. Everyone in town would be relieved the first big winter powder storm had arrived just in time for the holiday skiers.

"Welcome my brave rancher. You have overcome the fierce Christmas blizzard to be with us. I will warm you with my best Spanish brandy for this noble effort before we see the hot golden sun god again." Adrianna's tongue teased Cooper's ear as she retreated to her chair.

Cooper's jeans stirred as he refocused his eyes on Gary, avoiding Sue's stare. "Sorry I'm late but the steering went out on my Jeep near Sundance Auto Repair and I had to walk all the way into town."

Before Adrianna could speak Sue said in a stoned voice,

"Thought real cowboys towed a horse in a trailer everywhere. But I hear, you're a skiing cowboy these days."

Cooper didn't want a rerun of his last conversation with Sue so he popped Adrianna's gift onto the table although he had intended to present it privately.

She gasped, "Cooper what have you brought me in such a special small box? I will open it later under my tree with you at my house where your present awaits our return."

Before Cooper could respond or Sue could counter, Gary handed Cooper a vile and said, "Merry Christmas. The snowballs are inside. Eat first and try them when you're under the tree with Adrianna. It looks like a very special night for my two favorite Colorado friends."

"Thanks," Cooper said, not knowing the term snowballs meant a mixture of coke and heroin popular in the edgy Hollywood crowd. "It's been a long day with the drive through the storm."

"Even Jack Dempsey needs a night off of training from boxing," Gary winked with a knowing laugh. Adrianna looked at Cooper quizzically but didn't rejoin Gary. Cooper signaled his acknowledgment with a half-smile to Gary but ignored Adrianna's quizzical look. Cooper began to eat, his alibi secure, as the revelers veered out of control snorting lines of coke openly on the table while a bottle of brandy was passed mouth to mouth in the candlelit room. Adrianna's wool skirted knee pressed his thigh as her hand stroked it.

An hour after the restaurant closed Cooper and Adrianna, wearing only the green turquoise ring, made love nude on the rug in her living room. She and Cooper had done half the vile of the snowballs and he was to high too think. All he could comprehend was her soft full breasts in his hands and a hard nipple in his mouth.

The blizzard rattled the windows but the fire warmed their bodies as Cooper covered her with his strong body by the Spanish tin and silver ornament laden Christmas tree. Cooper's fear of losing the YBarC gradually abated as the strong drug of her sex mixed with the snowballs obliterated his conscious mind while she stimulated his testicles with the ancient magic Hopi ring.

TWENTY-THREE

The Bowl

Cooper, wearing his new Vuarnet sunglasses, rode the chairlift and reviewed the events of New Year's Eve in his mind. He and Adrianna had gone to the ball in the World War II Quonset hut, which had been the high school gym since 1950. Most of the town, including the younger holiday skiers, had turned out for the volunteer fire departments annual fund-raising bash. Adrianna wore a stunning sleek floor length light wool black dress. Her right ring finger showcased Cooper's grandmother's ring in the low dance floor light.

Cooper saw Lonnie Jr., Sam Jr. and Jesse Smith talking at the bar where the firemen served Coors beer. They danced to Texas swing. A sterling silver flask filled with bourbon in his tweed sport jacket's inner pocket nested next to his .22. Gary and Sue danced by them, buzzed from coke, followed by Brady and Kara. The clock struck midnight and a net full of red, white and blue balloons were released from the rafters. Adrianna gave Cooper a long warm tongue-to-tongue kiss. Cardboard horns tooted around them and the revelers ushered in their hopes for a prosperous New Year. Cooper and Adrianna danced across the basketball court. Adrianna kissed Brady and Cooper kissed Kara. Most of the crowd was fueled with alcohol, pot or coke. It was ski town chaos in the crepe paper decorated gym.

Cooper felt a hard tap on his shoulder and he guessed it was Gary cutting in to kiss Adrianna. He felt her breasts float away as he turned. His body recoiled defensively. The swirling crowd trapped him as he faced Jesse Smith chin to chin. Jesse's blue eye blazed with fire as he stuck a legal-sized envelope into Cooper's hand, but Jesse's hand still grasped a letter-size one.

"Fuck you, Cowboy, this is notice to quit the Y Bar C. You are hereby served a foreclosure notice with all here present to witness on the first day of the year. In my other hand I have an injunction barring you from the bank, my office, and within two hundred feet of Lonnie's and Sam's houses. You violate it, you go to jail."

Cooper was pressed so tightly against Jesse by the on- looking crowd that the attorney was not able hand him the small envelope. Cooper hard-shouldered Jesse to his left then hit him with a right uppercut to the balls. He slumped in slow motion onto the old gym's hardwood floor. Cooper had never liked bad manners in public. He moved to shield Adrianna from the fray with his tall body.

"Bet you serve the restraining order first next time, big city lawyer."

Cooper felt his arms being pinned behind him by two young broad shouldered bearded firemen. "Take this bullshit outside, Cowboy, and get the hell back to the Saddle Tramp Bar where you belong."

Adrianna saw Cooper start to lose control and said firmly, "Let go, Chad, or your house account is history. He didn't start this. The crooked lawyer on the floor was rude."

They hesitated a long second and then freed Cooper. Just then Lonnie Jr. barreled through the bystanders with the longhaired deputy town marshal who had given Cooper the parking ticket.

"Arrest the deadbeat asshole," he demanded. "We got an injunction barring him from touching Jesse."

The deputy marshal, armed only with a flashlight surveyed the scene quickly then asked, "You that Cooper guy that owns the Y Bar C ranch?"

The whole gym went quiet as Christmas mass; all eyes were on Cooper. The deputy marshal stooped and picked up the small envelope and opened it. Cooper tensed, thinking about shooting his way out if he attempted to handcuff and arrest him.

"Says here you are enjoined from assaulting Jesse and Sam Jr. who is over there by the bar and Lonnie. It's the judges signature all right!"

Before he could make a decision Adrianna, stepped between them and said, "Jesse never gave Cooper the little envelope, only the big one, that's why you found it on the floor, Mark. He shoved Cooper in the back and knocked him into me, which started all this. You can't arrest a man for that."

The deputy marshal paused confused by the contradicting witnesses. Lonnie Jr. helped a white-faced Jesse to his feet.

The deputy played for time. "Anyone see it differently. If you did. speak up now."

Cooper saw Gary slide Sam Jr. out the fire exit with Sue, presumably for a toot and a hot tub. Gary's cutting horse move impressed Cooper. The drunk and high crowd edged closer, breaking into an old west versus new west stand-off. Only Adrianna, in her revealing dress, stood between the two sides. The deputy marshal applied his nonviolent '60s college civil rights sit-in training and concluded, "Then it was self- defense but the injunction is hereby legally served and I'm ordering both parties off the Fireman's Ball premises now."

Before anyone could react, Adrianna boomed in her lilted voice, "Drinks are on the house at the Bistro bar until closing time."

Half the crowd bolted for their wraps and coats because the locals knew she had the best liquor in Telluride. She grabbed Cooper's arm firmly and pulled him toward the front exit as Lonnie Jr. watched with a frozen look of hatred on his tanned face.

The cold northwest wind hit Cooper in the face as the warm air was sucked out of his lungs when they exited the gym door.

Cooper was still hotwired. "Why did you lie to stop me from just shooting Lonnie Jr. and ending the game? The bastard set me up publicly."

Emotion chocked her voice, "You spoiled brat. If a Spanish or Indian man had struck Sam or Jesse with his fist or shot up Lonnie's new house they would have buried him under the jail by now. You better stop bulling your way through Telluride. Use your prep school-college educated head. You let that son of newly rich white trash boy Lonnie Sr. sucker you into shooting anybody and you will serve hard time in Salida. You western Colorado boys are about to be out of fashion in the big ditch except to load lifts and pound nails."

Cooper was surprised at the depth of her anger. Logic returned to his voice. "So you figure, it's Lonnie Sr., just like my uncle and Liz do."

"Unless you have an iron skillet for a brain, Lonnie Sr. means to kill you if he can't buy you off. Sam and Lonnie Jr. got less brains than Sue."

"This legal-size envelope contains my eviction notice."

Adrianna stopped in the snow and turned to face him. She grasped both of his bare frozen fingers in her black deerskin gloved hands. She looked him in the eyes and asked, as the moon popped over Ajax peak, "What are you going to do about it, Cooper?"

The moonlight illuminated the white clock face on the courthouse. Cooper looked into her doe brown eyes that radiated strength. "Mano et mano until the old bull is dead. I ride the open range on earth or in heaven."

Adrianna's eyes burned deep into Cooper's soul. "Honor before life. That is the path of a great man. I ride with your brand from this moment. I am your lover and a secret silent assassin if you call me to fight."

Cooper was stunned again by Adrianna's clear courage and iron will. She had offered him total allegiance in an Anglo fight. She drew a line in the snow with her boot and stepped across it.

"Tonight, I cross this border to fight with you against our mutual enemies. The Anglo land and water speculators have stolen southwestern Spanish land grant rights since 1848. Drink my blood for strength."

She pulled a small penknife from her leather purse and cut her right index finger through the deerskin glove. When the blood formed on her exposed fingertip she lifted it to Cooper's lips. He tasted her salty red blood, their energy fused. The bitter cold northwest wind blew snowflakes against their faces as the warm blood coursed down his throat, renewing his center for the fight.

"Lift your ski tips up," a lift attendant yelled. New Year's Eve vanished from Cooper's thoughts as he glided across the fresh silky snow. Brady's other guest for the day was Rob Kells, a freestyle skier, motocross racer, and an aerobatic hang glider pilot. In Cooper's mind that was the equivalent of winning the all-around world cowboy championship in a year when the rodeo clowns were on strike.

Brady said, "Here's the plan, Cowboy. We're going to warm up on the big bumps then walk up with our skis on our shoulders to the top of the Gold Hill's hang glider launch site. Then we are going to snow launch and hang glide into the top of San Joaquin Cular on skis."

Cooper gulped, "I'm game for the ski part but I don't know how to hang glide so deal me out."

"That's covered. I have a tandem rig on the top of Gold Hill," replied Brady.

"Then deal me in but it sounds more dangerous than bronco busting."

"If you can break a wild horse then this is cruise control. Wild horses scare the piss out of me," asserted Kells.

"Every man's got to be afraid of something, my grandfather used to say. Only the dead morons failed to admit it," Cooper reflected.

Cooper rode the lift up with Kells who probed, "Here you deballed Jesse on the big eve. He's the playground snitch around here."

"You know him?"

"You bet," answered Kells. "He got an injunction against our hang gliding club, The Telluride Air Force, to stop us from winter launching off the top of Bridal Veil Falls. The mining company owns the only access to the historic Tesla powerhouse and the waterfall. Lawyer buddy of mine flew in to represent us but the local black robe was clearly surfing for the silver and gold moles. We argued the Utes still owned the column of frozen water that they consider sacred. Some old-timers say the Bridal Veil icefall is a Ute God. They believe their treaty with the white man doesn't cover Bridal Veil since they don't sell their gods. We lost in the local court on plain old trespass charges and the hometown courtroom fix."

Cooper was impressed by Kell's quick mind and frontier sense of justice. "Jesse is a fixer. You're dead right about that. It's a shock to see a kid from our generation already on that path. He's glued to my ass like a heat seeking missile. Too bad Brady can't take him tandem hang gliding with a trick harness."

Kells said, "I like you already. Jesse tried to get me banned from the mountain after I cut his skis tails last month and face planted him down a steep slope."

"Looks like he failed unless you have a stunt double."

"Fortunately, Lonnie Jr. likes all the publicity I get for his big snow pile and his secretary likes skiing Bear Creek with me when he's out of town. If you go skiing with her take your lambskin condoms because she gets off doing it standing in the pines on a steep tree run," Kells offered.

"Interesting," replied Cooper deadpan.

Brady, Kells, and Cooper skied to the trail for Gold Hill. The ski patrol had already towed the two hang gliders up for them behind a Ski-Doo to the launch area. It was one step at a time in ski boots at 12,000 feet in the thin cold air. Cooper was number three in the marching order so he easy stepped into the boot prints Brady made ahead of him. A half hour later they had reached the launch and set up the triangle shaped Wills Wing hang gliders.

"We're going to fly sitting straight up with our skis dangling below us," Kells instructed. "This makes launching tricky. We both have to ski off at the same speed and sit down at the same time on the bar. Too early, and we nose dive. Sit down too late, and you spin us hard back into launch. Since you break broncos I know you'll sit down on time."

"Used to outrun YBarC bulls as a kid game. It required diving under barbwire fences, which developed my timing."

The twenty-year-old Kells said, "Kind of like that, only you just sit down and let me fly once we're airborne."

Cooper snapped to full alert when Kells yelled, "All aboard on a ten count. The wind is perfect for takeoff."

On the count of zero they skied like madmen off the steep slope of Gold Hill and almost magically went airborne. Cooper crossed himself, Catholic style.

"Good enough view, Cowboy? Bet you can see your ranch from up here real good," Kells yelled over the wind as he circled the hang glider up toward Brady who was now on a glide path to the landing zone.

"I can see almost all of the YBarC. Too bad our hands can't use one of these to spot stray cattle. What's the landing plan, or are you just going to drop me like a ski bomb?"

"We're going to soft land on the chute's flat ridge top and away from its knife edge cornice so our weight doesn't break it. Then we tear down the gliders and tie them down real good so they are still here tomorrow when Brady and I hitch a ride near here on a snowmobile and fly them to town."

At two thousand feet above Gold Hill, Kells leveled off the hang glider and started a long glide across a deep canyon to the top of what looked like a thin football field. Cooper could see the snow-covered San Juan Mountains from his cramped seat as the wind roared against the gliders wing. The narrow cular looked like a roofless tunnel that opened into a natural bowl. Cooper knew each layer of untracked snow below them rested dangerously on the previously deposited layer always ready to set off an avalanche. Fresh snow in the cular indicated it was avalanche prone if the sun heated it too fast. Cooper did not want to hear the thunderous crack that signaled sure death in the bowl. He watched Brady approach the dangerous landing field with apprehension as the bright midday winter sun reflected off his glider.

Brady skidded down the snow runway veering close to the cornice's edge for a few yards until he lifted his skis a few inches off the windblown surface and realigned the glider. He used up the entire snowy flat-topped surface before he nosed the hang glider to a hard stop on his skis.

Cooper heard Kells instruct, "Buckle your ski boots tight; we're number two on approach for the snow zone."

The hang glider dove toward the landing zone. Cooper refocused as the snow's crusted surface rushed to meet their skis. Cold air filled his nostrils and the low winter sun blinded him. Kells first tilted the triangular wing left and then right until it reached the edge of the aircraft carrier-like snowfield. They flew full power on a centerline approach. Kells piloted them like an eagle diving for a jackrabbit. They came in flat-winged. Suddenly Cooper felt his skis glide across the surface of the snow.

"Stand up now, Cooper," Kells yelled as they skied shoulder to shoulder down the snow runway to an easy stop.

They let the glider wing fall perfectly behind them on the almost windless ridgeline with their view from the top of the winter world.

"Well done. Welcome to the Banana Belt. It's a special club and you just became a member."

The hot jocks like Kells and Brady called Telluride the Banana Belt because of its great snow, warm sunny winter days and cheap living. The current chairman of the club had just acknowledged Cooper's membership, but Cooper knew something Kells did not realize yet. In the boardrooms of the bank and Ajax Ski Corporation, the elimination of the Banana Belt Club was already being planned by the moneymen.

"Saddle that horse up again. It's the first time since I broke my first horse that all my cells have been awake at the same time," Cooper shouted over the wind.

"Time to stow the gliders. Brady drops in first. When he is midway down, Cooper, you drop in behind him. I'll ski clean-up so if anyone has a yard sale before we reach the bowl, then I'll ski down the surviving gear."

Brady started to fold up his hang glider. Cooper helped take down the large tandem glider and tie it down to metal stakes they pounded into the hard snow pack. Then the group checked their ski gear, tightened their bindings, shortened their goggle straps, and turned on their locators in case of an avalanche.

With a whoop, Brady jumped off the cornice and plunged airborne twenty feet straight down with his knees tucked parallel behind him. Cooper skied a few yards down the curved razor edge of the cornice and chose a less airborne route. Before he could ski off its edge, it cracked like a rifle shot and broke off, cart wheeling him into the bowl. He caught an upside down glimpse of Kells before the sluff avalanche carried him downhill toward Brady. He swam on his stomach and tried to regain control. Cooper knew he had violated the cowboy rule, which was never to ride your horse to the edge of a steep canyon to look over. Brady accelerated to escape the wave of snow that carried Cooper, who was now swimming on its surface trying to roll back onto his skis upright.

Cooper took a deep breath and pretended he was remounting a galloping horse. He centered his mind and forced his strong legs to lift him upright. He balanced and half way down the thousand foot shoot the sluff avalanche stopped and Cooper regained full control of his skis. A half minute later he stopped next to Brady at the top of the empty pristine bowl with its deep powder.

"Bet you won't forget to jump the cornice next time, Cowboy. When I say follow me, do it like Simon Says, not a golden retriever looking for a place to pee."

Brady had never dressed him down before, so Cooper knew he had screwed up totally.

"Glad you're happy to see me," Cooper laughed to break the tension just as Kells soared fifty feet into the air off the cornice edge, landing right of the gnarly snow that Cooper had agitated. With a dozen lightning quick powder turns he stopped an inch from Cooper's skis.

"Good recovery, Cowboy; Brady here is the best ski-teach in the big ditch. You can ski with us any day; just jump the edge of the cornice next time so we don't have dig you out."

"I'm gone," Brady laughed and he dropped into the wide bowl's waist deep powder snow and skied in easy turns down the bowl's perfect fall line. Cooper followed and Kells dropped in behind him. Cooper instantly knew he liked backcountry bowl skiing as much as he liked cowboying and that was a very scary thought because knew he needed to spend all of his time ranching.

TWENTY-FOUR

After Hours

Cooper passed his days in January by sleeping until nine, catching the lift up the mountain at eleven and skiing for four hours in the Colorado winter sunshine. He called Polecat from the inn or from the pay phone in the hallway at the New Sheridan Bar. He usually ate dinner with a local or two from the bar crowd. Around ten each night he met Adrianna and happily shared dessert with cognac. Their chaser was a line or two of her endless supply of coke. Cooper had learned the Bistro's high dollar coke dealers paid cash with a coke tip. Adrianna bought gold bars from her family mine with the off-the-books cash and stored them in the safe.

After Adrianna locked her office and the restaurant they usually closed down the New Sheridan Bar followed by a late party in a local's house. The deputy marshal occasionally stopped by for a line of coke and a bindle to go.

Telluride's after hour's parties were a closed society that required a local sponsor like Adrianna to gain entry. Pot permeated the bedrooms and coke dust flaked across the bathroom counters until sun up. Cheap liquor lined the kitchen tables like a contraband tribute to a Plains Indian chief. Talk was endless, loud, and full of high-octane opinion, merciless gossip, and pure intoxicated fantasy. Cooper usually had to pee outside since the bathroom doors were always locked. Sex was casual but, like coke, behind closed doors. Telluride had a five to one ratio of single men to women.

Cooper noted that Gary and Sue were regulars on the party circuit and they publicly seemed to be a number again. Brady and Kara appeared for the weekend blowouts. Lonnie Jr. and Jesse Smith were noticeably absent from the light white powder circuit but Sam Jr. occasionally made a guest appearance with Sue if his wife was out of town.

Cooper was solo when he ran into Sue one late night in January. After a short cocaine-high chat they had locked themselves into guest bedroom of a restored Victorian house that was the talk of Telluride.

"Word out on main street is that Sam Jr. has you broke like a saddle bronc, Cowboy. That True?"

Cooper, who had been drinking since four, said, "That shit head's so weak he couldn't turn you bottom up if you were floating in a hot spring, let alone break a cowboy."

"He tried in the hot tub but he can't get it up unless I blow his brains out. He's a limp dick these days like a lot of boys in Telluride. They've been mixing too much coke and booze for too long. Watch out or you'll be next."

"Never happen."

"Bet a gram your dick is getting real hard right now, Cowboy."

"Gut check," Cooper almost whispered as the words escaped.

"You're just like any other range bull. Why are you locked in this bedroom with me under the pretense of doing a line instead of a bump on the bed?"

"Got me," Cooper's resolve starting to fail.

"Do a Sue bump, Cooper," she commanded and rolled over onto her back pulling her knees in the air. Her short skirt flopped back revealing her pantiless blonde vee. Cooper's resolve failed and his senses warped in the room's candlelight. Cooper entered Sue almost in a trance as her smooth thighs surrounded him.

"Deeper, Cowboy," she purred.

"That was beautiful, Cooper," she whispered as she blew warm air in his ear twenty minutes later. He rolled on to his back seeing shooting stars and Sue pulled her skirt almost shyly over her thighs.

"The real thing is always the real thing no matter how hard you try to ignore it. Remember tonight and the first night with me. They will be in our dreams forever. I have one perfect skill. Fucking. But I am ready to learn a new one. Try me on the ranch, Cooper. I ride well. I ski fast. I will keep you warm and happy on long ranch nights," she concluded with a sad chuckle.

She continued her monologue. "Think it over Cooper, this is your last party favor. Take me to your ranch and I will dry out fast, I promise. I just want sunsets in the saddle not coke and booze to pass my jail time in the box canyon. Put these breasts under a red flannel western shirt and you'll be the only man who ever sees them again. Put me in jeans and I'll only take them off for you. I'll bear you a junior cowboy. Think it over, Cowboy. Adrianna is only interested in you to settle an old score," she finished with new strength in her voice.

Cooper eyes were locked into Sue's and his breathing had almost stopped. He visualized Sue on a ranch paint horse relaxed in the saddle next to him on a bluff watching an orange sunset over the purple La Sal Mountains. Her blonde ponytail peaked from under a straw cowgirl hat.

His tongue flickered in her ear as he whispered, "Sunrise in my room at the inn first."

"No mas Cooper tonight. I will stay clean starting at sunrise."

"You stay clean a couple weeks and you can start exercising the winter horses with Kara. I'll show you the ranch's best sunset spot. But there can never be coke on the YBarC."

"Deal." And Sue closed her eyes and dreamed of freedom on the range.

Cooper awoke alone in his inn room at four in the afternoon; Sue had left while he was sleeping. He showered and then called Arizona. Polecat reported the increased security for the herd had scared off any more rustling attempts but an early calf had died of rattlesnake bite. Cooper assured Polecat his Uncle Harvey was diligently working on refinancing for the ranch even though Cooper knew things were moving slower than even his uncle had expected. Cooper had sold his great-grandfather's Navajo rugs through a dealer to the Southwest Indian Museum in Los Angeles for $19,000. He had wired the money to his uncle for the purchase of Liz's annuity. Cooper still had a few other ancient Indian artifacts he could sell in an emergency but he was running out of other ideas. The fabled lunch pail gold nuggets had not materialized. Cooper's grandfather had paid cash for the small gold nuggets that Telluride's underpaid miners smuggled home at the end of their dangerous shifts. They had fake bottoms in their lunch pails.

The early morning events with Sue unsettled his empty stomach. He wondered if Gary was the puppeteer or if Sue had simply yanked his chain because she wanted to even the score with Adrianna. But Sue's pitch to take on the lonely tough role of a ranch wife had raced through Cooper's head to his heart. Cooper decided to monitor Sue through Brady but try to keep his zipper up. He would have Kara, Brady's girlfriend, probe how Sue had afforded a horse on the very expensive Scottsdale riding circuit which she had described to Cooper.

The phone rang and Adrianna was on the line. "Meet me fifteen minutes before midnight at the restaurant."

"What's up?" Cooper inquired.

"Be there and no questions now. Don't bring anyone and be sober please." The phone line clicked.

A second later it rang again and Cooper's uncle was on the line. "Cooper, I'm returning to Denver tomorrow for one last try. The nastiness of this foreclosure fight has everyone spooked. Everyone who does due diligence and calls Sam Jr. receives a bad mouthing about you and the ranch's current condition, which scares them off. They don't want to be stuck with a note five years out that a fourth generation kid can't pay. The Denver crowd also believes the ski area in Telluride will never amount to anything with Aspen and Vail already well established in the shadow of Denver and Stapleton airport and Interstate 70. They figure you should take Lonnie Jr.'s offer as a negotiated settlement and get out while there's cash on the table. Then, if you still want to ranch, take the 1.5 million net dollars and buy a big working operation in New Mexico for thirty-five dollars an acre where taxes are cheap and the weather is warmer."

Cooper responded firmly, "Make the trip to Denver, please. I want to die on the YBarC, not in a stranger's house down south. I can hold out through June before we have to throw in the hand, but let's stay at the table for one more deal of the cards for Grandfather."

"I'll do it for you and my dead brother. I'll fly up tomorrow and call you in a couple of days."

103

"Did you take care of Liz's deal?" Cooper asked.

"It's done. A twenty thousand mini tax-free AAA government bond fund pay out to a zero coupon for five years. After that she's back on your tab and social security."

"Thanks," Cooper replied. "Go with God. I have a rope on Sam Jr. that he won't feel. I'll call if he makes an unexpected move."

"So far it's all by the book, just legal foreclosure filings by that kid, Smith. August one is all I can buy you unless Sam Jr. drops dead."

Cooper wondered if Sue could blow and toot Sam Jr. off the planet. When Cooper didn't respond, his Uncle Harvey hung up. Cooper opened the drawer of the nightstand and pulled out Sue's nearly empty vile. He emptied the coke into the black cap and snorted it. The phone rang again.

"Hi, you want me over easy or sunny-side up for breakfast, Cowboy?"

"What's up?" Cooper smiled, playing with her line.

"Me silly, I'm returning your call to Gary you left on his answering machine."

"Good girl, but it's Gary I want to talk to, sweetheart."

"Funny, he's in Mexico again. Back maybe in a week. If you're really in a hurry he'll be at the Norwood airstrip at midnight next Sunday when his charter pilot Mick drops him off," Sue advised with a laugh.

Cooper knew Sue had dealt him an ace from under the deck. Mick, an ex-Navy aircraft carrier pilot was landing a tail dragger plane with ski skids on the snow-packed Norwood, Colorado runway at midnight. It meant Gary was flying cocaine straight in from Mexico.

Cooper replied with new respect for Sue, who had put herself in danger to pass on the information. "It can wait."

"I can't," she giggled. "Meet me after hours at Connie's house. Be coke free and don't be late. My period starts tomorrow and it's never late." The phone went dead.

Cooper wondered why Sue had suddenly betrayed Gary. How could the information help save the ranch? But it advanced her new hold on him. If she would snitch on Gary, she could bleed Sam Jr. for Cooper. He wondered for the first time if Sue was really a very clever girl stuck by unfortunate circumstances in a bad dance hall, or was she only a very clever whore. Liz had been a very clever model until she became a society bride that had inadvertently set the YBarC's decline in motion. Cooper's father's existential choice of his mother had shot a poison arrow into the heart of a western dynasty. Cooper wondered if Sue could be the antidote or was she a second deadly arrow. He would see her again tonight.

At 11:45 p.m., Cooper knocked on the locked door of Adrianna's restaurant as the sound of Austin country western music mixed with the laughter seeped out of the New Sheridan Bar. The western mountain town's social drinking was in full swing as the minus ten degree night air burned his lungs. The door opened and Adrianna beckoned him into the dark small bar.

"Follow me to the kitchen quickly and be silent."

Cooper followed her through the dark empty restaurant and he stayed close to her silhouetted form as she pushed open the double kitchen doors. A hundred candles flickered in the still warm stainless steel kitchen. She was barefooted in a knee-length white summer cotton dress.

"Sit down crossed legged in front of the altar," she commanded. The altar was composed of candles on large upside down restaurant stainless steel pots.

"I must start. There is a very special astrological alignment of the planets occurring over Telluride right now. Remain silent and watch. Do not interfere or you can die." Adrianna began to dance backlit by the glowing alter behind her. Her nude body bounced under her shear cotton dress. A minute into an ancient Spanish chant she lifted up a stainless steel pot and pulled a hobbled and muffled red rooster from under it. She rang its neck and danced under the shower of blood that spewed into the air, which speckled her dress and splattered Cooper's cowboy boots.

Suddenly, she changed the chant to English for Cooper's benefit. "Gods of gold and water, curse Sam Jr., Lonnie Jr. and Jesse Smith. Dry up their seeds of life. Freeze their hearts and lungs. Take this blood to satisfy your thirst until you devour these earth demons."

Adrianna collapsed face forward into a trance on the floor between Cooper and the altar. The candles burned wildly. Cooper smiled to himself. If the curse didn't work and his uncle failed, maybe Adrianna could just poison the trio next time they ate in the town's best restaurant. Then he silently blew the candles out one by one. He slipped out the office door to his sunny-side up rendezvous with Sue. The women had become his allies in the quest to defeat the evil spirits in the box canyon.

TWENTY-FIVE

Cow Art

Adrianna and Cooper sipped cheap California Champaign during the opening for Bobby Ray Kids' collection of cowboy paintings and black and white silver print landscape photographs. He had painted and photographed the YBarC in the 1950s when he cowboyed for Cooper's father and grandfather.

"Hello there, Cooper," an old cowboy's voice boomed as Bobby Ray approached in a traditional white rodeo shirt and wide brimmed Stetson.

"Bobby Ray, it has been too long a time. This is my friend Adrianna."

"Pleased to meet you, ma'am. Any friend of the YBarC is a friend of mind. Cooper, I visited your mom in Montrose on the way over. She looks tired," he probed.

"She's trying to adjust to life in town but you know she's never been happy since dad died."

Adrianna cut in, "I'll refill the Champaign glasses while you all catch up. Your work is fabulous. I'm going to purchase 'Full Moon Over the YBarC' for my cantina," and she darted away.

Bobby Ray's face turned from a smile to a frown, "Rumor is the weasel town banker here is trying to steal the YBarC."

"Yeah, it's an old-fashioned brawl."

"Polecat called me and said payroll checks are sometimes long arriving. That true, Cooper?" he asked tersely.

"Yes and I'm down to a dwindling calf payment and running short of ideas," Cooper admitted in a whisper to the old family friend. "I just sold Great-Grandfather's Navajo blankets so Liz will have an income while I turn the operation around or lose it."

"Don't talk that way, son. Your Grandfather would never let it happen and you got a lot of him in you. Hear you refused to fight the Federal Government fuck up in that 'yellow' Vietnam country. Your grandfather hated the USA government with every ounce in him. The Feds sent Walker Evans out to take pictures of us during the dust bowl. My family was dying on daddy's farm that the government ag agent picked out for him and told him to plow under the prairie grass and plant wheat. We had no cash or food. Jest ate dust. They jest sent us to the plains to die like the buffalo."

"Well, the bank's not going to get the YBarC while I can still ride a horse and shoot."

"That's more like it. Come by here tomorrow. Pick up that oil painting called Wild Horse Canyon. It's the last one from my YBarC days. Call Ned Turner in Santa Fe. He will pay $15,000 cash no questions asked."

"You can't do that, Bobby Ray."

"Your Granddaddy knew I was the son of a sod buster and he gave me the only chance I ever got after my daddy died. You use that cash to pay Polecat and the boys while you and Harvey fight them weasels. I got no children; an old debt is even, son."

"Thanks from my heart, Bobby Ray. I know grandfather's up there on the north mesa ridgeline watching me fight," Cooper tried not to tear up.

"Got to go say hello to that Denver art dealer over there and flatter him a bit." Bobby Ray shook Cooper's hand and was gone.

Cooper's payroll problems were solved until the cattle were shipped back to the ranch.

Sam Jr. walked through the gallery door. Cooper saw him out of the corner of his eye. Cooper walked toward him intending to knock him through the Gallery's plate glass window onto east Colorado. Four steps away from Sam Jr., Bobby Ray separated Cooper from Sam like a cutting horse.

"Sam Jr., you're not invited to this picnic while my work is hanging." Bobby used a firm forearm to shoulder him out the door.

Before Cooper could find a path around Bobby Ray, Adrianna steered Cooper to the open bar in back of the room. "You go after him in public and the marshal will have no choice but to jail you," she reminded Cooper.

He ordered a double shot of bourbon and tossed it down.

TWENTY-SIX

The Brown Palace

Cooper and Uncle Harvey met with his father's former polo teammate at the Denver Petroleum Club men's only dining room. Black and Hispanic waiters in cotton shirts buttoned to the neck and white gloves silently served the heavy set, rugged middle-aged men who either ran the regional operations for the major oil and natural gas companies or wildcatted prospects. The conversations were low, guarded, and secure at the corporate tables, while the wildcatters pitched deals with animated hand gestures.

After ordering a round of Whiskey and water and the rib eye steak lunch special, Bill Williams started in, "Cooper, your father was the best polo player of the first half of the century in Colorado."

"Thanks, I loved to watch him as a child. I will pass your thought along to Liz. It will mean a lot to her."

"Harvey," he shifted the conversation abruptly, "have you explained the basic deal points and legalities to Cooper?"

"Yes, the YBarC will be a Federal Sub S corporation with forty-nine percent of the voting shares to you, forty-nine percent of the voting shares to Cooper and two percent to me until the first mortgage is paid off in full. Then you get five percent of the voting shares and their profits annually redeemable by the YBarC for a $200,000 one-time, cash payment. If the ranch is sold before the first mortgage is paid off, you get the equity kicker, not the $200,000."

"That's correct. You understand the deal, Cooper. It's front-loaded with high interest because of inflation and back-loaded for risking my family money."

"Yes," Cooper replied.

While their waiter served a drink to each man the conversation lapsed.

Cooper continued, "I would like $800,000 at prime plus two, not four, with interest payable annually but principal due after year two in payments of $200,000 a year. I will wave a draw and work for expenses only until the loan is repaid. My personal expenses will not exceed $20,000 a year."

Bill Williams countered, "Harvey will be the board chairman and I want a $800,000 key man life insurance policy on Cooper with a prepaid ten-year term. You need new trucks to operate plus new fences. You can have the $800,000 at prime plus three, which is more than the current market value of the ranch with its debt if you can find a buyer besides the Ajax Ski Company."

The waiter arrived with salads and bread sticks. Cooper replied too quickly, "That will work."

Uncle Harvey's glance told him he just lost a half point of loan interest by not buttering a bread stick and letting Harvey wax over the iceberg lettuce.

Cooper could not stop thinking out loud, "I can cut costs even more with good rolling stock and have a happier foreman and crew."

Uncle Harvey interrupted, "I was figuring prime plus two and a half points based on the quality of your collateral."

"Can't do that, Harvey," Williams quickly countered.

"Inflation is too damn unpredictable with this Democratic big government crowd. The Federal Reserve is too political for me. The current prime barely covers the real rate of inflation. I've got to cover my ass, pardon my French, with three points above prime or I might be making a gift to the YBarC, not a loan." He chuckled at his wording. "Don't mind being a white knight as the Wall Street boys say but I'm not a Dutch uncle."

Cooper grimaced. Silence prevailed while the white-gloved waiter served their steaks.

"Well, Cooper," Uncle Harvey said after a long chew on a big bite of prime steak, "it's a fair deal and a good deal for the YBarC. If you agree I'll finalize the legal documents next week."

Bill Williams raised his tall ice tea glass. "That dog will hunt. Here's to the next fifty years of the YBarC."

When Harvey walked into the lobby of the Brown Palace Hotel, Cooper was happily visualizing handing Sam Jr. and his gang a $600,000 plus interest cashier's check.

"Taxi's waiting for us, Cooper. Some Negro girl clerk at the Secretary of State's office held me up an hour on a technicality."

"They are called Black women up here in Denver now." Cooper rose from the cowhide leather sofa and followed his uncle.

The grizzled bellman loaded their leather luggage and Cooper's sleeping bag into the cab. Cooper traveled with emergency landing snow survival gear. An airplane lost in the Central Colorado Mountains during winter could take days to find.

As the yellow cab sped toward the airport Uncle Harvey stated, "Weather's closing in fast from Utah. The Four Corner's high pressure has collapsed on schedule for a big March snowfall. I can't fly you to Montrose, only to Fairplay. You can spend the night at the hotel and meet Judy. She's my new 21-year-old manager."

A half-hour before dusk, Cooper and Harvey flew at 4,000 feet over the snowy mountains in the twin engine Cherokee. Harvey had arranged for the state to construct a runway before he retired from the legislature. Except during hunting season when it was busy, the runway mainly served as his and the surrounding ranches' private airstrip. The state highway department had to snowplow the runway for ten years at no expense to the town or county.

The thick black cloud front line was closing rapidly from the west as the plane flew in and out of a series of gray clouds. Harvey was silent as he struggled to find an altitude to avoid icing. Cooper listened to the chatter of the Denver air controllers. He was not worried. Harvey's twin turbocharged pressurized plane could climb above bad weather. The radio crackled and a Denver air controller ordered all eastbound and westbound commercial flights to divert. Stapleton airport was closing in the blizzard conditions and thick winter fog.

Cooper realized a retreat to Denver was cut off and the wings were icing. Harvey frantically worked the controls in search of clear air. Suddenly, the right engine exploded into an orange fireball as Harvey fought to control the airplane. He feathered the right engine to cut off its fuel but it was too late. The right wing burst into flames and the plane went into a blind high-speed glide as the strong left engine struggled to keep it airborne.

Harvey radioed, "Mayday just east of the Fairplay airport…flight plan one niner six," three times into the radio.

He pushed the good engine past its redline as they both searched for west light as the plane rapidly descended toward the spot where the Fairplay airport should be located. Finally, it punched through a storm cloud layer a thousand feet above a mesa used for summer pasture. The mesa was east of the airport and it was covered with six feet of snow pack. Harvey feathered the good engine and glided toward the ground at 120 knots per hour.

The plane threw up a giant rooster tale of snow as it landed and the windshield imploded. Powder snow rushed into the mortally wounded plane at high speed and filled the cabin, blinding Cooper and suffocating him as it filled his mouth. After a long moment, the plane stopped skidding but not before its wings were torn off. A few seconds later Cooper heard the muffled explosion of a wing tank safely behind the plane's fuselage, which had remained intact although it was filled with snow.

Cooper blinked open his eyes, cleared his mind and determined his body was intact although his left knee ached and his mouth and ears were filled with melting snow. He slowly raised his gloved hands through the powder snow and cleared his mouth with two fingers.

"Harvey, you okay over there?"

But he received no reply. Cooper quickly and carefully began to clear the wall of cold snow between himself and Harvey. Seconds later, he uncovered the left side of Harvey's face but it was ghostly still. His eyes were shut with no signs of breath. Frantically Cooper pushed snow away from Harvey's neck and then his head and finally his upper chest. The controls had been driven into Harvey's chest. Harvey's fate was sealed.

Cooper realized he could die of hypothermia. He needed to secure his sleeping bag and wait for search and rescue. He hoped it would be sooner rather than later as he started to dig toward his zero degree sleeping bag. Tears fell into the cold snow for his lost Uncle. Dark descended on the windblown mesa and snow started to fall at an inch an hour. Cooper hoped the plane's emergency beacon had survived the crash landing or he was going to be snow camping for the night.

Cooper woke to still blowing snow and darkness. A quick check of his watch's glowing dial read only 3:17 a.m. He was warm and made a mental note to replace the cowhands bed rolls with these modern down filled sleeping bags for their spring and fall ranch work. Suddenly, the sky lightened and the mesa was awash in moon shadows through the airplane's undamaged side windows. Cooper hoped the moon's appearance signaled the storm's end and the start of a snowmobile search and rescue from Fairplay and a helicopter search from Breckenridge. Using the bright moonlight, he found a flashlight, three flares and a small first aid kit in a metal box on the left passenger compartment door. He tied on his red bandana to cover his ears under his cowboy hat and stepped out onto a severed wing strut. He lit a flare and tossed it a hundred feet in front of the plane, well away from any aviation fuel. The waterproof encased flare sizzled as it landed in a foot of new powder but burned brightly in its snowy crater. Cooper next took a long drink from the icy emergency canteen and heard his stomach growl. Even with the flashlight's help, he couldn't locate the emergency food supply.

He guessed Liz was driving the authorities crazy by now since he hadn't called her from Fairplay. Even if the emergency locator beacon was damaged, Denver's FAA flight controllers would know they had not completed their flight plan after their Mayday radio transmission. Once the Denver papers and TV stations figured out it was former State Senator Harvey Stuart who was downed, the Governor himself would personally take charge of the search effort. Cooper worried about Adrianna and Sue's reaction to the news.

While the flair still produced its eerie battlefield glow, Cooper climbed back into the wounded aircraft after he pulled Harvey's body out of the plane through the pilot's door and covered it with snow. He undressed and settled into his sleeping bag to await daybreak. Cooper did not want to risk frostbite with sun up in three hours if the weather stayed clear. He fell asleep identifying constellations out of the passenger window in the pristine Colorado mountain air.

When Cooper woke again it was daylight, but it was snowing again, limiting visibility. The temperature in the plane was slightly warmer. After he dressed, his thorough search of the plane's rear passenger luggage compartment produced a large zip lock bag of dried fruit of unknown vintage. Cooper carefully opened the bag and tasted what turned out to be still edible dried bandana slices. He munched on a dozen more slices before he had a gulp of his icy water. The survival breakfast only made him wish for a sack of Liz's pancakes doused in Vermont maple syrup with a mug of steaming coffee.

After breakfast, he wrestled a new ROCKY MOUNTAIN MAGAZINE from his cowhide briefcase and started to read it in the plane's dull interior light. The cover story was on the coming World Speed Ski Racing Championships at Silverton, which only made the plane seem colder to Cooper, who wished he had the annual SPORTS ILLUSTRATED swimsuit issue instead. It continued to snow lightly all day long. Cooper wondered whom he could retain to represent him legally now that Harvey was dead. He decided he would call Ted Bayou, a Grand Junction ranch broker. He had brokered the last grazing land purchased by the YBarC while his grandfather was alive and he was a trusted family advisor. Cooper wondered how the voting control of the new corporation would be decided now that Harvey was dead.

Out of boredom Cooper rifled Harvey's briefcase. Beside some air maps, he found a year-old Time magazine and a small Sony transistor radio, which to his amazement, burst into a country music song when he turned it on. After a ten minute salute to Hank Williams, a special news bulletin interrupted the program from a Salida, Colorado station.

"Update," a gravelly voiced country DJ squawked. "The missing plane piloted by former State Senator Harvey McCloud Stuart with his nephew Cooper Stuart, operator of west Colorado's YBarC ranch, may have been located. The FAA in Denver picked up its emergency transponder signal intermittently about a half hour ago. I know all you Christian listeners out there are praying for the safe return of the good Coloradoans to their family. We will update our listeners hourly. Now back to Hank Williams Jr., the country tradition lives here on your dial." Cooper laughed, and tears rolled down his cold cheeks as the announcer's words reminded him that Harvey, Colorado's best rural legal Mr. Fix-It, lay dead in a snowy temporary grave.

As night two arrived, Cooper silently prayed that the snowmobiles had a true compass. He had given up trying to find the emergency transponder to insure it was still sending a signal. He had lit his second flare. Snow covered the debris path behind the plane. The sight of orange suited search and rescue workers on thundering snowmobiles would be welcome even if they had to wait to daybreak to drive him out to a hot shower and a dinner at the Fairplay Hotel.

The light powder snow fell straight down in the windless aftermath of the snowstorm as the temperature plunged. Cooper snacked on the last of his dried bandanas and a Snickers bar he had found under Harvey's seat. Cooper switched on the six o'clock radio news but the cold had killed its weak batteries. Only his Swiss watch Liz had given him for a Christmas past still worked.

The plane was colder the second night as arctic air drifted in behind the low pressure as it exited Colorado for the Great Plains. Cooper had to wear his clothes in his sleeping bag to stay warm. He knew he wouldn't freeze to death but it was going to be an uncomfortable night's sleep. He wore his sorrel boot liners, as well as his wool ski cap. Cooper drifted off in fitful sleep, thinking about the hot springs at Ouray, Colorado, where Liz had often taken him for a swim as a boy.

He awoke to the sound of the fuselage shaking and braced for an avalanche in his confused state. Then he heard a rhythmic pounding on the pilot side door as the roar of a snowmobile engine broke the silence of the mesa. Cooper opened the passenger side door to the sound of voices and a flash light beam blinded him.

He peered into the cold blonde bearded face of an exhausted 200-hundred-pound search and rescue volunteer who yelled, "You alive and well in there?" His voice cracked from emotion.

TWENTY-SEVEN

South Park Funeral

Cooper stood at the head of Harvey's coffin on a windy overcast day in the cemetery behind the postcard perfect Presbyterian church in Fairplay. Two hundred mourners had assembled from all over Colorado, including the Speaker of House of the state legislature and the chairman of the Colorado Bar Association. Both Denver newspapers had their political reporters at the funeral.

It was clearly a changing of the guard as Cooper surveyed the weathered men in the crowd who mostly wore cowboy hats and expensive custom western boots. Liz was stunning as always in a designer black wool suit with a long open black Russian fur coat. She had arrived only an hour before the funeral in a chartered airplane from Montrose airport because the highway mountain passes remained closed. The storm had dumped four feet of snow onto Telluride's ski slopes.

Harvey's hotel manager, Judy, stood on Cooper's left. Adrianna had arrived unannounced at the front desk of the hotel during the wake at the courthouse where Harvey's closed coffin had lain in state the night before. Adrianna wore a beautiful silk dress with a long black wool shawl. Judy was dressed severely in a long black wool skirt, a black silk blouse, a navy blue wool coat and a dark blue pillbox hat and veil.

A large but uncarved slab of pure white marble lay by the gravesite. Judy had the Marble, Colorado, slab trucked over from the hotel where it had been stored for new front steps for ten years. She had hired a local gravestone cutter to complete it after Harvey's funeral. Harvey had been instrumental in helping Colorado's only marble quarry from going under on more than one occasion by having the state prepay large marble orders for its buildings in Denver.

The Presbyterian minister finished his benediction and turned to Cooper, who had been designated to deliver the only eulogy.

Cooper wasted no time in the windchill and said to the gathering, "My uncle Harvey Stuart, your neighbor and law maker for most of his life, was a good and decent man of the old west. His wife Mary, who is buried here beside him died, ten plus years ago and they never had any children. You all here in Fairplay and in the State of Colorado were their family as well as their friends. He loved you and was always fair and honest in his dealings for you. He died riding his favorite mount, his well-worn twin Cherokee, almost within sight of town on a clear day. You will miss him and I will miss him."

A strong long cold gust of wind hit the crowd as Cooper decided to end his simple eulogy. "We say goodbye to his body today but his spirit will ramble through Harvey's old hotel forever to watch over Fairplay and keep a keen eye on our lives."

The women in the crowd sobbed openly while the men mostly looked away as they shifted their boots on the frozen ground. Each steel-eyed man seemed to be wondering when his marker would be called. The cold wind blew thirty miles an hour across the frigid high plain called South Park. Everyone in the crowd had buried a baby or a relative or a friend in the vast empty and often brutal expanse of the west on a cold gray winter day. They were proud hearty tough pragmatic survivors of a pioneering western century of droughts, dust storms, floods, wind driven fire storms, mining cave ins, economic busts, endless isolation and in a couple cases, the last Indian raids on the frontier. Cooper shifted his gaze to Adrianna as she made the Catholic sign of the cross.

The pine coffin was lowered into the grave with rawhide lariats by the local members of the Colorado, Cattlemen's Association. A local Boy Scout bugler in full dress winter uniform played taps. Cooper feared that Telluride and the other resort towns like nearby Breckenridge were about to overwhelm the honest western culture of rural Colorado that Harvey had worked so hard to maintain. The two-bit drug dealers, land speculators, petty criminals, and big city financial swindlers had swarmed into Colorado's ski resort economy for the first time since the mining boom that crushed the Ute Indians in the late 1800s.

The Cattlemen's Association President ended Cooper's foreboding thought as he tossed Harvey's lariat into the grave. Cooper tossed in his uncle's favorite gray dress Stetson as the laborers began to fill the grave with the hard-frozen high plains soil. As the crowd departed Judy tossed a red rose into the grave. She leaned against her mother crying. Adrianna stared blankly at him, dry cheeked. He took Liz's hand gently and walked her toward the hotel in a cowboy booted lock step before anyone could approach them.

Cooper watched Judy manage lunch for a 100 plus mourners in two shifts in the Hotel's wood paneled dining room. Cooper joined the second seating with Adrianna after Liz departed for her charter flight back to Montrose. Cooper had just finished a rib eye steak when Judy informed him that a Mr. Bill Williams was on the hotel desk phone.

Cooper excused himself and walked out to the front-desk to take the call. He heard a dull roar in the bar but the lobby's overstuffed leather couch and chairs were empty.

Cooper picked up the battered black plastic phone and said, "Hello. Cooper speaking."

"Wait a moment for Mr. Williams, sir, please." There was a click and then silence.

Ten seconds later a voice boomed, "Cooper, you there?"

"Yes sir, we just buried Uncle Harvey."

"My condolences and my family's condolences. Your uncle was a great Coloradoan, a good statesman and attorney. He got my oil leases with the state of Wyoming in the Powder River Basin straightened out or I would have lost them." He paused and it seemed he wished he could take the words back. "I have to leave for Cabo San Lucas to fish in an hour or I would have driven down."

"Uncle Harvey had a great send off. He would have understood because he always said take care of your main business first and best. I'm taking your loan papers to a family advisor in Grand Junction to review. Harvey's notes from our meeting survived the crash."

"That's why I called, Cooper. I sure hate to do this over the phone, but the deal is off. I know it's a double blow and my timing is terrible, but without Harvey as Chairman and watchdog, I can't risk almost a million dollars."

"Harvey always said a deal's a deal, don't you agree? The paperwork just backs up the handshake. The YBarC needs this loan or we could go under. It's too late to back out. We can agree upon a fair replacement for Harvey, I'm sure."

"Your witness to the deal is dead, son. He was a material element and my attorney concurs. Nothing has been even initialed, let alone signed. It's your word against mine, Cooper," he said in a suddenly cold voice.

"In a San Miguel County Courthouse my word still means a lot," Cooper threatened.

"I doubt that, son," he countered delivering an unexpected knife to Cooper's ribs. "My son John just played a round of golf with Lonnie Jr. who is hustling him to build a hotel for the ski resort. He says Lonnie alleged you are a coke addict and even in a condo construction development deal with the town's main drug supplier. Says you hang out with a former Scottsdale prostitute. Lonnie will get me affidavits to this if you take me on legally, boy. Goodbye."

Cooper heard another voice in William's office say,

"That's enough. We're legally protected."

The line died, as did the loan.

Uncle Harvey's credit for the save on William's oil leases had died with him and was probably the secret that had allowed him to strong-arm the loan. Cooper knew if he sued for enforcement of the contract they would allege Harvey was the key man and also smear him publicly statewide. Sue's well-used pussy had come back to haunt him, and Gary was in trouble with Lonnie Jr.

Adrianna walked up to Cooper as he hung up the battered phone. She instantly read the betrayal and rage in his eyes and led him without a word down the hall to her room. She made love with him and he napped until it was time for him to walk next door to Harvey's law office for the reading of the will.

At the reading, only Cooper, Judy, the county judge and his secretary were present.

As the will was read section by section, it became clear to Cooper that Harvey, like most men of the people, had died in near bankruptcy. Harvey had always believed it was far more important to have political power and community respect than a fat bank account. He believed you rarely had both in the same lifetime. He had about ten thousand in cash, which he left to Judy as working capital for the hotel that he also left to her. The judge and his secretary both gasped when the will revealed that Judy was his daughter. Cooper realized why Harvey wanted him to meet her. They were cousins. The townspeople would be shocked. Cooper knew the hotel had a first and second mortgage on it and had lost money for years but Harvey wouldn't close it because it functioned as Fairplay's community center.

Harvey left his law books to the county and his office furniture to the judge's son who had just started a law practice. Cooper inherited the airplane that had already been declared an uninsured total wreck by the FAA inspectors. He also received a free room and three meals a day in the hotel for life, twenty five percent of the hotel's net annual profit as long as Judy owned it, plus antique furniture from Harvey's apartment in the hotel. He left his penny mining stock to the University of Colorado rural scholarship program and Jeep Wagoneer to Judy. The longtime clerk at the hotel received his ten-year-old red Cadillac sedan. Judy's mother received Harvey's undivided half share in the 160-acre ranch near Breckenridge where Judy grew up.

Judy sobbed quietly while the silver-gray-haired judge looked ashen. Cooper figured the judge didn't like the duty of informing the local paper that Judy was Harvey's secret daughter. He knew the Denver papers would pick up the story and probably print it even though Harvey was dead. Cooper walked Judy back to the hotel that bordered the courthouse grounds. A five o'clock wind blew snow into their backs and pushed them along.

Judy said, "I'll make the hotel work even if I have to sell a few antiques to recapitalize it. What are your plans Cooper?"

"I plan to have Adrianna drive me to Grand Junction at first light and meet with Ted Bayou, the last living friend of my grandfather who still owes the YBarC a favor. Maybe he can help me find a solution for the YBarC's financial problems."

"I know you are probably surprised about the state of your uncle's financial affairs. He never paid any attention to them. He seldom collected a legal bill if a client couldn't afford to pay him. He gave away room nights to anyone in the county who needed a roof over their head. He only cared about keeping the hotel open for the town, fuel for his airplane and putting me through college. The airplane engines needed an overhaul a year ago according to an FAA notice I found on his desk one night. He called someone in Denver who got him an extension. His only hobby and expense was an occasional trip to Santa Fe where he and his late wife bought antiques. I suspect your bequest will provide you with some short-term money for the ranch. I argued about canceling the airplane's insurance after the last steep increase a year ago but he said it was a waste of money now that big city juries were handing our general aviation liability awards like popcorn. He did keep the theft insurance on it because he flew it to Denver so often. He said a plane up there was stolen by a Florida drug ring."

"That's my uncle all the way. My grandfather never carried a dime of insurance on the YBarC until the state made him pay workmen's compensation or go to jail. He claimed he never hired a cowboy who planned to injure himself and if one was killed on the ranch it was between god and the cowboy."

She laughed as they approached the side entrance to the hotel and its bar, which still produced a roar. Pickups, Jeeps, and cars were still parked around two sides of the hotel.

Judy said "goodbye" at the bar entrance.

Cooper walked to the front of the hotel to avoid condolence drinks at the crowded bar. He passed Adrianna's door as he silently walked to his room.

Dawn came early. Cooper was dressed in a warm sweater, jeans, cowboy boots and his bomber jacket. He fired up his uncle's Jeep Wagoneer to drive to Grand Junction. Adrianna had left to visit her father at Red Cliff.

Cooper walked into Ted's office at 11:30 p.m. and quietly outlined the YBarC situation. He figured Ted had heard most of it through the ranch intelligence network.

After listening patiently to Cooper's presentation, he said, "Boy, you done dug a deep hole in life and now the sides are falling in fast." He smiled sympathetically. "All I can do is liquidate the YBarC fast, which is to your benefit way I see it, while Marshall Fielding, my son-in-law who's an attorney here in town, holds the wolves at bay."

Cooper looked at him in shock. He had been hoping for a miracle. "That all you can think of?"

"That's it, boy, and if your grandfather had not been one of my best customers, I wouldn't get in this bear pit, no way at my age. Fight like this might stop my ticker cold."

"So what can you get me end of the day?"

"Got a client in Midland, Texas, more oil money than God. He'd take 29,000-acres, the mother cows, half of the water rights, the winter lease hold, plus Polecat," He laughed at his joke. "Unless you plan to shoot him at closing. You keep the two Wilson Mesa sections near the ski area for speculation and your family Victorian on thirty-five-acres with an easement to the state highway. I auction the other half of the water to the highest bidder. That's got to be Lonnie Jr., I figure, because, son, he needs it bad to peddle that elk pasture 'round them lifts. I can ring him with a couple of buyers from the water districts down-river just to keep him honest but not to outbid him so he can't steal your rights."

"So what do I get net?" asked Cooper.

"One hundred dollars per acre including half the water, four hundred dollars per pure bred YBarC mother cow, maybe five hundred thousand at auction for the other half of the water rights less the loan balance, less legal, less an eight per cent reduced brokerage fee. You know ten is regular."

He continued without a calculator. "Two and a half million less change in cash dollars, tops, plus your hold back of them summer grazing sections with Aspen trees on Wilson mesa near the ski area. Near future, they'll be worth $500 an acre to them city ski developers with well water rights only and that mesa aquifer is shallow in a real dry year when you need it."

It was the Lonnie Jr.'s deal all over again, although Cooper suspected he could not revive it because they thought he was on the ropes. Cooper knew the Midland buyer would be all cash, not terms, because Ted's client list bought that way and refinanced their deals later if they wanted cash back after closing. Cooper saw Ted's logic in unlocking the hidden value of the YBarC water rights. The buyer, he figured, would run the ranch to maintain its agricultural tax status and wait for the ski area to go big time like Aspen. Then he could sell it for a profit.

"Well, boy, what's the verdict...death by hanging or bullet to your head before the pose rides you down? Devil's choice they called it during the depression." He spoke without joy in his old voice.

"I'll take my chances with a shootout with the posse, but I will need Marshall Fielding."

"He's yours, young and hungry for a west slope fight. I knew'd your decision. You're jest like your Grandfather. But remember, son, the west is changing again. Can't cut a no good thief's throat as easy as the ol' days. The law be on you too fast to blink. You change your mind, I'll retire on your commission before this old body turns to dust. I have been preserving it with a pint of bourbon a day too long."

His eyes fell on a faded framed black and white picture of Cooper's grandfather and himself shaking hands on a long forgotten deal.

Cooper stood up silently, deliberately not breaking his family friend's thoughts about days long past. He exited the office and stepped out into the winter west wind off the eastern Utah mesas flanking Grand Junction. The muddy brown Colorado River roared in his ears, as he stood alone on the bleak winter Colorado Plateau with only the spirit of his grandfather and the bravery of his father to guide him. He was a lonely rancher fighting to save his legacy and create his destiny. He was prepared for an epic battle and he heard the sound of six guns as his step quickened toward the spirit horse that appeared in the gray clouds on the horizon.

TWENTY-EIGHT

Ute

The sky was cold blue as Cooper drove toward Montrose. Ted Bayou's old-timer's stare had burned into Cooper's mind. Cooper remembered the beaver had been nearly exterminated first, followed by the elk, then the Indians, the wild horse herds and now it seemed cattle were next. His family's way of life for the last hundred years was being put into play by remote ski resorts that were connected with cheap oil for airline routes to teeming cities in an emerging global economy. He had narrowly avoided America's latest military adventure, which was financed by rapidly growing Federal Government bond debt and force fed to the American public by Washington and Wall Street.

About a mile south of Montrose, Cooper realized he needed a stretch and a drink of water. A historic marker sign caught his eye. The Ute Indian Museum was at the next right turn. He had driven past the small yellow brick building his entire life without stopping. Cooper, like all Colorado natives, knew the history of the Utes was tragic but he was in no hurry to honor their treaties or return his ranch land to them. Cooper slowed the powerful Jeep as he signaled a turn into the museum's small parking lot.

The crushed creek gravel parking lot was empty as Cooper walked through ghosts of the Winnebago RVs which surrounded the Utes each summer. In the frontier days, it had been the Utes who had surrounded the covered wagons during their summer treks west. The gold and silver mining interests with the help of Denver tabloid newspaper headlines featuring Indian frontier raids, rape and torture, had driven the Utes from the region. A legal aid attorney would have gotten their trumped-up charges dismissed in a modern Colorado court. The New York, London and Hong Kong gold mining interests had used the Calvary and militia to knock the Utes down like bowling pins before Colorado received its cherished statehood.

Cooper's family had never fought the Utes. His great-grandfather had purchased the YBarC directly from Brigham Young and the Church of Jesus Christ of Latter Day Saints, which colonized the Paradox Valley region after the Utes were moved to three reservations. Cooper's great-grandfather became a Mormon convert before the sale of the ranch. He promised the Salt Lake City church hierarchy he would maintain their perimeter defense against the Christian homestead settlers and missionaries if they would sell him the Y BarC on very favorable terms. Historically, most of the Y BarC foremen and hands had been Mormons although Cooper and his father had only attended Mormon weddings and funerals.

Cooper pushed his thumb down hard but the museum door was locked. Cooper tried one more time in case the latch was frozen but the door remained tightly shut.

He was walking back toward the Jeep when he heard a strong deep voice behind him over the wind, "We're closed for the winter but come and warm your hands."

Cooper turned to face a thirty-something handsome male, presumably Ute Indian. Cooper walked into the museum's entrance feeling lucky for the first time in weeks.

Before Cooper could introduce himself the Indian spoke, "Your timing is perfect blue eyes. We need a stranger to critique our postmodern Native American art exhibit. We're trying to get away from the old style three by five postcards, pots, blankets, and trade bead displays. I'm Joe Bear Spirit from the Mountain Utes. I might be your brother if you have lived around these parts more than three generations."

Cooper's mind flashed on a news article that the hippie movement had awakened America to its swept-under-the-carpet Indian history. The once proud Indians lived on alcohol-riddled reservations on pitiful Federal Government stipends. Pretty, longhaired, brown women were West coast vogue. He did not approve of the treatment of the nearby Utes and Navajos. Even Cooper's great-grandfather, who had been born into an immigrant Scottish family, believed the American Indians were treated worse than the British treated the Scots and the Irish.

Cooper stood facing the first Ute he had ever met who wasn't at a roadside stand selling pottery or dancing at some pioneer days event.

"I'm Cooper Stuart, a traveler today and maybe soon to be a man without a country, too," he joked with bitter irony before he could check his tongue.

Joe Bear Spirit sized up Cooper for a long moment, which ended when a younger female worker in a beaded deerskin dress walked into entrance area unannounced.

"Betsy, meet Cooper, our soon-to-be critic. Cooper, meet Betsy, who is from the Museum of Natural History's Ancient People's staff in Denver. She's on loan helping us spend our pitifully small BIA grant."

She smiled hostilely at both Cooper and Joe Bear Spirit. Cooper tried to charm her, "Hello, Betsy. Mighty glad to be of service since I was hoping to see the museum on my way back to Telluride."

She replied coolly, "Follow me after Joe Bear Spirit gets you some hot tea." She pivoted on her perfectly beaded moccasins as Cooper's eyes followed the rhythmic swing of her very round bottom.

"Cooper, you no steal squaw," Joe Bear Spirit laughed as he interrupted Cooper's stare.

She slammed the door that cut their view with a definite finality. Joe Bear Spirit walked silently to a small table and poured Cooper hot tea from a stainless steel Kmart pot into a pottery cup with a Ute design glazed on its side. Cooper observed, "You two are not exactly firing on all cylinders here in Montrose."

"You are a quick study under that cowboy hat. She wants to stick to exhibiting trade blankets, old pots, and grave robber's artifacts with revisionist messages for the Ma and Pa Kettle crowd. I want to exhibit current Ute crafts and paintings with the ancient peoples rediscovered trash. We are a living nation of people. She is only half Cheyenne by her mother, which makes her a tribal member at birth but her daddy was an anthropologist at Yale University."

Cooper instantly began to like Joe Bear Spirit. He was at once calm, well spoken, direct, and at ease with his power in the present situation.

"I am the great great-grandson of Chief Ouray, the same name as the town except we don't live there anymore. We were thrown out of our adobe house near a hot spring by the U.S. Calvary after the White River Massacre even though we didn't start it."

Cooper's knowledge of Ute history was hearsay evidence at best. His years of boarding school in New Mexico with its Apache and Comanche frontier stories had colored his thoughts.

Joe Bear Spirit sensed Cooper's mood change, "Follow me, Mr. Cooper, to the contemporary art gallery. You can view trade beadwork another day for the dollar admission fee."

Cooper followed him through a newly painted fireproof door but stopped cold in his tracks. The artwork in the room astonished him. He was surrounded by contemporary Indian oil paintings, modern pottery, and abstract stone sculptures. His eye stopped suddenly on large oil painting that centered the room's chaotic energy.

Joe said, "My young brothers and sisters have been busy between bouts with firewater and BIA mineral lease royalty fraud. The latter is more dangerous than the former."

"This is astonishing," Cooper replied, having only seen the work of the ancient Indians in the Denver Art Museum. "Is this work from Colorado?"

"Yes, it is from the Ute reservations at Ignacio and Cortez. Most of the artists are high school dropouts and their work is original. Animism is the foundation for our religion. We can turn ourselves into animal spirits. I am named for the spirit protector of our people, the Grizzly Bear as Anglos call him now, driven from Colorado by the miners and ranchers."

Cooper replied reflexively, "You're right on that point. A grizzly sow can kill and eat a calf a day. There is not much profit in raising calves for the bear market."

Joe parried defensively. "We know who profits. You graze our hunting lands. We get a pittance for our oil and gas leases on the reservation from our BIA negotiated leases. It's illegal government negotiated theft."

"You would like my late grandfather; he hated the Federal Government, too. He claimed they would ruin the West someday."

"They done ruined it, Lone Ranger," Joe mocked. "The Ute's Bear Spirit is coming back on a big wind to blow the factory whistle and the white man will be gone in a fierce gust."

His words struck at Cooper's heart, not his head.

"Legends are legends, Cowboy, but the old powerful spirits are here wandering on the land. See the running horse on the red orange painted canvas that is guided by the blue wind. The Ute and the horse will always be one with the wind, undefeatable like desert cactus flowers."

Cooper froze as he realized he was in the presence of an ancient messenger. The exhibit was not about grave art or trade trinkets but power, history, vision, and spiritual apocalypse.

"I saw the painting of the spirit warrior horse once before, on my family ranch. It was my father and his prized polo pony riding with the wind on the polo field." Cooper felt tears in the corner of his eyes and his heart began to pound.

Joe picked up his trance. "And one day they both rode off the earth into the wind forever leaving you to walk the earth alone until this day when you tied your pony to a strange Aspen tree and walked into a cave to find shelter from the pain and the wind."

Cooper blurted, "You know the story of my father and Sugar Cube."

Joe replied, "I know of all true spirits who inherit the wind. After today you do not have to ride alone. I will join you when my work is complete at the museum. You are the lone blue-eyed stranger of legend chosen by the great Bear Spirit to help guide me and my people from slavery into the warm current of the summer west wind."

Joe simply vanished. Cooper stared at the vacant place he had occupied in the center of the gallery. Cooper was supercharged with power for the first time. His father and Sugar Cube had simply ridden off the earth into the west wind forever leaving Liz to nurture Cooper.

The door opened and in walked Betsy who didn't even notice Joe was gone. "Seen enough, Cowboy? It's time to ride your pony far away from here. This stuff is drugged out reservation space junk. The young Utes watch too much TV, drink too many six-packs, and eat too many frozen dinners from the trading post. Joe performed his disappearing act again while you were hypnotized by his mobile home living room painting." She turned and walked through a small office door that locked behind her with a loud click.

Cooper triggered the fire exit alarm when he left, just to piss Betsy off.

TWENTY-NINE

Deuces Are Wild

A t 4:00 a.m. Cooper startled upright in the inn's cast iron bed and whipped his .22 out from under his pillow as his eyes blinked open in the dim light. His pistol was pointed straight at Sue's blonde triangle as she discarded her bikini panties at the foot of Cooper's bed. She was high on cocaine and reeked of expensive scotch. Her pin-up girl breasts were lit from the street light below the window.

She said, "Don't shoot me in the pussy, Cowboy or you will ruin the fun." She laughed wildly.

Cooper replaced the pistol while Sue bound onto the bed and went to work on his dick with her warm soft mouth. Cooper, exhausted from Harvey's funeral, drifted back to sleep and half dreamed he exploded into her throat.

A couple hours later Cooper woke from a dream about being evicted from the YBarC. He had yelled in his sleep, which woke Sue who rolled over onto her stomach exposing her rounded hips in the east winter morning light.

She stared at Cooper's penis. "You turning into a limp dick, Cooper. Wake me up early if you are hard as a rock ready for a poke. That Spanish witch whore put a magic spell on your dick while she's out of town."

"Funny, maybe that is the problem."

She shot back, "I think they are deballing you like a steer, Cooper.

"That what Sam Jr. saying in his hot tub visits?"

"They've stopped since you left town. His wife followed him over to the house from the bank last Thursday and surprised us in the hot tub with a Polaroid camera flash. She popped through the alley door that Gary always leaves unlocked. She hurled a chair at me while Sam's dick was still in my hand. I dove under water as the chair hit Sam in the forehead. When I came up for air, she hauled Sam Jr. out by his dick that was still ram rod straight with cum coursing."

Cooper started laughing uncontrollably.

"She drug him bare assed naked out the open alley door, tripped him and he fell backwards into the snow. She snapped another Polaroid before she started kicking him in the groin while he rolled in the snow screaming. Then she jumped into their Wagoneer and drove it straight at him. At the last possible moment she turned the steering wheel hard left and roared through the hot tub room's glass window. I dove through the kitchen door for safety."

Cooper could not stop laughing.

"Suddenly, a marshal arrived and maced Sam Jr.'s raging wife. She was trying to back the Wagoneer out of the hot tub and run over the marshal. But he dropped the mace when he saw my beach towel slip off. Then Sam Jr.'s wife tried to set the hot tub room on fire by lighting the gasoline dripping from the Wagoneer. Just then a second marshal arrived with a drawn gun and yelled, 'Freeze everybody or I will shoot.'"

Cooper laughed so hard that tears ran down his cheeks.

"I got Gary on the line for the marshal who told him no way he would press charges against Sam Jr. or his wife even after the marshal insisted he should see the damage. So in the end, all the marshal could do was drive Sam Jr. home in my towel with his sobbing wife handcuffed in the front seat."

Cooper started to regain composure, mainly because his sides hurt too much from laughing.

"Well, Cowboy, that runs out the meter. I have to meet Gary's flight. You'll have to wait for a roll in the hay with me." She pointed between her legs. "Cooper, if you can't stick it in my wet pussy, legs wide open or bottom in the air, ranch or no ranch you are no good to any woman. Watch it or you'll end up in Scottsdale like those actors from Hollywood who can only get it up for each other in their poolside cabanas while I watched them."

Cooper mused that Sue had inadvertently given him a clue to her past. "Which actors?"

She dodged, "They'll be in Telluride soon enough. Just a day or so after the heroin and a film festival arrives. Watch out for the blonde one who won an Oscar. He sun bleaches his pubic hair and likes urban Arizona poolside cowboys big time."

Cooper moved to the edge of the bed as Sue started to put her bra on very slowly and very deliberately.

She blurted out, "You got it all Cowboy, big ranch, good looks, fast Jeep, big time western family name, which old-timers can barely whisper around here without looking over their shoulders. Wake up, Cooper. The rest of us live paycheck to paycheck and suck up to a Sam Jr. for a living."

Cooper yelled, "Gimme a Break!"

"You take their cash for the YBarC, baby Buddha Cowboy, and they'll find a way to steal it right back. You have been using Adrianna and me as entertainment when you come to town to pout. Cut the judgment shit, Cooper, and choose a new team. Your cowhands aren't going to win in Telluride. The white gold boys mean to bury you in a shallow grave on boot hill in a no name pine box."

Half nude and mad she was the prettiest girl Cooper had ever seen. Her energy radiated from her blue eyes.

"Look at me, Cooper, I can help you. I can be your scout on the street. I grew up on it. Cut the Spanish princess loose. Rumor is her daddy's mine is broke and she is the payroll money scout." She pulled on her faded jeans skirt. "Besides, what you really need is under this skirt for long cold nights and strong perfect children. Loneliness will finish your heart faster than the Telluride gang. This is my final offer, Cooper."

Sue bolted through the unlocked door tears in her eyes, leaving it open as her footsteps retreated down the hallway. For the first time, Cooper realized Sue loved him, but his head warned that her lifestyle and blurry unspoken background were as potentially dangerous to the YBarC as her street sense could be helpful. He had never questioned that her sensuality launched him into the stars.

Cooper's Jeep purred in high four-wheel drive as he and Gary pulled up in front of George Creed's rusting Quonset hut that housed his snowmobile repair shop in Delta, Colorado. Gary had met the recent transplant at the Bistro bar. They were late because a bitter cold northwest wind had turned the highway into black ice. Cooper and Gary let themselves in through a red metal door. A Telluride real estate speculator and trust funder, a Delta stranger, and George sat around a battered card table playing poker with two empty scarred gray metal folding chairs. A Coleman lantern hung over the table, providing light, and a case of Coors long necks sat on a warped wooden cable spool. Empty beer bottles were already three deep in front of each player.

As Cooper sat down George said, "Meet Elmo, he owns the Dairy Queen here in town and likes high stakes poker, barely-legal naked teenage waitresses, bourbon and good cocaine. You know Dillon, I presume. He just bought a snowmobile from me."

Gary said, "Straight poker, nothing wild, no limit tonight. I feel real lucky."

"Fine with us," George's voice sounded strained. "You boys look like you need a bump after the drive."

He produced a vile from his vest pocket and passed it counter clockwise, and each card player did a double bump without hesitation until it reached Cooper. He paused. His iron clad rule was not to do coke or any drug with strangers but he was tense from the knuckle gripping drive from Telluride. He snorted a satisfying bump.

Before Cooper could enjoy the rush to his brain a flash bulb exploded in his eyes, temporary blinding him, and a voice from behind him in the dark recesses of the Quonset hut yelled, "You are under arrest, Cooper Stuart, for possession and use of a Federal and State of Colorado controlled substance. Hit the floor spread eagle. We know you are armed and we will shoot to kill."

Cooper felt the .22 pistol in his bomber jacket inside pocket and blinked to clear his vision. The command had placed one of his adversaries ten feet behind him in easy killing range. Cooper calculated that if he rolled to the left behind George, Gary would take the bullet giving Cooper a dead bead on the target from the muzzle flash. But killing a cop meant the electric chair.

Cooper stood up slowly and raised his open palms. Then he kneeled and lay spread eagle as instructed on the cold, hard, grease-stained cement floor. He gambled they would not shoot him with witnesses in the room. A rough set of hands frisked him and fished out the small pistol.

"Got you on a concealed weapons charge, too. You gonna shoot up the poker game if you lost? Been waiting to bag me a YBarC rancher for forty years and change," the cop said as he snapped the cold steel cuffs hard on Cooper's wrists and expertly sunk an elbow deep into the small of his back sending blinding pain down Cooper's legs.

"Everybody else here is under arrest too but George. You all will be booked for misdemeanor gambling and released on your own signature by the magistrate until your court appearance. Its Cooper here we want. George, who is an informant for the Colorado Attorney General's Office, will testify Cooper here has been using the YBarC landing strip to supply Telluride with coke. Plus, now we got this picture of him using the stuff. Anybody here who doesn't testify to that fact will get a possession charge added to the gambling one and join Cooper in the state slammer in Salida, Colorado. The redneck and half-breed Ute inmates his great-granddaddy stole the YBarC from will finish this draft dodging boarding school puke-off for the government with a shank at no charge after they widen his asshole by a mile or two."

The sound of two additional sirens ended the officer's tirade as Cooper began to slowly blackout from the blow to his kidneys.

THIRTY

Jailbird

The cold breakfast in the Delta county jail was inedible, especially with the smell of vomit wafting from the adjacent drunk tank. Cooper had slept fitfully under a surplus Army blanket on a steel bunk with a thin mattress because the magistrate had refused him bail. The other three poker players had been released on the misdemeanor charge of illegal betting inside the town limit. It carried a maximum fine of $500 dollars and ten days in jail. The magistrate mumbled that he couldn't remember when anyone had been charged under the 1920s ordinance.

It was clear to Cooper that he had been set-up. He had followed the bait like a mouse straight to Delta where the YBarC had no political clout. Worse, Pete Simple turned out to be the arresting officer. Cooper's grandfather had paid Sam Jr.'s father's Telluride bank fifty cents an acre for the Simple family's foreclosed farm on Wilson Mesa near the end of the depression. The San Miguel County sheriff was ordered to evict the starving family after the bank foreclosed on their note. Sam Sr. had foreclosed on them and many other sodbusters on the mesa after they failed to pay their loans. But rapidly rising land prices near the ski area were opening old wounds.

Cooper ached from the manhandling Pete had given him with his nightstick in the back seat of the police cruiser. Cooper still couldn't pee from the assault on his kidneys and his forehead was bruised from being hurled into the cell's concrete wall.

Pete had jeered, "You draft dodging, dope using puke, I am going open the door on the next turn and kick you out and me and Jake will shoot you for escaping. That will save the county and the state some money, you no good land-thieving Stuart." Cooper had wisely kept his mouth shut.

Cooper called Ted Bayou at his Grand Junction office at 8:00 a.m. sharp and he picked up the phone. "Hello," Cooper had not wanted to make the call but there was no one else he trusted.

"Howdy, Cooper. You ready to sell today? Good day, before they raise interest rates again because of the damned stagflation."

"No, but I need your son-in-law to drive down to Delta and get me out of jail," Cooper mumbled.

"Why you in jail? You run one of their famous speed traps drunk in that Jeep hot rod of yours?" he laughed.

Cooper gulped, "Worse, I got busted in an illegal poker game and George Creed, the snowmobile repairman, put some cocaine on the table. Pete Simple is trying to settle a score with my grandfather."

"Them Simples got some power in Delta these days. Oldest one is Mayor and his son Pete is the deputy marshal. You got big trouble, son. They still publicly claim Sam Sr. and your granddaddy cheated them. With them rising land prices on Wilson mesa because of the ski area it will be riling them up again. I avoid them like bad medicine. The ol' man's almost 95 and still sharp as a Sheffield razor."

"Well, with Uncle Harvey gone I don't have an attorney."

"My son-in-law, Marshall, will drive down pronto and bail you out. You sure got more snakes in your bed than pillows, boy, so you got to be careful where you sleep."

The phone went dead.

Relieved, Cooper hung up the jail house pay phone, which was in the common area of the cell block. He started to walk back to his cell, when the back of Pete Simple's hand cracked against his jawbone so he reflexively brought up his hands to protect his face.

Pete yelled, "Don't you attempt to hit a law enforcement officer boy."

He struck several heavy body blows from a nightstick the size of a little league bat. Cooper began to blackout and started to collapse onto the concrete floor.

He heard a very distant voice say, "Don't you ever raise a hand to a Vietnam vet."

Two hours later Cooper regained consciousness on his hard steel bunk. Blood still trick-led from his bruised nose and swollen mouth. His ribs ached and his forearms were black and blue. The cell door suddenly opened and an older man with a doctor's bag walked in as Pete Simple leered from the cellblock hallway.

"Doc here will fix you up for your hearing. You touch him and you go out of here in a body bag like that wetback boy. Doc, you fix Cooper here up real fine. Someone already tipped the Grand Junction paper and TV news hounds."

The doctor was clearly cowed by Pete but he did a workman-like job on Cooper's wounds as he examined him. Pete tapped his nightstick against the cell dull gray bars.

"Pull off your shirt, son, so I can tape up a couple cracked ribs before you try to walk and tear up the cartilage worse."

Cooper had felt them wiggle but ignored the pain, "Can I ride, Doc."

Pete cut the Doc off, "He ain't going to be working his ranch ever again, Doc. Just riding jailhouse bunks 'til his headlamps go off."

The Doc remained grimly silent.

Suddenly a new voice said, "Shut up, Simple. Don't ruin my case. Got a confession all typed out for the prisoner to sign. Hello Cooper. I'm Dan O'Connell, the Delta County

Prosecutor. Soon as doc fixes you up from your punch at Pete, you sign the confession, do a year of state time in Grand Junction Jail, not the big house in Salida."

"Where's my attorney?" Cooper demanded.

"You mean that greenhorn deed filer from the grand junkyard? He called me an hour ago and said his daddy-in-law tried to pressure him into defending you on a trumped-up dope charge. He said to tell you he is a real estate and corporate attorney. Go find a drug lawyer in Denver. Not any on the western slope, except maybe that longhair hippie lawyer down in Telluride. Also, he said to tell you his new real estate client on the slope is the Ajax Ski Company. He will be representing them on matters before the BLM district office."

Doc's hand stopped. His eyes signaled he was bandaging-up a corpse.

Pete cut in, "You bring that hippie attorney into Judge Parker's court room and he will add time to your sentence." "Shut up," Dan exclaimed. "Take a walk, Pete. Get a drink of water. Doc will be okay and I'm not going into the cell."

Doc said weakly, "Let me check your hands, boy, make sure they're not broken."

"So what's the verdict, Cooper? You want to stand trial with a hippie drug lawyer. I hear the YBarC's dead broke. It would have killed your Uncle Harvey's heart to see you in this cell. He was a fine attorney. Tell you what, I'll plea-bargain you six months in jail and six months probation. Sign it in the courtroom after the judge explains it to you or you risk twenty to life if you go to trial on these charges. Judge already sent two longhairs from Aspen last year to the big house for peddling cocaine and pot here. See you in court."

"Fuck you. I am a rancher not a cocaine dealer. The drugs were George's and the whole thing is a set up."

"You're finished, Cooper. Doc, get him ready for the press. I hate these new portable color news cameras. His bruises will show. Enjoy Pete's hospitably 'til the trial. You will never make my bail," and Dan walked away.

"No broken bones in your hand son but I don't know why not," Doc reported. "Be careful in here, Pete means to kill you and it won't be the first prisoner carried out of here with a blanket over his face on a stretcher," the gray-haired Doc whispered.

An hour later Cooper stood shakily before Judge Parker. "You waive counsel, Cooper, or I will appoint one. I can't wait all day for your decision."

"I want an attorney but need to make another call," Cooper demanded.

"You are charged with possession and distribution of cocaine, hitting an officer of the law in an attempt to escape from jail, and swearing at an officer of the court. You plead guilty or not guilty?" he thundered as the reporters scribbled in the cheap knotty pine-paneled courtroom.

"Not guilty," Cooper said firmly. "It's a set up by a lying informant and Pete Simple is trying to settle a family score," Cooper asserted.

"Another outburst, son, I will hold you in contempt. You are charged with very serious violations of the state criminal code. Your bail is set at $100,000 cash, no collateral or bonds until trial in two weeks. I will appoint an attorney for you tomorrow if you don't retain one by noon," and he banged his gavel down.

"That's not fair. Everyone else in the poker game was released on their personal signatures. I am not fleeing anywhere, I have a ranch to operate," Cooper yelled.

"You're a flight risk, Cooper. The DA says your ranch is in foreclosure and you have strong ties to Fiji. We don't want the expense of sending Pete out there to haul you back. My son died in Vietnam."

Pete and the bailiff walked up behind Cooper and started to snap on leg chains.

He heard Liz crying, "I'm here, Cooper."

"Judge, I am Max Cleavel from El Paso, Texas. I am here to get Cooper out of jail now and defend him."

"You best return back to fucking El Paso, mister. You will do Cooper here no good in these parts," Pete growled.

Max cut him off and authoritatively said, "You threaten me or touch my client again officer and I will be in Federal District Court in Denver this afternoon and get a civil rights restraining order against you being within a mile of me and my client."

"I don't have to take this off no out of state lawyer. I will stop this arraignment on security reasons," Pete shouted.

"You deprive my client of his constitutional rights and I will have this case dismissed by lunch time. Judge, please order this marshal to leave the courtroom. He is menacing my client. Judge, my client never legally pled because he had no attorney present, so his bail is not set legally."

"Bail is set. Appeal what you want, wherever you want, counselor," the judge laughed.

"Then order your bullying marshal out of here, so I can confer with my client."

Pete Simple turned bright purple and fingered his pistol trigger guard. Liz was sobbing quietly unable to speak as she clasped Cooper's aching bruised hands. All of her motherly energy passed from her heart and soul into Cooper.

The DA, seeing his case going down the drain ordered,

"Simple! Out of the courtroom before you destroy this case on constitutional grounds."

"He beat me," Cooper yelled pulling off his orange jail top. The reporters grimaced and scribbled on their note pads.

The judge angrily ordered, "Simple, leave or you are in contempt. The bailiff will sit in on the meeting with the DA, Cooper Stuart and his attorney."

Simple stomped out and the judge took his leave.

Max spoke confidently, "The excessive all cash, no bail bond requirement is illegal but it will take a week to appeal it in state court and we can't risk leaving you in jail another night. Dr. Blacker already talked to the local Doc and we understand your problem with Pete Simple. Ted thinks he will kill you before you can be tried and he apologized for his son-in-law's actions. Dr. Blacker is wiring the money for bail but it may not reach Delta 'til tomorrow."

"You're a quick study, Max," Cooper replied.

"Oh, Cooper, I love you and I need your father so much now." His mother squeezed Cooper's hand and he ignored the pain. The DA walked over and interrupted, "Not that easy. We found a kilo of cocaine in a sealed plastic bag in the gas tank of your Jeep, plus we have the Polaroid of you snorting coke."

"The poker game is entrapment and won't stand-up in court. George is an informer. It's a swearing match between Cooper and Pete on the attempted escape and Doc will testify on the beating."

The DA countered, "Mr. Cleavel, may I call you Max."

"No, I prefer Mr. Cleavel as is the custom in criminal law cases."

The DA turned red, "I guess you'll paper me to death on this case. The county will scream when they see what it costs to prosecute against a famous law firm. It's already costing us a bundle to defend the hardworking marshal's office against the Justice Department on the Mexican farm worker's death."

"Not my problem, sir," Max replied, matter of fact.

The DA shuffled his cheap cowboy boots uneasily, then sat down in the empty chair beside the bailiff.

Dan opened the new poker game, "I deal your client out nolo contendere for six month's time in the Grand Junction jail."

Max said deadpan to Cooper, "That means you neither plead guilty or not guilty and serve 180-days hard time. I will stipulate that Colorado State police transport you to Grand Junction after we walk directly from the courtroom to a patrol car. Also, Marshal Simple may not be within a thousand feet of this courthouse."

"I don't like your demands, Mr. Cleavel, but I am here to save the taxpayers of Delta money on a Telluride mess and a resulting show trial."

Max gunned him down, "I am sure you would rather spend your time campaigning after you sell the newspapers this deal." Liz started sobbing.

Max raised the table stakes on cue, "Your call, Cooper, it's your life. You stand trial on these facts and you will walk a free man and we have cash bail being wired to Delta, but you are jailed here for the night."

"I will take my chances in the courtroom with you and twelve decent Western Colorado men and women. Their pussy witnesses and paid informant won't sway anyone."

The DA lost it and yelled, "You use profanity one more time, and you are back to the cell block ASAP."

Max cut in, "He will not use first amendment protected slang again, sir, but any future harm to my client in the cell block and your local Doc and I will hold a press conference about Cooper's condition and you can forget about running for State Senator. I have a tape recording of his call from Doctor Blacker in San Antonio."

The county court clerk walked through the courtroom door trailed by Pete Simple and she ordered, "Cooper is free to leave with you right now. Bail has been posted on the original bond in the form of $100,000 in gold bars by a resident of Telluride." Max said, "I am walking out of here with my client now. His mother will sign for his personal effects and receive them from your jailer."

"He leaves with me to get his effects. That's the procedure in my jail," asserted Pete Simple.

Dan O' Connell was speechless with his game plan in shambles as Max stood abruptly and pulled Cooper up with his right hand. He picked up his expensive calfskin briefcase and led Cooper toward the door as Liz scrambled to follow.

Pete screamed, "Wait a second, you can't take my prisoner." He started to reach for his pistol but the DA's hand stopped him cold.

Max ignored him and led Cooper through the door.

The DA yelled, "You are technically free on bail, Cooper, but we will see you in court. Your big city defense attorney cannot save you from Delta justice."

As they walked out of the courthouse, Cooper saw Adrianna standing next to a repainted armored truck. A Spanish driver held a 12-gauge shotgun next to her.

Adrianna beamed, "Gold's better than water here in Delta, Cooper."

Max looked a little dumbfounded. A Denver newspaper reporter ran toward Cooper with a photographer leading the way as a bevy of flash bulbs went off.

Max moved between Cooper and the onrushing reporter as the impromptu press conference began on the steps.

"My client has been falsely charged on the word of an unreliable, government informant who entrapped him in a private poker game after the tragic death of his uncle and mentor, a revered Colorado politician. Delta's law enforcement officials must not be allowed to engage in this kind of illegal and immoral behavior no matter how important it is to stop the trafficking of drugs. The constitution prohibits the use of entrapment by the police to stop personal grudges from being settled by officials like Pete Simple through illegal arrests and the illegal beating of Cooper in his jailhouse. He is a hard working fourth generation Colorado rancher who has been harmed by the overreaching of the law."

A television cameraman shot close-ups of the shirtless Cooper's bandaged ribs and bruised hands. Other TV cameras rolled as more flash bulbs popped.

A reporter yelled, "So you are alleging the Delta City government set up Mr. Stuart?"

"That's what entrapment means, sir," replied Max. "The government had no case against Cooper so Pete Simple set one in motion to settle the depression era family farm foreclosure."

"Good story, boys," shouted Dan O'Connell as he descended the courthouse steps. "I pledge to suspend and investigate Pete Simple," he paused with the reporter's attention now riveted on him. "You all want to try this case on the courthouse steps, that's all right with me. Did Mr. Cleavel tell you the state trooper's detective unit out of Grand Junction found a kilo of cocaine in Cooper's Jeep's gas tank? We have a second reliable secret witness who will testify it was unloaded from a tail dragger on the airstrip at the Y Bar C, which happens to be Cooper's ranch of record in these parts. I'm dropping all of the poker game and jailhouse charges against Cooper Stuart. But I will prosecute the felony distribution and possession of a kilo of cocaine, a controlled substance, under the Colorado penal code, which by statue is twenty years to life in prison. We intend to offer no plea bargains in this case and it will be tried in Delta County, you can bet on that Mr. Cooper Stuart."

Cooper blinked in disbelief at the DA's lie. Dan turned on his heel and climbed into the driver's side of the black Chevy sedan and roared off. Cooper was cold to the bone now, still in a jail uniform.

Max confidently asserted in a loud voice, "The secret witness will probably disappear mysteriously after the election and after we prove Pete Simple had access to the Jeep before the state police searched it. I'll put an investigator on it immediately. Planted evidence by corrupt policemen is the staple of B movies and real life."

The reporters all scribbled his remarks on to their pads and scrambled to make deadlines.

Max turned to Adrianna, "Thanks. Pete might have killed Cooper if he had to wait for the wire transfer from Texas. We will replace it with cash tomorrow."

"Lucky for Cooper it was a gold shipment day. My father diverted the mine's armored truck from the Grand Junction airport to the court clerk," she smiled.

Liz said emotionally, "Thanks dear, you and Max have saved my son's life."

"Let's get out of this god forsaken town and have lunch at the Cattlemen's Cafe in Montrose across the county line," Max suggested. "Dr. Blacker's Lear is there and I am leaving for Texas at 4:30. The Montrose bank can messenger over a cashier check to replace the gold bars tomorrow. Your driver might as well spend the night here. I'm advising all Stuarts and their allies to stay out of Delta."

Cooper's naked stomach was growling, "Great idea. I'll treat after I put on some warm clothes. I have a thousand in cash, which was my stake in the game."

"Our stake," Adrianna corrected Cooper. "But, you are out of the poker business. It was my mistake introducing George around town after he fixed my chef's snowmobile."

Cooper noted that Max's eyes just crossed Adrianna off the secret witness checklist, her bail non-withstanding. Cooper realized Max instinctively trusted no one, which was a trait he instantly needed to adopt.

THIRTY-ONE

Ute Reservation

From his room at the Telluride inn, Cooper completed a call to the Colorado Highway Patrol office in Grand Junction to arrange for the return of his Jeep. Cooper called Polecat in Arizona and he briefed him on the Delta events. Polecat had no love for the Simple clan but Cooper could tell by his reaction he was pissed at his involvement in a boozy coke-fueled card game. Polecat had always strictly enforced the YBarC "Saturday night in town blow off steam" policy. But no drunkenness or drug usage by the outfit's cowhands was tolerated on the ranch. Cooper asked the winter hand and his wife to ferry the Jeep from Grand Junction through Gateway to avoid Delta. Cooper checked on Liz, who told him Dr. Blacker had refused to let Cooper or her pay Max's retainer or sign a note for the bail money. Cooper resisted an urge to ask Liz why she and Dr. Blacker had not married after the doctor's wife had died.

Cooper walked down the empty hallway and his broken ribs shot pure pain through his body. He took deliberate steps down the inn's steep narrow Victorian staircase. He hugged the oak banister for extra stability, aching with each step. Skiing was not happening for a couple of weeks but he could cowboy with his ribs taped and a shot of bourbon.

Cooper found his way to the front porch and gazed at the pink snow covered face of Ajax Mountain just as the western sunset kissed it good night. When Cooper lowered his gaze, he saw Joe Bear Spirit's brown Ute eyes. Joe was standing on the blue painted pine steps of the inn dressed in a pair of faded Levi's, elk skin high top moccasins and a deerskin shirt. He had a string of grizzly bear teeth around his thick bronze neck. His long jet-black ponytail was framed by the pale azure twilight sky.

A startled Cooper asked, "What are you doing here?"

Joe replied, "I have come to teach and guide your battered spirit and help heal your body. I arrived as an albino grizzly bear hidden by the white snow of winter; that is my cover and roadway."

"I apologize. I've been impolite. I'm surprised to see you in Telluride. My surprises have not been pleasant lately."

"It's okay, Blue Eyes. You have suffered much at the hands of your enemies. You have

135

tasted powerlessness for the first time and you hate it. You must be careful with hate amigo or you will become what you hate."

"How do you know about my arrest?"

"We have newspapers on the reservation, plus radio and TV, just no power over our lives. Be alert Cooper. They are baiting you like a white hunter baits a bear for his client to shoot and kill."

"How do you possess all this wisdom? We talked for five minutes at the museum."

"I know much about the spirit currents of the world, Blue Eyes, and yours is almost dead. It must be revitalized or you will leave the earth soon," he said with a calm, holy voice.

"So what do you propose?" Cooper quizzed.

"Come to the Ute reservation on Sleeping Ute Mountain with me. The grizzly bear spirit will appear for our purification ritual. In Ute legends, it has been said the bear spirit appears after the last spring snowfall. I will call him from his sleep in the white winter to help you. I believe you will be an ally of my abused, cheated and enslaved nation if we can help you survive your ordeal and defeat your enemies."

Cooper was astonished to be invited to a sacred ceremony on the reservation by a man he barely knew, but the Peace Corps had taught him the power of native traditions.

Joe Bear Spirit continued, "I saw a vision in the world while I last slept. In our culture the white man's physical or real world is the Ute dream world. During sleep a Ute Indian enters the real world and leaves the dream world that I am traveling in now. That is why our traditional Ute culture can never co-exist with the white or European cultures. We cannot participate in the destruction and possession of all things in nature."

"The government forced my grandfather to build fences at the end of the open grazing era. Other than the fences, the Y Bar C has not disturbed its land. We deliberately under graze our land and have always protected wildlife habitat."

Joe interrupted, "We must travel soon. Nightfall will cover the valley. Travel light and bring only one change of spare warm clothing."

"How are we going to travel?" Cooper asked hesitantly.

"Are we going to turn into bears?"

"Not now, you are not ready. We will drive down to the reservation in your ranch pickup."

Joe disappeared, leaving only the mist from his mouth hanging in the frigid winter air. The pain from his jail beatings, which had dissipated while Joe was present, returned.

Cooper wired money to Polecat from the Western Union office and walked next door to the Telluride bakery, which was housed in a ramshackle tin building. Cooper needed fresh donuts and a cup of hot coffee before he tackled the drive from Telluride to the Mountain Ute's reservation near Cortez. Next, Cooper stopped by Gary's house to get an update on the condo project. He was seriously considering withdrawing his money. Neither Gary nor Sue were at home even though the hot tub room door was ajar. Its window was ply boarded.

He closed the hot tub room door and walked down Oak Street to Adrianna's bistro. The chef informed him she was at home. Cooper called her from house reservations phone and she answered after eight rings.

"Good afternoon," Cooper chirped and then white lied to cover up his Ute Reservation trip. "I am too banged up to ski so it's back to the YBarC in an hour."

"Well, you know I would accept an invite but it's Arizona Days and the Telluride is packed with ski brats and their bored suntanned moms from Phoenix, Tucson, and Scottsdale. Business is booming except the moms cannot get it through their bleach blonde heads I am the owner, not a waitress."

"Thanks. Went to a boarding school friend's wedding in Tempe a few years back. The coeds wore short shorts and halter tops, no underwear," Cooper teased. "I don't remember a single conversation."

"Cooper you are bad."

"By the way, father needs the gold back or I meet his payroll next week."

"No problem. Max finally made the assholes accept the cashier's check today. The gold will be released tomorrow. Hear anything on campus about who the secret witness might be?"

"Not yet, but the box canyon has ears. Father always said, when cash or gold is missing from the mine headquarters, look at the fingers on the desk nearest the safe first. Keep your eyes on the snow as they say on the mountain."

"Your father is a wise man. I want to meet him," Cooper said too casually.

"You will meet him if you travel to Red Cliff to ask for my hand in marriage. Until then you are a business friend of mine and he is a mine owner from the old world upper Spanish class. Call me Monday."

Cooper pondered her message but marriage was not a priority. At a swap shop, he bought a battered rifle to replace his pistol and rifle that were being held in Delta's evidence room. He returned to the inn and packed an old saddlebag with a change of clothes. Cooper was securing the Marlin 306 on the pickup's gun rack when Joe Bear Spirit reappeared.

"The sun is in a low position in the western winter sky. Our shadows are long and the dream world will vanish soon. Tonight, you enter the real world to regain your power."

Cooper and Joe Bear Spirit, in near total silence, hurled toward Rico, Dolores, and Cortez on an empty state highway. The snowplow had cut steep walls of snow that lined Lizard Head Pass, and reminded Cooper that the southern San Juan Mountain high country had blizzards. The studded snow tires sang against the frozen roadbed that had merged with patches of black ice five miles north of Rico. Cooper's eyes were fixed at the edge of the headlight beams at fifty miles an hour. The night was so dark that the red sandstone cliffs north of Delores were invisible to the eye. An occasional window light from the small homestead ranches along the Delores River provided the only reminder of modern civilization. The night's winter silence recharged Cooper's heart and his brain. A new energy began to emerge from his spirit's center.

Two hours after leaving Telluride, Cooper and Joe turned into a rutted reservation road. The lights of Cortez shimmered like industrial diamonds on the mesa below them. Rumors were that the reservation's Anasazi ruins rivaled those at Mesa Verde National Park.

Joe Bear Spirit spoke for the first time in two hours as the cold potholed gravel road jarred their young human bones.

"Brother Blue Eyes, we are at the cliff dwellings. Follow me after you park next to the stock tank. Be very careful during the descent on the old dry pine ladders since we will have no light."

"Tonto, now that we're on the reservation, just use sign language," Cooper dryly quipped.

Joe smiled, "There are a few missing rungs. Miss one and it is a five hundred foot drop."

Cooper grimaced remembering, "Polecat's father found some unmapped ruins on the ranch's extreme southern boundary. We kept them secret to keep the government out of our chaps and the pot diggers off the YBarC. Nothing big, probably lookout posts to warn the Anasazi around here about invaders."

"You are mostly correct."

"Let's descend before my battered hands get any colder," Cooper complained as he pulled on his leather gloves.

"Check, Blue Eyes." Joe slipped over the corn snow ledge and disappeared into the dark without a sound.

Cooper carefully fished his left leg over the cliff face until it found a rough-hewn pine rung. He gripped the thick ladder top with his now gloved hand as the wind blasted sandstone dust into his face. He disappeared over the edge of the mesa into the quiet solitude of the hidden windless Canyon. The down climb was cold, dark and arduous. As they dropped silently their feet rhythmically found creaky pine rungs. After five minutes of silent terror, Cooper landed with a thud after he had slid the last twenty feet fireman style because of a broken rung. He was silently happy to be alive with only a scraped chin from his misadventure.

"Good recovery. I have seen Ute's perish from a slip like yours from higher on the ladders. The broken rung is a bad omen but your recovery signifies that you are a great warrior whose spirit has much work to do."

"Great news," Cooper replied, still shaking. "Where to now on the magical mystery tour?"

"Look up," Joe said reverently when on cue the moon broke the mesa edge and illuminated the canyon in pastel hues. Cooper gasped as he stared up at five stories of matchless cliff dwellings with smoke rising from twenty plus apartments.

"The old ones are here tonight because it is a full moon. They are descended from the Anasazi, as you Anglos call them. They abandoned their stone cities during the great drought that lasted four hundred Anglo years in ancient times. Their descendants from the pueblos return here but fear the spirits of the dead who remain here. They invite the Utes to join them. First we must cleanse your spirit in a sweat lodge. You enter wearing only a loin cloth to protect your seeds from the hot steam."

He handed Cooper an old deerskin loin cloth from his nylon daypack.

"Any other tips?"

"Be silent and follow me to the old ones. If you live, your warrior spirit will be revitalized. But if you die your spirit will be blown by the mesa winds lodging in river valleys among the Aspen and pine forever guided by the stars, warmed by the sun and protected by the snow."

Joe turned on a dime and Cooper followed him one step behind so as not to lose him in the shadows. Cooper saw the symmetry of the extinct civilization everywhere. The mesa shaded the cliff houses from the blazing summer sun and sheltered them from the wind and snow in the winter. The spring fed creek with its bottomland's fertile soil nurtured primitively irrigated corn and beans in the summer. Primitive check dams irrigated their crops. Stone walled granaries stored the corn and beans. The ladder roads provided safety from predators and the cliff cities were hidden from roving enemy eyes.

The stone houses stored the south sun's heat and the warmth of their pinion fired kivas. Secret seeps in the canyon's sandstone walls supplied additional drinking water, as did the seasonal creek that cut the sub canyon. Game roamed the mesa and was easy to hunt even before the arrival of the horse. There was order in the sweep of his peripheral vision but something had gone very wrong here seven hundred years ago. Now the ancient ones had secretly gathered on the sacred reservation site away from the regulations of the National Park rangers, the archaeologists and prying anthropologists.

Cooper faced an elk skin teepee secluded by a half block of stone dwellings in disrepair. He felt a silent vibration that chilled him to the bone. Joe signaled and Cooper peeled off his clothing layer by layer starting with his sheepskin jacket and ending with his Swiss watch. It was the first loincloth Cooper had worn since Boy Scouts when he had dressed as a Sioux Chief for a play at the Norwood Elementary School. The near zero wind lashed at his bare back and he was happy when Joe finally opened the teepee's flap door and signaled him to enter.

Four Ute men sat against the teepee sides. An old man with a sun cracked face and a long gray ponytail sat by the hot rocks. Steam curled toward the teepee's conical opening at the junction of its Aspen poles. The glow from the large hot river rocks seemed supernatural.

The man on Cooper's right played a small drum, providing a mystic rhythm for the gathering. Cooper's eyes strained in the low light and his mind started to clear. Joe Bear Spirit's presence floated away. The steamy moist heat filled Cooper's nostrils as the YBarC floated away. The steam warmed Cooper's bare chest, thick muscled thighs and his brain as he descended into a trance. Cooper floated into space as warriors arrived one by one. The drum stopped suddenly and a stone pipe with a large bowl appeared. The old man filled it with brown shavings that were combusted by his stare. He smoked the pipe first and then passed it counter clockwise. Cooper smoked a hit without hesitation and it burned down his throat and down into his lungs, causing him to cough violently, breaking the silence.

A half second later, tantalizingly bright lights flashed in Cooper's head in dizzying patterns like explosions of dying galaxies past and future. Supernatural spirits of the dead began to talk a language so ancient and so earth simple it was easily understood. Cooper's body rocketed down river valleys at high speed and then soared into the clouds, changing shapes easily in the wind before it ascended a high mountain. Thoughts collided like atoms and exploded like electrons at the bottom of a waterfall. Colors flowed like rivers, bloomed like flowers and exploded like spring blizzards. Faces flashed past in flames, centuries were heartbeats.

Then it all stopped on the top of a boulder-strewn escarpment where Cooper's grandfather sat.

He spoke, "Stand facing the west wind, Cooper, and you will become one with nature. That is your honor, your strength and your destiny."

Then Cooper fell into a deep sleep for a day.

THIRTY-TWO

Joe Bear Spirit

Cooper jolted awake in the teepee. A small pinion fire in the center of the teepee had replaced the hot steaming rocks. Joe knelt next to Cooper holding an ancient cooking pot of steaming elk stew. Cooper's blinked and adjusted to the low light. The Old Medicine Man gave Cooper a hand-carved wooden ladle of melted snow to drink from an ancient clay water pot. Cooper reeked of sweat from the steam heat but his body felt lighter and refreshed. His mind had been cleared of the Telluride toxins - cocaine, alcohol and pot - by what he suspected had been a mushroom-based drug.

The stew filled Cooper's hollow stomach along with wild berries and spring water.

"Your journey was long, Cooper, into the ancient land before our people came to the San Juan Mountains. You have experienced virgin wilderness, seen first animals, and waded pure streams," the Old Medicine Man said as he gave Cooper a ladleful of water.

"I understand the origin of life now and my body, mind and spirit are connected again," Cooper gazed into Joe's coal- pupils in the flickering orange firelight. Its translucent smoke produced a hologram as a shaft of the rising sunlight poked at the teepee opening.

"Your spirit has been purified by the Old Medicine Man or the Shaman as we sometimes call him, the last Ute descendent from the ancient ones. His magic is the science of the wilderness, his spirit both man and animal, his knowledge encyclopedic about the earth, his history oral and his footprints blow away with the wind," Joe replied.

"I can return to the ranch and Telluride now and fight like a warrior with clear vision."

"You have one more step to make tonight before you are granted the magic of a Ute spirit warrior. You are now purified for the rite."

Cooper continued to eat. He was content to wait to ride into the wind bravely and achieve victory.

Dusk came, Cooper wandered through the recycled cliff dwellings and its invisible spirit population looking for Joe Bear Spirit. He had given his Swiss watch to the Old Medicine Man as a token of appreciation for his successful magical journey. Joe silently appeared and lead Cooper up six ladders to a group of Ute warriors who were dancing around a giant bonfire of pine logs.

As the blue-black night sky descended, a chief with a ten point elk headdress led the dancers to the beat of an ancient log drum. Suddenly, ancient warriors appeared from the openings of the cliff houses dressed in deerskin clothing and sat in a circle around the dancers. Their death masks revealed they were not from the present century but were time travel warriors. After an hour of dancing and drumming, Cooper saw a massive column of white smoke rise from the fire and form a three story grizzly bear. Warriors dressed as mule deer, elk, eagle, hawk, beaver and big horn sheep danced just out of reach of the bear's giant claws. The ancient animistic spirit warriors chanted in unison. Cooper transfigured into a Ute Spirit Warrior dressed as a mountain lion. He danced around the Ute Bear Spirit inhaling the misty smoke. As he danced he became a mountain lion and the seated ancient warriors stroked his golden-brown winter coat.

The massive Bear Spirit slashed at the sky with paws that reached the white streaked Milky Way. Suddenly the moon popped over the mesa edge and the ancient ones vaporized with the Bear Spirit, leaving a dazed Cooper dancing alone at the edge of the Ute warriors who stopped at the last drumbeat. Cooper's mountain lion head fell to the earth as his human eyes searched the horizon for a trace of the vanished Bear Spirit. Joe tapped gently on Cooper's shoulder and took his hand. Cooper visualized being a mountain lion again and they jumped twenty feet up and landed gently on the mesa rim above a cliff dwelling.

"The ancient ones have granted you the earth magic as a Ute warrior. Use it only for fighting great evil, never as play."

"I promise. No party tricks at the New Sheridan Bar."

"Misuse the power even once, and it is gone forever, just an invisible memory."

They drove into the sub-zero night while Cooper took a mental inventory. His wounds from the Delta jail beating had completely healed; his body had a renewed physical grace and power, and his eyes saw beyond the headlight beams. He was at peace again.

THIRTY-THREE

The Return

The Jeep whined in low four-wheel drive as Joe Bear Spirit and Cooper plowed their way through fresh powder on the driveway to the YBarC after a day of skiing. Cooper noted the winter hand had not plowed out to the county road, usually the first chore of the day after a heavy snowfall.

"I volunteer to snowplow the road," Joe volunteered.

"I can use all hands. A Person could think about a Ute raid on Telluride to burn the bank to the ground, scalping Sam Jr. and carrying off all the bleached blonde skiers!" Cooper said dryly.

"American Indian Movement tried that at Wounded Knee and the Feds countered with gunships straight from Vietnam. I slipped through the federal lines twice."

"That sounds dangerous."

"Very like Wounded Knee and Hill 407 in Vietnam where one in five Marines in my unit walked off under their own power. I was the regiment scout with C Company when we assaulted a ridge with hundreds of dug in North Vietnam regulars because an ROTC First Lieutenant from Oklahoma ignored my scouting report. He called me a half-breed coward. Later I flew a medivac helicopter in 'Nam."

Cooper powered the Jeep over a rise and the brick Victorian came into view. The curtains were closed and there were no tracks in the snowy driveway.

"The winter hand should have checked the headquarters by now. Something may be wrong. Move behind the Jeep quickly when I stop." Cooper pulled his new short barrel rifle from the back of the Jeep with his right hand as he slid to a stop in neutral.

He left the engine idling and unsnapped the cold steel door handle. He and Joe moved quickly behind the Jeep into deep snow. He lever actioned a bullet into the rifle chamber. Joe crouched silently, weaponless, next to him, his breath barely visible in the bitter cold moist air. Pine tree limbs swayed around them, their branches flocked with fresh snow. Cooper signaled Joe to remain behind the Jeep and then crossed the open front yard, hopped onto the covered porch and pulled a key from under the snow-coated doormat. Cooper knew the back kitchen door was usually unlocked but he wanted to maintain line of sight with Joe. Cooper opened the iron door lock and slid down the entranceway hall to the library where the gun safe stood solidly against the wall. Cooper's Grandfather had given him the combination written on a box of Marlin 306 bullets for his tenth birthday. He had memorized it for life.

The propane gas furnace's blower cut on. Cooper made a mental note to restore some of the wood stoves and burn ranch wood next winter. Liz wasted thousands of dollars on propane heat. Cooper reached for the combination lock and his eye caught a handwritten note Scotch taped to the desk. Cooper relaxed his trigger finger and picked up the rough brown grocery sack the note was written on.

"Dear Liz and Cooper, Quit on Saturday and couldn't reach nobody by phone and didn't want Polecat to talk me out of it. Late pay was okay but the Delta thing isn't. Can't work for no drug dealer. I hear people do coke openly in Telluride like it is okay. Thanks for the good years. Sure wish your grandfather still ran this outfit. Send my last paycheck to Box 43 Paradox, Colorado. Thanks and please find God."

Cooper realized his own behavior caused this mess, and the one in Delta. A shaken Cooper walked to the open front door. And in an anguished voice said, "All clear. We're the new winter hands. Problem is, I barely remember what happens here in the winter while the cattle are sunning themselves in Arizona."

"We'll just play hearts, listen to the March storms howl across the mesa and feed the horses. That's what we used to do down on the res," Joe laughed.

Dawn came early for Cooper as the sweet odor of Ute camp elk stew lingered in the old house. They had breakfast listening to Montrose country music radio and then divided up the chores. Cooper took the mechanical chores by default because Joe chose the outdoor fresh air ones. The propane tank level was a day or two from empty. The restoration of the wood stoves was urgent since there was an accumulated decade supply of quartered pine, pinion and juniper behind the ranch house. He discovered the phone was out of order probably because the continuing snowstorm had downed the line. The electric well pumps were working and the emergency generator had a full fuel tank. The ranch's always-hopeful TV aerial had been blown sideways in the high winds. Cooper could not remember it ever receiving anything but static-riddled pictures from Grand Junction so he didn't plan to climb the steep snowy roof to right it.

Joe found the dozen winter horses in their warm stalls in the main barn and refilled their feed bins with oats as a treat. He then tested the water in the hot spring house. The slight smell of lithium and sulfur wafted through the cold air above the clear 105 degree water that took on the hue of its red sandstone walls. The spring was the ranch's secret treasure but well known to the Utes who once camped around it. Finally, Joe walked a two-mile perimeter in ancient trapper snowshoes around the headquarters checking for human and animal tracks.

At noon, they met back in the headquarters kitchen for venison steaks, baked potatoes and a Key Lime pie Liz had left with a note on it in the freezer.

Joe sipped hot tea from an ancient English teacup and reported, "Human civilian tracks that are not your cowboys' a mile west at the main headquarters' pasture fence. They were put down between snowstorms probably by Sorels, maybe about the time we arrived. Anglo steps deep at the heal."

"Interesting. Let's set a watch tonight. Snoop by day, trouble by night. I have to go to Norwood tomorrow because the phone line's down. This afternoon we have to reinstall three wood stoves and check the fireplaces."

They both startled as they heard a big engine coming up the ranch driveway too fast in the snow. Seconds later the gun safe was open and Cooper walked onto the headquarters front porch with a Winchester rifle in hand while Joe covered him from an open front window. Cooper had a nylon ammunition belt pulled across his bomber jacket. A shiny new Grand Wagoneer roared into Cooper's view and he identified Jesse Smith behind the wheel with a uniformed Pinkerton Guard in the passenger seat. Cooper stood on the marble steps with his finger on the trigger of his Winchester rifle. The Wagoneer slid to a stop fifty feet from the steps, its engine running as the two men in it talked. Finally, Jesse stepped out, tanned as usual, wearing a tweed full-length topcoat with a small brim Austrian hat and new Sorels. He leaned on his heels, clearly not happy to find Cooper at home.

He yelled over the engine as Cooper levered a bullet into his Winchester, "I have a notice of a hearing to post on your door. The bank wants this ranch put under a bank appointed receiver, Cooper. You are under indictment for a felony and the bank doesn't want its assets dissipated for your defense."

Jesse paused, waiting for the Pinkerton guard to get out of the car, to post the notice. Cooper fired a Winchester round through the Grand Wagoneer's window destroying it and temporary blinding the armed guard. "You are trespassing on posted YBarC ranchland."

A blue-faced Smith dived for the rear of the Grand Wagoneer as the Pinkerton guard dived into the snow.

"Run, or you'll leave here boots first for armed trespass."

They ran through their tire tracks down the long driveway as Cooper levered in another round. He fired a bullet at the Grand Wagoneer's gas tank. It exploded in flames. Jesse and the Pinkerton guard never looked back as they cleared the low ridge.

Joe walked out the front door with a frown on his face, "You need much teaching Blue Eyes. This will solve nothing."

"You're dead right, but it sure was fun."

Cooper and Joe rose at dawn to do the morning chores before they drove into Norwood. Cooper fired up the ranch's faded blue Chevy pickup with the snowplow attached to its rusted front bumper. After he plowed the driveway, he chained the burned-out Jeep Wagoner to the straight six-cylinder truck and towed it out to the front gate. He left it on the county road's shoulder. Then he rounded up Joe and they drove to Norwood on a clear cold day. At the ranch gate, Cooper saw a deputy sheriff pull over behind the burned Wagoneer. Cooper gunned the Jeep's engine and turned out of the driveway.

"Hello, Janet," Cooper said as he walked to the front counter at the telephone office. "Got a line problem on section 106 of the YBarC between the county road and the house. Can you get to it today so I can work the headquarters phone?"

"Do what I can Cooper but you're three months behind on the YBarC's account," she replied matter-of-factly. Cooper laid the two folded $100 bills on the counter.

"Thanks," she said, "That'll keep Denver off my back. The college grad managers up there don't know calf payment schedules."

"Got to get over to Telluride to check on some business so we best be on the road."

Cooper stopped at the inn to check his messages while Joe looked for a part-time weekend bartending job. Cooper could only pay him $50 weekly, room, board and gas money until the herd returned. Max had called; he had found a state ruling that might get Cooper's case moved to another venue and out of Delta jurisdiction.

Next he read a message, "Received the wire transfer. Thanks. That will hold us for four weeks. Polecat."

Finally, he read a message from Liz, "Couldn't reach you at the ranch. Driving over this afternoon now that the highway is plowed. I need to pick up some spring clothes."

Cooper did not want Liz to be alone at the ranch all night, but he wanted to have dinner with Gary at Adrianna's restaurant and get an update on the condo deal.

Cooper called Gary on the front desk's phone. "You okay for dinner at Adrianna's at five so we can go over your payout projections on the condo project?"

Gary hesitated, "Make it seven, I scheduled a presale closing at six. Things are really moving. You'll be happy when you see the spreadsheet projections. A record number of skiers here this month with these storms and they are not all Tempe, Arizona coeds. Got some credit card skiers whose condo deposit checks will clear." Gary could reduce any information to the crudest terms, but Cooper was delighted by the report.

"Sure could use a payday."

"Count on it, partner," he replied. Cooper projected a May payday when he needed to move the YBarC herd back from Arizona to the ranch.

"Good work, Gary," Cooper blurted out. His grandfather would never have been that generous before a check cleared.

"See you at seven."

"Make it sharp. I have to get back to the YBarC early." Gary hung up.

Cooper walked over to Adrianna's restaurant admiring Telluride's freshly red painted brick courthouse on the way. County tax collections must be up; it had never been painted in his memory. He entered the restaurant from the alley door and was delighted to surprise Adrianna in her office.

"Hello, Cooper," She jumped up to hug him. "You know your phone is dead at the ranch."

"Storm damaged the line. Grandfather ranched in the early days without one and did just fine."

"You have plans for the afternoon?"

"Not until seven here with Gary for dinner. I need a reservation and you are invited to join."

"Good then. Let's go skiing in perfect spring snow, then a hot tub at my place."

Cooper and Adrianna spent the next two hours on the slopes skiing March powder. Back at Adrianna's house they stripped and enjoyed a long hot tub together as her laughter relaxed him. Afterwards they retired to her bedroom where her warm tongue and ruby lips aroused his manhood. Time fled like a horse thief.

Cooper awoke later, alone, and he showered. He bumped into Joe on the way back to the restaurant.

Joe announced, "Good news. I got the weekend job drawing draft beer for skiers at the local beef and brew hangout from four 'til closing. Tips are good, I am assured. The manager wants me to try out tonight from seven 'til nine. Haven't bar tended since college at CU in Boulder so I'm a little rusty."

"Meet me at the inn at nine and see if you can get part of your tip as a couple cold ones for the drive back. We'll crank the heater up all the way."

To Cooper's surprise, Gary was sitting at the bar uncharacteristically on time.

"Hello, Cowboy," he loudly greeted Cooper, which meant he was already high. Gary took a long sip of his vodka martini.

Sue caught Cooper's eye next as she blustered, "It's Cooper in prison. I mean person. Where's your ball and chain?" Gary turned red immediately and glared at Sue.

Adrianna walked into the small bar and announced, "Drinks are on me. What are you all drinking?"

"Nothing," Cooper replied, miffed at Sue, not divulging his Ute purification rite. Sue attacked again with the hated Adrianna now in the scene, "That part of your parole, Cooper, not drinking and on Adrianna's leash?"

Adrianna, who expected the worst from Sue's trash mouth, blushed while Cooper shifted on his cowboy boot heels.

Gary quickly changed the subject and stared at Sue, indicating she'd regret it after they left. "Weather sure nice and warm down in Phoenix. I played golf every day last week. I won almost a $1,000 on putting bets. Phoenix is going to be a good market for Telluride real estate but not once the weather heats up. This is the best month to sell, so I am here until closing day. I have to crack the whip on these novice Telluride real estate brokers. They get one commission in their jeans and they start spring skiing and partying again."

Sue stared at Gary in silent disbelief, guessing he was lying.

"Good idea, so pedal to the metal," replied Cooper.

Sue queried angrily, "You fuck all those black and white girl cows yourself, Cowboy?"

Adrianna pounced like a mountain lioness, "He couldn't tell your pussy from a mother cow's. I hear around town your ass is always in the air with some local bull rooting around in it." She turned and walked briskly thru the "employees only" door. Sue turned sugar beet red and swung a fist at the spot where Adrianna had stood. "That bitch," she cried almost inaudibility and whispered, "she stole you from me, Cooper."

Gary's tanned face tensed as Sue turned and ordered another double martini. Cooper involuntarily put a hand on Sue's shoulder. Tears were forming in Sue's eyes. He once again realized her deeply felt emotion for him. He felt guilty he had always equated their relationship with coke and sex.

Gary got up, "Excuse me, ladies and gentlemen, I have an urgent call to the men's room. Sure you're drying out tonight, Cooper?"

"Yes I am."

Gary quickly walked away and Sue turned toward Cooper and stared into his blue eyes, "You could have been my salvation from indentured servitude. I would have killed for you, Cowboy. Take me back to the ranch with you and you will never regret it, Cooper. I am in love with you." Tears rolled down her soft cheeks.

Cooper was moved deep within his soul by her honesty and he replied without hesitation, "Joe and I are leaving for the ranch at nine. The Jeep is parked in front of the inn. Bring a sleeping bag. It's cold ride in the rear of the Jeep."

Sue was not sure she heard Cooper correctly.

He continued, "Joe is the weekday winter hand now. You can cover for him weekends while he pours beers in town for extra cash. It's cold rough work and no coke allowed. No one's ever broke the 'no drugs' rule on the ranch. Break it, Sue, and I will kick your perfect ass all the way back to Telluride."

"I get it," she replied still in shock. "I made all A's in high school before I dropped out to suck and fuck and deal for Gary. He has changed since then. There is a lot you don't know."

She became silent as Gary returned, his gaze fixed on Sue. He barked an order, "Back to the house, Sue. I have a package being picked up and I want you to be there tonight, babe."

"I do believe Miss Adrianna, chief witch of the Telluride realm, has ordered me out of her lair."

"Don't push it, babe. There is a Quaalude in my desk drawer. Take it and cool out while I dine with Cooper and go over some numbers. Maybe I can coax him back for a hot tub with you. He's not married to Adrianna yet and you are persuasive sans clothes."

Sue slapped Gary so hard it knocked him into the bar and his arm shattered her martini glass. She walked out without another word as the other patrons watched in silence.

"She is finished," he mumbled. "Let that little cunt freeze for a week in a ski bum shack and she'll crawl back."

Cooper tested Gary, "I just hired her if she can stay straight."

Gary turned white but didn't immediately respond. "Like I said, Cooper, she hasn't been straight since sixteen and she can freeze to death on your ranch for all I care."

Dinner went better as Gary explained the new spreadsheets. They projected Cooper would get his $50,000 principle back by early June when construction financing kicked in and a $15,000 profit distribution from presales in May. A final $50,000 in profit was projected for late November when phase one construction was complete and the buyer contracts closed. The condo project had become the YBarC's working capital. Cooper departed in a good mood after Adrianna's long goodbye kiss.

At nine o'clock Cooper met Joe at the ice-covered Jeep but he didn't see Sue until he opened the brittle leather and plastic windowed door. She was curled up on the backseat floor asleep in a sleeping bag, wool ski cap pulled down over her ears. Her soft relaxed breath in the translucent light produced a soft fog on each exhale. Sue stirred when Joe and Cooper climbed into the Jeep.

Cooper said, "Joe, meet Sue. She's your weekend relief, weekday cook and housekeeper. Sue, meet Joe Bear Spirit, an all-American Ute and the YBarC's winter hand."

Sue's blue eyes were as wide as sage grouse eggs as she stared at Joe's round brown face and black ponytail.

Sue said intuitively, "So he's your new secret weapon, not me. I will be damned, Cooper, you can still surprise a girl."

"Ranch's secret weapon," agreed Joe. "But as of tonight, also the new weekend bartender at the Steak and Brew Saloon. I'm the equal opportunity poster boy for Telluride."

They drove a long hour on black ice roads to the ranch turn off. Light crystalline powder snow started to fall at the ranch gate. The conversation had been loud over the roar of the glass packed mufflers but entertaining and frank. Sue's voice was clear and warm from the back except when she grimaced occasionally when Cooper hit an icy pothole. Cooper drove slowly down the snowy covered ranch road following Liz's tire tracks. As the Jeep came over the last low mesa ridge Cooper saw an orange glow from the headquarters site. Alarms bells sounded in his head.

Cooper sped up as Joe saw the glow and yelled, "Fire Cooper!"

Cooper blazed toward the brick house. A moment later Cooper visually confirmed the century old headquarters was on fire. Liz's car was parked in front of the porch steps.

Joe asked, "You have water and fire hoses?"

"My mother is in the house," Cooper shouted over the roar of the Jeep. "The hoses are in the white shed with a red roof on a steel roller out back. Take Sue with you. Their hook up is at the well's red pump house just inside the door on the left. Hook up the hose, turn the valve to the left and then hit the big red pump switch button. I have to find Liz and make sure she is safe."

"Put a wet handkerchief over your nose," Sue advised Cooper. "Here's my flashlight."

Cooper's heart raced as he braked to a stop a few yards from the yellow brick house. He jumped into the crusted snow as Joe and Sue clamored out of the Jeep and raced toward the back yard. Cooper yelled at the top of his lungs for Liz. A wall of heat hit him as smoke tore at his lungs. He coated his blue skiing bandana with fresh snow. He raced through the unlocked front door to search for his mother.

THIRTY-FOUR
Smoke Jumper

The heat from the old cast iron doorknob penetrated Cooper's gloved hand as he pushed open the unlocked door. He momentarily froze as he scanned the main staircase. It would take Joe and Sue too long to start the pump, unroll the heavy fire hose and start up the back stairs off the kitchen. He pulled off his nylon ski jacket and tossed it in the snow. Acrid black smoke was pouring from the front attic vents, indicating the fire was now spreading to the second floor. Cooper raced through the front door into the dark hallway. He turned on the hall lights, which flickered but still worked. His eyes burned as he opened the hall closet and groped for the small fire extinguisher. He found it and raced across the wide pine planked hallway floor to the base of the wooden staircase.

The lights flickered again and then dimmed gradually, creating an orange smoky hue in the hallway. Cooper started up the staircase but was slowed by swirling flares that pierced the ceiling. He used the fire extinguisher to put them out as he climbed step-by-step and shouted for Liz. He had seconds to find Liz as the bone-dry century old ranch house began to combust. He heard the Jeep start up and deduced the bunkhouse phone was still out so Sue was driving to the nearest neighbor to call the volunteer fire department. Cooper lunged into the hallway that linked the five bedrooms. Liz's bedroom was at the end.

Cooper shouted, turning his head to the left toward the back staircase, "Joe, do you have the hose?"

There was no reply; he dropped to his knees seeking breathable air but the smoke still choked his lungs so he got onto his stomach and crawled toward Liz's room.

He called as he crawled. "Liz, can you hear me?" Again, he heard no response as he wormed down the hallway.

Suddenly a polished pine floor plank burst into flames ahead of Cooper, forcing him to spray it with foam so he could continue his progress. The last of the foam dribbled out but the flame temporary disappeared in front of Cooper.

"Liz, are you trapped in your room?" There was no reply. Cooper yelled, "Joe, I need the kitchen fire extinguisher!" Silence again greeted Cooper as the fire lapped at his feet.

The stairwell was being consumed behind him. Cooper crawled the last fifteen feet to Liz's room.

After an eternity, he reached the white painted door and with a final lung-busting burst of adrenaline stood up. He opened the white-hot knob and burst into Liz's smoke-filled bedroom, ignoring the pain in the palm of his hand. He reached Liz's bed in two long strides.

Suddenly Cooper heard the large kitchen fire extinguisher slide down the length of the hallway as Joe shouted, "Grab the extinguisher! The pump won't start. I have to retreat before the back stairs catch fire."

Cooper ran to the burning bedroom door and grabbed the extinguisher as it skidded to a stop. He turned and walked back into the smoke-filled bedroom and sprayed its foam all around Liz's bed. Finally, the smoke cleared a little as he reached her and extinguished her burning wedding ring quilt that his grandmother had hand sewn.

Liz was unconscious and badly burned. Cooper tossed the empty fire extinguisher through the west window of Liz's bedroom. It shattered, releasing a black plume of smoke into the frigid night air. As the smoke exited, it expanded Cooper's field of vision. But the blast of cold air ignited the Victorian cloth wallpaper in Liz's bedroom, lighting it up like the Fourth of July. Cooper inhaled deeply once, scooped up his still unconscious mother in his arms and after one massive stride, followed the fire extinguisher's path out the west bedroom window. Cooper was airborne momentarily with Liz secure in his arms as stars appeared on the winter night horizon line. He fell two stories, gambling the steep roof's winter snow pile had accumulated enough to break his fall. Cooper and Liz landed with a dull thud as he sank waist-deep in snow, cradling Liz. His mother lay like a sleeping goddess on a soft white mat of crystal white snow in the early morning moonlight.

Cooper's burning lungs heaved for fresh air. The landing had knocked the smoke out of his lungs. His eyes fought to open as tears wiped away the smoke but not its acrid smell or sting. Liz remained motionless. The fire eerily illuminated the yellow brick that still provided Cooper protection from the smoke and flames, which were devouring the house's innards. Cooper eyes cleared and he saw Liz's burned body and still beautiful face as she struggled to breathe. His heart broke as he reflectively kissed her charred cheek. He started to give her mouth-to-mouth resuscitation.

After a couple of long minutes Liz's lips moved ghostlike, her eyes opening slightly, her pale blue pupils dilating with the last energy of her life. She whispered, "I love you, Cooper." The words whispered like alpine waterfall spray, audible only to the spirit absorbing them. "Live strong like your grandfather; embrace the spirit of your father."

She died in his arms. Her spirit rose into the Milky Way on the path of the new east moon. Cooper held her lithe body in his arms against his chest. His heart broke into a thousand pieces as his mother left him alone on the earth. No sound rose from his parched throat but if it had the wail would have silenced all living creatures with its despair.

Long moments later Cooper closed his mother's delicate eyelids and let his fingers rest on her still warm lips. Cooper said goodbye to her forever for the first time in his life as the fire crackled so loudly overhead it returned him to the horror of the night.

Joe ran toward Cooper and ordered, "The house's brick walls are going to cave in. Move away now!"

"Mother's dead," Cooper almost whispered. He scooped her up and struggled through heavy snow pile as Joe shoveled a path to carry her body away from the home she had raised Cooper in.

The west wall collapsed; a curtain of bricks came down where Liz had died.

Joe intoned, "Breathe, Cooper, take the pure night air into your lungs and purify your spirit."

Then Joe chanted an ancient Ute song that rose into the night sky following Liz's departing spirit. Headlights pierced the smoky yard as a rescue 4x4 followed by a fire tanker truck and a deputy sheriff's 4x4 rumbled into the front yard. An EMT and Sue ran toward Cooper and Joe. Volunteer firefighters pulled a black hose from the pumper truck.

Sue stopped to look at Liz, then stepped toward Cooper, and whispered, sobbing into his ear, "I'm sorry Cooper, your mom's dead because of a fake meeting with Gary."

Cooper, shocked and exhausted, whispered in a hoarse voice, "There is no condo project? It's a shell game?"

A sobbing Sue nodded "yes."

"Don't tell him I know," Cooper rasped with revenge in his thoughts. "You owe that to me for keeping his secret."

An hour later the fire was reduced to smoldering sporadic flares. Twilight revealed the north, east, and south brick walls that remained as a monument to the Stuart family.

The sheriff approached Cooper, "I need to ask you some questions. I got Joe's statement and I need yours for Liz's inquest. She tell you how the fire started before she died?"

"Liz was too far gone. Joe saved my life."

"Son, I got to conduct an investigation since there was a death," he said in a cold tone. "You are under indictment over in Delta, short of money, and this house is insured."

Cooper's eyes narrowed as he looked the sheriff straight in the eye and rasped, "Grandfather and father paid to keep you in office. This is still the YBarC and don't you forget it."

Cooper turned and walked away with the sheriff's gaze piercing his back. Joe left to search for tracks in the snow along the fence line.

Near sunup, the volunteer firemen departed. Only the gun safe had survived intact, according to the fire chief, but it was too dangerous to unload it. In it were the YBarC's remaining guns, ammo, cash, deeds, family jewelry and records. The house's collection of antiques, western art, and five thousand mostly first edition hardback books were a total loss. Cooper had left Liz's body in the care of the family's longtime funeral home in Montrose. Cooper assumed the insurance policy on the house and its contents was in the safe.

While Joe, on snowshoes, was checking the perimeter of the headquarters' fences, Sue was grocery shopping in Norwood. The fire had destroyed a year's supply of game, fish and beef in the four freezers. Cooper planned to enter the house at sundown and move the gun safe's contents to the bunkhouse office safe even though the sheriff had yellow taped it. A state patrol arson investigator was due from Denver in a day or so. A U.S. WEST telephone lineman had hooked up the bunkhouse phone.

The Montrose country music station, over the office radio, blared a report that the grand jury had quit hearing testimony on the still unsolved Bill Daniels murder.

The telephone rang and it was Polecat. "My cousin called me. First time I have been able to get through in three days. I'm sorry 'bout your mom, Cooper. I'll be up for the funeral." Cooper knew that was mostly a nice white lie since Polecat felt in his heart that Liz had wrecked the ranch.

"That's not necessary. I need you with the herd until we know all the facts, too much bad luck around these parts. You are the YBarC's field commander and we are at war." Cooper was emotional but firm.

"What facts?" Polecat queried carefully.

"A hunch," replied Cooper knowing Polecat would talk to his cousin again who was a direct link to the Norwood gossip circuit on her four-party line. "I got a Ute Indian tracker out on the fences."

Cooper gambled that if a local had burned the headquarters to settle an old score, gossip might carelessly make him show his hand.

Cooper changed the subject, "Have the calf report notarized and sent certified mail to me in Norwood next week so I can use it as collateral." Cooper paused as he heard two engines approaching the bunkhouse. "Please tell the hands to give the flower money to the Norwood school library. It just lost the family book collection, which Great-Grandfather started and Liz willed to it." Cooper hung up as the engines shut off.

Cooper was amazed to see Sue climbing out of his Jeep and Adrianna climbing out of her Wagoneer. Cooper met them at the door hoping to defuse any tension between them.

Adrianna uncustomary blurted out, "Cooper, I am so sorry for the loss of your mother...Su Madre is dead...poor hombre."

"She was in Norwood at the gas station getting directions to the ranch when I stopped to fill up the Jeep," Sue stated coldly. "She followed me here."

Sue walked into the bunkhouse dining room. Adrianna threw her arms around Cooper, pressing her soft breasts into his gray cotton work shirt. Sue slammed the door so hard it shook the old log building. Adrianna sobbed; she'd come to pay her respects because she was a princess, not the common criminal Cooper now knew her friend Gary to be. Tears flowed down her dark cheeks landing on Cooper's shirt as her heavy breasts heaved.

Sue shattered the moment when she opened the office door, "You two going to help me carry the groceries in before they freeze?"

Adrianna pulled away and almost stopped weeping on cue, "No, Miss Sue, please finish your chores while I help Cooper make funeral arrangements."

Once again Adrianna had sunk a silver dagger into the new winter hand's heart.

An hour later, Cooper and Adrianna emerged from the office with most of the funeral arrangements set. Liz would be buried in a traditional pine box in the YBarC cemetery. Adrianna had also reached Dr. Blacker in El Paso.

He said on taking the call, "Hello Cooper. Max working hard for you?"

"Yes, sir but this call is not about Max," Cooper choked back tears as he gave the doctor the bad news. Cooper knew in his heart Liz had planned to be with Dr. Blacker in his retirement and that moment would never come now. He'd hung up the phone before Cooper could say goodbye.

Joe Bear Spirit appeared at the bunkhouse dining room door. Snow and icicles covered his braided black hair.

"Adrianna," asked Cooper, "please could you cook up some Spanish grub while Joe and I compare notes?"

A tired Joe sat down in a battered captain's chair and Cooper sprawled onto a well-worn cowhide couch with oak wagon wheel arms.

"Two sets of tracks in the snow, both Anglo in Sorels. One is about six feet, two hundred pounds and the other shorter, lighter, both male, paralleling the driveway boundary fence from the east last night about nine o'clock before we arrived," Joe continued as Cooper listened in almost disbelief.

"Their tracks merge into the well house tracks where the firemen's boot tracks obliterate them but they were pointed toward the kitchen door. I found this on the trail." Joe produced a cheap, lighter fluid can wrapped in a green bandana. "It's empty. The bandana's mine to protect fingerprints. I cannot see any. It looks clean to my eyes, Cooper. Give it to the Highway Patrol fire investigator, not the sheriff. It makes sense because the fire was so intense on the kitchen's north wall when Sue and I entered it. The kitchen door was unlocked."

"One of Liz's bad habits is leaving the kitchen door unlocked. Her dog stayed in Montrose. Her neighbor has him. She probably dozed off reading in bed."

"There are no tracks out. They were here when we arrived so they had to leave with the volunteer firemen or they're still on the ranch," Joe asserted.

Cooper was chilled by the idea, "Let's search the bunkhouse rooms and the out buildings."

Cooper loaded a Colt 45 that Polecat kept in the desk drawer for payday protection. The ranch payroll was always cash. Cooper remembered it had been used once in 1952 when Polecat wounded a cowhand when he pulled a knife and tried to rob the payroll.

Cooper and Joe stopped in the kitchen where food was cooking but no women were present. Joe froze and turned an ear toward the dark hallway that led to the ten bunkrooms. He smiled, "They are in the bathroom together. I hear the blonde peeing."

Cooper challenged him, "How can you tell which one is peeing? That could be perverted."

Joe said deadpan, "She is younger and her pee hits the toilet water harder." Cooper smiled thinking about Sue's perfect plumbing.

"Amazing. You listen to the whole earth with your ears. I am glad you are on my team."

"Yes, Anglo, that is how I live. Try it and you might live longer."

"And better."

Adrianna and Sue emerged from the bunkhouse bathroom. "Stay in the kitchen; we might have intruders. Joe and I have to check the bunkrooms then the out buildings," Cooper said.

"The fire was no accident, was it, Cooper?" Sue asked.

"Too early to tell," Cooper dodged. "Just stay put."

He and Joe inspected the bunkrooms one at a time. Only number one, where the winter hand stayed, had been disturbed. The search of the out buildings went slowly but other than some unusually stacked hay in the main shed, Cooper and Joe could find no evidence of recent visits. The mystery deepened since Cooper did not believe the two men had walked out backwards to cover their tracks.

Dinner passed with a temporary truce between Sue and Adrianna. Joe entertained the group with Ute stories and legends. Then he explained the Ute death beliefs, which provided some relief for Cooper. The ringing phone was ignored by all and after dinner Cooper assigned bunkrooms with Joe in one, Sue in two, Adrianna in nine and Cooper in ten with the bathroom separating the two groups. The long hallway created some privacy.

Cooper sat in the foreman's office to collect his thoughts while the trio headed toward their rooms. Cooper left the door open and lit a kerosene table lamp that had a very smoky globe. He twirled the loaded Colt 45 as thoughts collided like billiard balls. He could not remember a clue from the night before that would have placed an arsonist on the ranch. Who was the state's secret drug witness for his Delta trial next month? Was there a link to the fire? Why had Gary lied to him and set him up on the Condo project? Was Gary linked to the fire? Was Sue still in Gary's camp, a double agent? What was Gary's hold over Sue besides coke, or was it that simple?

In the yellow glow of the oil lamp, Adrianna suddenly appeared in a long white sheer nightgown. Her dark brown nipples and black triangle took Cooper's breath away.

In a ghostly manner, she whispered, "I will help you get your money back from Gary. Sue told me the sordid story." Without a word, she walked to the swivel chair and spun Cooper toward her. Cooper stopped spinning the Colt 45, its barrel pointed safely toward the tin plate ceiling. Cooper emptied its chambers, the bullets rolling across the floor. Adrianna faced him standing, her more than ample breasts against his lips. She pulled the gun barrel toward the tip of her triangle as her left hand slowly raised her nightgown. Cooper's tongue tasted the salt of her nipple through the expensive lace. She started to gently rub the gun barrel's front bead site against her clitoris as her full lips caressed its muzzle. Her right hand easy unbuckled Cooper's jeans and slowly unzipped them. She began to arouse him with gentle fingertip strokes.

156

She took the gun from him and laid it on the desk as her secret sweet scent was revealed in the cool night air. She mounted Cooper as he sat in the chair, its back tilted against the lip of the desk. Her full wet lips engulfed him and bathed his senses. She rode him like an angel of mercy; his deep penetration caused a tidal flow of hot juice that flowed onto range rider's thighs. Her powerful convulsive orgasm vanquished the tragedies of his life momentarily from his mind and his young spirit exploded in orgasmic response. Then Cooper slumped unconscious with his head against her full breasts. Adrianna silently rocked him. Their bodies were united and their souls bound together as the soft yellow lamplight bathed them.

THIRTY-FIVE

Gray Sunday

His Cousin Judy stood on Cooper's left with Adrianna on his right. Doctor Blacker stood next to Judy with the group of two hundred plus silent relatives, friends and neighbors at the YBarC family cemetery. It was a dark gray March day on the mesa with a snowstorm approaching from the west. Row upon row of men in dark western cut suits and black cowboy hats accented the women in black wool coats and hats. All the color from the YBarC range had vanished at the hour of Liz's burial. Six tall stout neighboring ranchers stood ready to lower the pine box with three rawhide ropes. The grave had been blow-torched and dynamited into the rocky frozen ground. Joe provided cover with a Winchester rifle a half football field away on a rusting elevated tin water tank. Sue covered his back. Naked gray cottonwood limbs blew in the wind around the iron fenced in graveyard. A Marble, Colorado, slab marked each gravesite. Liz was being buried on row three next to Cooper's father. Cooper already knew he would be buried on row four. This section of the ranch provided the inhabitants of the graveyard an eternal sunset view.

The Presbyterian minister droned to a close with the Lord's Prayer, which was heartily recited by all in attendance. When the prayer ended a hundred black cowboy hats swung with rough hands back to their owner's heads. In the knifing wind Cooper watched the mountain peaks weep for Liz, the mighty Ajax to the east, Lone Cone to the south, La Sal peak to the west and North Mountain to the north. A few in the throng had known Liz well but most only in passing. Most came in mud-splattered pickup trucks for the Stuarts, not Liz. A few came on horses which whinnied in the corral by the burned-out headquarters house. The horses could smell death and the mourner's mood in the wind.

Cooper started his eulogy holding the book Brigham Young had given his great-grandfather.

Cooper began, "Liz Stuart, my mother, your neighbor and operator of the YBarC after my father and grandfather's deaths, lies here burned to death in a headquarters house fire. I will carry on the traditions and operations of this ranch as she asked me to do before she died. The circumstances of this fire are open for investigation and I believe my mother was murdered by arsonists."

The crowd gasped; the sheriff shuffled his boots and looked away.

"The YBarC's enemies are loose in this county and I will not rest until this range war, which started in Paradox is won. I swear to bring to justice my mother's killers, the cattle rustlers who brazenly stole YBarC stock and the men who framed me in Delta," Cooper intoned. "I will rebuild the YBarC, its herds and its headquarters. I will ride with my hands with Winchesters on our horses until we revenge these attacks. This community is my witness. I swear to destroy my mother's killers and the ranch's enemies as my great-grandfather and grandfather did in their day. Take this message to the far reaches of the western slope to every ranch, homestead and town. From this hour, any man, who enters the YBarC without my consent will be shot to death without warning."

The crowd stepped back, fear in their eyes.

Cooper continued, "This is a range war until death. Now pray silently with me for Liz's spirit before you return to your homes. The YBarC will be posted no trespass to all county outsiders."

The six pallbearers lowered the coffin into the grave after a short prayer. Cooper stepped forward and shoveled the first dirt onto Liz's coffin. He looked up and saw Joe Bear Spirit covering him with the Winchester as the silent crowd wandered toward their pickups. The sheriff walked slowly through the departing crowd with two deputies flanking him.

The sheriff said, "I'll take you in if I hear anymore incendiary talk from you in public. I forgive your emotion today only because it's your mother's funeral. Hear me, Cooper Stuart."

"Pick your side, sheriff. I will not call off the war until you find my mother's killers, my cattle and the men who shot at Adrianna and me on the Utah line. Nap time is over."

"Don't insult me, Cooper. It's not 1892. I am warning you, operate outside the law and I will get your bail revoked. Your mother probably died in an accidental kitchen fire. Tracks your hand saw were probably just a couple neighbors walking in."

"Thanks for stopping by," Cooper abruptly walked past the sheriff to gather up the women and Dr. Blacker who had lingered by the gravesite until the last shovel of mesa dirt covered the pine box. Joe continued to cover Cooper's back from the rusting high tin water tower. The snow blew in with blinding bitter cold gusts.

"So it's range war, Cooper, like your great-grandfather. Count me in. You need family to help," Judy said loyally.

"Yes, but you are back to the Fairplay Hotel tomorrow until you get it straightened out financially. Maybe Dr. Blacker here or one of his friends needs an investment. Talk to him tonight. You got number six in the bunkhouse. Storms too bad to drive or fly out tonight. You are all guests of the YBarC. Doc you have room number eight."

Dr. Blacker replied, "I will stay, but no range war for me, Cooper. I'm tired of sewing up gunshot wounds. I will try to help Judy with the hotel. You have Max until the Delta thing is over. He is convinced you were framed."

Cooper replied, "This is Liz's last ranch day. I call a truce 'til sunup. I will drive Judy, Joe and Sue back to the bunkhouse. Adrianna, you take the Doctor. Norwood ladies will have left enough food for a Calvary detachment."

Cooper walked back toward the gravesite with Judy, the visibility almost zero. Judy handed him a snowflake speckled red rose and he tossed it onto his mother's grave. Joe and Sue approached the gravesite with tears in the corner of their eyes. Cooper wondered if Liz's spirit had channeled Sue to replace her beauty on the rugged YBarC.

Cooper fielded condolence calls in the office from old family friends from Montrose, Grand Junction, and Denver while he reviewed the ranch accounts.

George Ball, the president of Ranch and Farm Insurance in Denver called, "My condolences Mr. Stuart, we will be sending you $30,000 accidental death insurance. Liz had a triple indemnity $10,000 life insurance policy. Soon as I get the coroner's finding, the check's in the mail. However, the bank in Telluride wants the whole $50,000 of fire insurance proceeds."

"No way, we paid it. Besides, your agent let Liz underinsure the headquarters the last ten years. I want to rebuild as soon as possible."

"Wait a second, Mr. Stuart. Our company sent Liz an annual letter asking her to let us review the coverage and she never responded," replied Ball matter-of-factly.

Another one of Liz's business mistakes surfaced as Cooper regrouped, "That's on the YBarC then, but I want the fire insurance proceeds the day they are legally due. The insurance policy was never pledged to the bank."

"It will take two weeks for the adjustor's paper work after the inquest. So, if no court order is in the bank's favor, the check goes to the YBarC."

"I will make sure there isn't one. Goodbye," Cooper angrily hung up.

Cooper thought about it. Thirty thousand would get the herd back, pay more overdue bills and carry the ranch through summer. The sale of the painting had cleared up back pay. But $50,000 fire insurance payout with the $50,000 he was determined to recover from Gary could help attract a new loan to free YBarC from the bank. He then joined the mourners for dinner. The neighbors had dropped off a supper of pinto beans, pickled wild asparagus, Palisade canned peaches, smoked duck, venison stew, elk steaks, and cherry cobbler. Table talk centered around good times past and everyone collectively avoided the past three days and the future. Judy warmed to the group and Joe Bear Spirit flirted with Sue. Adrianna seemed preoccupied with her restaurant. She was interrupted three times by calls from the hostess. Cooper regaled the group with Liz's ranch tales.

After dinner, Sue and Joe left to complete night chores while Cooper cleared the plank table; Judy and Adrianna washed dishes in the porcelain sink. Adrianna and Cooper talked briefly before she turned in early. He had begun reading a Zane Gray novel when a woman's soft footsteps approached the locked office door and an almost inaudible knock followed.

He unlatched the iron lock and opened the oak door slowly. Judy waited to be invited into the dimly lit office. She was wearing a full length tattered terry cloth robe and bedroom slippers, with her long black hair braided to her waist. Cooper assumed she wanted to talk about the ranch privately and signaled her to enter. He closed the door behind her and retreated to the desk chair.

She walked across to him frowning, "Do you really think the YBarC was burned-out?"

"Yes, Joe found two sets of tracks to the house from the corral fence. Question is, why didn't the sheriff find them and who were they? The fire blew up too fast for a stove burner fire with all the windows closed for winter. We're keeping the empty lighter fluid can secret around here for a while. I don't want it tampered with." Judy's eyes widened, as Cooper continued, "I want the life and fire insurance proceeds to bring back the cattle, pay the cowboys and run the ranch for the summer."

She whispered, "I can help you with money, too."

"The hotel's underwater in debt."

"I have an offer on the antiques that your uncle willed you. I held up shipping them until I could discuss it with you."

Cooper had forgotten about the antiques Harvey had left him. "How much?"

"Thirty thousand dollars net after the auction and maybe more." Cooper was surprised and his eyes showed it. "They're Spanish colonial. Father bought them in the 1950s and they have appreciated."

"That's good news," replied Cooper, "but you keep the antique money to operate the hotel and pay down debt."

"That's too generous, Cooper," Judy whispered.

"They belonged to your father."

"How much is the insurance money?" she asked.

"Thirty thousand accidental death, which gives the ranch operating cash through the summer and $50,000 fire. Plus, I intend to get my condo investment back from Gary. Sam's bank is trying to freeze the fire insurance as part of the foreclosure. He may win that round, who knows, but we have a record high calf rate."

"How'd you pull that off?" she asked, impressed.

"Switched to artificial insemination where necessary. Polecat and Liz were calving at seventy-eighty percent. That's one reason we're so far in debt. Calving rate stayed the same for ten years but supplies and labor skyrocketed. This place has been run like a retirement home."

"No reason you need to continue bad management."

Cooper smiled, knowing that the pretty business head on his cousin would save the hotel.

At dawn Cooper drove Dr. Blacker to the Montrose airport where his Lear Jet was fueled to return to San Antonio. The San Juans were bright white after three days of March snow. They discussed Cooper's pending trial and the good doctor warned Cooper to stay clear of Delta and Sam Jr. until the trial was over. Cooper listened but kept his silence.

When Cooper returned to the ranch Adrianna had departed but had left a note. Her employees were skiing deep powder all day, skipping their restaurant shifts and causing chaos.

Judy was in the office going over bills. "Supplier patience is running out, Cooper, unless you communicate better. You owe about $5,000 overdue ninety days, $4,000 overdue sixty days, and $3,000 due now. I have made a lot of calls and mended fences where I could. $4,000 in payments when the life insurance check arrives will hold them off for thirty more days, and then you need to get $6,000 out. I have prepared a list for you to pay by date. I'll return in late April to redo the payables for you."

"Thanks. Bookkeeping has never been my strong suit."

"You had better learn or move me down here. Liz's Norwood bookkeeping lady can't appease angry creditors. My problem is, the hotel's also under water."

"I know, fences about gone, rolling stock whipped, irrigation ditches in bad shape, the headquarters burned, and the hay bailers qualify for the Smithsonian. First new fence posts in a decade arrive in a week. Once the ground thaws Joe and I will run a fencing crew to fix our weak points. I need your help."

Judy flashed a tight-lipped smile, her pink tongue darting through her lips, "I would like that a lot. I'm good with books and suppliers. I can string barbwire, too, and ride herd in any kind of weather."

"Deal, but only when the hotel lets you up for air. Can't lose both the family's assets in the same year. Let's eat lunch."

Sue and Joe arrived from a snowshoe survey with a diagram for fence line replacements. They seemed to like working together. After lunch Cooper and Judy returned to the office. She called the Del Norte mill and added five hundred more fence posts based on the survey. Then she dispatched Sue and Joe to inventory the YBarC barbwire rolls which were stored in a metal outbuilding behind the bunkhouse. The foreman's log showed 153 rolls on hand.

Two hours later, with a scratched cheek, Sue handed over a count of 32 rolls on hand in all outbuildings. Judy ordered five hundred more. Cooper made a note to talk to Polecat about the missing barbwire rolls. Liz's watch had been at the YBarC had been so loose he assumed the barbwire was on Polecat's fence lines. Judy insisted he get to the bottom of it.

Joe returned and announced he was moving an elk hide teepee to the YBarC to sleep in after the hands returned from Arizona. He asked Cooper if he and Sue could pick it up at the res since the snowstorm had paralyzed ranch operations. Cooper offered him his father's air stream but they opted for the teepee.

Joe replied, "You can stay in the teepee, too, Cooper."

"I'll take the Airstream."

"Funny, Cowboy. Once you go teepee you will never go back."

Sue laughed for the first time in a week and Judy blushed, hiding a secret thought.

Joe said, "We will feed the horses and be back tomorrow night. You hold the fort." He and Sue departed the bunkhouse with the sun starting to drop in the western sky.

The phone rang. A lady's voice reported while Cooper leafed through months old cattle reports, "Our annuity policy number 17832 deceased payee Liz Stuart is now assigned to Cooper Stuart. Is that you?"

"Yes ma'am," replied Cooper as Judy listened, her breast touching his broad shoulder.

"Then you get five hundred a month for the term of the annuity. We will mail you the transfer papers tomorrow. Fill them out, notarize them and attach a death certificate then return them in the enclosed envelope. Goodbye, sir."

"What's that about?"

"Liz loaned me most of her $50,000 'cookie jar' Salt Lake City bank account money to invest in Gary's condo project, with the profits to go to pay off the YBarC debt. I sold grandfather's antique Navajo rugs to the Southwest Museum and put the money in an annuity for Liz at $500 a month. Guess I saved the rugs from burning up, too. Bad news is, the condo project is a fraud to cover cocaine dealing by Gary, according to Sue. I have to track him down and get my money back."

"Can you cash out the annuity and pay a penalty. You need the cash now not five hundred a month."

"No, I set it up so Liz could not do that for ten years. Wanted to make sure she had a monthly income."

"Adrianna introduced you to Gary and Sue was his playmate?"

"You are quick," Cooper replied downcast.

"Run a hotel, see human nature at work every day. Sue the bait, Adrianna the go between and you the new mark in town," she said but realized she had gone too far. "Let's have a beer and dinner. Enough finances today."

Cooper agreed. He heard a ranch pickup leave with Sue and Joe as he found two leftover elk steaks in the bunkhouse fridge. Judy heated canned sweet corn in tomato sauce and baked two Idaho potatoes. They finished with leftover cherry pie.

Judy suggested cards after dinner and sat down across from Cooper at the bunkhouse game table with its cigarette burned, faded green felt surface.

"What's your game?" Cooper politely asked as Willy Nelson wailed on the radio.

"Strip poker," Judy said with a blush. "You game, Cowboy?"

The fire crackled as yellow light soaked the room and Cooper laughed for the first time since Liz died in his arms, thinking she was bluffing. "I call you. Your deal, nothing wild."

"No mercy," she replied surprising Cooper again. A half hour and two shots of bourbon later Judy was down to a pair of JC Penny panties, her hard pink nipples bobbing in front of Cooper in the low light as she picked up her hand trying to cover her breasts.

She was blushing as she giggled, "Cooper, I haven't won a hand in the last ten minutes. You stacked this deck."

"Poker is like that, cowgirl. You cut the deck." Cooper replied shirtless and bootless.

"You bluffing again?" she asked as he dealt her two cards and she played two queens.

"No, baby, I have three kings on the deal." He spread his hand over hers.

She gasped, "I don't really have to remove my panties, do I?" She giggled as she downed a shot of Bourbon from the half full bottle on the table.

"Bunkhouse poker rules require that you pay your bets," replied a tipsy Cooper with a smile. She slowly stood up and pulled her white panties down an inch at a time revealing her pencil thin waist and dark mystical triangle. Judy's panties dropped slowly over her firm thighs and then slid over her hard calves onto the bunkhouse floor.

"You win," she almost whispered, tears starting to well in her doe eyes.

"We win," replied Cooper. After a brief hesitation, she smiled and slowly but deliberately walked around the table. Judy kissed Cooper gently as her firm breasts pressed hard against his chest in the warm firelight. The snow snuffed out all sounds outside the bunkhouse. Judy started to unsnap his jeans as tears rolled off her soft cheeks coursing onto Cooper's taught stomach muscles. Her breasts brushed Cooper's forehead as she turned and bolted through the door. Cooper silently stared at her last poker hand and he flipped over the three-facedown cards. Judy had a full house, the winning hand.

THIRTY-SIX
The Fire Next Time

April Fool's Day dawned bright, blue, cold and calm with a foot of fresh powder on the mountain. Cooper viewed it from his room in the inn as he listened to the rusting cast iron radiator clack and clang. Adrianna, sleeping silently beside him, filled the room with her scent.

Cooper ran through his YBarC spring checklist in his head. Judy was handling the ranch accounts from the Fairplay Hotel office and Cooper had mailed her Liz's $30,000 term life insurance payout to keep the ranch running. The inquest had ruled Liz's death accidental from a kitchen fire of undetermined origin. Cooper's theory of arson died when the judge refused to admit into evidence the fingerprint-less lighter fluid can. The judge ruled a law officer or fireman would have had to find it for him to consider it evidence. The state arson investigator testified the fire burned so hot, it destroyed any evidence of arson. The Norwood volunteer fire chief, a high school physical education teacher and football coach, prevailed at the hearing. He testified that the volunteer firemen hadn't seen any strangers around the YBarC headquarters. He believed the two sets of tracks that Joe found were inconclusive because of the activity caused by fighting the fire. Cooper quickly concluded no one wanted to spend county time and money investigating a winter house fire. The bad guys had won the round but Cooper planned to avenge Liz's death.

Sue and Joe were working the ranch on a daily basis as they prepared for the herd's return in May. They had moved into the elk skin teepee and coupled. Joe was teaching Sue the Ute customs and religion during the long ranch nights. Sue was teaching Joe how to ride Anglo cowboy style while they worked the remuda to get it into summer shape. Cooper had hired a D-8 bulldozer to clear the burned-out rubble from the fire. The three stark brick walls towered quietly like a monument to the tragedy. He had moved the fireproof Browning gun safe into the bunkhouse office. All its contents had survived the fire without damage.

The fire insurance company had escrowed the house's $50,000 pay out until the foreclosure was completed by the bank or voided by a YBarC note payback.

Max was holding the bank's foreclosure at bay with complex legal maneuvers that promised to get the YBarC through the fall calf sales. He had developed a new legal theory for the ranch's defense, which was derived from the customary easement law that prevailed in the ranching west. He was arguing that by custom, the bank had rolled over the principle with only interest due annually for so many years that any change was a breach of an implied contract with the YBarC.

He argued that the YBarC, therefore, should have a reasonable mutually agreed upon workout plan for principle payments spread over a number of years. It was so novel that the Colorado Bankers Association had intervened on the bank's behalf to block it in court before it could become case law. They wanted absolute control over their rural borrowers even though they routinely provided loan workouts for their industrial, mining and Denver real estate clients. Max believed a good offense was the best defense and the threat of a YBarC victory might force the Bankers Association to bring the Telluride bank to heal. Cooper was free to ranch for the summer and he intended to do it well.

Max had pushed the Delta trial date back until June 16th. He had outmaneuvered the DA at each stage of the criminal trial process with discovery motion after discovery motion to delay the trial. He had still not forced them to reveal the identity of their secret witness but the case's cost had exceeded the counties annual prosecution budget. The local newspaper had started to question the cost benefit. Max was trying to force a no contest plea without Cooper admitting guilt or innocence with no jail time. Cooper, Adrianna, Joe and Brady continued listening to Telluride gossip to sleuth out the secret witness.

Adrianna stirred and pulled back the covers in the warm inn room. Cooper surveyed her beautiful naked body as he slid quietly out of bed. She had completed her off-season business plan at 3 a.m. and surprised him in bed. Her full breasts with their barrel nipples heaved with each breath. It had been the first time they had slept together since Cooper declined to move into her guest bedroom.

Cooper was also on a mission to find Gary, who had not returned his calls. A bartender who worked with Joe reported he'd seen Gary enter the still unrepaired hot tub room of his house very late two nights ago.

Adrianna reported that the lift side lot had reverted to its seller when Gary failed to convert his option into a purchase on March 15; Gary had lost Cooper's $50,000 deposit. A group of dentists from Grand Junction, with a loan from Sam Jr. had already contracted for the property to build a hotel.

Late morning, Cooper circled Gary's house but saw no sign of habitation. A pile of yellowed ROCKY MOUNTAIN NEWS newspapers on the front porch indicated he had been away a couple weeks. Cooper slipped into the unlocked hot tub room door. He found a bulky black plastic answering machine that had stopped taking calls. Cooper listened to a ten-minute tape of Gary's messages, half of which were from Cooper; one from Sue telling him she was happy working at the YBarC and would not be returning; one from Adrianna asking him to pay his overdue $563 account; one from Dillon told him there was an all-night party down the street; one from a real estate agent said he had twenty-four hours to cure the default on the lift side property option or it was being sold to the dentist group.

There were a dozen hang-ups and two party calls inquiring about his hot tub availability and refreshments. Cooper found frozen pipes in the kitchen caused by an open window over the sink. The expensive electric heat was set on seventy-five throughout the house. The hot tub was set at a perfect temperature so Cooper stripped down and climbed into it after turning the jets on full force. He called Adrianna on Gary's phone.

"I have a reservation for you over here in Gary's hot tub."

"Don't think so. I would rather ski," she said coolly.

"And miss a perfect hot tub in the warm April noon sun in the solarium?"

"No, Cowboy. You sneaked out this morning before I could talk to you about Judy and Sue."

"So no hot tubs unless I move in with you?"

"No more nothing, Cowboy, until you move out of the inn into my guest bedroom. No nooky, no free meals and no hot tubs at my place or any place. If you're horny, just hold your dick with your free hand and fantasize about Judy the bookkeeper and Sue the 'Cowboys and Indians' girl, not me," and she hung up.

Adrianna had decided to be jealous and put on her chastity belt, Cooper surmised. He called Judy long distance on Gary's nickel, "Hello, Judy, it's Cooper."

She answered, "Lunch time Cooper, call me back at two o'clock. The dining room is full with an old west bus tour."

Cooper decided to enjoy a long soak alone, enjoying the revitalizing sun pouring into the room. Then he showered and put his plan into action.

He opened the hot tub drain but left the motor running, contrary to the caution sign. He figured sometime in the next twenty-four hours the motor would go up in smoke, setting off Gary's fire alarm. Sue had told him she couldn't figure out how to reset it after she burned a roast in the oven. Cooper hoped a hot tub fire would attract the volunteer firemen and cause Gary return. Cooper closed the kitchen window, turning the faucets to drip position. Cooper intended to get his $50,000 back.

On Cooper's way back to the inn, he ran into Brady.

"Haven't seen you in a month of Sundays," Cooper quipped.

"On my way to find you. You have to look at these schematic maps."

"This must be hot if you are not skiing the fresh powder today. I'm tapped out if you are looking for an investor in a development project," Cooper replied, knowing half the Ajax Ski Company staff was shopping real estate development deals.

"No, everyone in town knows the banks foreclosed on the YBarC. To hear Jesse Smith tell it at the Sheraton Bar, you're on the ropes and being body punched hard."

"Maybe but there's bounce in the ring's ropes," replied Cooper casually. He didn't want to sound alarmed until he knew the reason for his friend's mission.

"Cool, Cooper. That's why I like you and a lot of other jocks around here do, too. You're the only one who stands up to the Ajax Ski Company, the land scammers and the BLM. All they want to do is make this place safe to bulldoze and kill the best ski town left in North America."

They walked the rest of the way to the inn, talking skiing. Once they were in Cooper's room, Brady insisted he lock the door. Cooper couldn't find the key so they tilted a chair under the old style cast iron doorknob.

Brady unrolled the maps on the surface of the made up bed. "I have to get these back to my girlfriend Kara at the Ajax Ski Company headquarters by four before Lonnie Jr. notices them missing or she'll lose her job and our rent money."

Cooper began to decipher the maps. They were incredible in scope and detail. They showed the integration of the YBarC holdings into the Ajax Ski Company resort master plan over the next twenty-five years in four phases. The Wilson Mesa grazing land was going to be a satellite town, served by mini buses, and the 30,000-acres of YBarC was going to be divided into hundreds of thirty-five-acre ranchettes. There was a water diversion plan that showed the YBarC San Miguel River water rights being pumped out at Telluride and diverted to a major ski village. Attached to the maps were spreadsheets, which forecast the profit on the YBarC land sales and Delores River water rights to be a cool hundred million dollars at build-out assuming three percent annual inflation.

However, a second spreadsheet showed that if the mine remained open and the YBarC kept its respective land and water rights, the development was choked off to five thousand peak residents and a peak visitor prediction of 3,000 skiers per day during holidays. Cooper noted sprawl versus common sense was the difference in the two plans in the arid region.

"Mind boggling," a shocked Cooper muttered. "They seize the YBarC through the bank and make a hundred million dollars in profit and turn Telluride into a small city without even a countywide vote."

"They bulldoze every run and turn some of the best skiing in the state into flat landers trails for Christmas and New Year's vacationers," asserted Brady forcefully. "They're already doing it in Vail, Aspen and California. They wipe out the mesas for subdivisions and drop the river level to a creek that won't float a kayak or support native trout in a drought."

"You stay here while I run over to Adrianna's and xerox these documents."

Cooper walked to Adrianna's office where he explained the urgency of copying the documents without revealing their source. She became an ally again when she read the executive summary and realized the scope of Cooper's predicament.

She volunteered, "The Anglo's have stolen land grants from the Spanish in New Mexico and southern Colorado through the banks and courts for a hundred years. It is the same game plan."

She swore silence as Cooper ran back to the inn with four o'clock only a half hour away. Cooper had hidden a set of xeroxes behind Adrianna's desk, securely taped to its back.

Cooper reminded Brady, "You are my link to the ski bums and the outdoor community in Telluride. Stand by for a secret meeting as soon as I figure out a plan. I am going to need your help to save the YBarC."

"We'll be there. No one moved here to recreate Vail, Aspen or Lake Tahoe except Lonnie Jr. and Jesse Smith. But it's really their dad's. They're only the front men."

"Thanks, I'm convinced now that my mom's dead after they missed a shot at me. Then Max spirited me away from Marshal Pete Simple and the Delta County Jail in the nick of time."

"Your mom was murdered?" Brady gasped. "The paper said a kitchen fire burned the ranch house down."

"Joe found evidence that points to arson."

Brady whistled and said, "This is big time, Cooper. I have to get these plans back or Kara will be fired or worse." Brady raced out of the room.

Cooper replayed the afternoon's events in slow motion to make sure he was not being set up again. When the tape stopped, he was sure he was not but Brady and Kara had stumbled into a very dangerous game trying to help the YBarC and defend their ski paradise.

Cooper put one set of the xeroxed documents into a brown manila envelope and addressed them to Max in San Antonio. He did not trust the Telluride post office so he drove the Jeep out to the almost abandoned mining town of Ophir, ten miles south of Telluride. Afterwards, he joined a group that was watching Jeff Lowe solo climb the granite wall next to the one-room post office. Cooper had heard Jeff solo climbed the 300 foot frozen Bridal Veil Waterfall in Telluride's east end the day before for ABC television.

At dusk, Cooper stood in front of the dilapidated New Sheridan Opera house and paid $5 to see a night of mountain films. He sat down a minute into a film about high altitude aerobatic hang gliding featuring Rob Kells. After the final scene, the lights came on and a filmmaker, Tom Deskins, appeared on the stage. He was from a group called Eco Warriors that were committed to preserving the western environment and, at this fundraiser, the right to launch and land hang gliders throughout Colorado. Cooper listened with interest as he spoke about Earth Day and the future use of solar and wind energy.

Cooper left his seat and waited off stage in a short line to speak with the filmmaker. A few minutes later Cooper introduced himself, "I have a problem you might have some ideas about. Also, the YBarC has a potential hang glider launch spot over on North Mountain you might want to scout."

Tom caught Cooper off guard, "We don't help ranchers. Cattle destroy public land. You are the enemy. I have to go." He walked toward the exit.

Brady intervened. "He's okay, Tom. Come have a beer with us and I'll explain."

"Only if you vouch for him," Tom replied and added, "Brady pioneered hang gliding off the Gold Hill launch site. That's 12,000 feet, Cowboy. I trust him always."

Suddenly, a siren shattered the night air. Cooper realized it was a full volunteer fire department alert. He raced to Colorado Avenue leaving the group behind and to his surprise saw the old drug store building was on fire. The turn-of-the-century, brick three story was already completely engulfed in flames on the top floor. The last thing Telluride needed was two fires, so Cooper raced back up Oak Street to Gary's house. He let himself in just as smoke was starting to curl from the wiring under the base of the hot tub. Cooper cut the master switch and poured a pitcher of cold water on the pump's housing.

Once Cooper was sure the pump had cooled down he raced back down Oak Street and discovered a volunteer fireman doling out emergency assignments. The cold wind tore at Cooper's face; twenty volunteer firemen grappled with two high-pressure hoses that poured a steady stream of water into the broken third floor windows of the old brick building. Cooper wrangled a section of the powerful hose as a yell came up from the growing crowd behind the two red pumpers. Cooper looked up and saw the flames jump from the third floor to the western style false front of the wood building next door. A 500-foot plume of smoke was now rising into the star strewn night.

THIRTY-SEVEN
The Last Tribe

Lunch began early at Adrianna's bistro in a private booth with its curtains drawn. The occupants were exhausted and their hair still had a smoky aroma. Brady, Cooper, Joe and the filmmaker Tom Deskins had been on the fire line until almost sun up.

Joe broke the ice with the cautious filmmaker, "Cooper tells me that you founded the Eco Warriors group. The southern Utes were once great mountain warriors after they stole the horse from the Spanish. History has forgotten our story because our Ute bands numbered only five thousand at peak, making it easy for the Anglo politicians and miners to move us out of the pristine San Juan Mountains."

Tom spoke with an intelligent southern accent, revealing a heritage in the old Confederacy, "I know little about your people except for the reservation signs near Bayfield and Cortez. For the past three years I've lived in Idaho making documentary films about skiing, kayaking and now hang gliding. I was a PT boat commander for two years in Vietnam. My great-grandfather ran the Union blockade of the port of Mobile for the Confederacy. Navy's always been a family thing but 50-caliber gunning of coastal Vietnam villages at night was not my idea of war."

"Very heavy man," Joe responded in a whisper. "I flew MedEvac Helicopters up north."

"Our karma. I found out one night we actually took out an orphanage. So now I kayak rivers and patrol mountain lakes to keep the polluters and dams out. Guess I can't kick the water thing. Probably will figure a way to launch a hang glider from my kayak," Tom laughed from deep in his belly to break the dark silence.

The curtain parted and Adrianna's arrival ended the discussion. She led a waiter who carried a tray of hot Spanish dishes. "This is my Taos brunch for the brave firefighters. Welcome to my La Fonda, Tom, your home on the road."

Adrianna completed serving her guests then slid into the booth beside Cooper and closed the curtain in the same motion. She pulled Cooper's right hand across her firm thigh, keeping her legs shielded by the tablecloth. The tip of his finger flirted with her panty seam.

"Enjoy the food. It's on the house, let's eat." She pushed her napkin into her lap, which dislodged Cooper's finger.

The silent hungry group tore into the Spanish style eggs and spicy sausage. She released her linen napkin teasingly.

"I have heard of your family," Tom said between bites.

"We must talk after breakfast privately. Your father's mine at Red Cliff is on our organization's list for polluting the Eagle River."

Adrianna seized the moment instantly and asserted, "He is an intelligent tough man from the old way but reasonable if he is doing something wrong that can be corrected. Come back to my office by the kitchen after brunch. I will phone him and set up a meeting."

"I can stop and see him on my way back to Idaho. We have a manual that demonstrates how old mines can install pollution control equipment and techniques at a reasonable cost. The mines here have polluted the headwaters of the San Miguel River for nearly a century. The tailings will be hot for a million years with their mercury, arsenic, lead and zinc leaching into the river and the wind blowing their dust into the air. It's too big a fish for our organization to take head on so we have asked the EPA to do some tests."

"You didn't have to drive here just for the mines?" quizzed Cooper.

Tom continued after a furtive look at the curtains, "There is a secret plan being discussed between the Ajax Ski Company, West Slope businessmen and the Colorado congressional delegation in Washington to dam the San Miguel River to create a recreational lake and cheap hydro power for a new ski city. The stored water could be filtered and treated for a new population of up to 20,000 people."

There was silence as Brady and Cooper glanced at each other.

Adrianna countered, "That sounds like an impossible task. Only eight hundred people live here now. In the off-season, I barely serve twenty people a night except for the Fourth of July and Labor Day weekend."

"We have the plans," Tom rebutted.

Cooper intervened, "A dam in Norwood Canyon was proposed in the depression as a public works project but nothing happened on it after World War II. The YBarC and the Lone Cone Ditch owns most of the downstream water appropriations. The mine and the town own most of the upstream appropriations. So how can they dam our water?"

"Easy," Tom countered. "Close the mine and buy your ranch's water rights or have the Fed's condemn both and write you a check."

"Wow. You know the bank is trying to foreclose on the ranch and grab my land and water rights for nothing?" replied Cooper. "The YBarC is a by-the-old-book ranch. It's more pristine than a National Park. We fuck it up and we're out of the ranching business. So how do I help the Eco Warriors stop the dam?"

"With a campaign to embarrass the Colorado Congressional delegation and the Ajax Ski Company if they pursue the proposal seriously. We'll strike first in the media and then we'll up the ante in Telluride."

"What do you mean 'up the ante'?" Cooper inquired.

"Cannot give you details, Cooper. All Eco Warrior operations are secret. They are designed like special opts in Vietnam."

Without a pause Cooper replied, "Count me in and I will ante up a hundred dollars to help the media campaign. Twenty thousand resort types will do more damage to Telluride and this region than the YBarC's herd could do in one million years."

Everyone applauded except Joe Bear Spirit who in his heart wanted the valley returned to the Utes.

The curtain parted and one of Adrianna's waitresses appeared with fresh coffee and a message, "Lonnie Jr. wants a table for twelve VIPs tonight. We're booked up tonight."

Adrianna started to say no but Cooper squeezed her hand and she replied, "Book it for 7:30."

Cooper addressed the table after the curtain closed.

"Let's have a spy serve the wine. Brady used to work here. Okay by you, Adrianna? Maybe tongues will loosen as the night progresses."

Adrianna replied, "Happy to have him for the evening shift."

"I like your style, Cooper," Tom, said. "Thanks, Brady."

"Maybe if they like my wine selections Lonnie Jr. will pick me to guide the group tomorrow," Brady volunteered.

"I will stick around for a debriefing tomorrow," said Tom. "Where can I stay?"

"Out of sight," Cooper replied. "The canyon walls have ears. I'll give you directions to the ranch. Take any empty room in the bunkhouse. Sue and Joe will fix your dinner. Thanks for brunch, Adrianna."

"To the firefight," she toasted.

The phone rang as Cooper entered his room at the inn. Adrianna boomed, "Big rumor in town that it was an arson fire last night. Lonnie Jr. had the building insured for $1 million. Word is that an installment note is due on the Ajax Ski Company next month."

"Thanks, I'll let Max know. Maybe he can get the state insurance commissioner to fuck with him. The plot thickens."

The phone rang ten seconds after he hung up. It was Polecat. "Who's this Judy woman?" he challenged in an angry voice. "She challenged the vet bill down here. She said it was padded."

"My cousin, and Uncle Harvey's daughter, it turns out."

After a long silence Polecat sharply queried, "She have authority to review ranch stock bills?"

Cooper answered calmly, "She's the new YBarC bookkeeper and controller. She has total authority."

"I don't like taking orders from no woman and now I hear a blonde and a half breed are the winter hands living in a teepee."

"Times they are a changing Polecat. Your nephew walked out on me. Maybe if he had been at headquarters Liz would still be alive."

Polecat retorted, "I have been on the YBarC almost fifty years, Mr. Cooper, and that's the first and last insult I'll tolerate from you. He quit because of late pay and your arrest up at Delta."

Cooper thought a short second about firing Polecat over the phone but he needed the herd back from Arizona so he merely countered, "Pay was late and he had a right to quit. Liz said the Vietnam War took a toll on him. Hopefully the church will help him. As for Sue and Joe, if they want to live in a teepee it saves heat in the bunkhouse."

"So be it. You're the boss of the YBarC."

"Judy has prepaid the Union Pacific today. Get ready to ship the herd back," and Cooper hung up.

After reading Judy's analysis of the past ten years of calf sale prices, Cooper spent the next two hours calling beef brokers throughout the west, announcing that the YBarC fall cattle were available for open bid for the first time since World War II.

At 4:45 p.m. as Cooper was about to leave for the New Sheridan Bar's spring wet t-shirt contest, the phone rang.

"This is Mosley Price out of Omaha, son. We have been your cattle brokers for almost 35 years."

"I know that, sir. My late mother and grandfather spoke highly of you."

"Sorry 'bout your mother. She was a fine woman and she had great style. My wife often copied her dresses. They cost me a bundle," he chuckled. Cooper remained silent. "I know what I heard is not true. The YBarC is going to open bid for its fall sale. That will disappoint the fine steak houses that buy your beef year in and out."

"It's true, times are changing. We've been under market nine percent and change for ten years for prime beef that every top steak house wants anyway. So, sir, if you want a ten-year exclusive on the YBarC cattle, we want a one-time payment of $100,000."

"That is highway robbery, son," he mumbled.

"That's business, sir, or bid for them at auction."

"You got me over a barrel like your grandfather did in World War II and you are chiseling out its staves."

"Got to go, sir. I have a cocktail party at five o'clock."

"Wait a second son. I'll send you a cashier's check for $50,000 for a ten-year exclusive at best market rates."

"You got a deal, sir, when the ranch receives the check. Thanks." Cooper hung up.

"Dunk shot," he yelled to an empty room.

Cooper pushed through the packed crowd as six mostly barefooted, well-endowed women climbed onto the gleaming waxed bar, wearing cheap white New Sheridan tee shirts and assorted colorful shorts. A roaring crowd of miners, drug dealers, locals, ski bums, and college boys slugged down drinks as the Rolling Stones played on the jukebox. The crowd stomped their feet as the women danced on the bar, their braless firm tits bouncing.

A bartender acting as MC yelled into an electric megaphone, "Five hundred dollar pot for the biggest wettest wildest best looking pair of breasts. You the lookers decide by applause...any ties broken with a topless dance."

The young thin buff blonde bartender stepped up onto the bar with a pressured seltzer bottle of cold water and sprayed the contestant's tee shirts one at a time to the delight of the howling crowd.

Cooper silently picked contestant number four as the winner and sipped a long neck Coors. She was a tall brunette beauty with 38C breasts and half dollar nipples, which were counter weighted with an ample bottom clothed in tight white short shorts that bled into long tanned firm legs. The crowd applauded at various levels as one through three were announced with a few funny catcalls spicing the judging.

Then the MC announced, "Number four, Sheila from Malibu."

The boys went wild. Number five barely got any applause while the crowd chugged their beers. Finally, number six, a five foot two blue-eyed blonde in cowgirl boots who was all thighs, breasts and bottom started dancing to Willie Nelson as they called her number and then she raised her t-shirt over her head. Her ample breasts bounced to the song as the crowd went into overdrive ecstasy. Upset of the year, Cooper thought, as the MC climbed onto the bar next to her with five new $100 bills. Lesson to be learned, Cooper mused. Play the game until the last hitter is out. This was how he was going to play the bank.

Number six pulled her t-shirt down and accepted the prize. She motioned Cooper to lift her down off the bar, which he did. Her wet shirt brushed against his chest.

"Buy me a drink, Cowboy. You got a jean jacket I can put on?"

"It is up front on a hook," Cooper offered. "Follow me close. These boys are all fired up."

Cooper turned and faced Adrianna who grabbed his arm, "Pardon me, cowgirl, Cooper is my bull. Here's his jean jacket. Leave it at the Bistro next door before you leave town. And have dinner on me, honey, to celebrate your victory. Let's go, Cooper, we have other plans."

Adrianna hauled him out by the arm as his cowboy boots skidded across the beer-splashed floor. Speechless, he turned to catch a final look at the perfect pair of aces as the cold air hit his shirtfront and the bar's door closed behind him.

Adrianna whispered, "Sometimes I think you walk the earth like a one-eyed bull that's been fixed for a rookie matador."

THIRTY-EIGHT

The Spy Who Came in from Pow

C ooper woke up early the next morning alone and relaxed. His body tingled. Adrianna had brought a graphically illustrated tantra yoga coffee table book complete with an entire chapter on erotic meditative massage. Adrianna and the magical book had knocked him out for ten hours.

The phone in Cooper's inn room rang; it was Max from El Paso. "I have the Delta prosecutor's Office covered, Cooper, if we can ID their secret witness. Do you have any good ideas yet on who that might be? It will be his word against your word so his character is the entire case. ID him and you will not stand trial."

"I have a hunch. In Telluride, the box canyon walls are so steep that even thoughts echo."

"Keep fishing, Cooper. Change your flies if you don't get a bite. You have a month or we have to prepare for trial. I do not want to chance a small-town jury against an out-of-town big rancher and attorney if we don't get a venue change."

Cooper felt the effects of Adrianna's massage start to wear off.

"I can buy you until Labor Day on the foreclosure under the Colorado bank statues. I can appeal it after the fact but no guarantee we can win. Message is, find new financing fast," Max concluded.

"You can't delay them until October calf and cow sales?"

"Yes and no. You will have a redemption period under Colorado Law until they buy their note back on the courthouse steps, but you'll need a hundred percent cash with interest and court costs. Any new lender or venture partner will know you're against the wall and extract control of your ranch on crippling terms."

"I get it. We're in overtime now."

"That's correct. Do you have money to run the operation this summer?"

"Enough as of yesterday. Picked up $50,000 for signing a new cattle sale agreement plus $30,000 from Liz's accidental death policy. I'm still looking for Gary to get my $50,000 investment back in his fake condo project. Then if we can get the fire insurance proceeds of $50,000 released, I have $180,000. That, according to Judy, completes the refencing, buys a new pickup, pays the help and bills and the bank interest through September. That would leave $70,000 plus the calf sales. Judy believes we could have $200,000 available to contribute to a refinancing deal by mid-October. Judy is working magic and her banker, Luke Ford, up in Fairplay is keeping the YBarC money safe. I think he wants to make a merger out of the YBarC, the Fairplay Hotel, with Judy and me and then get his $50,000 loan back out of the old building."

"Take that gal seriously, Cooper. She has a good head on her shoulders."

Joe and Cooper went skiing at noon when the spring snow softened in the warm sunlight. Cooper updated him during the lift ride.

Joe replied, "Noose is tightening like it did on the Utes before the White River massacre. The arrogant white Indian agent made the Utes try to farm for a living at the Meeker agency. The Denver boys wanted an incident so they could move the Uintah Utes to the Utah Territory and get on with gold mining. It made no sense to the Utes to plow up their grassland, which fed their horse herd, so they killed the agent and kidnapped his wife and daughters. The politicians finished them off with the black pony soldiers from Durango."

"So how does this affect the YBarC?" Cooper asked, shocked by the story.

"Telluride Mayor was in the bar last night with a couple local real estate types, big bellies and small heads, all talking big between trips to the men's room to dust their noses. They're going to change the Telluride Town council from three to seven and hire a city manager so they can control things. They want to run the hippies, ski bums, liberals, fags and Earth Dayers out of Telluride. Then they want to grab the small ranches and summer grazing land on the town's flanks for ten cents on the dollar compared to their future value. Problem is, the mayor can't even pay his monthly tab at the bar so he needs big money partners to pull the land grab part off."

"Democracy and capitalism at work and at play," Cooper grinned.

"They're going to call in good professional government just like the Bureau of Indian Affairs," Joe answered in jest.

At dusk, Sue walked through the bunkhouse door, red faced from riding fence lines in the spring sun. "In a week we can start refencing the lower HQ sections, then upper HQ sections in early May," she reported.

"Good. The herd's back May first," Cooper said.

"Best work I've ever had. I see more deer and elk tracks every day with a mountain lion tracking them."

"Add big horn sheep, bear, birds, trout and everyone is waiting for the Aspen and Cottonwoods to bud. Add sixteen hundred cow-calf pairs and the ranch will be humming."

"Will I be on for the summer?"

"Keep up the good work and it's a done deal. Stay off the white lady and you will be the first woman hand since my great-grandmother helped settle the place."

The phone rang and Sue answered, adding only a series of "yeses" before she hung up.

"Gary's back day after tomorrow. That was the girl you met with the razorblade and shaving cream on the San Miguel River the night you met me. She called to tell me Gary wants to see me and make up for mistreating me all these years. Start fresh. He loves me." Sue stopped near tears.

"You agree to see him?"

"Yes, only with her at her apartment to tell him goodbye and get my grandmother's ring back. I need to borrow a pistol. I want you or Joe at the door. He has bound me up before and hauled me away after shooting me with morphine."

"It's a deal, ladies first. But I want my $50,000 back."

"You won't get it. It's up his nose now or paid to the Colombian drug dealers. Gary is in for a quarter million of coke debt. He never has been able to clear his tab. He spends money like water in Scottsdale and puts a lot of product up friends' noses to hang with the rich winter crowd. The only reason he's alive is to help them take control of the Telluride coke traffic and cut out the Phoenix mob."

"You know a lot, Sue. You even safe for a second in a room with Gary?"

"No," she replied.

THIRTY-NINE
Dead Wood

Cooper headed toward the North Mesa to check his gates and ranch roads. The spring sun had begun to burn the snow off his higher pastures, turning them into mud soup. As Cooper cleared a rise on the narrow county road, a logging truck loaded with fresh cut virgin aspen came barreling up the other side straight at Cooper's Jeep. The truck driver braked hard but he was clearly not expecting a vehicle in his path. The truck's large polished steel bumper loomed directly ahead. Cooper gunned the Jeep's engine and spun into a high snowplow bank as the truck's massive steel bumper missed his door at eye level. Its fifty-foot logs sped by like a sack of missiles and its air horn blasted the pristine morning air. Cooper tightly gripped the steering wheel and used the Jeep's power to plow a half lane through the heavy snow. Wildly spinning rear tires brought Cooper to a halt as he steered back toward the plowed road. Cooper wondered who had cut early spring Aspen and if they had come from Forest Service lease land or illegally from the YBarC.

He knew this gravel section of county road was plowed because the county road boys did it on their own time to get some early fishing in the nearby reservoir. Cooper stepped out of the Jeep into three feet of wet snow and pulled an army surplus shovel and two short one-inch thick pine planks from the Jeep. He dug out the rear wheels and placed the planks under their front edges. Cooper feathered the engine carefully and when the rear tires rolled onto the planks, he gunned it and surged back onto the plowed highway.

Two hours later, after checking the melt off on his pastures and finding no evidence of logging on the ranch, Cooper was back in the bunkhouse office dialing the Forest Service number.

"What can I help you with, Mr. Stuart? I don't believe your operation has any Forest Service grazing leases in Colorado, just some on BLM land."

"Homework well done. I wanted to know if your office has issued a new permit for logging on Lone Cone Mountain. I have not seen an announcement."

A short silence followed, "Why are you interested? It does not affect the YBarC grazing. You own the low pastures on the north and west flanks and we own the high ground."

"One, because a logging truck loaded with fresh cut aspen logs ran me off the county road this morning. Two, a big cut on Lone Cone above the YBarC will cause run off into my water rights on Naturita Creek."

The ranger paused again and replied carefully in a bureaucratic voice, "There is a ten-acre test cut on the north side of Lone Cone which is bounded by your ranch. We do not need a public review for a test cut that small. The county bladed the snow for our test and we do not need YBarC access to reach the section that will be put up for a logging lease."

"It's soft wood with a single root for the entire grove. Cut a road though a grove and erosion starts," Cooper stated.

"Alabama Atlantic has a new process to chip and compact aspen to make construction board. My job is to make the Federal Government some money in this district and not just spend it. You boys out here have had a free ride too long on federal forest land."

"Study this one. You clear cut aspen groves and you will silt up the creeks and rivers. They hold unstable soils. You will put mud into Lake Powell above the Glen Canyon Damn that the Feds wasted tax money building."

"I do not need a lecture, Mr. Stuart. Alabama Atlantic wants to pay us good money for trash timber that has never had a good use until now. The construction industry needs pulp board and it will create new jobs for a county that has none since the uranium boom went bust."

"Aspen is a poor but cheap choice, it's like buying drugs. The money's gone tomorrow; nothing to show for it."

"Guess you would know that," he replied with sarcasm. "We'll give you a call when the public hearings start if Alabama Atlantic likes its test cut results, but I advise you not to piss them off since they will be cutting along your boundaries. They can be a good Forest Service lease neighbor or not. Goodbye."

Cooper reflected that Colorado's virgin pine trees lived in hundreds of miles of mine tunnels now. The homesteaders had also attacked the aspen to clear poor yield soils for farms after 1890, setting off more erosion until the dust bowl and depression ended their dreams in the 1930s. The forests around Telluride and Norwood were just recovering but it appeared the big timber cutting companies were tracking the trees growth with the Feds as their scouts.

Cooper drove in gusty winds to the outskirts of Telluride to find Joe. When he passed the new school on the west side of town, a helicopter swooped in low over the speeding Jeep. Cooper fought to control the steering wheel as the prop wash shoved it five feet into the oncoming lane. Cooper pulled to a stop on the icy gravel access road to the school and watched the flight for life helicopter from Grand Junction Hospital land on the baseball diamond. The sheriff skidded to a stop next to Cooper in a mud-splattered 4x4 with its red lights flashing.

The sheriff jumped out and ran to Cooper's window, "I need your V8 Jeep. Volunteer fire department boys got the ambulance stuck in the spring mud at the lift. Nine-year-old hit a tree skiing. Sure wish they would put football helmets on the kids up there."

"I'm good, but where's the local tow rig?"

"Down valley out of CB contract…towing a tourist out of a snow bank."

Cooper reversed out, spraying mud and a minute later was at the end of the road near the lift, his tail facing the stuck ambulance twenty-five yards away. The head of the mountain's snowcat operations walked up pulling a snowcat chain that was hooked to the ambulances steel front bumper.

"I'm going to hook the chain to your boat hitch. The ambulance has four-wheel drive so maybe you can pull it out. This kid is dying from a head injury. Every second counts." Thirty seconds later, which seemed like an hour to Cooper, the chain was secured. He feathered the engine to full torque in low four-wheel drive and put the Jeep's 302 cubic inches to work. The roaring muffled big V8 engine pulled the Jeep forward as the studded snow tires fought for a good grip on the muddy gravel road. The ambulance broke loose and Cooper pulled it forward at two miles an hour to pavement. Cooper helped unchain the ambulance and saw a tiny crumpled figure inside with a nurse and doctor working feverishly. Cooper, tearing up, followed the ambulance as it sped to the high school's baseball diamond. When the ambulance door opened a wind gust hit the helicopter and the pilot suddenly shut down the rotors.

The sheriff yelled to the pilot, "What's wrong, Fred?"

"Winds too dangerous to take off with all this weight…doc, nurse and patient plus life support gear. It could shear me in a big gust. I need to wait."

The nurse yelled over the howling spring wind, "He will die if we don't go now. He needed the neuro-surgeon in Grand Junction an hour ago."

The grim-faced pilot replied without emotion, "Ma'am weather kills more flight crews than accidents. I cannot trade your lives for the boy's."

"But he's the ski company owner's son," the doctor yelled.

Cooper digested the news, as the sheriff said, "Just like the rodeo, Cooper, don't matter how big your ranch is if a mean bull gores you in some small-town arena."

"Sure hope that little boy pulls through," Cooper replied. "Where are his mom and dad anyway?"

"In Houston. They left him with one of those Texas Mex maids. He skipped school on her," asserted the sheriff with total disdain. "My office cannot reach her but Lonnie's secretary thinks she's in Montrose at the grocery store."

The sheriff's radio blared, "Lonnie Jr., over sheriff, can you hear me?"

"Yes, sir. We're just trying to save your son's life like everyone else standing here. Your boy skipped school and hit a tree skiing at high speed. He's still alive, but the flight to life helicopter is grounded because of high wind."

"What the hell," yelled Lonnie Jr. through increasing static. "Let me talk to the doc and the pilot now. Where's Maria, his nanny?"

"Your Mexican girl is in Montrose shopping, according to your office," replied the sheriff as he handed his radio to the pilot.

"Then get that helicopter off the ground. I don't care how high the winds are. You all here me loud and clear. Sheriff you order it into the air," Lonnie Jr. screamed.

"Shear's too dangerous in this tight valley," replied the pilot.

"You take off or I will see that the FAA yanks your license," Lonnie yelled over the radio as the pilot handed the radio back to the sheriff.

"He won't fly Lonnie 'til conditions are right. There are three other lives at risk besides your boy, so try not to make matters worse."

"That son of a bitch," Lonnie yelled through the radio as Joe Bear Spirit walked up to the sheriff.

"I'll fly the bird out, sheriff," he stated matter of factly. Cooper's mouth dropped in awe.

"You might fly an eagle out of here, son, but not a million dollar Jet ranger," the sheriff replied as he dismissed Joe.

"I flew 2,000 hours as a combat medic pilot in 'Nam. Call the Pentagon if you wish, sir, but I can save this kid's life."

The sheriff took a minute to sort his thoughts out as Cooper silently nodded.

"Lonnie, got Joe Bear Spirit the Ute boy who works for Cooper. Says he flew 2,000 heli medical hours in Vietnam and he'll fly the chopper out pronto. I can commandeer the bird in the name of San Miguel County if you give me your word you will cover the damages if he puts it down bad."

"Let him fly it. I will cover your ass with the county commissioners and the bill," Lonnie said coldly over the radio.

The sheriff called the pilot over and stated with authority, "I am seizing the helicopter in the name of San Miguel County under the civil emergency statues of the State of Colorado. My newly appointed deputy Joe Bear Spirit will fly it to the Grand Junction hospital."

"I will disable it first, to stop this nonsense," the pilot asserted angrily.

The sheriff pulled his gun on the pilot, "You are under arrest. Handcuff him deputy!" Cooper watched in amazement as the deputy handcuffed the pilot to the sheriff's 4x4's cattle guard bumper. Two paramedics loaded Lonnie Jr.'s child into the helicopter with the nurse. Then one of the paramedics climbed into the helicopter. Joe jumped into the pilot's seat and fired up the helicopter. Its rotors set off a tornado of swirling snow. The pilot looked on with dismay. Five minutes later with thumbs up through his window Joe lofted straight full power to two hundred feet and rotated at a forty degree angle into a sudden gust of wind that blew Cooper against his Jeep. The helicopter seemed to stall, caught like a seagull in a big wind gust. It wanted to flop over and fall to the ground as the rotors fought for an invisible grip in the sky.

At the last fraction of a second before disaster struck Joe found some extra power and rotated it back to a plane with the ground. He flew nose first into the next gust that was mercifully lighter and the airship started to gain altitude in the tight valley. After two more strong gusts rocked the bird it disappeared down valley still gaining altitude to climb over the 10,000 foot high Hasting Mesa and head north 100 air miles to Grand Junction's regional hospital.

"That Ute did fly like an ol' bald eagle out of here," the sheriff admitted.

The radio crackled its cord stretched taut from the dashboard. "What's going on sheriff?" Lonnie asked.

"Ute Indian magic, that's what. You had to be here to see it. Your boy got a fighting chance now, by God."

Cooper drove to Adrianna's bistro for lunch and called the Grand Junction tower from the restaurant. Joe had landed like an eagle in high gusting winds there. The boy was still alive when he was transferred to the hospital ambulance and had awakened briefly to cry for his mother.

Cooper was half way through lunch when Adrianna brought her long cord phone to his booth.

Lonnie Jr.'s voice boomed, "Thank you for pulling the ambulance out of the mud. And thank your Ute hand for flying little Lonnie out. We just landed in my dad's Lear jet at Grand Junction. If Joe wants a good paying job at the ski company, he has it. You tell him that, Cooper." Lonnie paused to catch his breath.

"I'll pass that on to Joe Bear Spirit but he doesn't expect a reward."

"It don't mean nothing is resolved between you and me, Cooper, but I will take this truce to make a final offer of two million dollars for the YBarC. My daddy will guarantee the bank note and you get all cash, no stock, thirty day closing for the ranch, no survey to close and you keep the cattle. We will feed them 'til you find a new ranch or lease. That gets you a big ranch in New Mexico, Arizona or Wyoming and off the hook with Sam Jr. Jesse's dad can set it up so it's a tax-free swap for the new place. Call me in a week and think real seriously about my final offer. Western Colorado's done for big ranching forever. You boys just took the land from the Utes to hold it for the ski tourist industry. Second homes are the cows of the future, Cooper."

The phone went dead before Cooper could digest the offer.

FORTY

The Last Chance

Sue arrived in town in the ranch pickup as Cooper left the Bistro. He flagged her down to tell her about Joe but she had already heard a news report on the radio. According to the report, Lonnie's son was out of the woods, but he would have a bad headache for a couple months. The radio also reported that Lonnie's Mexican housekeeper had been picked up by the INS in Montrose and she was awaiting deportation.

Three hours later, Cooper and Sue met Joe after a deputy sheriff dropped him at the inn. They outlined their plan for Sue's last meeting with Gary at her friend's apartment on East Colorado.

Joe said, "I'll take the fire escape on the alley end of the hall. Cooper will cover the front stairs to the East Colorado entrance to the building. He will move into place on the upstairs landing after you enter the apartment."

"Sue, I still don't see why it is necessary for you to personally see Gary," stated Cooper. "He's out of your life. You are a YBarC hand."

"He promised to bring me my great-grandmother's solid gold wedding ring. We were engaged a couple years ago; I gave it to him for his pinkie finger. It's the only thing I have left from my family. She wore it when she sailed around the Horn with my great-great-grandfather to San Francisco in 1851. I took it from my mother's jewelry box when I ran away from home."

"I understand. It's a talisman…you must get its power back," replied Joe.

"Then we're set for six sharp. Sue, I hope you remembered the pistols I left in the bunkhouse office," Cooper reminded.

"They're in the second drawer of the dresser," Sue replied.

Cooper opened the dresser drawer. He pulled out a handmade circa 1920s leather double saddlebag and emptied its contents on the bedspread. Its tarnished silver buckles were heavy and still strong after fifty years. Family lore was they had been Blue Bob Thompson's, the YBarC's gun hand. He gave Sue a small short barrel .32 caliber gun. He and Joe took traditional well-oiled glistening Colt 45 pistols and loaded five bullets with the hammer on an empty cylinder. They put extra bullets in their jean jacket pockets.

Cooper continued, "We only shoot if he attempts to kidnap Sue or pulls a gun on us. We break down the door and rescue her if she is not out in five minutes."

"Ten," Sue replied. "I need to discuss something else."

"Five," Cooper shot back. Sue hid her gun in the inside pocket of her ski parka. Cooper strapped on a gun belt and holster. He put on a duster while Joe did the same.

Ten minutes later they were walking down Colorado Avenue like old-time YBarC gun hands to settle a range dispute. Joe and Cooper ducked up a side street as Sue continued toward the red brick building's entrance. They watched as she entered the open door foyer and disappeared up the wide wooden plank steps.

Joe continued up the side street and disappeared into the alley. Cooper rounded the corner and continued to the entranceway where Sue had disappeared. A few shoppers were strolling down the almost dark street with bulging bags in hand. Cooper tipped his hat to them as he disappeared into the entrance and quietly ascended the steps to the landing. He glanced at his father's Bulova watch and quietly sat down on a step and waited. His eyes locked onto doorway number 204.

After four minutes and no Sue in sight, Cooper moved silently step-by-step toward the door in the hallway lit only by a hanging naked light bulb bathed in dust. The patterned strip of carpet was threadbare with muddy footprints. With thirty seconds left Cooper heard a muted voice as he approached the red paneled door. Cooper prepared to kick the door down if it was locked. At the five-minute mark Cooper pulled the Colt 45 and cocked it. Joe vaporized into Cooper's vision as he flew down the hallway. Cooper tried the worn cast-iron doorknob but it was locked. Before he could kick it open, Joe flew by him and hit it like a blocking back with his shoulder. The cast iron lock popped and the old pine paneled door burst open. Joe exploded into a high tin ceiling living room. Cooper stepped in right behind him with his gun leveled for action.

To Cooper's astonishment, Gary was standing over Sue who was bound and gagged on the carpet. Gary held a syringe in his right hand, dripping a white diluted paste. There was a lit candle and a small copper cooker on the oak coffee table and an open briefcase with bundles of hundred dollar bills. Cooper aimed the gun at Gary's head and squeezed the trigger halfway.

"Drop everything, you son of a bitch or I will blow your brains out," Cooper said clearly.

Gary looked at Cooper with coke-crazed eyes, "You won't do that, Cooper. That's murder one and you will never get your fifty thousand back from the condo project. Now you and Tonto get out of here and I will forget this happened. You are out of your league, as usual. This is not, I repeat not, your affair. Sue girlie is going home to ranch in Phoenix for high hooker dollars. That right, Sue?"

She nodded her head yes slowly as blood oozed from an exposed vein on her left forearm.

Cooper's first shot blew apart the syringe, splattering its contents all over Gary's wool ski sweater. The bullet hit the exposed brick wall and ricocheted dangerously across the room as Joe ducked for cover. Joe pulled an elk antler handle knife from his buffalo hide belt and started to cut Sue's hands loose.

Then he pulled the duct tape from her mouth as she gasped for air but whispered, "No, Cooper. I need another hit of heroin I am only halfway high," and she started to cry.

Gary watched frozen as Cooper said, "Get her out of here, Joe, while I deal with Gary. I don't want any witnesses."

"You are not taking her anywhere boys or you will be another fifty thousand big ones poorer. That is what it will cost me to buy her out of her contract or it's my skin."

"What contract?" Cooper asked in shock.

"She is a white sex slaver...owned by Joey Banana out of the Chicago mob and run by one of his soldiers in Phoenix by the name of Tony 'Blade Man.' She was loaned to me so she could kick smack up here in Telluride and get back to work in the Scottsdale hotels at $250 dollars a night while she has that tight little pussy and those pouty teenage looks. This girlie's been tricking for the mob since she ran away from home at fourteen to marry me. I traded her for $50,000 in coke to start my business after I hooked her on smack," Gary finished with a mean smile.

Cooper's second shot sliced Gary's fine woven ski sweater across his chest as blood formed in the foot long graze. Joe retaped Sue's mouth and hands then threw her over his shoulder while she half-heartily struggled.

"You are an asshole, Cooper. Joey and Tony can find the YBarC easily and your ass is grass if you take their blonde dolly. She was due back end of ski season, Sunday. These are real bad boys, Cooper, not cowhands with pop guns to shoot rattle snakes."

"You're out of here, Joe. Toss me your knife."

Joe accommodated and slid out the broken door with Sue securely over his shoulder as Cooper caught the knife, elk handle first.

"Give me Sue's ring or I will cut it off."

Gary pulled the gold ring off and tossed it to Cooper, who caught it with his left hand. Cooper stuck the knife in his belt, dropped the ring in his shirt pocket and then stepped over to the briefcase and loaded five thin bundles of cash into his duster pocket.

Gary yelled, "That's five large of Telluride drug money I owe the boys in Phoenix, Cooper."

"I'll take it off your tab, Gary. Call it interest. I want my fifty back in ten days. Got to ride. Neighbors probably called the marshal by now. This is for Sue." Cooper stepped toward Gary and pistol-whipped him before he could raise his arm in defense.

Gary crashed unconscious onto the coffee table.

Cooper pulled his cowboy hat low over his eyes as he ran down the hallway to the alley exit.

A female tenant emerged from an apartment behind him and yelled, "I called the marshal's office. You coke dealers are ruining Telluride night and day."

Cooper caught Joe in the alley two blocks west heading for Cooper's inn room. He ordered, "Straight to the Jeep. A neighbor woman called the marshal. Gary's out cold. I am carrying $5,000 in cash. They'll set up a roadblock when they figure out what happened but that will take a while. It's a mess in there. Looks like a drug deal gone way south. No one knew about us tagging along so it's back to the YBarC. We'll overnight at a line shack and establish an alibi while Sue here sobers up from the smack. Some canned grub is stashed there for the summer hands. Leave the pickup truck at the inn. We'll take the Jeep. Need it in the spring mud on the line shack road. She all right?"

They moved out of the alley and walked a quick half block to the Jeep. The marshal's lights were flashing in front of the brick building three and a half blocks east of them. Joe put Sue down gently in the back compartment and wrapped her in his duster. He kissed her on the forehead and zipped down the rear window.

Cooper started the engine and they eased out of Telluride using back streets until the school. They pulled onto the state highway and accelerated toward Norwood into the moonless night. A Colt 45 was under each front seat. Joe had pulled the .32 pistol out of Sue's ski jacket pocket, placed it in the glove box. Cooper's Winchester was loaded, lying behind the driver's seat. They were ready for Joey, Tony, Gary or anyone else who wanted to mess with them.

FORTY-ONE

Closing Day

Cooper woke up at dawn on Wilson Mesa in the old homesteaders cabin his grandfather had named Theodore Roosevelt. It was the same two-story house that the Simples had lost on the Telluride court steps in the depression. Polecat's ranch hands kept it in good repair for the summer months when the YBarC grazed fifty pairs to protect the land's agriculture tax status. In the fall, it was a rustic elk and deer hunting lodge for the YBarC hands since it abutted the national forest.

The kitchen had a black cast-iron wood burning stove, a bevy of cast iron frying pans, blue tin plates with chipped hand painted rodeo riders stacked on shelf with the tin coffee cups, and yellowing plastic handled silverware. The Kerosene lighted house had a kitchen, dining room, and parlor downstairs plus three bedrooms upstairs. An outhouse rounded out the amenities. A propane tank provided power for a generator that powered the erratic well's electric pump. The mesa sat astride a giant seam of federal coal and had poor seasonal aquifers that failed in drought summers. A mega wood stove provided heat. Cooper, Joe and Sue sat around a small pine plank pioneer table that had a fold up pine bench on each side. Sue, still affected by the heroin, quivered next to Joe Bear Spirit in the kitchen.

Cooper asked, "You okay this morning, Sue, or do you need to see a doctor?"

"I don't need a doctor, Cooper, but I am real scared. Been off H since I came up here with Gary. Been off coke at the headquarters. I got very high last night, it's fucked with my will power."

"After the ski area closes today, we'll go down to the reservation and let the Medicine Man dry you out the old way. We had our own druggies before the white man or the Spanish came."

"Okay by me. Just be back by mid-April to start refencing the headquarters sections," added Cooper.

"Roger, Lone Ranger, I can use real dollars now that the bartending job is over until Bluegrass Festival weekend in mid-June. Back in a week." Joe ducked out the kitchen door to go to the outhouse.

Sue looked uneasily at Cooper, "I heard Gary yelling at you. What did he tell you all?"

"Everything. You hook for the Phoenix mob. White sex slave was the term he used."

"It's true," she sobbed silently. "Gary kidnapped me from my poor parents, hooked me on heroin at fourteen, worked me with their top clients in Scottsdale."

"That's a tough one. Maybe you need help from the FBI." Cooper was deadly serious now.

"I can't stay with you or Joe. They'll come after you," she sobbed.

"Fuck them," Cooper replied in a steely voice.

"Lonnie Jr. already hired B mobsters to hit me at the Utah line. We ride for the Brand. You are a YBarC hand."

"They'll fuck with Gary big time. He was supposed to dry me out in Telluride and get me back for the spring golf season in Scottsdale. I'm the nineteenth hole, you see." She did not crack a smile.

"The pistol-whipping last night was just a warning. I want my mother's $50,000 back."

"They'll come for me whether Gary pays my contract off or not. Two girls that ran away disappeared without a trace. Lonely desert graves near Phoenix or Vegas, the phantoms say." Sue's face turned white and her blue eyes saddened.

"You're safe with us. Tell Joe everything on the drive to the reservation."

"I will. I would rather spend my last days here in paradise than hooking in five star hotels until some wiseguy sells me to a mob snuff film."

Joe walked into the kitchen as Cooper almost retched from Sue's latest revelation.

"You going to ditch any evidence that we were in Telluride last night?" asked Joe.

"Yes, pistols stay here in a hiding spot in the wall. If the law thinks this was our caper no use giving them evidence. Even if Gary turned star witness they would have to arrest the quarter of the town he sells coke to. No one would be left to run the resort," Cooper laughed and walked out the cabin door into a brilliant purple sky day under the mesmerizing snowcapped Wilson Peak.

Cooper had arrived back at the Wilson Mesa cabin with Adrianna near 7 p.m. in the ranch pickup. He had called her from the pay phone on the sunny mid mountain deck after he had skied down for a beer and to hear the cross-dressing Grand Junction rock band that was playing at the season ending party. Cooper's tongue flickered against Adrianna's caramel vaginal lips in the low orange lamp light as the coil springs creaked in rhythm with the wind. Her smooth contractions began as Cooper's palms continued to open her soft light brown thighs. Her stomach muscles tensed in a climatic orgasm while her long fingertips stroked her dark brown nipples that floated on her breasts, before her eyelids involuntarily closed. Cooper too, drifted off slowly with her sweet taste on his lips.

Around nine the next morning Adrianna woke Cooper from a hazy wine doused sleep with a long kiss and then she burst into tears. She sobbed, "I have to tell you something, Cooper. Wake up now."

Cooper scrambled his brain cells and signaled with a cupped hand around his ear he was kind of awake.

She sobbed, "I am pregnant. I cannot keep it a secret from you any longer."

Cooper gasped, shock seeping into every crease of his being. No way was he ready to be a father. "Well, the Supreme Court just made abortion legal although you could always get one down on the Navajo Reservation."

Adrianna burst into uncontrollable tears as her heavy breasts heaved under the worn-out quilt. She cried nonstop for five more minutes before she blurted, "It's against my Catholic religion, Cooper."

"Not mine, but I'm only half the decision," Cooper replied emotionally. "So, let's get out of bed and after a cup of cowboy coffee think it over with clear heads."

Adrianna composed herself. She sat up and let the quilt fall away from her large soft breasts as the sun bathed her from a frosted window. Cooper looked away to avoid being seduced.

"I know this is a surprise and the timing is not good for you, Cooper, and we have never discussed marriage. So, if in a week you don't want to marry me then I will think about aborting our little baby."

"The answer will be probably be the same in a week, Adrianna. I have only known you for six months and there is a full-scale range war in progress. Currently, I am getting the shit kicked out of me so a quick marriage with immediate fatherhood is hard to grasp."

"It's to death for you in this range water war, like for the Spanish matador in the bullring. Isn't it, Cooper? Spanish wives only sit in the shade in the stands," she replied, realizing his situation and mood.

"You understand me precisely. Shoot to kill from now on, not to wing your attackers. Wounded enemies will come back to ambush you."

"So you are never going to back off, not even for a family. Lonnie, Jesse and Sam openly say in my restaurant that they are going to destroy you and erase the YBarC from the face of the earth. So the matador or the bull must die," she repeated knowingly and bitterly. But her love for Cooper burned like the flaming pueblos. God might allow her to lose this baby to save this great love but only this one baby.

Cooper was sipping coffee at the pine table while Adrianna cooked a Spanish omelet using the dinner leftovers with a half dozen eggs she had brought from town. Cooper heard a 4x4 approaching on the snow packed road. He rose and pulled the loaded Colt 45 from behind the kitchen cupboard and put it in his jeans waistband. He pulled a short barrel Marlin 306 off the kitchen wall's gun rack and handed it to a now alarmed Adrianna who was not a stranger to a rifle.

"Cover me from the window. Shoot to kill if it's Gary's gang opening fire. I'll explain why later. If it's the sheriff, keep a bead on him but do not shoot even if he pulls his Colt 45 on me."

190

Cooper heard the vehicle pull up about twenty yards from the line shack and shut off its engine. He heard three doors open and slam shut as he avoided the window.

Through a battery powered hand held bullhorn, Cooper heard the San Miguel County sheriff intone electronically, "Cooper, if you are in there, come out with your hands open in front of you. I am here to question you about a fracas on East Colorado two nights ago."

Cooper pushed open the line shack door slowly and stepped out to face down the sheriff, his Colt 45 visible in his waistband.

"I will discuss it with you all. My winter hand has a rifle sited on your forehead. Keep your guns in your holster or we all will be buried on YBarC property, which you are trespassing on," Cooper retorted calmly as he surveyed the sheriff flanked by two deputies, their pistols still holstered.

The sheriff paused for a very long moment, county ranch history reflecting in his old eyes. "You got a point, son. You are alibied up, I know. Your brand don't talk to the law. If that greenhorn coked-up marshal in Telluride wants to question you about some drug deal gone bad, he can drive out here. Tell Adrianna to drop that site off me. She probably can't shoot a lick."

The sun glint off Adrianna's rifle barrel disappeared from the cabin's window.

Cooper countered, "Then, you drive out of here."

"You sure pushing the decency envelope, Cooper, but the YBarC always has. Problem is, it's not 1891 anymore."

Cooper asserted coolly, "Law of the open range still lives on YBarC holdings. My hands still ride with guns."

"So be it, son. That attitude will get you a pine box shortly. Your great-granddaddy, to protect open grazing, had his gun hands kill a county deputy and a homesteader on this very spot. Then they run off his family so there were no witnesses to testify against them. Bet you don't know that part of the story."

"That's your hearsay version sheriff. I know the family lore."

"Tell the lady inside to cover her ears. Blue Bob Thompson the YBarC's top gun hand from the Wyoming Territory and his New Mexico rifleman Turquoise Sanchez, raped the homestead woman in front of her three children in this half built cabin. Then Blue gunned down her husband and the deputy when they rode in on mules and her husband raised his shotgun in defense of his wife. The YBarC gun hands left her and the children on the mesa hog-tied to each other in October. They were nearly frozen when a trapper happened along and brought them into Placerville where a relative put them on a train for Denver and then back to Illinois. Their relatives back east would not let them return west to testify, fearing for their safety. The mine owners and the cattlemen did not want a trial but wanted a message sent to the homesteaders to stay out."

Tears started to well up in Cooper's eyes but he blinked them away. The family version had never mentioned children or rape. Officially Blue Bob had disobeyed orders by pulling a pistol on the homesteader who had panicked and raised his shotgun. Blue Bob had gunned him and the nosey deputy down.

"So, son, the YBarC has always been a tough outfit, some say savage. So, I'm backing out of here. I retire in a year to Tucson. I'm not going to throw away a forty-year pension fighting the YBarC. Marshals in town are no match for you, Cooper, but you have bigger problems. The replacements for them mine owners are the snow miners and real estate speculators." The sheriff turned on his heels and the deputies followed him. The 4x4 U turned out in a spray of snow and mud.

Cooper said softly, "Gather up the food, the other Colt 45 behind the cupboard and our belongings, Adrianna."

He walked over to the well shack, opened the door and picked up a five-gallon can of gasoline for the generator.

Adrianna walked out the door with her Spanish black leather overnight bag over her shoulder, the pistol and rifle, Cooper's sheep lined jean jacket and a bottle of red wine. She was startled to see Cooper dousing the windward west side of the line shack with gasoline.

"Does it hurt that much Cooper?"

"I can't change history and everyone involved is dead but no one's goanna ride line or hunt out of this cabin again." Cooper tossed a lit match onto the gasoline-coated logs and it burst into flames. Cooper and Adrianna walked to the pickup and climbed into it. As Cooper drove away he watched the unchecked flames devour the line shack in the rearview mirror as a plume of brown smoke rose against the white snow into the crystal blue-sky. The line shack had become a funeral pyre for his family history.

Cooper walked into the bunkhouse late afternoon as the phone rang.

"Hello Cooper, let me introduce myself. I am Todd Smith Patrick, an acquaintance of Brady from Ski School. Never met you but I thought I would let you know I have established a real estate agency in Telluride with some dough my grandfather was kind enough to leave me. It's called Big Sky Real Estate."

"Don't waste your pitch on me. I have a mortgage to pay off on the ranch before I buy anything in Telluride. Call the skiers who buy condos."

"Not trying to sell you today," Todd replied happily like a golden retriever wagging its tail. "I have a proposal. My dad and his Dartmouth ski race team pals want to buy the YBarC and break it up. They will pay you substantially more than the two million Lonnie Jr. has offered you."

"Todd, get the hell off my phone line and do not introduce yourself to me in person unless you like to box." Cooper mused to himself that by mid-summer lift attendants would be calling, hoping to get finders fees for selling the YBarC. Cooper then rang up Judy.

"How's Fairplay. I need a quiet corner room."

"Spend a day with me and my mouse ears at the Fairplay Hotel and you will know all the no good that all these landless lost souls are up to."

"No thank you, ma'am, just prefer living on the open range."

"You cut loose Adrianna yet Cooper? She is an Arab mare that won't gallop a wild river to save a herd. She's looking for you to save her, Cooper. I overheard a conversation in the hotel lounge that her family mine is busted unless the government lets the price of gold float."

"I don't have a dime to invest in the gold business."

"Then she'll walk at some point, Cooper, and cause your heart a lot of pain…but pain never killed anyone in your lineage, Cooper," she said sharply. "I'm coming down next Monday to work on the books. Maybe we can spend the full moon night up at the log house on Wilson Mesa."

"Can't."

"Why?" she challenged.

"I burned it to the ground a few hours ago to free its tortured ghosts."

"Harvey always said you would if you ever found out the truth. See you next week, Cooper."

FORTY-TWO

White Death

C ooper, Joe, Sue and four hired fence hands worked fourteen-hour days during the last three weeks of April, refencing and cross-fencing the ten sections close to the YBarC headquarters while Judy ran the ranch office. It snowed, hailed, rained, the sun shined, and the southwest wind blew hard while the tired crew toiled sometimes under pickup truck headlights seven days a week. The spring mud hampered operations, coated work boots and caused stuck pickup trucks. The barbwire cut through the crew's rawhide work gloves, scarred chaps and gashed small cuts under ripped denim shirts. Tons of pale green posts arrived weekly from the sawmill to fence forty miles of five-strand barbwire for winter range. After a week of fencing the crew was in football shape.

Judy had convinced Cooper that the rising cost of sending the herd to Arizona each winter was too expensive. He planned for the first time in the ranch's post-World War I history to grow enough irrigated alfalfa hay during the short summer to feed the mother cows over the next winter.

Adrianna had closed her restaurant for Telluride's off-season and returned to Red Cliff to help her father with the mine's financial problems and to have an abortion at the hospital. She skipped the family priest confession day. She planned to reopen her restaurant in mid-June for the town's first ever Bluegrass Festival. Judy ran the logistics and the financing of the refencing like an Army quartermaster. Her nightly log recorded the progress made in the YBarC pastures. During Judy's second week at the ranch, she asked Cooper to come into the bunkhouse office. Cooper, fresh from a hot shower in clean jeans and a wrinkled plaid cowboy shirt, fell into the old cowhide leather chair. Judy pulled what looked like a check out of the desk drawer. Cooper's eyes followed her fine boned long fingered hand as it brushed her white pleated blouse stretching over her firm breasts.

"Cooper, lady luck, just came our way. The antique broker I hired to sell Harvey's antiques made $31,700 net. I will pay off the hotel's bank loan. According to my budget the accidental death insurance proceeds will cover bringing the herd back, summer payroll, and there is six thousand left for a new pickup, which I ordered from Grand Junction this afternoon, ten percent off list. All the fence accounts and ranch supply accounts will be paid up to date as well as the Arizona crew's back wages."

Cooper, who had avoided the tantalizingly beautiful Judy after dinner for days, looked at her with amazement and respect. The lady from Fairplay could crunch numbers like an accountant, make a penny scream in a deal and ride the ranch like a pro rodeo barrel racer. Her being his cousin notwithstanding, he knew his grandfather would pick her as the mistress of the YBarC.

"That's the best news the YBarC has had since I returned. My hat's off to your deal making. The first round of fencing will be finished May 1st when Polecat brings back 1889 mother cows and 1806 February calves. With the newly fenced ten sections and normal irrigation water for hay this summer, we'll keep 400 heifer replacements and expand the herd back to 2,000 mother cows. The saved transportation costs next year plus a bigger herd will put the ranch back on a profitable course even if beef prices continue to cycle down. The hands will refence the grazing boundary's as they move the calf/cow pairs this summer."

Judy replied, "You should build the herd up to 3,000 mother cows over the next three years. You have the irrigation water to grow enough hay to carry them. This place has been running at half speed since Liz took the reins. Polecat quit on her ten years ago. He's just been collecting a check and I believe building up his own place for retirement with YBarC supplies. I am auditing the last ten years of ranch account records. In a week or so I hope to have the tally. Right now, all I can tell you is the work logs and inventories do not account for the incoming supplies."

Cooper weighed the information quietly, "Working the fence lines tells me you are right. Not much new but mostly rusty ol' patch wire used for most of ten years. Hope you can finish the audit before Polecat returns with the herd. Forgot to tell you there is five thousand in cash from the busted condo deal in the safe in a yellow envelope. Use it when you need it for supplies."

"The audit will be done Friday. Tonight, let's celebrate the auction with a toast to Uncle Harvey. Dinner is on me." Cooper nodded in agreement.

After their steak dinner in Norwood, they returned to Cooper's Airstream and he pulled a bottle of reserve twenty-year-old bourbon out of the cupboard. Two straight shots later, Judy put her thin muscled arms around Cooper's strong tanned neck and kissed him hard. Her pink tongue filled his mouth and she took his breath away from his sore body as his mind shut down. He slowly opened her white blouse button by button and then popped the front snap on her bra. Her firm breasts pressed against his hands as her pink nipples rubbed against his palms. He snapped open her beltless faded jeans and pulled down the zipper. He found a black silky triangle as his hand pressed against her flat hard stomach. Her jeans slid off her flat hips as she unbelted his jeans and pushed them to the floor. His hard dick filled her narrow warm canal in one strong thrust. Cooper lifted her onto her tiptoes as she braced her hands against a smooth, cool aluminum door. His thrusts lifted her into the air and she moaned in pleasure as her juices washed over his thighs and she rode him like a fine horse. Their orgasm was mutual and long as she screamed in delight to consummate their wild coupling. They were wild horses on the windblown mesa.

The herd arrived at the Grand Junction railhead on May 7. Cooper, Judy, Joe, Sue and the newly hired summer hands met Polecat's crew with a fleet of cattle trucks, the new and old pickups and Cooper's Jeep, five shotguns, six repeating rifles, a dozen pistols with leather holsters and assorted beat up cowboy hats. The transfer of the cows and calves to their YBarC summer pastures went flawlessly with the exception of the usual cattle truck flat tire. Duties were assigned to the summer crew and complaining about the increased irrigated hay operations started immediately. Cowboys always preferred open range work to farming. However, full pay envelopes helped the cowboys' mood, with the exception of Polecat who had started to chafe when he felt Cooper's new bit firmly in his mouth.

Judy remained in the ranch office after Polecat's administrative duties were abolished. Judy had agreed to stay until the hotel reopened Memorial Day weekend when the summer business picked up. Sue and Joe bunked in their teepee, which had been moved to a secluded Aspen grove near the headquarters. Drugs, rock and roll and alcohol had been eliminated completely from Cooper's ranch life. They had been replaced with fourteen-hour workdays, home cooked meals and nights with Judy to the beat of Austin country music.

FORTY-THREE

Snow Cones

The Montrose radio station was calling for two feet of heavy snow in the Norwood area with drifting up to five feet. The YBarC herd was in the low spring pastures, which ranged from seven to eight thousand feet so the calves were at risk. Most of their mothers had weathered a late spring snowstorm. It was going to be a long day and night until it stopped snowing and the May sun went back to work.

Judy had grown up on a ranch and knew it would be a hellish night. She and Cooper changed into winter range clothes and pulled on their blue oilcloth slickers. They rode the south sections until midafternoon in a blinding blizzard. The herd was split into units of 350 pairs in each double section. Joe and the hands had dropped fifty-yard long strips of hay near the cattle's water tanks to keep them bunched. Judy and Cooper pushed panicking strays back into the two herds all day long.

At three o'clock the storm started to lift as a patch of blue-sky appeared over the La Sal Mountains. Judy stayed with the sick calves while Cooper rode back for the new four-wheel drive pickup truck and horse trailer. Three hours later Cooper and Judy unloaded nine sick calves at the headquarters' corral's sick pen where the vet was already attending to three-dozen calves from the higher north sections. Polecat was in irrigation boots helping the vet. Cooper and Judy left the experienced team with the calves and returned to the Airstream for dry clothes and dinner before they relieved Joe and Sue at eight o'clock.

Cooper and Judy took a hot shower together since the Airstream had a small water tank. They soaped each other's long smooth muscled backs but were too exhausted to play. While Judy dried her black hair, Cooper cooked a hearty ranch dinner of fried eggs, rib eye steaks and hash browns served with orange juice and coffee. Half way through dinner the ranch lost electric power so Cooper went outside to start the propane generator. Judy ate in her heavy flannel robe and they went over the cowboys' night hawk work plan. Judy would rest until ten o'clock and meet Cooper in the lower of the two north sections. He would leave a hot walkie-talkie for her. They both thought the moon would be out because the snowfall had almost stopped. The crews had to keep the cattle from standing and freezing to death in snowdrifts during the night when the windchill would drop to minus

20. Polecat's crew, which was already exhausted, would rotate onto the easier southern sections where the snow was not as deep. Joe and Sue would tag team Cooper and Judy on the northern sections at 2 a.m. and they would switch again at 8 a.m. It would be a long dangerous night on the YBarC.

Cooper stopped at the bunkhouse to check on Joe and Sue, who had moved in from their snow collapsed teepee. The Utes had wintered in the southeastern Utah desert for a reason. Polecat and a cowboy were snoring away in their rooms and two top hands had already left for the south sections. Dirty dishes and cold food were still on the bunkhouse table. Joe's door was ajar and Cooper looked in and saw him sleeping, but Sue was missing. A perplexed Cooper walked into the office where a kerosene lamp flickered. A note on his desk from Joe said Sue had been too tired and wet to ride back to headquarters so he had built her a fire in line shack two and left her in a sleeping bag that was stored there for emergencies. Could Cooper take her dry clothes and coffee so she could ride back to headquarters?

As Cooper was leaving the yellow-lighted office, the phone miraculously rang.

Adrianna chirped, "Amazing I got through. The YBarC phone line is always first to go in a big storm. Denver radio says it is the worst May blizzard since 1922 on the west slope. Is it really that bad, Cooper?"

"Worse than bad."

"Well, the kissing cousin does come in handy when I am out of town Cowboy Cooper," she accused angrily.

"Judy has done a fantastic job restructuring the ranch's administration and financial operations," countered Cooper.

"For free I bet…family duty…code of the Anglo west." She was in tears.

"I have to saddle up and check on Sue up at line shack two. We'll discuss Judy later."

"No, we won't, Cooper. I had an abortion last week." The line went dead. Cooper's tears froze on his cheeks as walked out of the bunkhouse into the minus 5 windchill.

An hour later a cold Cooper rode up to line shack two after checking the split northern herd and prodding tired cold calves and mothers to their feet. If they slept on Cooper's watch they were going to sleep standing. Kerosene lamplight flickered in the old fashion glass pained front window. Cooper knocked and then entered the cold room. Sue was shivering in a summer weight sleeping bag.

"Help me please Cooper I cannot get warm enough to ride back to the headquarters. My clothes are still damp and I am out of firewood."

"Let me refuel the fire; I have a spare pair of Judy's jeans and a sweater in my saddle bags."

Fifteen minutes later a blazing fire had warmed the rustic cabin and Cooper had boiled a pot of coffee. Sue sipped a tin cup of coffee and had stopped shivering in the dry sleeping bag. Cooper had her boots on the hearth and her duster, clothes and underwear on a rope line in front of the stone fireplace. He put on his now dry duster to leave. To his surprise Sue clamored out of the sleeping bag buck naked and pranced like a pony over to the hot fire to warm up. She surprised Cooper with a full-frontal nude view of her range-hardened body. Her perfect body never failed to arouse Cooper.

Everything was round where a woman should be round; flat and hard where a woman should be firm, and sexy everywhere. A month of fencing and range riding had made a perfect body into a living sculpture. The silky vee of her triangle caught the soft firelight and accented her smooth lips where they disappeared between her soft thighs. Cooper remembered the sweet perfection of Sue's pink opening. That thought momentarily stopped a bone tired Cooper in his tracks.

"Still the most magic body of all isn't it, Cooper?" She said matter-of-factly, standing dead still as her breasts rose and fell with each breath and her light brown nipples visibly hardened.

"Yes, ma'am. I have never seen a woman as perfect as nature made you."

"Another lifetime for us maybe, Cooper," she said prophetically. "Not this one."

An hour later Cooper heard his walkie-talkie squawk and a static-laced Sue's voice reported her safe return to headquarters. At ten, Cooper's walkie-talkie squawked as Judy spurred a fresh ranch quarter horse and rode out to meet Cooper. He was busy pulling nearly frozen calves back onto their hooves or reuniting them with their mothers for warm milk.

A white-faced Judy spurred her reluctant horse into the minus fifteen degree windchill as the new ranch pickup approached, pulling a long horse trailer. At the wheel was Johnny, a long time YBarC top hand and a legendary Colorado team roper from Olathe, Colorado. Judy reined in her horse and let the pickup roll up to her.

Johnny rolled down the window and finally his frozen jaw loosened enough to spit out the last of his tobacco. "Got six more sick ones back here, Miss Judy. Polecat and Bobby tending to five more. We got two dead calves and one mom to the south. She was a first timer. Our older moms are jest fine but pissed, pardon my French, ma'am, to be back up here from the sunny state where they wintered."

"Good work Johnny. You all hold down the south until sun up. The vet's scheduled again for six at headquarters. We got his first stop. I am riding north to help Cooper."

"You can night hawk with me anytime Miss Judy. You handle a horse as good as any cowboy on the place."

"It would be a pleasure, Johnny." She knew that was his highest compliment short of one regarding roping. She tipped her broad brimmed cowgirl hat and spurred her reluctant horse back into the wind.

One hour and three walkie-talkie conversations later, Judy found Cooper wrestling yet another almost frozen calf to its feet. Cooper had five calves confirmed dead but his mother cows were mostly fine. Eighty years of YBarC breeding had produced a hearty strain of range cows. One storm, no matter how fierce, was not going to knock off the ranch's herd. He spoke to Judy through a frozen jaw and cracked lips, "Got a couple more sick ones by the tank with their mothers but the herd is veteran and tough. Polecat has our first-time mothers to the south where there is always less snow."

"Johnny brought in five more sick calves to headquarters, reported two dead."

"If we lose ten or less that's the best we can hope for in this snow. It is going to be a couple long nights."

"I'll ride the other section…radio you if I need help. Might like these Motorola radios better than you."

Cooper cracked a cold smile, "Good thing they can only squawk then."

"Vaya con Dios, Cowboy." Judy spurred her horse into the wind with her saddle rifle and its worn leather case bouncing against her horse's flanks.

The temperature was now minus 15 and the windchill was minus 30 when Joe saddled two rested but cold horses. He loaded the horses into the eight-horse trailer behind the new double rear wheeled pickup. Fresh horses were being trailered out to the tired cold cowboys and nearly frozen sick calves were being brought back to the ranch headquarters' barn. He radioed Cooper and Judy but they did not reply. He assumed their batteries were dead from the cold or they were working low ground out of line of sight. Johnny did reply and confirmed Judy rode out at ten and that he and Polecat had moved half the southern herd into an arroyo to protect them from the wind. When Bobby arrived to tend them, Johnny and Polecat planned to do the same with the other half. Joe signed off as Sue clamored into the truck's cab with a genuine look of serenity on her face for the first time since he had known her. He perceived something spiritual and magical had occurred in the snowstorm. He knew the Ute gods often brought important messages to the chiefs in the most adverse of weather conditions. Major spring snowstorms had a reason in the pantheon of the tribe's life and health. They never occurred randomly.

Cooper had just completed pushing his herd away from the water tank and into a draw. They could drink at sun up, he figured, but the wind was god-awful. Even with his bandana over his nose he could not move his mouth anymore. His toes and fingertips were also aching. Suddenly, he heard the double-barrel retort of Judy's saddle rifle in the adjoining section. He pulled out his radio and forced his lips to move but his battery was dead. He realized he should have kept the radio inside the duster so his body heat could have preserved his battery power.

Cooper gave the herd a couple of minutes to settle down from the gunshots. Cooper wheeled his horse easily without a sound and rode to find Judy. Halfway to her section boundary line Cooper picked up bear tracks in the deep snow. It was a mature male with about four hundred pounds of well-muscled killing power. Cooper spurred his tired horse into a gallop in the snow. The bear's tracks continued a couple feet to the right of Judy's horses hoof holes in the snow. Cooper reached the section's partially open gate that was stuck in deep snow. The tracks picked up again on the other side of the gate. Cooper yelled into the wind for Judy as he galloped through the snow. In the moonlight, he saw a bleeding dead calf fifty yards ahead. The bear had mauled it in the deep snow. Cooper followed the bear's tracks at full gallop and suddenly Judy's downed horse emerged into full view bleeding from the neck. Cooper's heart raced and fear settled into his cold brain. Judy's lanky figure emerged waist deep in the snow; the cattle bunched a hundred yards behind her. She was standing beside the dead bear, which was face down in red snow.

"I'm mostly fine. Took a second shot to his head to stop him. My horse took the swipe to his jugular but stayed on his feet until I could dismount. He saved my life by not going down in the snow. I can't pull the trigger." She started to cry.

Cooper dismounted and knelt by the fatally wounded quarter horse. He closed its eyes carefully. He patted its head and calmed it in a whisper. He stood and with one eye on the still nervous herd Cooper chambered a steel tipped bullet, but wished he had a bowie knife. Cooper shot Judy's horse knowing they might be dead next if the herd stampeded. He hoped the deep heavy wet snow would hold the cattle in place. The herd stirred dangerously, started to settle but when Judy's radio crackled with Joe's voice, the herd stirred again.

Cooper mounted his horse in one motion and reached down with a strong arm to pull a still sobbing Judy up behind his saddle. Judy put her hands around his waist and he spurred his panicked horse toward the open gate a hundred yards across the pasture. He prayed the horse did not stumble under their double weight and go down. He wanted to be behind the closed gate as the herd stampeded. The pinto somehow always found his footing with only one heart-stopping slip. Cooper and Judy raced through the open gate and he reined the horse to a slow stop. He dismounted with Judy and they forced the red gate closed in the deep heavy snow. The herd surged slowly through the snow and into the gate but it held.

"Glad you are a good shot, Annie Oakley. I'll make that bear into a rug for you."

"I love you, Cooper. Let's get to that warm pickup. We've had enough of this snowstorm tonight. Sunshine always restores hope after a snowstorm."

FORTY-FOUR

Sleuth

E arly Wednesday morning Cooper's phone rang in the Airstream. "Hello Mr. Stuart, I am Laura Daniels, the widow of Bill Daniels."

Cooper searched for the appropriate response and wondered why she would call after all these months. "Sorry about your husband's untimely death. I hope your family is getting along okay."

A proud western women's voice replied, "We'll make it. Our families pioneered Montrose. We have seen hard times before but that's not why I called. I came across a carbon copy of a memo while I was preparing to store Bill's home files yesterday. It mentions the YBarC but I know Bill was not working for your ranch when he disappeared. I did his bookkeeping. I will read it to you in confidence. I don't know who else to call."

"You have my word, ma'am," Cooper was interested now.

She read in an unemotional monotone, "The memo is titled, 'Date: August 5 1975 - Field survey for LJR/LSR/SJR,' I don't know what that means?"

"I do. Please continue."

She continued, "(1) YBarC ranch owns the fifty percent high mean average cubic foot draw of the middle San Miguel River flow for beneficial use by a water court adjudicated water allocation to the Delores River intersection. (2) August to October; the proposed planned Ajax Ski Company home community of up to 20,000 units in the east end of San Miguel County will send the San Miguel River water flow underground in low rainfall years from Sawpit eight miles west of Telluride to Nucla thirty miles west of Telluride with the current town of Telluride and gold mine water allocations. (3) Add the senior YBarC Lone Cone Mountain and Naturita Creek surface flow irrigation rights and there will be no trout fish life in the San Miguel River in any drought year. (4) There will be no ranch livestock or irrigated hay farming in San Miguel County or southern Montrose County except Lone Cone Gurley water share irrigated hay farms. (5) The planned density coupled with population density and snowmaking for 1,000 acres of skiing will severely damage aquatic and wildlife in the region. Sewerage treatment waste and septic tanks will pollute the San Miguel River basin year around plus its ground water in the San Miguel and Delores River basins.

(6) I can only recommend a bi-county cap on growth immediately to protect these water resources if no purchase of the YBarC water rights by the Ajax Ski Company occurs. If no purchase occurs, then I recommend only a cap that allows two thousand homes. Note 1: called LJR on this 8-19; he was upset and unpleasant and suspended my confidential $1,000 per month retainer for the water resources study. Note2: The San Miguel River below the uranium mill at Uravan which Lonnie Sr. owns measured higher than permissible levels of radiation."

Cooper replied, "LJR is Lonnie Jr., operator of the Ajax Ski Company, your late husband's consulting client. Bill's notes for his report indicate what my grandfather knew when he bought most of the middle and lower San Miguel River water rights before and during the depression. It's a fact that 18 cubic feet per second of mean annual flow will not support much life, cattle, people, or trout with a highly unpredictable 12-inch annual rainfall, which totals 25-inches of rainfall when snowmelt at high elevations is added. Why he measured the radiation level below Uravan is puzzling. The result is alarming!"

"So what are you saying, Mr. Stuart, exactly?" she asked with a foreboding in her voice.

"That someone murdered your husband thinking they had the only copy of this report."

Her voice broke into sobs, "Do you want this carbon copy, Mr. Stuart? Please help my kids and me. Bill's life insurance is still being held up because of the Coroner's ongoing investigation. I have no tuition money for my son to attend Colorado School of Mines in the fall."

"You have my word. Please do not discuss this with anyone. Your life could be in danger. If Lonnie Jr. or his father ordered Bill's murder they are lethal. They have already tried to ambush me and probably killed my mother by setting the YBarC headquarters house on fire. I will send Joe Bear Spirit, my trusted Ute ranch hand, to pick up the carbon copy. You and I must not be connected. What is your address in Montrose?"

She burst into uncontrollable sobs.

Cooper walked over to the teepee and gave Joe his secret Montrose mission instructions. Then he stopped at the bunkhouse office and checked the April snowpack report that indicated above average irrigation water for the summer. Next he drove to Telluride where he found Colorado Avenue deserted. He parked in front of Adrianna's Victorian house. Cooper planned to discuss the abortion and end their romantic relationship. He knocked but when no one answered, he let himself in through the unlocked door. The house was eerily dark with its heavy velvet ruby curtains drawn tight. The hallway seemed ghostly to Cooper as he opened the leaded glass French parlor doors. Adrianna was reclining on a mauve leather Spanish chaise lounge surrounded by a ring of thick black candles arranged in an oval. Her black velvet robe was open. The smokeless orange flames threw a golden hue onto her nude body. She had shaved her striking jet-black triangle and recreated it in smeared red lipstick. She opened her eyes and Cooper saw the orange candle flames dance in her dark brown pupils. Her black hair was in long braids that covered her nipples.

"Do not speak, Cooper. It's over...our baby's gone forever."

"I'm so sorry," Cooper mumbled in a soft voice as the emotion hit him like lightning on the open range.

"No. You're not sorry or you would not have made me take its life. We are finished. I don't ever want to see you again. Please leave my house."

"Let's talk, we are both upset about this."

"Talk about...what? Death, evil spirits, religion, my sin, down on their luck ranchers, low gold prices and the pleasure you got fucking me? Get out!" Anger flared from her nostrils.

Cooper retreated two steps, "I will leave in peace."

"Muerte, hombre. Go to your cowgirl cousin so she can produce a four-eyed baby for you, Senor."

Cooper froze.

"I see in your eyes that you want to hit the woman who let your baby be murdered to hide your shame but your heart stopped you," she screeched with fire in her voice as all reason left her. Adrianna's eyes became hard like Toledo steel.

"That's enough. I'll talk to you when reason returns."

"You will talk to me in hell for making me sin against God."

Without warning she raised her hidden right hand, which had been resting on the oak floor and expertly hurled a pearl-handle Spanish dagger toward Cooper. Its sharp Toledo steel tip was aimed straight for his heart, as he reflexively dove to his left. The tip of the dagger pierced his shirt and impaled in the flesh on his right upper arm. Cooper landed hard on his side.

"You bitch witch," Cooper mumbled under his breath.

"You still think I am just another mare at the YBarC waiting to stand stud for the white stallion?"

Blood soaked his blue denim shirtsleeve. After he steadied himself he winced as he slowly slid the dagger out of the burning wound.

"Feel the pain, Cooper just like the burning in my belly and my soul when the baby died." She started to cry.

Cooper walked over to Adrianna and kissed her forehead.

"I'll keep the dagger for now. Vaya con Dios."

Joe and Sue had TV dinners ready in the Airstream when Cooper returned to the ranch. He'd concealed the county nurse's bandage on his arm by wearing his jean jacket. They played hearts and recounted blizzard stories. After Sue left for the teepee Joe handed Cooper a brown envelope stamped CONFIDENTIAL and sealed with red candle wax.

"What gives, Richard the Lionheart?" Joe mocked.

Cooper did not unseal the envelope. "The memo is the smoking gun that proves Lonnie

Jr. or his dad killed Bill Daniels or had him murdered. Problem is, I can't prove it unless we can locate the original and prove that Bill delivered it to Lonnie Jr."

"Bill Daniels was just another white man who helped steal Ute water rights," replied Joe coldly. "But the Lonnies are evil in its purest form, true black spirit warriors, who come to destroy some of the Ute's most sacred valleys and mesas."

"I will need your help if a path to the original memo reveals itself," Cooper replied.

Later he hid the brown envelope behind the Airstream's small refrigerator after wrapping it in aluminum foil.

FORTY-FIVE

Festival

Early June days consisted of fourteen hours of backbreaking fencing in the beautiful North Mountain pastures. After the fencing was complete and the cattle were all herded to their grassy summer range, Joe returned to the Steak and Brew as a bartender on weekend nights. Judy arrived Friday noon before the Telluride Bluegrass Music Festival and spent the afternoon updating the ranch books while Cooper rode the range with Polecat.

On the way to Telluride, Judy opened the conversation, "Forty-eight thousand cash left. Fencing on budget. You will make October okay but unless you get an advance against your calf sales or the fire insurance money the financial storm clouds are back. That includes the twelve month bank interest-only bank payment Max says the court will require until the legal fight is settled."

"Sure would be nice to have the fire insurance settlement," Cooper replied as Judy's Wagoneer motored through Placerville.

"It's yours rightfully. But Max says you need a signed release from Sam Jr. It's in my overnight bag in the back."

"I'll work on it. Give it to me at the inn," Cooper said with an edge in his voice. Judy had been raised not to ask a man about unvolunteered details.

Joe Bear Spirit made sure the hostess gave them the Steak and Brew's best table for two. A few minutes after they were seated, Joe signaled Cooper from the bar to look to his right. Waylon Jennings, his band and two long-legged Austin Texas blondes were seated in a red upholstered booth. Judy's mouth dropped wide open.

Cooper said with excitement in his voice, "There's not been a name star in town since the Opera house shut down after the silver crash of 1902."

Joe stopped at their table and whispered into Cooper's ear. Cooper rose from his chair pulling Judy along by her hand.

They followed Joe over to Waylon Jennings' booth and Joe introduced them. "This is my friend Cooper and his girlfriend Judy."

"Good to meet. Ute Joe here says you operate the legendary Y Bar C outfit. Sit down and join us," his harmonic voice boomed.

"It's music to my ears," Cooper smiled as they pulled up chairs.

"Joe Bear Spirit here says the town posse is closing in on you, Cooper. My friend Joe Ely says bankers been driving good ranchers and farming men to ruin since the big depression."

"We're holding the loan rustlers off at our fence lines but they are devils in the wind for sure."

"Well, we're going to dedicate a song to the YBarC tomorrow at the Festival."

"Tickets are in my wallet."

"You'll be down front and backstage, too. Glenda here will take care of that. You ride the range, you're the band's guest," Waylon said with delight.

"Thanks, maybe you boys can all come out to the YBarC Sunday for a barbeque. Our headquarters house burned to the ground but we have plenty of bunkhouse space."

Waylon answered with a broad smile, "We been on the road three months. We need a night away from smoky bars and bright town lights."

At closing time, Cooper sent Judy back to the inn without an explanation. He followed Joe out the bar's back door to the alley where he was locking up.

"Meet me at the back alley door to the bank tomorrow at noon. Sam Jr. always works Saturday morning until noon closing and leaves via the alley door after he sets the alarms. Judy brought a fire insurance release that I need him to sign. You are the witness."

"See you at noon." Joe departed the alley in the opposite direction from Cooper's route to the inn.

The next morning, Cooper walked into the alley behind the bank and saw Joe waiting. Cooper approached the door and handed Joe a red bandana. They both pulled the bandanas over their faces like range cowboys in a dust storm. Suddenly the door opened and Sam Jr. stepped into the alley. Cooper came out from behind the open door and stuck a very sharp hunting knife into Sam's crotch from behind.

"I have a paper for you to sign or you will be a steer for the rest of your life. Do not turn around, just sign the page on the clipboard and date it. Use your ball-point pen."

"You cannot get away with this, Cooper," Sam blurted out.

"Your word against mine and my witness' signature. So sorry…now shut up and sign."

Sam signed as Cooper pressed the knife blade up slightly. Joe stayed hidden and silent behind the still open steel door.

"You mother fucker. I will finish you for this. The fire insurance money will not buy you one extra hour on the YBarC," Sam angrily yelled.

"Time to say goodbye." Cooper pushed Sam back inside and turned the key that he'd left in the door's lock.

Joe signed the witness blank and departed without saying a word. Cooper cleared the alley and ducked into the unlocked door of the empty U.S. Post Office and mailed the form. Then he met Judy at the festival where they listened to country bands on a blue-sky summer day.

Around midnight, a slightly beer high Cooper and Judy were back in their room at the inn. Judy stripped off her cowgirl clothes and reached for Cooper's Junior High Rodeo belt buckle. There was a hard knock at the room's door. Cooper opened the door as Judy stepped behind it. The town marshal looked sternly at Cooper.

"Sam Jr. alleges you forced him to sign an insurance release and locked him in the bank."

"You know he would say anything about me. He's trying to steal my ranch."

"Mind if I search your room? I already searched your Jeep."

Cooper shook his head, "You got no warrant; besides, I have an alibi witness."

Judy stepped out from behind the door in a bra and panties; the marshal's jaw dropped. "Cooper was in bed with me or at the festival all day from sun up 'til now, Mr. Telluride Marshal. No cowboy could pass up a day like that, could he? Fact is, you're keeping us out of bed right now." She stepped back behind the door.

"Peep show over...time to go back on patrol," Cooper said with a smirk.

"I am going to nail you someday Cooper and the sheriff is not going to save your out-of-control cowboy ass. Rich kid ranchers and drugged out ski trust funders are not going to run Telluride."

"Night! Go look for some drug dealers. Or find yourself a whore or did you run them all out of town to protect the skiers and condo queens?"

Cooper closed the door in his face. As footsteps departed down the hall, Cooper playfully pushed a giddy Judy onto the bed.

Waylon Jennings' bus parked in front of the YBarC bunkhouse around noon on Sunday and set off an epic twelve-hour party. Polecat and the hands saddled horses, guided an early summer fly-fishing group, and barbecued an entire steer using a washtub of Cooper's secret sauce. Cooper drove Waylon on a Jeep tour of the ranch; cold beer and bourbon flowed in the bunkhouse but Cooper requested the band keep its pot in the bus. Sue and Judy made potato salad, coleslaw, baked beans, fresh bread, and blueberry cobbler. Joe led the horseback sunset tour that ended with a western sky that blazed orange, gold, purple, and pink over the La Sal range, Blue Mountains, Lone Cone Peak and Wilson Peak. After a gigantic dinner on tin plates, the band played a few cowboy songs. During the final honky-tonk number the two girls, who had been cheerleaders at the University of Texas, jumped onto the bunkhouse table and high-kicked out the grand finale jam session in tight blue jeans. They nearly set off a bourbon fueled cowboy riot in the bunkhouse.

When Cooper awoke at dawn in Judy's arms, he heard the bus's diesel engine roaring like an African lion on the dead quiet ranch as it drove off for a Twin Falls, Idaho club date.

Judy, too, soon left in a cloud of fine summer ranch road dust.

Ten minutes later Joe Bear Spirit knocked on the Airstream door and entered. "Big news in Telluride."

"What now, a golf course so the miners can use their sledge hammers for putters after the day shift gets off?"

"Close. The mine's closing up for good. Price of gold, silver, lead and zinc are too low, plus the EPA is trying to put its Utah smelter out of business by forcing it to modernize to cut air pollution."

"They say," Cooper, mused almost to himself, remembering an economics class at college, "eight companies based in Denver, London and Cape Town control the world's gold production and sales. It's easier to post higher prices in London by closing down older mining districts. First it was Cripple Creek, Central City, Rico and now it's Telluride. Bet it's Leadville, Silverton and Ouray next."

"Maybe you're right but this is good news for the Utes. The mine owners and railroads drove us out of the Colorado mountain ranges. The crooked Denver politicians and speculators helped them. So fuck them all, including the miners. They all stole Ute land. They polluted Ute rivers."

Cooper's mood changed, "Utes want the YBarC's water rights back, too. Is that really your point?"

"Yes."

"Help me save the YBarC and the Utes can have half the ranch's Delores River water rights if you can figure out how to divert the water south to the res."

"You serious?"

"Dead serious. The ranch can install modern irrigation equipment and cut its hay growing water usage. Judy gave me a USDA report about it. Ski resort speculators get this operation, the Utes will never see a drop of water."

"I'll talk to the chiefs. It's the best offer an Anglo ever made. The U.S. government has never delivered the southern Utes their treaty water from the Animas River at Durango. You loco?"

"No."

"More news, I am shifting to Adrianna's as the night bartender weekends for more pay. No more Steak and Brew." Joe disappeared out the Airstream door as Cooper frowned.

The next morning, Cooper ordered Polecat to cut out the mothers that did not calve this year.

"Why the cut out this early?"

"Because miners, many of them sons and grandsons of YBarC beef customers, just got fired. Winter is coming in four months. The YBarC is going to give the ones with families a quarter cow until they find new work."

"Your grandfather and father would have done the same thing, Cooper. YBarC fed many a starving child and family during the depression and the union strike. One starving teenager even lived here," Polecat paused, and quickly changed the subject. "Your grandfather believed well paid miners would eat more beef."

Cooper was straightening up the Airstream, when Max called. "The fire insurance check's on the way. Courier is delivering it. Meet the four o'clock Frontier Airline flight at the Montrose airport and sign for it. It is an irrevocable cashier's check," he laughed.

"Thanks again, Max. One down and one to go. We find out who Delta's secret witness is and 'none' to go," replied Cooper.

"Roger that, Cooper."

FORTY-SIX

The NTSB

T he phone rang early at the YBarC headquarters' office and the call was from the National Transportation Safety Board.

"As you probably know, by law the NTSB investigates and files a report on all aviation accidents, general aviation included, to improve the aircraft and better prepare pilots."

"Good, a wise use of tax dollars for once."

"First, as you know, Harvey Stuart was not your blood uncle. He was legally adopted on April 21,1932 at the age of eighteen by your grandfather. Our investigation discovered this since you referred to him as a blood relative. Anyway, the thrust of our report is a ninety percent probability the navigational instruments were tampered with on his plane and that is why he missed the runway and crashed landed, the snow storm notwithstanding."

After a long stunned silence Cooper replied, "You mean someone sabotaged the plane's instruments? My uncle Harvey was adopted?"

"Adoption is not our line of work. Basically, there is a ten percent probability the instruments were not properly calibrated during the last maintenance check, the records and flights subsequent to that FAA mandated overhaul do not support that hypothesis. We believe someone intentionally sabotaged the instruments."

"You have a suspect?"

"We only investigate and file an aviation accident report. We have already informed the FBI and today we will inform the Attorney General of Colorado and the crash site county sheriff. The FBI lab found no fingerprints on the instruments except for Mr. Stuart's, which means they were probably wiped clean. The FAA will be kept informed by the FBI but we will not be directly involved in the investigation unless aviation technical analysis is requested."

"When will the Denver newspapers have this story?" asked Cooper.

"In two days our Public Affairs Office will release the report and a cover press release," his official voice returned. "This call is a courtesy only so you and your family don't have to hear the report on the evening news first. Please call my office if you have any other questions after you receive the full report by certified mail. Good day, sir."

Judy went into telephone shock when Cooper relayed all the news to her by phone. He belatedly realized he should have driven to Fairplay.

She went in and out of teary outbursts and asked, "Do you think they were after you or Harvey? Are you sure he's not your blood uncle? That means we're not real blood cousins."

"No one knew I was flying back to Fairplay but Uncle Harvey."

"Then why Harvey?"

"Barring some Fairplay local legal revenge or a grudge against our clan, it was possibly to stop him from helping me save the YBarC."

"Then they almost killed you, too," and she sobbed again.

"Precisely, two for one. Splendid serendipity," Cooper asserted with an Edgar Allen Poe chill in his voice.

"Who, Cooper?"

"The gang of three in Telluride but more probably Lonnie Sr. It's his style I hear."

"I have to go cry for an hour for my father, Cooper. Then I have to laugh because we are not blood relatives. Now I'm just another woman trying to marry Cooper Stuart and become mistress of the YBarC. If you can handle that, Cooper, then I will handle the press here in Fairplay when the story breaks. Uncle Harvey was a big fish in these parts. It'll be a big story."

Cooper was relieved the cousin barrier had evaporated so his developing relationship with Judy would not set off another explosive controversy. He had become very dependent on Judy to help run the ranch and with her cowgirl clothes off he had little resistance to her powerful allure. On the matter of Uncle Harvey, he needed to talk to Polecat when he came off the range. His recent words, "one starving teenager," played over and over in his mind. Why had his grandfather concealed Harvey's true identity and Liz, too, if she knew?

An hour passed and Joe drifted into the office to get out of a gusting wind. Cooper brought him up speed on the NTSB news.

"Need a couple weeks off to do some AIM work, Cooper. Know you need me on the ranch, but it's a must do."

"Where?"

"The Southern Ute res. We want our treaty water back from the Animas River."

"So what's the plan? Raid the wood burning train between Durango and Silverton and scalp some tourists?"

"Funny. Study all the old treaties; specifically, all references to the Animas, the Piedra, the Delores, San Miguel and the Florida Rivers and work out a law suit the old fashioned Anglo way with maybe a demonstration in Durango to gin up the media. Hadn't thought about attacking the train though."

"You are goanna stir up old hate among the farmers, ranchers, townies, rafters and kayakers down there."

"Fuck them," Joe responded not smiling anymore. "They drove the Utes south to the desert rim and then stole our upstream water. Time to call the game."

"If the courts hold for the users, what then?"

"United Nations."

"What in hell?" Cooper gasped.

"Ask for protector status under the charter like the former European colonies did after World War II."

"You mean what I think you mean?"

"Right, get Britain, France even Russia put in charge of the Ute Territories, then declare our independence as a sovereign nation under the UN charter that the USA signed."

"That's a nuclear bomb not a Molotov cocktail," Cooper reflected. He was trying to remember his international political science class.

"You got that right. But a hundred years of patience has gotten the Utes nowhere…time to call the game - winner take all."

"What about the YBarC water rights I offered you?"

"We're looking into a water swap that might make them work for us."

"So I see you when I see you. Ride with the wind." Cooper reached into his jean pocket. "Here's a couple hundred in advance wages."

Joe took the money and silently disappeared. Cooper considered Joe's words carefully. Everyone wanted the YBarC's water, every drop of it. He wished Joe well in the dream world and the real world. He would need both as he helped organize the Utes.

FORTY-SEVEN
The Skunks

Cooper arrived at the Fairplay Hotel the night before the ROCKY MOUNTAIN NEWS featured the NTSB findings on its front page. Cooper was pictured in front of the bunkhouse wearing one of his grandfather's beat up beaver cowboy hats that had survived the fire.

The sub headline read, "Rancher points finger at modern day land and water grabbers." The story disclosed the ranch's foreclosure, the headquarters' house fire that Liz died in, the ongoing investigation of attack by the gunmen on the Utah line, the rustled mother cows and the rejected two million dollar offer from Lonnie Jr.

Then Cooper was quoted, "Lonnie Jr. is the sheep. It's Lonnie Sr. who is the wolf. He has a bootlegging conviction in Cortez. He sold booze on the Navajo res. Hoods are hoods forever."

The Colorado Attorney General announced he was forming a special task force led by the State Police to investigate Harvey's death. The Attorney General stated, "No current or former public servant will be murdered on my watch in Colorado without frontier justice being served on the perpetrator."

It was a beautiful blue-sky June morning but it didn't take long for the switchboard at the hotel to light up. The first call for was from Jim Mudd the Denver oil, gas, and coal magnate.

"Cooper sorry to read this story about your uncle, but do the Fed's have a lead or are you just wildly finger pointing?"

"As they say in poker, let the cards fall where they may when the game is called."

"Wild statements can ruin a man's reputation," he warned coldly. "That Cortez history about Lonnie Sr. is old news, son. He is a big time operator these days. The cow shit is long off his boots."

"He's a small-time scavenger and as crooked as the San Miguel River."

"Be careful what you allege."

"FBI will call you. You're on their list. You were our last meeting in Denver."

"You son of a bitch, Cooper. You defame either me or my corporation in this witch hunt and you will hang. You fucking ranchers are blocking progress all over the west, slowing oil

214

and gas pipelines and drilling, open pit coal mining, timber cutting, ski resort and suburban development while you run a few cows and ride the range for sunsets. Western Colorado will be through with all of you soon. Take Lonnie Jr.'s check and get the hell out of the state."

"You're nothing but a Denver Chamber of Commerce booster. You and your pals stay the fuck out of western Colorado," and Cooper slammed the receiver down.

"You are our Sunday regional story. Headline will be MURDER IN THE OLD WEST - MODERN DAY LAND GRAB OR REVENGE!" The ROCKY MOUNTAIN NEWS reporter said as he tapped an agitated Cooper on the shoulder.

Cooper turned. "What's the revenge angle?" Cooper asked surprised. "Your researchers or stringers have something interesting?"

"Mr. Peter Simple says his family's ranch land was grabbed in the depression by the YBarC for fifty cents an acre paid in rolls of quarters."

"It's public record," Cooper asserted.

"Do you know that Mr. Simple's brother works as a security guard in the general aviation area at Stapleton airport where you and your uncle took off?"

"Very interesting fact…you have more?" Cooper asked as the news bombshell sank in.

"Yes, off the record. He travels on weekend flights as a personal bodyguard with a Mr. Jim Mudd, a Denver oil, gas and land speculator."

Cooper remained silent.

"Our Denver sources say he canceled a potential refinancing of the YBarC after the plane crash and that you and Harvey met with him the same afternoon you flew back to Fairplay, Colorado. Cooper, do you want to go on record about what was discussed in that meeting and whether he knew you were flying to Fairplay later that afternoon with your uncle?"

"We agreed on a loan to the YBarC. Uncle Harvey was going to review the paper work in Fairplay," Cooper answered, reflecting on the call he had just received from Jim Mudd. "He didn't know I would be on the plane to Fairplay. That was not discussed at lunch meeting."

"That's odd. Our sources also say Mudd is late on a payment of five million dollars to United Copper's founding family for a mine that he bought."

"Interesting, is there more?"

"Yes, United Copper holds a recorded first mortgage to secure a private placement for two million dollars in the Ajax Ski Company in Telluride. They also have call warrants for the Ajax Ski Company's common stock."

Cooper was speechless. "Jim Mudd called five minutes ago and threatened me if I didn't shut up. He made a verbal deal to bail out the YBarC with Uncle Harvey and me in Denver. He knew Uncle Harvey was flying back to Fairplay to finalize the paperwork. The NTSB has the unsigned draft of the YBarC loan agreement that was pulled out of the crashed plane. Harvey never disclosed he had a loan with a company, United Copper, that owned a portion of the Ajax Ski Company."

"So do you believe he was setting you up for a future foreclosure?"

"But why murder Uncle Harvey and cancel the loan? Easier to make the loan and then legally squeeze me out later if the YBarC faltered."

"So back to the Simples. They knew your Uncle's plane was in Denver. They may have known you and your uncle were meeting Mudd. Plus, they had already set a trap for you in Delta."

"With my grandfather and mother dead, the Simple family goes after me and then Harvey. Can you find a link between Lonnie Sr. and the Simples?"

"Good idea but a tough one, any other pertinent revelations?"

"Not at the moment but talk to me again before your deadline."

"Deal."

"Jesse Smith on the line," the desk clerk chirped.

"Hello Jesse. You can read line type, I presume."

"Screw you, Cooper. You libeled my client for the last time. I'm getting an injunction barring you from Telluride and San Miguel County."

"Matter of public record. Lonnie Sr. served hard time."

"Those records were recently sealed. How did you get them?"

"Grandfather kept a copy of the Cortez newspaper article in his fire proof safe because Lonnie Sr. owed him for some cattle he resold to the Navajos when he went on trial."

"Look Cooper, Cortez loves Lonnie Sr. these days. I have the newspaper's microfilm of its coverage. Have you given the article to anyone?"

Cooper lied to set a trap, "Xeroxes to the Denver papers."

Jesse screamed into the phone, "We're going to burn you alive for this."

The trap worked. "So you missed the chance to kill me and burned my mother alive. You are a dead man walking, Mr. Smith." Cooper hung up, shaken that his suspicions were correct.

A well-dressed beautiful Judy walked in from the dining room where she had met with a group of local officials.

"They're forming a special county fund to help investigate my father's murder."

The desk clerk frowned, "FBI on the line."

Cooper signaled Judy to listen in on the switchboard line.

"Good morning, Mr. Stuart. We need to meet with you on the NTSB matter. Two agents are coming down from Denver," he intoned in a base mid-Atlantic voice.

"Sure. Fairplay Hotel lobby at 2 p.m."

"I must warn you, threats against upstanding citizens with Federal Government uranium processing contracts will not be tolerated by the FBI in the interest of national security in our fight against communism, especially by someone under indictment."

"What's that got to do with sabotaged airplane instruments?" Cooper tersely responded.

"Everything. We are investigating a tip that your cocaine suppliers tried to murder you on that flight because you have not paid for their last shipment to you."

"You boys have been chasing communist spies and bugging black ministers too long. We're on the same team. Let's try to solve Uncle Harvey's murder."

"No, we are not on the same team, Mr. Stuart. You are a draft dodging, Indian loving, drug pusher and I intend to help put you behind bars. You continue to smear loyal Americans like Lonnie Sr. and deputy Peter Simple and Jim Mudd and we will get you for treason too. Good day."

"Got to go, Judy, before the FBI gets to the office safe first. I should have kept my mouth shut. They will destroy the original Cortez newspaper articles. You entertain the federales and the press. Boston black tea and crumpets should do."

"Funny, Cooper. I suppose you are Paul Revere. One if by land, two if by air."

Cooper chartered Fairplay's only plane for hire. Fortunately, it was a tail dragger that could land on the YBarC's rough dirt strip. He knew the landing would attract a hand and he could commandeer his horse for the short ride to the bunkhouse office. He would have the plane stand by to fly him to Norwood's grassy strip.

Two hours later the plane bounced up off the YBarC's rutted dirt strip on its way to the Norwood airstrip with the newspaper file stuffed in Cooper's shirt. As the turbocharged single engine plane flew over the ranch entrance a black government sedan with a slew of radio aerials turned down the ranch road. Cooper figured they had national security search warrants so he had already sent Polecat and the hands out to the North Mesa so they would not defend the bunkhouse. He posted Sue in the office by the open safe door after he pocketed Gary's remaining three bundles of cash and the manila envelope with the Lonnie Sr. article.

Cooper paid the pilot in cash at the Norwood grass strip and hitched a ride into Norwood's one block town center. He commandeered the hardware store's Xerox machine and made ten copies of the key articles. Then he bought ten manila envelopes and headed for the post office. He mailed five, including one each to THE MONTROSE NEWS, THE DENVER POST and ROCKY MOUNTAIN NEWS. Then Cooper hid the original under a reward poster on the Post Office Bulletin Board and walked thru town putting five more in random local mailboxes addressed to the Fairplay Hotel and to himself at the Montrose Best Western. He gave a teenager in a red pickup a ten-dollar bill, which got him a too fast ride back to the ranch with hot-rod unmuffled cutout pipes roaring all the way.

When Cooper walked into the YBarC's bunkhouse office he found Sue picking up the safe's contents, which were scattered on the floor. After they replaced its contents and Gary's cash, he closed the safe and spun the combo lock. Sue told him the G-Men had verbally abused her with sexually charged comments. He called Judy and had her arrange for the pilot to pick him up at first light to fly him back to Fairplay. He sent Sue to the safety of the Airstream until the hands returned from the far reaches of the YBarC for dinner. He told her to pick up the original of the article in Norwood when things cooled down.

Cooper walked into the Fairplay Hotel lobby at 9:00 a.m. where the FBI agents were waiting. Judy was talking to Mr. Wilcox, the reporter from the ROCKY MOUNTAIN NEWS. All eyes turned toward Cooper, looking cool in his Stetson summer straw cowboy hat, bootcut jeans and Lucchese dress boots. The gray-haired G-Man with the pockmarked pasty complexion spoke first. "We want to talk to you alone. Let's go up to our room."

"You got a warrant?" Cooper asked with a grin.

"No."

"Then no go. Lobby is fine with Judy and Mr. Wilcox sitting in," Cooper replied coldly.

"You start cooperating."

"Or what?"

Two Colorado State Police detectives walked into the lobby just when Judy angrily ordered, "Start solving my father's murder or get off the hotel property now."

"These Federals bullying you Colorado citizens?" one of them asked, not amused. "This is a state and county matter. We will solve it."

"Bob," the senior FBI Agent asserted, "this is our case, now."

"Wrong," replied Bob. "This is our case, according to the Attorney General, a close friend of State Senator Harvey Stuart. Let's mosey on outside and talk this over so we're not in earshot of the ROCKY MOUNTAIN NEWS. We like Mr. Wilcox, but he'll print our conversation word for word."

The four officers exited the hotel.

"Our tax dollars at work," Cooper quipped. "Grandfather was right."

"Typical," replied Wilcox. "Attorney General wants to run for governor so he wants the headlines from breaking this case. Pardon my language, ma'am, why are Feds trying to screw you, Cooper?"

"Lonnie Sr. is a patriotic anti-communist and a big time government uranium mining and milling contractor. Peter Simple is the born again Christian and John Bircher who set me up in Delta."

"Then you are in hot water," the balding reporter opined with a frown.

"So I skip Vietnam for the Peace Corps and get set up in Delta. They have me on banana peels," Cooper mused out loud.

"I know you didn't kill your uncle; he was helping you save the YBarC. So, who did, Cooper?"

"All roads lead to Rome and Rome wants the YBarC land and water rights - Lonnie Sr. for his son Lonnie Jr., his front man."

"Well, now," Wilcox countered, "you on the record all the way."

Cooper calmly replied, "All the way."

"OK. Anything else I should know?"

Cooper recapped Joe Bear Spirit's finds after the fire that killed Liz, the Utah ambush with Adrianna, the rustled mother cows and the poker game at Delta.

Then he added, 'off the record,' as newspaper reporters say, "Jesse Smith, Lonnie Jr.'s Telluride attorney, basically admitted over the phone he had the ranch house torched."

Wilcox departed to drive to Denver to work the story. Quiet returned to the lobby; darkness enveloped South Park as it had for millions of years. Judy disappeared into the kitchen to arrange dinner for herself and Cooper in the now closed dining room.

Just as Cooper started dessert, the desk clerk entered the dining room. "A Miss Adrianna, sir."

"Cooper, you have to help," her stressed voice crackled in the phone.

"The pricks from the FBI threaten you?"

"No, it's about Joe Bear Spirit. He didn't return to bartend last night. No one can find him. He disappeared after a water meeting in Cortez."

"Shit. I'll be in Cortez by noon tomorrow. Meet me at the cafe on Main Street."

"Please pick me up in Telluride; Joe has my Wagoneer."

"Okay, try to relax. Joe is tough and his magic can probably make a Wagoneer disappear, too."

"Don't joke. You know they're after him because of you."

"Time out! He's trying to cut off water to half the 'powers to be' and towns in south-western Colorado. See you at ten o'clock sharp." Cooper hung up and was surprised to find Judy listening behind him.

"She get questioned?" Judy inquired.

"No, Joe Bear Spirit's gone missing," Cooper, replied now depressed.

"Cooper," Judy almost whispered.

"Let's hope it's one of his Ute magic tricks."

As Cooper finished dessert, Jumbo Roberts, captain and chief criminal investigator of the Colorado State Highway Patrol, and Bob, a sergeant, pulled up a chair. Judy excused herself to get them dessert and coffee from the kitchen.

Jumbo began, "Cooper, I got rid of the Feds for now. Told them I would make you my material witness if they didn't hightail it for Denver."

Cooper nodded thanks but said nothing.

Jumbo continued, "A person is trying awfully hard to bankrupt your ranch and kill you. I read the Utah State Police file, the NTSB file, the arson report on the YBarC headquarters fire and the State Brand Inspector's report on the rustled cattle on the way down here."

"Have you reviewed the inquest reports about the death of my mother?"

"Bob here briefed me. He's an arson expert. County boys say accidental, but he thinks not."

"That leaves my indictment in Delta," Cooper fished.

Jumbo reflected and answered Cooper with a smile,

"Oldest trick in the west is to kill an enemy in a friendly poker game. Shift the venue at the last minute. Many a mining claim and ranch water hole changed hands that way."

Cooper tested the two hundred-forty pound, 6'2", blue-eyed state patrolman again.

"I was in the Peace Corps, Captain; some folks don't like that."

"A lot of folks don't," he said coolly and dodged. "I don't give a shit about your opinion on the war. My only boy died there so there ain't gonna be another Jumbo Roberts wearing a badge in Colorado and toting a peacemaker."

"Sorry."

"Don't need your pity, son. He made his decision. You made yours. Why we got a constitution and laws. I am sworn to enforce them for everyone."

Judy arrived with a sterling silver dessert tray and a pot of fresh coffee.

"Who do you think is behind all this Cooper?" Jumbo asked flatly.

"Lonnie Sr., Lonnie Jr. and their attorney Jesse Smith are behind everything but the poker game. Sam Jr., the YBarC's banker, is their pawn. They want the YBarC. The Simple family set me up in Delta and had access to the plane. That's personal, probably."

"Why the Simples? What's the YBarC connection?" Jumbo probed while the sergeant took notes.

"My great-grandfather hired the gunslinger Blue Bob Thompson to run a Catholic sheepherder and his family off Wilson Mesa near Telluride. They homesteaded on YBarC open summer range. Blue Bob got wild drunk and gunned him and a deputy sheriff down, raped his wife in front of her children. The Simples bought the homestead later for a dairy farm. Then my grandfather bought the homestead from the Simple family for fifty cents an acre and back taxes in the depression."

"Well, Cooper, you just closed two open historical murder cases at the State Capital." There was shock in his voice as the sergeant fidgeted nervously and then excused himself to the men's room.

Jumbo looked Cooper straight in the eye, "The Colorado criminal historians who have tried to solve this puzzle for decades have been in denial that Mormon ranchers would gun down a Catholic sheepherder and a county deputy to protect open grazing."

"I burned the homestead cabin when the facts surfaced," Cooper replied.

"Well, Cooper, your brand's a tough outfit. I reckon you have two choices. Sell the YBarC and I will investigate and solve your mother and uncle's deaths if I can pick up the cold trails."

"And the other?" Cooper asked, not liking the first one.

"Hold your poker hand, meaning the ranch, and I do the same while trying to keep you out of prison and alive." Jumbo looked at Cooper as if he were an eight-point bull elk in hunting season.

"I will throw in with you on number two," Cooper replied.

"Figured. We brought one of them Army surplus bullet proof vests down for you."

Jumbo laughed and Judy became translucent white.

Jumbo continued, "Your Uncle and Judy's father oversaw the highway patrol budget in the State Senate for ten years. You will not have any trouble with my men. Harvey raised us up to a living wage with good medical and fair pensions. Bob returned to the table. Now, please excuse us. We have to get over Hoosier Pass to Breckenridge Ski Area to investigate the theft of a snowcat. We'll be in touch." As afterthought Jumbo said, "I cannot protect you if you get involved with your Ute hand in his water war path down south. Water runs way uphill toward money in this state."

After the officers left Judy asked, "You trust him Cooper?"

"As much as any lawman who balances the law with politics at his level," Cooper reflected.

"He's Colorado to the bone."

"That's the conundrum," Cooper answered.

"I don't understand."

"I don't know if Colorado knows what Colorado is anymore."

FORTY-EIGHT

The BIA Surprise Party

C ooper was just north of Cortez driving at a very high speed. Adrianna was riding shot-gun. They had both avoided mentioning Judy or Sue.

"Joe last called from a pay phone at the Cortez Best Western after a meeting chaired by the attorney for various water right's holders. He said everyone at the meeting was angry at him, including ranchers, farmers, real estate developers, local political types, white water guides, and even the Mesa Verde National Park manager. The Bureau of Indian Affairs, or the BIA as we call it in these parts, was monitoring the meeting."

"Besides stealing water, the Utes must be burning ranch houses and kidnapping white women if everyone is so angry at them again," Cooper deadpanned.

"No jokes, just find him."

"Did he say where he was going next?"

"Mexican Hat in Utah."

"That's way off the Ute Mountain reservation. Why there?"

"Meet with the Navajo AIM members to get them to join the Ute Water Coalition."

Cooper let out a low whistle, "Shit he is trying to start an Indian war."

"Maybe."

Cooper pushed the high clearance CJ5 to the max and three hours later they rolled into the outskirts of Mexican Hat. He drove straight into the narrow parking lot of its only motel near where his San Juan River rafting trips had ended. They both noted Adrianna's Wagoneer was parked in front of room twenty next to a shiny black late model four door Ford.

They checked in as Mr. and Mrs. Whitewater, cash in advance for one night. Cooper sensed high-powered binoculars on his back. He fumbled with the key in one hand and put his other hand on Adrianna's butt as they entered the yellow-walled room with its cheap Sears art deco kit furniture. She pushed him away angrily as the door closed. Cooper looked out over the San Juan River through the big picture window.

"Play along, Adrianna, or Joe is another dead Redman. They are watching us. A late model BIA pickup followed us to the motel entrance from the outskirts of town. No Navajos here just 'bad Injun agents', like Joe says. Stay visible in the window. I'll pick you up when I have Joe."

Cooper slipped out of the picture window's view line and then out the door ducking behind the Jeep. The wall of dry hundred degree desert heat hit him. In one motion, he grabbed his Winchester rifle from the Jeep's open back compartment and ran in a zigzag pattern. Cooper barreled into room twenty's door shoulder first and knocked it off its hinges. He levered a live bullet into the short barrel Winchester as he burst into the room facing three blue-jeaned, white shirted men with brown leather shoulder holsters.

"Don't move," Cooper ordered. Joe rose from a cheap pine chair.

"Good to see you, Lone Ranger." Joe gathered pistols from shoulder holsters and then the walkie-talkie on the coffee table.

"That's federal property. You can't take it," an overweight agent blurted.

"Party's over boys. We like warrants, court orders, even the right to an attorney and all the other constitutional formalities," Cooper lectured sternly.

The walkie-talkie squawked in Joe's left hand, "The white male is missing from room four."

"We're going to nail you, boys," a Fed shouted.

"Bring the loot. Get 'Ms. Bistro' in room four. We are out of here," Cooper winked.

Cooper shot out the front tires of the black sedan. Joe pulled Adrianna out of room four and locked the BIA guns, walkie-talkies and car key in it. They climbed into the Jeep and raced out of the parking lot toward Bluff, Utah.

"Good thing we paid cash in advance," Cooper joked.

"How'd you find me?" Joe quizzed.

"Adrianna informed me you were meeting the Navajo Nation Council's Waterkeepers here. Only one motel," Cooper replied.

"There must be a Navajo American Indian Movement informer working for the BIA. They never showed. The war between the Utes and Navajos continues," Joe said sadly.

A quarter mile east of Bluff, Cooper slowed and turned through an open rusting red gate onto an unmarked desert dirt road.

"They will call the FBI and cover the state highway through Blanding and Montecito so we are cutting through the Anasazi back country to the southern La Sal Mountain flank and then through Disappointment Valley to the YBarC. Enjoy the view but it will be bumpy and hot. We'll eat Adrianna's picnic lunch in an Anasazi cliff dwelling."

The hot afternoon sun scorched the bone-dry red sandstone country as they 4-wheeled through the sculpted cliffs the Anasazi had once called home.

Cooper stashed the Jeep in the mouth of a shallow arroyo for a midafternoon lunch in a ruin with rock art. Then he followed Cottonwood Creek to the edge of the cedar trees at Blanding, Utah. It was a dusty trip as they drove rutted Jeep roads across the forested eastern flank of the Blue Mountains to Monticello, Utah, where they crossed to the Lisbon Valley

Road through Summit Point. This route avoided the highway and the Ute Reservation at Blanding. Cooper and Joe alternated at the wheel, their eyes at the edge of the headlights in the cool night air. At dawn Joe dropped Cooper off about a half mile from the ranch's main gate so he could approach the bunkhouse from the west pasture with the Winchester rifle. Cooper feared a BIA ambush. Joe drove to Telluride with Adrianna.

Cooper field-glassed the bunkhouse and saw no sign of activity except Sue hanging out sheets and towels on the clothesline.

He walked up to her Indian style and she jumped when he said, "Hello, the Fed's been here."

"Quiet with your gang gone. Trouble seems to follow you when the Spanish witch is around. Where's Joe?"

"Just recaptured him from the BIA. He's driving to Telluride to drop off Adrianna. The BIA has her Wagoneer in Mexican Hat."

"The gold witch is bad medicine for Joe. I want him back in my Teepee."

Cooper and Sue left on horseback midmorning trailing two packhorses. The low east sun backlit the green cottonwoods as they headed up into the high country. It was going to be another dark blue-sky day with 75 degree temperatures. They rode into the shimmering Aspen groves and through grassy wild flower meadows. They crisscrossed a rushing clear cold mountain stream and then rode into virgin Spruce and Pine. Three hours later they arrived at line shack three. While Sue unloaded the supplies, Cooper met with Polecat on its steps.

"The rebuilt fences cut calf loss by eighty percent. Ninety percent of the mother cows will send calves to market come fall," Polecat asserted. But before Cooper could thank him he said ruefully, "Been with this outfit fifty years after another winter. Forty-nine good ones but this one's getting squirrelly."

"Pay not late again?" Cooper asked.

"Not that. Judy running the ranch books best in years. Pay on time, horses shod, Sue keeping us well supplied. No injured summer hands except a barbwire cut or two so far. Only had to put one horse down that broke a leg in a prairie dog hole a week ago."

"Then what's bothering you Polecat?"

"You," he said coldly.

"That so?" Cooper said defensively. "Guess I am not working hard enough to pay off the debt you and Liz ran up."

"Enough of that Cooper. I carried out her orders to keep this operation running 'til you were back and took over."

"You did that," Cooper said flatly.

"Word in Norwood and Durango you involved with your Ute buddy in this water rights thing. Even promised them some of your granddaddy's hard won Delores river rights to the Injuns. Plus, people say you smeared the Simple family in the Denver papers. You know how to attract lightning, son, like a lone pine on a mesa."

"And you don't want to get struck riding next to me."

"That's about it."

"Don't blame you. I've been thinking about how to avoid being a lightning rod and still keep the YBarC. Maybe marry and stay on the range and out of Telluride. You finish the fall roundup and if you still want out then you can retire with your fifty-year pension. Granddaddy paid it in full to the U.S. Trust Company before he died. It's waiting for you the day you ride off the YBarC."

"That's fair, Cooper. The Stuarts always been fair. I'll think it over some. Got to get back out on the range."

After lunch on the line shack porch, Cooper and Sue spent a breezy warm blue-sky afternoon checking on part of the herd, which was grazing in the Aspens near line shack one. Then they rode back to the bunkhouse with a stop to skinny dip in a windmill-powered stock tank to cool off.

An hour before sunset a day later, Cooper and Sue finished loading four of the YBarC's horses into a long trailer with three Winchesters in the tack box. Cooper planned to take Brady and Tom Deskins' Eco Warrior friend, George, up to Blue Lake by horseback after a secret meeting to discuss water rights at the Alta Lake abandoned mine bunkhouse. He had called Joe Bear Spirit to meet him as backup. Cooper was in full outfitter garb which included a red bandana around his neck, one of his grandfather's battered Stetson hats, a blue plaid cotton shirt, bootcut jeans and thick leather ranch riding boots. He figured the rig and the outfit would get him past the Feds if they still wanted to play. Sue thought the entire disguise was foolish.

At sundown, as the high thin clouds turned bright orange and red over the La Sals, Cooper pulled out of the ranch gate. A few minutes later he was in low gear as the old pickup groaned against the weight of the four-horse trailer as it descended the Norwood Hill toward Placerville. The highway with its steep grade never stopped trying to peel off the unstable canyon cliff as it descended to the San Miguel River. There were no guardrails and several pickups with horse trailers had jackknifed on the descent and one rolled into the river a thousand feet below. Cooper reached the bridge at the bottom of the mile long steep grade with the pickup's brakes white hot. He pulled over to let them cool down and drank a shot of bourbon from his flask.

Twenty minutes later he passed the church camp on the river, its cabin lights lit up with kerosene lanterns. Ten minutes later he rolled into Placerville but decided not to stop at the store for a cold soda because he might be recognized. Cooper headed up the San Miguel River canyon toward Society Turn three miles west of Telluride where he would turn toward the Alta Lakes mine road. As he slowed at Sawpit, a flashing red light pulled out of the store's parking lot and he carefully slowed to a stop.

A Colorado state trooper approached, "You got a taillight out on the right side the horse trailer. Just a reminder."

"Thanks, officer. Got a spare in the trailer." The officer then handed Cooper a manila envelope and walked away without a word.

Cooper realized Sue was dead right on the disguise and opened the sealed envelope.

The note was from Jumbo Roberts. "No news on the NTSB-FBI criminal investigation yet but the Denver Simple has gone missing. Remember you are in grave danger if you get involved in the Indian water rights thing. Get the Ute off your ranch. Delta Simple asked for State Police help on your drug indictment. I refused the request. Stay away from Adrianna, your Telluride restaurant owner friend. Feds have a bead on her because she is helping the Ute Indian. The Santa Fe FBI office telexed us that she was involved in the Tierra Amarilla, New Mexico armed courthouse takeover for Spanish land rights in 1967 where a jailor was wounded. She is a member of the Northern New Mexico 'land or death' movement. Her case is still open. Jumbo."

"Whew," Cooper said to himself as he burned the note.

Cooper pulled onto the steep gravel road the Forest Service maintained to the Alta Lake mine's abandoned bunkhouse. It had withstood years of heavy snow. As the truck whined up the steep grade with the horses rocking the trailer, Cooper tried to force Sue's almost oracle advice out of his mind - "End the odysseys with the Utes, Adrianna, and Brady's Eco Warrior friends, then ranch the YBarC. Marry Judy and never set foot in Telluride again."

Cooper's pickup whined into the gray rock tailing piles that dotted the ruins of the abandoned mining camp. Cooper's headlights flashed on a row of decaying miners' houses with peeling yellow paint, tattered screens, and broken windows stood like silent ghosts to better times. At the end of the row of houses, across from the avalanche battered mill, stood the two-story miner's dorm. Cooper parked and circled the building with a Winchester 30-30, but detected no one on the first floor. He walked up the covered outdoor staircase to the second floor bunk area and opened the door with his rifle leveled.

"Cooper, you are dead," Joe Bear Spirit whispered over the wind and beamed his flash-light down at Cooper.

Cooper spun 360 degrees but saw no one until he looked up into the exposed wooden rafters. There was Joe sitting in deerskin moccasin feet with a Winchester on the wide center beam.

"Good one," Cooper countered realizing Joe had just given him a no cost lesson. "Who is here?"

"George and Adrianna. She is representing the 'Give me land or give me death' Spanish settlers' claims, the Tierra o Muerto movement. But they live on old Ute lands. The Spanish settlers hated the Utes who kidnapped their women and children into slavery. Conversely, the Spanish bought Ute slaves from the Navajos at the Taos Indian Slave market."

Cooper thought this was a strange historical alliance, "Where are they?"

"Third room on the left," directed Joe. "But make this meeting fast. My father called from the res. The FBI was at his house looking for me."

Cooper walked into the dusty wood-paneled darkened bunkroom on his left, lit only by a candle lantern.

A voice said, "If I may introduce myself, I'm George. Good to meet you, Cooper. Better for Brady not to be seen with me around Telluride. Someone might connect the dots. Let's start the powwow."

Cooper squinted to see Adrianna sitting on a bunk with only mattress springs. Cooper nodded as his eyes adjusted to the dark room. She said nothing.

George continued, "Tom Deskins sent me to outline the plan. The Eco Warriors and allied groups will help Joe try to get back one hundred percent of the water on the Animas, Piedra and Florida Rivers for the Utes. The pioneer Spanish families get all the Chama River water rights back. The Utes must agree not to build the Animas River diversion dam in Durango. Both groups release their existing water rights back to the towns along the river at prevailing market rates."

Cooper, hoping he could leave, asked, "So why am I here?"

"The Utes get the YBarC water rights on the Delores. The YBarC keeps its San Miguel River water rights with the condition of keeping it undammed, plus its Lone Cone Ditch shares. The Eco Warrior's donors give you $600,000 for the Dolores River water rights, which is what you owe the bank. Everyone wins."

"Good plan. The YBarC will ante up but what if the governments kill the deal? The YBarC needs a $600,000 check drop dead at the bank by October, according to our attorney."

"War council then for the Utes?" George questioned.

"Who leads the negotiations?" asked Cooper.

"Joe Bear Spirit," George confirmed.

"They could bury Joe Bear Spirit and maybe Miss World Spain with him," asserted Cooper.

"That's not funny, Cooper," Adrianna said tersely.

"Then we will supply Idaho's only Indian friendly water attorney to front Joe. His name is Lance. He is a former World Cup kayak star and he wants to run for his father's Utah U.S. Senate seat someday. He is quietly trading the Eco Warriors free legal work for future campaign help. The Telluride gang can't reach him," asserted George.

Before Cooper could respond Joe said from overhead,

"That works for me. I can use legal help. How will we communicate?"

"No one calls me. Use Lance for everything. I will have him call Joe in a week," replied George.

"Let's get out of here now. The Ute spirits tell me it is time to ride," Joe Bear Spirit said suddenly and the meeting adjourned abruptly.

In minutes Cooper had everyone on the saddled quarter horses. The Jeep and the pick-up truck were stashed off the road in a stand of tall pines.

"Stay head to tail behind me on the trail and no flashlights. Blue Lake is a hard ride in the dark, about 13,000 feet above tree line. No one can trail us tonight without good horses and a Navajo tracker."

Cooper rode his favorite Paint for the occasion because he trusted the Indian ponies sure footing. Joe rode drag for the dangerous night ride to their campsite by Blue Lake to throw any pursuers off their trail.

FORTY-NINE
The La Sals

A t dusk the next day, Sue was rubbing down the horses in the headquarters corral with Joe. Cooper was in the bunkhouse office returning a call to Gary at the Red Rock Inn and Golf Club in Phoenix.

"Just a moment, sir," an operator chirped.

"Cooper, let's forgive and forget," Gary, very high, chimed as Cooper heard splashing in the background.

"You have my $50,000?" Cooper asked coldly.

"Yes and no," Gary replied coyly.

"Let's hear about the 'yes.'"

"I'm with Joey and Tony. They miss Sue so they are willing to loan me $50,000 to pay you off and we get the girlie."

"Keep talking," Cooper replied as his mind raced through options to save Sue.

"Joey wants to visit Telluride in a couple days, maybe park some money in real estate. We will fly up in his twin. Wants to ski even though it's July."

"Perfect," Cooper lied to set his plan in motion. "Sue is in the La Sal Mountains with one of my hands and a hundred pairs of YBarC cattle on leased summer high mountain pasture. There is good July heli skiing nearby. Joe Bear Spirit will rent the helicopter at the Montrose airport. You fly in there in two days at 8 a.m. We all fly over to the La Sals, make some runs, then I trade you Sue for fifty thousand big ones."

"Deal, that'll work my boy. See, you are finally tired of Sue. She's high maintenance. You want us to fly you out one of these poolside babes with balloons for breasts?"

"The heli's already crowded. Maybe next time."

"Okay, see you Friday morning in Montrose. But no dollars 'til we get Sue. Joey will be packing, so no Sundance Kid stuff." The phone went dead.

Cooper called Joe into the bunkhouse office, "Call Montrose airport and rent the helicopter for Friday. We are going heli skiing with Gary and Joey. We'll work on a war plan and a Ute curse to save Sue from Joey while she stays here at the ranch. Let's get some dinner, first."

Cooper continued his thought as Joe blinked, "I hope you can fly upside down and empty the change out of their ski jacket pockets on the way to the north face of the La Sals. It will make heli skiing safer."

"I'll do that for Sue," Joe Bear Spirit replied.

The Friday morning sky was bright blue as the sun warmed the tarmac and the rusting Quonset hut that housed Montrose's only helicopter. It was mostly used for geological or pipeline work by the west slope oil and gas companies. Its fuel truck had already left for La Sal Junction where it would refuel the helicopter for the trip home. Cooper and Joe's skis leaned up against the side of the hut glinting in the low morning east sun. Joe was helping the charter company pilot roll the Bell helicopter out onto a red circle on the tarmac. Cooper had kept Adrianna and Sue completely out of the loop. Adrianna and one of her waiters were in Mexican Hat picking up her Wagoneer. Cooper had sent Sue to the safety of line shack three to work with Polecat and a hand. Judy was in Pendleton, Oregon with a college barrel racing teammate enjoying a much-needed vacation at the annual rodeo.

Cooper had paid the pilot $1,500 cash, plus given him an insurance certificate that allowed Joe to fly as a ranch employee. After fueling the helicopter the owner-pilot checked Joe out at the controls. Then the owner-pilot jumped into his yellow 427 Chevy convertible with dual cutout pipes and roared out of the Montrose airport to go water skiing. Cooper and Joe went to work on the back right hand seat behind the pilot where Joey would be sitting. They loosened the bolts that held the safety harness in place. A half hour into flying, the helicopter's vibration would take care of the rest. Then they removed the rear doors, summer heli skiing style, for easy exits and strapped their skis to the metal basket attached to the helicopter's skids. Just as they finished, a twin turbo engine plane landed on the main runway and taxied up to the helicopter's apron and cut its engines.

The charter pilot remained on board as Gary and Joey climbed out of the plane onto its wing, pulling skis and boot bags from the luggage compartment. Then they stepped onto the tarmac and slowly approached Cooper while scanning the area. Joey wore a one-piece black ski jump suit unzipped to the waist, which revealed a bare hairy chest. There was a bulge under his left shoulder. Cooper wished he had Jumbo's bulletproof vest under his blue nylon spring parka. Gary approached Cooper with a black Mexican leather briefcase in his left hand. Cooper saw that Joey a "wiseguy" in Phoenix's rumored mafia had arrived.

Gary opened the conversation, "Hello boys, you are right on time for a Friday payday."

"Heli ski day," Cooper corrected.

"Right on, Coop," replied Joey in a Jersey City accent. His pinkie diamond ring glinted in the low sun.

"Joey, I presume." Cooper barely resisted an urge to kick him in the balls and smash his pocked marked jaw into the tarmac. "Nice ring."

"You Bear Spirit the Indian heli pilot?" Joey asked, eyeing him carefully.

"Joe Bear Spirit helicopter pilot ready for take off." Joe mumbled in an affected Ute English accent.

"These guys look okay," Joey said to Gary, his face businesslike as his bull neck bulged with each staccato sentence, "but, pat them down just in case. No wire mic and no guns."

"Inside the hangar, please. Too many eyes on the tarmac with the helicopter fueled for a summer ski trip," Cooper ordered.

"Okay, but if you are wired or packing, we walk," Gary asserted.

"Any other special instructions? It's hard to hear up there with the doors off for skiing?"

"Yeah, Cooper, you stay and walk out with the money after we get Sue girlie. You are done fucking my girl for riding lessons. Injun Joe flies us back here," snapped Joey, while Gary patted them down.

"I'll ride Sue's horse out," corrected Cooper.

Joey looked at the helicopter. "This no door thing."

"Standard for summer heli skiing," Gary assured him.

Joey hesitated, not wanting to look stupid. "Okay then. I want it to look routine in case the Feds or local cops are watching. Let's get out of here. My one piece is getting hot."

"Not 'til I see the money," Cooper replied.

Without a word Gary placed the briefcase on the army green metal desk in the hangar and popped it open. The money was all there with a couple vials of liquid next to it.

"Good to fly," said Cooper keeping his voice calm. Cooper strapped their skis to the basket and stored their boots in the helicopter knowing it was all a charade. He had figured out their plan. Joey planned to shoot him in the head once they had Sue. There was morphine with the money to knock her out for the flight back to Phoenix. Joe Bear Spirit would fly them back to Montrose with a gun to his head. Then Joe Bear Spirit would end up in a desert grave in Goldwater land. The Phoenix pilot was on the mob payroll for big charter flight dollars for his silence. Cooper heard Joey tell the pilot to be fueled and cleared for take off in four hours. Joey was the last to board sitting behind Joe so he could watch Cooper. They lifted off for the hour flight to the La Sal Mountains.

Cooper silently wondered if it would be his last flight ever. He knew the margin for error was super thin but he was confident in his planning. Only he and Joe knew that the helicopter's owner-pilot had left his Army pistol ducked taped under the passenger's control panel dashboard in case they encountered a bear in the La Sals. As the copter flew west over the Uncompahgre National Forest, Cooper rehearsed scenarios in his head. They were all very dangerous.

The late spring snow had produced a deep July snow pack. As they flew over the north flank of the La Sal mountain range Cooper felt a tap on his shoulder. He turned his head to see Joey leaning forward straining his harness. Cooper silently prayed it did not come loose prematurely. Joe Bear Spirit flew calmly up the bench of Mt. Peale toward the top of the snowfield at twelve thousand feet.

Joey yelled menacingly in Cooper's ear, "I want to see my whore now. Fuck this ski stuff. This is fucking close enough to the white-faced peaks. Fly directly to Sue." Joey's face was framed in suspicion.

Joe Bear Spirit averted his calm eyes to Cooper, who gave him the thumbs down signal for immediate action, which he could not hide from the mobster.

Joey yelled, "You are a dead fuck, Cooper."

Joe Bear Spirit banked the helicopter hard left into a climbing hammerhead roll at forty-five degrees at twelve thousand feet. The G force pinned Gary and Joey to their seat backs. Joey pulled his gun from his shoulder holster but it went sideways in Cooper's peripheral vision as the gun retorted at almost point blank range. The safety harness bolts held as Joey strained to regain his balance and fire again. The bullet grazed Cooper's headset's right ear-piece, shattering it as it pierced the helicopter's thick windshield. Gary struggled to hold on to the briefcase. Joe Bear Spirit pulled the helicopter from a sure death spiral at the top of the stunt spin hammerhead maneuver as it stalled and he rolled it back to the right forty-five degrees as it fell tail first toward the bench of the mountain.

Joey wildly tried to aim the pistol at Cooper to fire a coup de grace shot. Finally, the bolts holding his safety belt vibrated loose and Joey, almost in slow motion, leering at Cooper for a long moment, fell out of the open helicopter passenger door firing wildly into the dark blue high altitude western sky. His terrifying scream lasted for seconds as he plunged to his death two thousand feet below into a snowy wilderness cliff face. His shattered body would vanish into the stomachs of the mountain's predators and scavenger birds. His empty pistol would rust in silence.

Joe righted the helicopter and stopped its backwards slide in the thin air with a series of precise maneuvers in the variable cross winds of the mountain's steep side. After the stomach turning half-minute the ship returned to normal flight mode, moving away from the mountain. Cooper pulled the pistol from under the dashboard and pointed it at a white faced speechless Gary. Urine spotted his jeans, and his white knuckles gripped the briefcase.

Joe said over the radio, "Two thousand for the windshield, Cooper, and two hundred for the headset. FAA approved gear. You cannot get them in an auto store."

"Worth every penny," declared Cooper still tense from the close range gunshot miss. "Briefcase Gary, please."

Cooper pointed the gun at Gary's open door. Gary got the message and handed it to Cooper, who stored it under the dash in a mesh compartment with the flight maps and a first aid kit. Joe started a slow turn back over the bench of the mountain.

"The boys in Phoenix are gonna fuck you up real bad for this, Cooper. Sue is not worth dying for, Cowboy," Gary asserted in a shaky voice as Joe continued to slow the helicopter as it flew down the east side of the mountain on an air route toward the fuel truck.

"We are going to have a talk, Gary. Unfasten your seat belt and climb out into the ski basket on the skid. Hang on to the door frame tightly unless you want to make this a no return flight," Cooper shouted over the wind and engine as he unbelted and turned to face Gary.

The pistol was pointed dead into Gary's wide-open eyes. Gary, terrified unfastened his harness and climbed carefully out the open door into the basket holding the doorframe with both hands.

"Please, Cooper, don't dump me."

"No intention, Gary. Joe's going to fly real slow and smooth so we can talk on the way to the fuel truck. It's confession time. Tell all to the priest and you get absolution," Cooper mocked.

"Condo project was a scam for Joey. Twenty per cent to him off the top...fuck the suckers and the rest to pay my coke tab," Gary's hair blew flat backwards across his head.

"Good one on me. Sort of a test market project for the mob in a ski town," Cooper laughed.

"Kind of like that. My hands are cramping, Cooper."

"Tell me something I don't know and you can come back inside and fly home with the charter pilot. Otherwise you use up your last life."

"I'm so sorry, Cooper," Gary whimpered, bursting into tears as Joe came around into the sun on the south side of the La Sals and headed due west toward the fuel truck with the fuel gauge reading almost empty.

"Peter Simple made me set you up after he caught me with two kilos of Joey's coke at the Delta airstrip."

Cooper froze, the info hitting him like a sledgehammer. He had Delta's secret witness on the helicopter skids.

He said over the headset to Joe, "Gary's the DA's secret witness in the Delta arrest. Pete turned him after a drug bust."

Joe concentrated as he flew the helicopter over a dangerous ten thousand foot ridgeline on a direct route to La Sal Junction, the fuel tank reading empty. The helicopter strained to hold altitude in the midday sun.

Cooper yelled, "You're the secret witness who put the kilo of coke in my Jeep's gas tank?"

"Yes, please let me back in the helicopter, Cooper. My hands are numb."

"Gary, you are truly a bad man. Absolution is real tough but you have earned a ride home. Max can deal with you," Cooper yelled as Gary stopped crying and his right hand reached inside the helicopter searching for something to grip. His hand was out of Cooper's reach.

Suddenly the helicopter jumped five hundred feet straight into the sky as Joe radioed, "Hit...big south side Ventura...huge thermal. Hang on! It may tear our rotor off!"

At the apex of the hot column of invisible air rising off the crumbling exposed rocky southern face of Mt. Peale, the ship plunged a heart stopping thousand feet until the rotor found cooler thicker air. Cooper watched, pinned to his seat by the G forces, as Gary's hands lost their grip on the doorframe and he fell backward onto the basket and then bounced into thin air. Gary's body fell a thousand feet and rag dolled across a scree covered slope. It set off a scree avalanche and his body was covered in seconds as the helicopter engine missed. A two hundred foot plume of brown dust rose from the mountainside.

"Ute curse," intoned Joe without emotion as they sped toward the refueling tanker truck ten air miles away, the engine coughing the last half mile.

While the helicopter was being refueled, Cooper and Joe explained to the refueling truck driver that the gun the pilot had loaned them went off when Cooper pulled the military issue automatic weapon out to scare a bear away from the ski landing zone. Cooper reiterated he and his insurance company would pay to replace the windshield.

While eating a greasy cheeseburger and fries provided by the refueling truck driver Cooper said, "I might as well take a first descent ski run in case we need an alibi. We have the bird all day."

"You're nuts, Cooper. The afternoon snow could slide. It's sun baked by now. We are base bound. You have a plan if they send anyone else after Sue?"

"They won't. But we'll keep Sue safely on the ranch for the rest of the year, maybe longer. Judy is meeting me at the Best Western tonight in Montrose on her way back from Oregon."

"How do we deal with the Phoenix pilot?"

"Leave the cover story to me. As soon as we land go to my pickup at the side door of the hanger. Pull the rifle and cover me from the hanger. If he pulls a weapon, shoot. I doubt that he's mob - probably cash only, no flight plan pilot for hire. Probably flies coke for them, too. He won't want to attract the local law."

"Roger, Cooper, let's go home. The west has two less bad guys."

"So it does. But it always keeps attracting more black hats. It's the curse of this beautiful country where we should be able to live in peace under the big blue-sky."

The charter pilot had the twin parked on the apron, his props spinning for a quick take off. Once the helicopter blades rotated to a stop, Joe jumped out and headed for the Jeep. Cooper climbed down and made a zero with his thumb and forefinger and signaled the pilot to take off. The pilot stared down at Cooper from a hundred feet away and feathered his engines.

He climbed out on to the wing and yelled, "Where are my passengers? I have four listed for the return."

"Gary and Joey had us drop them with the girl at the Moab airstrip. They're all driving back to Phoenix together in a rental car. The boys wanted some R&R with her," Cooper lied and deliberately omitted Sue's name.

Cooper saw the pilot's eyes find the bullet hole in the helicopter's windshield.

"Shit," Cooper gasped, realizing Joe should have landed it away from the planes line of sight. The pilot's arm went back into the plane as Cooper yelled, "There is a 30-30 aimed straight at your head. Climb back into the twin and takeoff."

"This isn't, 'Nam," he shouted back.

"Well it kind of is. Local DA doesn't like drug pilots." Cooper tossed two pairs of skis, boots and poles onto the apron and then walked backward to the hanger. He could see Joe's site on the pilot's forehead from the shadow of the hanger.

The pilot pulled an empty hand out of the plane palm up and Cooper smiled to himself. He jumped off the wing and loaded the ski gear into the empty twin. He turned and gave Cooper the finger then climbed into the plane. Two minutes later he taxied to the runway.

Cooper looked at Joe and quipped to break the tension,

"Body count two for the mob and zero for the cowboys and Indians. Was hoping he would leave the skis for the free box in Telluride. Make some ski bums happy."

Joe lowered the rifle when the plane was airborne.

"Where's our next skirmish line?"

"You're on R&R. Take five hundred out of the briefcase for the insurance deductible and leave it for the heli company with a note and an extra hundred apologizing for my Peace Corp military pistol incompetence. Take a thousand for the Ute water fund, that's your pilot fee for the day and bring me the briefcase. After we push the ship back in the hangar drop me off at the Best Western. You take the pickup back to the ranch tonight and sleep with one eye open. We'll break the news to Sue tomorrow at dinner when she gets back from line camp three. I suspect Max will call soon with a Delta case dismissed message. The secret witness is sequestered, as they say."

"Roger that, Cooper. Time to stop being an eagle and return to the Bear Spirit world. There is too much death and destruction around these whirlybirds," Joe grimaced.

Cooper did not reply. Cooper's thoughts about Judy in the sack at the Best Western already danced in his head. They started to replace his visions of death and near death above the high snowfields of the La Sal Mountains.

FIFTY

Too Beautiful to Lose

C ooper walked down Colorado Avenue after breakfast at the Iron Ladle and refocused his thoughts on the YBarC. On the way to pick up his Jeep at the Bistro he noticed a new hand painted wooden sign with a miniskirt for a logo over a storefront shop that read Mountain Girl Things. Cooper wanted to give Sue a freedom present when he broke the news about Gary and Joey. Also, Judy's birthday was in August and Norwood was short on shopping. Cooper walked into the store's open door and was greeted by a blue-eyed middle-aged athletic blonde.

"Got anything for cowgirls?"

"Underwear or outerwear," she gave a wry smile.

"Outerwear," blushed Cooper.

"Bet you are better with underwear, Cowboy. Just got a shipment of Paris bras and panties. Sure beats the stuff in Montrose and Grand Junction but over there are some classic shirts from Rockmount Ranch Wear in Denver," she teased again.

"Please pick out two women's Rockmount cowgirl shirts."

"Need sizes," she replied a little disappointed.

"Five-two, perfect thirty-six, 120-pound blonde and a five-six, 34-long-legged ex-barrel racer black headed beauty."

She walked over and picked out two classic cowgirl cotton hand embroidered shirts and brought them over to the cash register.

"How much I owe you?"

"Fifty cash and no tax."

Cooper completed the purchase, "Good luck with your store."

He walked out whistling into late morning summer sunshine and almost knocked down a frantic Joe Bear Spirit.

"Fuck, I've been on your trail for five minutes. There's been an accident," Joe said urgently.

"Who? Where?"

"Sue on the creek side of Specie Mesa section of the YBarC. Two hikers saw a horse and a blonde cowgirl go down in a slide over the red rock rim a thousand feet above them. They hiked down to the highway and flagged a passing driver to call for help. Search and rescue called Adrianna who sent me to find you," Joe reported.

"Let's ride. Search and rescue there?"

"They should be at the rim by now."

Cooper and Joe roared out of Telluride in the CJ5 at eighty miles an hour. Forty danger-ous high-speed minutes later they reached the canyon rim with their adrenaline pumping. They looked down in anguish at a 500-foot-long slide zone of dirt, rock, and scrub oak. They saw a team of four San Miguel County Search and Rescue members digging frantically with portable shovels two hundred feet below them in unstable landslide debris. A horse's hoofed lower leg pointed at the big blue-sky in a stomach-wrenching angle out of the dirt and rock rubble. Cooper and Joe knew instantly it was Sue's line horse. Cooper charged past a deputy sheriff who tried to stop him. Joe followed with a rifle in hand to shoot the horse. Cooper had Sue's silk cowgirl shirt stuffed in his heavy denim work shirt. Cooper and Joe carefully worked their way down a 200-foot-length of climbing rope to the rescue site.

"Do you know if this is your hand's horse?" asked a gray bearded giant of a man who was captain of the San Miguel County Volunteer Search and Rescue.

"It's Sue's. Where do we dig?"

"Help complete the arc next to the guy with the blonde beard. We hope she's alive un-der the horse where there may be an air pocket," the rescuer reported.

Cooper nodded, moved to his position and began to dig. Joe started to remove rubble with his hands. Everyone dug silently and carefully, trying to clear the debris from the buried horse without setting off another rockslide, which could bury the rescue team. Tension filled the air when from time to time a menacing rock broke loose and bounced by the rescu-ers' yellow hardhat-protected heads. Gradually the horse head and the outline of its body appeared from a rocky hell. The mare's body was broken but her lungs still heaved. A tan leather saddle appeared with a blood-soaked cowgirl boot still in the stirrup. A long minute later a dusty shattered woman's wrist appeared. The team's EMT carefully crab legged over to Sue's wrist and checked it for a pulse as Cooper held his breathe.

Joe looked on silently. "A weak pulse but a pulse. Get her uncovered fast. She needs blood and oxygen."

Four more search and rescue climbers arrived at the site and in five minutes the team had Sue's broken body uncovered with one leg still pinned under the horse. Her blood streaked tangled blonde-haired head faced uphill in debris. The well-trained YBarC mare had fought successfully to keep her footing and protect Sue all the way down the slide until they both were covered with rocky debris. The horse's head started to move as the EMT began to give a barely conscious Sue mouth-to-mouth resuscitation. A small portable oxygen bottle and mask were being lowered down by rope. She was covered with blood, red sandstone dust and dirt. Her blonde hair was matted; her eyes were closed and bruised black. Cooper, closest to her, cradled her head gently in his hands. Joe and the rescuers began to inch toward her one at a time to free her pinned leg. Another rock broke loose above them and everyone ducked as it tumbled past the rescuers.

"I have to shoot the horse or she may attempt to get on her feet and set off a big slide," Joe said.

"Heads up team. The shot could send loose rock down but Joe's right," Cooper advised.

A shot rang out seconds later and the brave YBarC horse was relived of her misery. The shot caused Sue to blink her eyes wide open as she looked up at Cooper. Sue was audibly breathing.

The EMT waited for the oxygen that was a half-minute away. In a child's voice too weak to hear beyond her lips Sue whispered, "You rescued me again, Cooper. I love you."

"You are free Sue. Gary and Joey are off the earth. I will get you out of here," Cooper said in a low voice smiling to give her strength and courage.

"That's not in the stars. I just waited for you to come."

"Here's your freedom present for your next dance," Cooper whispered, fighting back tears as he pulled out the cowgirl shirt that was stuffed in his jean's waistband and laid it against her hand.

"You're the only one who really cared. Save the west, it's too beautiful to lose," she barely whispered as Cooper waved the oxygen mask away. Sue's eyes closed.

Cooper's eyes filled with tears as Sue's spirit arose into the deep blue Colorado sky, her head in his hands as he kissed her goodbye. The rescue team levered the dead cow horse just enough for Cooper and Joe to pull Sue free. Cooper picked up her broken body in his arms and held it until a mountain gurney could be lowered to start her last ride home to the YBarC headquarters. His tears washed the dust from her beautiful peaceful face.

FIFTY-ONE

Rock Sculpture

The day after Sue's burial in the YBarC cemetery, Joe and Cooper drove south on Highway 191 toward the town of Bluff, Utah south of Blanding. Joe had insisted they go to the desert to cleanse their young spirits of the three ghosts. Bluff was a turn of the century irrigated Mormon settlement on the San Juan River bordering the Navajo reservation. They planned to turn south at the Hatch Trading Post and drive thru Monument Valley to Kayenta, Arizona on the northern Navajo reservation.

Joe drove while Cooper mentally outlined a plan to have Judy alibi his date with Lonnie Jr.'s office safe. Kara and Brady had exchanged the safe's combination at Sue's funeral for three month's rent money. Lonnie Jr. had fired her after she resisted his advances. If he found the original of Bill Daniels' water memo in Lonnie's safe, Cooper planned to turn it over to Jumbo Roberts personally at Colorado State Police headquarters in Denver.

While eating Navajo tacos at an outdoor stand in Bluff, Cooper and Joe met two Flagstaff, Arizona coeds who were hitchhiking to Cortez. They had completed a summer internship at a nearby University of Northern Arizona archaeological site in the Anasazi ruins north of Bluff on Cottonwood Creek. Joe offered them a ride. They threw their aluminum-framed backpacks with desert sleeping bags through the Jeep's rolled up back window and climbed into the rear seat. Their matching blouses were tied off above their tan safari shorts exposing flat brown stomachs. Their straight black hair in pony tails was tucked under straw cowboy hats, which had hatbands with the University of Northern Arizona logo. Cooper flipped on the Jeep's radio and tuned in a FM country music station. The blue-eyed coed named Celia asked Joe, "Are you going to the Valley of the Gods? I've only seen the monuments from the state highway."

"We're climbing a monument to hold a Ute ceremony to purify our spirits," Joe replied.

"You aren't dope dealers meeting a plane on a desert strip?"

"No, a working rancher and a Ute Indian water right's organizer but definitely not young Arizona Presidents Club candidates," Cooper said over the wind.

"Funny. Mind if me and Ali hang out and sightsee."

Joe replied, "Okay, but spirits are spirits and I can't control their power."

Joe downshifted and slipped the Jeep into high four-wheel drive as he turned onto a sandy unmarked road. Gradually they gained on a giant monolith of red sandstone towering above the desert. Its sun drenched flat top was the size of an aircraft carrier. Its steep walls were isolated from nearby monuments by a sea of red sand. A crumbling sandstone Mormon trading post came into view. Joe followed the track to the base of the monument's southern wall. The midafternoon sun baked the red sandstone, throwing off heat waves with fiery mirages.

Joe drove around to the cooler shadowed northeast side and parked by a low cactus patch. He ordered, "We climb here."

Celia and Ali's eyes opened wide.

"Follow me up the secret steps. Don't look down. The hand carved steps and handholds will lift you to the top," Joe instructed.

The coeds scrambled over the Jeeps tailgate and rubbed each other down with suntan oil. They pulled blue bandanas out of their backpacks and tied them around their foreheads, ditching the floppy straw hats. They tightened their hiking boot's laces.

"Follow me," Joe ordered. He led the party to the bottom of the steep sandstone wall, which had an almost invisible trail of cut steps and handholds.

It rose in a zigzag pattern across the monument's shadowed face. He silently led the party up the wall, hands leading feet toward the sky. The pitch of the holds was perfect and the sandstone cool to the touch. In line under Joe's elk hide moccasins was Ali then Celia with Cooper in rough leather cowboy boots in drag position. They slowly snaked up the rock face. Cooper looked up at khaki short clad tanned legs strong from hiking and climbing. At the summit Cooper passed around his leather strapped two-quart canteen he had carried over his shoulder. The sinking southwest sun drenched the monument top in orange light while a soft west wind caressed its smooth surface. A 360 degree view swept the Navajo nation around Kayenta.

Joe pulled an old aspen log drum and a worn hard wood stick from a crevice. He gave the seated group a mushroom sliver from his deerskin neck pouch. The coeds were not strangers to mushrooms. The effect was an immediate blinding red flash as Joe started the drumbeat. Cooper and the coeds levitated onto their feet. Cooper felt detached from his body and danced with the coeds through the first stage of the desert sunset. Suddenly spirits in animal forms began to appear and joined the dancers. The group removed their clothes and danced in the natural world. Cooper passed the canteen around and the coeds doused their chests. The water droplets rolled down the curve of their breasts in rivulets, flowed around their nipples, slowly coursed over their stomachs and disappeared between their smooth skinned orange tinted thighs. The low sunlight backlit their erotic bodies as they danced to Joe's drumming. As sun's last rays bathed the group, the girls suddenly turned into large red tailed hawks and glided in chaotic swooping circles around Cooper and Joe in the cooler twilight air. Their sharp claws narrowly missed Joe and Cooper on their tight passes.

As the final single ray of sunlight disappeared into the blue-black night sky, the silhouetted twin hawks glided over the monument's edge and disappeared.

"What happened?" Cooper quizzed.

"They were spirits," Joe answered as the Ute drumming stopped, "who met us in the dream world."

"So we did not turn two Arizona coeds into red tail hawks?" Cooper confirmed.

"The dream world spirits took human form," Joe explained. "They brought me a message. No more treaties. The Utes must have water or perish."

"Ute War."

"An ultimatum first," Joe responded.

"Then war if no water?"

"Then war," Joe's words echoed off the sandstone monument top. His eyes blazed like hot charcoals.

Cooper and Joe started the long moonlit climb down. Joe refused an exhausted Cooper's request to turn into hawks and fly down. An hour later with raw hands, cramping feet and burning legs, Cooper reached the Jeep. The coed's backpacks had disappeared.

Cooper, tired and achy, quipped, "If you turned the coeds into hawks please turn them back again so they can give me a back rub in a hot tub."

"Time to return to the ranch, Cooper. Judy can give you a cowgirl backrub."

A young beautiful Judy rode Cooper high and hot in the Airstream at high noon on Sunday. Her thick black hair bounced in delight to his strong thrusts. His thumbs and fingers almost touched as he gripped her waist. Her rider's thighs gripped his muscular legs. Judy's strong orgasm accented her fluttering curled eyelashes as it sensually erased Cooper's tension. Judy rolled over while Cooper, breathing hard but smiling, drifted into sleep under her tender watch.

Cooper approached the deserted Ajax Ski Company headquarters at 8 p.m. on the new moon. The beat-up ranch pickup skirted the chain-link gate and slowly drove up to the pine day lodge and adjacent corporate offices. Lonnie Jr.'s darkened second story office window overlooked snow-capped Mount Wilson. Cooper's eyes panned the empty parking lots C then B and finally A for any sign of a security guard. Brady Fox had assured him at Sue's memorial service that there were no security guards in the off-season. A couple of log light poles sprayed yellow beams onto the day lodge's empty picnic tables. Kara had informed Cooper that Lonnie Jr.'s family was attending the last night of the Chamber Music Festival at the Opera House.

Cooper parked beside the headquarters building in Lonnie Jr.'s reserved space. He used a small screwdriver to pick the decorative ironwork lock. He let himself into the entrance hallway. His high-powered flashlight found the polished pine plank steps to Lonnie Jr.'s office at the end of the hallway lined with ski posters. A German Shepherd dog the size of a two-man pup tent bounded down the steps and viciously bared its yellow stained teeth. The growling dog lunged and bit him. Cooper's gloved hand pulled a Colt 45 from his hip holster and he knocked the dog out cold. Cooper shined the flashlight onto his jean clad right thigh and found a blood-spattered tear. He sat on the stairwell and tightened a bandana around the wound and quietly waited ten minutes with the flashlight off in case of additional security.

He climbed the steps with a throbbing thigh and used a screwdriver to take Lonnie Jr.'s standard hinges off his dead bolted office door. He pulled the door off its frame and propped it against the reproduction deco-patterned wallpaper. Cooper's flashlight scanned the office's modern furniture and finally rested on a Lange ski boot poster whose blonde Austrian model had her black jump suit unzipped to her nipple line. It was signed, "Denver Ski Show, you are my Telluride good luck ski guy, Tina."

The six-foot high antique bank safe with its gold lettered American Bank of Cortez 1928 logo, sat against the wall across from the picture window that let in the dim yellow light. Cooper spotted the flashlight on the safe's dial, and then rotated the combination 9L-22R-36L-44R-5L. The safe door shifted. He turned the brass levered handle and it swung open, its old dry hinges squeaking. The flashlight beam guided Cooper to a corporate charter binder, black leather bound board meeting notes, a corporate seal, some rubber stamps, two leather bound check books, a rubber banded stack of deeds and leases, $50,000 or so in hundreds, a bottle of rare expensive Mexican tequila, a dozen unopened sheepskin condoms and two large manila envelopes. Cooper opened the top manila envelope with a bulge and emptied its contents on the Oriental rug in front of the safe. Out popped a gold bracelet with "Tina" engraved on it, followed by an 11 x 7 color nude photo of the poster girl. Cooper flipped over the photo and read it out loud.

"Absolutely hot night at the Brown Palace, honey. Hope you choose me as Telluride's ski poster model next season. My phone number is area code 213 ALL REAL. Reaches me in Malibu this summer because Austria's so boring. Come out for a week and I will make it wet and wild. Diamonds are a girl's best friends, Tina!"

Cooper opened the other manila envelope in silence and pulled out the original Bill Daniels' water memo to Lonnie Jr. The final memo had a cover letter from Bill attached to it with a rusty paper clip.

Lonnie Sr.'s signed handwritten note was on the bottom of the cover letter. "L Jr., this water report must never see the light of day. I am having BD x'ed out by contractors who have helped with a uranium lease holdout in the past. Lance has us covered with the environmental pests. Lonnie Sr."

Next Cooper found the final proof he needed that Bill Daniel's memo was stamped, "RECEIVED BY AJAX SKI COMPANY/PRESIDENT'S OFFICE."

Cooper whistled in awe and started to stand up. He felt a small round gun barrel against his right temple.

"Back up slowly in a squat, Cooper, and hold the envelope over your head," a voice calmly commanded.

Momentarily confused, Cooper followed instructions a millisecond from assassination.

"Now pull out the Colt 45 pistol in your hip holster butt first with your thumb and forefinger and drop it behind you."

It fell with a thump onto the oriental carpet and its well-oiled barrel shimmered in the dim yellow light. Cooper, astounded he was not already dead, used the five seconds to plan. His mind worked real time in slow motion.

"Now face down on the carpet, palms flipped up at your sides, toes turned out spread eagle, your mouth open hard against the fibers."

Cooper, completely defenseless, flashed on the YBarC and said a silent "I love you forever" to Judy as the assassin kicked the Colt 45 out of Cooper's reach. Then he kicked the flashlight, shattering its lens and bulb against a desk leg.

"Who are you?" Cooper played for time.

"A fair question since you will be dead in a minute or so. Lance is the name. I'm George's Eco Warrior attorney. I'm a black operative for U.S. nuke security interests. My father is the Senator from Utah that I will replace some day." Cooper tried to speak but the carpet's fibers chocked him. "You are wondering why you are still alive?"

A perfectly still Cooper listened as the Lance monologue continued, "I need the location of the carbon copy of this original report so they both can be ashes. You do not get your life back but Judy gets to keep hers." Lance picked up the original memo and set it on fire with a Zippo lighter.

Son of a bitch, Cooper wanted to scream.

"You have my word on Judy, otherwise she dies slowly and horribly. When they find her it will look like a sex maniac kidnapped her from the hotel," Lance said coldly. "I cannot let you blow a national security problem wide open, Cooper, over the Ajax Ski Company's fight to obtain your ranch's water right's. Lonnie Sr. has been dumping illegal radioactive waste in the San Miguel River but we have to protect him. We have a Cold War to fight. By the time I finish the count of ten, you turn your head slowly and tell me where the original carbon copy is hidden, or you die painlessly. But if it is not there, then Judy dies Comanche style… one…two…"

The numbers came quickly. With only three left, Cooper rolled over hard and pulled a cheap .22 pistol from his cowboy boot top and it retorted. Its small soft hollow point slug went directly through Lance's forehead at close range burrowing in his brain, tearing an ever-expanding bloody hole. Lance's brain began to shut down one function at a time. Cooper rolled to his left as shot after shot from Lance's automatic pistol randomly sprayed the office.

"Warlord," Lance mumbled. He dropped the pistol and pitched over backwards dead as the ashes from the Bill Daniels memo floated to the carpet.

Cooper limped out of the Ajax Ski Company headquarters. He drove toward Norwood with no evidence to convict Lonnie Jr. or Lonnie Sr. He reached the Airstream and his alibi, Judy. He knew he had to tell her the entire story because she thought he had gone to a meeting with Joe Bear Spirit at the Telluride Inn's small conference room on Ute water rights issues. Judy patched up Cooper's bleeding thigh with her trembling but strong fingers as she recapped his story.

"So you shot Lance in self-defense and saved me, too, but Bill's original water memo with both of the Lonnies' signatures burned to ashes."

"To ashes."

"He say anything else before he died?"

"Warlord."

"That's you, Cooper?" Judy guessed.

"Probably."

"Lonnie Jr. knows?" asked Judy.

"Maybe…probably."

"We are dead?" she clasped Cooper's hand tightly.

"Not yet."

"Why not, Cooper? If they were willing to kill me to get you to give up the memo copy, it has to be more than water for Ajax Ski Company development now."

"They have probably been dumping radioactive waste into the San Miguel River just above the Delores River confluence at the Uravan Mill, probably since the early 1940s."

"They're poisoning part of the upper Colorado River system," Judy replied with disbelief.

"Basically for National Security reasons. A bombs and H bombs for the cold war, and cheap fuel for nuclear power plants."

"Oh my god, Cooper. There is no place to escape. Lonnie Jr.'s connection then is his dad, not the Feds?"

"Correct again. It's Lonnie Sr. who legally owns the subsidiary corporation that does the Atomic Energy Agency's dirty work at Uravan and dumps radioactive waste in the river at Uravan. That's why Lonnie Jr. needs the YBarC's San Miguel River water. Its upstream from the Uravan mill."

"Joe knows all this?" she asked.

"Not yet."

"He's dead, if you tell him," she gasped.

"Two counts. His ultimatum is coming on the Ute water rights."

"The Utes are going to war for water."

Judy pressed her breasts into Cooper's gray-work-shirted chest sobbing. Cooper held her against his aching body until she fell back asleep. Her white cotton nightgown was wet against her nipples from her love tears for Cooper and Joe. Cooper dreamed about Joe Bear Spirit leading a Ute war party. The Lonnies' bloody dripping scalps were on his warriors' spears.

FIFTY-TWO

Bad Salt

J udy and Cooper galloped their paint horses up to the headquarters corral. They had ridden to the flank of Lone Cone into the aspens where they picnicked. Cooper had buried
the cheap .22 pistol in the grove. On their ride back to headquarters, they had counted over
two hundred elk cows and calves in a single herd. They tied the sweaty horses to the corral
fence as the sheriff pulled up in his dusty 4x4. Cooper's short barrel Winchester 30-30 was
in a saddle holster on his paint within easy reach.

The sheriff approached with a tense smile, "Good afternoon, Cooper and ma'am. You
out counting elk for the hunting season or calves for shipping?"

"Both. Best elk calving rate in years. All that late spring snow made good high country
grass. If this is social, sheriff, Judy will make some dinner while we have a whiskey," Cooper
replied.

"No time for that, Cooper. You in Telluride last night?"

"No, right here in bed with me. You want the details?" Judy giggled.

The sheriff blushed, "I figured you would have a tight alibi."

"Why do you care if I was in Telluride?"

"Can't say," he muttered sheepishly.

"Well, we got to rub the horses down before they cool off any more," Judy said.

"Good afternoon," Cooper added.

The sheriff shot them a look for being summarily dismissed.

Copper watched Judy dress to leave at first light for the Fairplay Hotel. She highlighted
her coal brown eyes with mascara. Cooper listened to Montrose country music radio as he
ate ham and eggs.

The deejay announced in a special report, "Forty-seven rock and roll concert attendees
arrested on drug possession charges in Telluride last night. The promoter skipped town with
$20,000 dollars in unpaid bills, according to a local source. A campfire spread out of control
in Ilium Valley and burned a hundred acres before it was contained by local volunteer firefighters near the church camp."

The phone rang and Cooper turned off the radio to answer it.

Max was on the line, "Cooper, a Motion to Dismiss your charges filed in Delta. Their secret witness has vanished, I gather. You are a free man. Now, find a new loan for the YBarC. Can you get your hands on the original Bill Daniels' memo? His wife called me about it."

"Ashes to ashes and dust to dust," Cooper replied, not trusting the phone line.

Max remained silent.

Cooper added, "What about a loan from Doc Blacker?"

"He was just diagnosed with long-term progressive vision loss and will have to retire from surgery. I'm putting all his assets into a tax-free foundation for brain and spinal injury research. Now that you are cleared of the Delta charges, I will propose you for a board seat. We need someone who understands ranch, polo and rodeo injuries. Stay out of Delta."

Cooper dialed Adrianna to see if she had any news from Joe about his water meeting at the reservation, but she did not pickup.

An hour later Polecat burst into the Airstream door and the almost never profane Polecat yelled, "Fucking assholes, they cyanided the salt licks on the Wilson Mesa grazing sections. We got eighty pairs dead. Eighty mother cows and eighty five-month-old calves. The hands are replacing all the salt licks."

Cooper's face went white.

"When's this gonna end, Cooper? Ain't been nothing like this since the sheep wars."

"It's not going to end until I'm dead or Lonnie Jr.'s dead," Cooper replied coldly.

"This isn't 1890. You can't ride into Telluride with Blue Bob Thompson and kill him. Me and the hands aren't gunslingers."

"Guess that's the difference between being a foreman and a ranch operator these days. I'll ride in alone."

"Person's gotta do what a person's gotta do. I'll get on the phone with the sheriff over there and the Colorado State Brand Inspector and file the cattle reports," asserted Polecat.

"Bring a temporary hand on to help. Joe is missing again."

"Joe's a no good Injun; they been missing a long time. Nothing you can do about that. Get rid of him permanent, Cooper. He is stirring up old water feuds. Folks know the YBarC is harboring him, maybe even helping him," Polecat ranted.

"You just quit, Polecat. Bury the cows. I'll take over Friday sundown. That's your last day on the YBarC."

Polecat went red-faced speechless then blustered, "You and your no count mom wrecked this operation in ten years flat from the day we buried your grandfather. Ruined your family's life work. I don't want to ride for this outfit no more." He stalked out of the Airstream and gunned the pickup truck engine as he sprayed gravel; dinging the Airstream's aluminum siding.

Cooper dressed in rough country cowboy gear and backed the Jeep up to a single horse trailer by the corral. He loaded a fast quarter horse with good rocky terrain footing into a single horse-trailer. He walked over to the equipment shed and unlocked it. He loaded a case of dynamite into the Jeep that was left over from blasting fence post-holes on the north range's rocky escarpment. He took a full roll of fuse wire and drove off the ranch.

An hour later, Cooper parked the Jeep in the backcountry behind the Uravan uranium mill and unloaded the already saddled quarter horse. He filled the battered saddlebags with dynamite sticks, fuses and fuse wire. He had a Winchester rifle in a saddle holster and the Colt 45 in his hip holster. He spent the late afternoon slowly working the horse through locals only canyons on old Ute trails until he saw the mill's southern security fence from a low ridge. Lonnie Sr.'s Universal Atomic 100,000 square foot plant was a quarter mile from the Atomic Energy Agency's main mill. At five o'clock the mill whistle sounded and two hundred union workers walked to their pickup trucks in groups and drove out the main gate to Naturita, Nucla, Gateway, Paradox, Redvale and Norwood, Colorado. Cooper tethered his quarter horse and ate beef jerky, canned bake beans and white bread followed by a double shot of whiskey from a sterling silver flask with a chaser of YBarC sweet spring water from his canteen.

Sunset came and departed in the beautiful red rock river valley. Through binoculars, Cooper watched the armed security Jeep patrol until midnight under the star filled sky. Then the guard parked the red security Jeep by the flood lit main gatehouse and settled into a card game with another guard. Low clouds from the south began drifting over the half-moon sky. Cooper rode toward the half mile long south fence after he burlapped the quarter horse's hooves. The silent-hoofed horse carried Cooper up to the 10-foot-high chain-link fence with razor wire strung across its top. Cooper cut a crawl hole in the unelectrified fence and hobbled the horse. He knew the muffled echo of the San Miguel River that flowed by the plant's north boundary would obscure the sounds of his movements. He carefully placed the heavy saddlebags over his broad shoulders. He moved quietly across a hundred yards of open space to the Universal Atomic building's backside. The card game continued in the gatehouse; southwestern Colorado's isolation had made this little known Cold War outpost careless.

To his surprise, Cooper walked right into the building through an unlocked back door. He watched for a guard dog but none appeared. He used his stubby hunting flashlight to find the big stainless steel centrifuges in a locked thick-glassed windowed airtight room. It looked like a multimillion dollar machine.

Cooper very carefully set the dynamite under the glass window and attached a 10-minute fuse that he lit with his Zippo lighter. Cooper exited the back door and saw the red Jeep's headlights reflect off the west canyon wall. Cooper had timed the guard's rounds; he had five minutes to reach his horse and ride safely into the draw. He reached the fence in a minute and rode off. He heard the guard's walkie-talkie crackle in the moonless night sky as the red Jeep pulled up to the hole in the security fence. As Cooper worked the horse toward the top of the low mesa ridge, he heard the bark of a guard dog that must have been patrolling in the jeep. When he silently topped the ridge, he saw the main gate was locked down and the plant site was lit up like Christmas. The two guards found Cooper's boot prints with an oversized flashlight beam when the dog neared the back door. The Universal Atomic plant blew up in a fireball explosion that launched the one-story centrifuges through the steel roof like rockets. The dog and the guards were blown into the chain- link fence. Secondary explosions ripped through the building as a hideous fireball burned five stories into the sky. Its heat wave warmed Cooper in the cool night air on the low ridgeline and backlighted his escape into the series of interconnecting canyons. Cooper continued to hear muted explosions for half an hour with the fading sirens of firefighting equipment.

He rode up to the Jeep in Gypsum Creek Gap, loaded the horse into the trailer and cut back to Lone Cone on an abandoned grazing track. He turned onto the county road around the west side of Lone Cone where it bordered a YBarC section. He established residence in a line shack near Miramonte Reservoir just before sunup. He dropped the worn saddlebags, deerskin gloves and his boots down an abandoned stock well after he unsaddled the horse. He got another pair of ranch work boots, a Winchester rifle, and his bedroll from the Jeep.

After a couple hours of sleep, Cooper cooked a bacon and eggs breakfast, unhooked the horse trailer and drove up to the high point on Mountain Lion's Lookout above the lake. He tuned his transistor radio to the Montrose country music radio station.

The deejay was practically yelling into the station mike, "…Uranium ore processing plant blew up last night. Two security guards and their dog suffered lacerations but were treated and released from Montrose Hospital, we are told by a spokesman. The Colorado State Patrol found a cut in the chain-link security fence. Sabotage is suspected, maybe by angry union workers that were laid off last month. The union is in litigation with Universal Atomic over what it calls illegal layoffs. Lonnie Halstrom out of Houston, Texas owns universal Atomic. He is a well-known western slope native of Cortez, Colorado. There will be a press conference at the Nucla high school gym at noon. The governor is helicoptering down from Denver."

After mending barbwire fences for the morning, Cooper rode back to the bunkhouse office. The phone rang as he walked into the small travel trailer. He picked it up.

"You fucking, no good, Stuart bastard. You're just like your great-grandfather and grandfather. You high-handed fucking big ranchers are dinosaurs. You're a walking dead man. I got no act of war insurance up there with all that security. Twenty-five million up in smoke," Lonnie Sr. sputtered.

"Since you called, have your son send me a check for eighty moms and calves he had poisoned on Wilson Mesa. You can also send the check to me for my grandfather's cows that you never paid for. You come at me old man, I'll shotgun your nuts and guts old west style and your kid's nuts and guts, too."

"I got ten gun for hire Texas assassins like your family's gunslinger, Blue Bob Thompson," Lonnie Sr. hissed like rattler coiled under sagebrush. "You ain't ever going to see me boy, just one of them."

248

"Then I guess they'll bury your son with his boots on in Telluride," Cooper had ice in his veins.

"You and that fancy El Paso lawyer who has been fronting for you are finished," yelled Lonnie Sr.

Five minutes later the phone rang again. Cooper answered, "Your daddy already called," and the line went dead.

After lunch Judy called with alarm in her voice, "There is a report in the Denver paper 160 YBarC cattle were poisoned on Wilson Mesa."

"Bad news travels fast. Poisoned salt licks dropped across our fence lines. Polecat retired himself yesterday. He has no stomach for it anymore. I've been on a downed fence-line all morning," Cooper complained.

"Noon radio news says the uranium mill blew up at Uravan."

"Just got a call on that. Good end to a bad penny."

"I'll move down Saturday," Judy volunteered.

"No, after Labor Day. We cannot afford to lose the hotel's income." Cooper didn't want to risk losing her in an open range ambush. "Stay put."

"I have to check in a guest. Goodbye," Judy said, sounding disappointed and the phone line kept clicking. Cooper heard a familiar motocross bike pull up to the bunkhouse.

"Cooper, it's Brady."

"Come in."

A dust-covered Brady walked in.

"They're questioning everyone you know in Telluride," Brady squeaked, his mouth dry.

"Who are 'they'?" Cooper asked.

"FBI and the sheriff and the marshal's office. Adrianna alerted me so I went out the back window of my house and rode the mountain trails here. What's going on?"

"Maybe it's about the poisoned cattle."

Brady blurted, "You blew that uranium mill!"

"I'm a cowboy, not a mining explosives expert. They probably blew it for insurance."

"Lonnie Jr. probably blamed it on you."

"Want a shot of bourbon? Your voice is cracking from the trail dust."

Cooper drove his Jeep onto the Wilson Mesa with a paint horse in his single horse trailer. Tommy Lee, the new foreman, was using a front-loader to drop the last of the poisoned cattle into a building-size trench. Cooper unloaded his saddled horse and mounted it as Polecat performed his last day of work for the YBarC. Polecat was splashing cans of high-grade gasoline over the carcasses. Then he lit the pit. Yellow flames shot into the air as the funeral pyre sent a pillar of stinking smoke into the sky. The southwest wind blew it into Telluride's box canyon. All three men avoided eye contact, saddened by the needless slaughter of helpless cattle. From horseback Cooper surveyed the sacks of lime that would be spread on the remains before a D6 Caterpillar covered the mass grave. Cooper signaled his departure with a wave of his hand and rode southwest on Wilson Mesa toward a steep Jeep trail that dropped into Ilium Valley. As he rode away, Cooper saw the USDA cattle inspector arrive with the Colorado State Brand Inspector to check the disposal of the cattle. It was Polecat's last task to handle the YBarC's federal and state paperwork.

At 4:30, Cooper rode a YBarC paint horse up the sidewalk to the open door of the New Sheridan Bar and carefully walked the horse a hoof at a time into the 25-foot tin ceiling barroom. He was eye to eye with a life size oil painting of a reclining nude prostitute on a purple Victorian couch.

The Finn bartender without even looking up, asked, "What will it be, Mr. Stuart?"

"Best Canadian Reserve Whiskey you have on the back bar, no ice sir."

The gray-haired Finn poured a double shot of 20-year-old whiskey from a dusty half full bottle and set the tumbler on the bar five feet below Cooper, who reached for a twenty-dollar bill.

"That will be on the house Mr. Stuart for the mining families the YBarC fed when the Denver mining company bastards laid them off for good."

Cooper nodded, slid sideways in the saddle as his horse eyed the bartender and he picked up the fake crystal tumbler of bourbon. He straightened up tall in the saddle raised the glass to make a toast as the bar's clientele silently stared at him.

"To range war and death to Lonnie Jr. for poisoning my cattle."

A gasp rose from the entire length of the bar. But a slightly drunk ski bum quipped, "He'll take your season's pass away for that toast, Cooper," and laughter broke the tension in the bar room.

A town deputy marshal ran through the open double glass bar doors and ordered, "Get this horse out of here."

A junior real estate agent caught the deputy marshal's eye, "He accused Lonnie Jr. of poisoning his cattle and said he planned to shoot him in a range war."

The deputy walkie-talkied for back up and moved to Cooper's horse's right flank. He saw the Colt 45.

"Now out of here with the horse and gun or I will arrest you. This is not 1890 Cooper." The marshal's comment produced guffaws around the bar.

Cooper backed the sure-footed Indian paint horse out the open double doors and into the street. Jesse Smith arrived and had a whispered conversation with the junior real estate agent. The chief marshal arrived and conferred with the rookie deputy. Jesse Smith ordered, "Arrest Cooper; he carrying a pistol in town."

"No go," replied the chief marshal. "He's on a Colorado state highway, where it's legal to ride a horse and carry an open weapon in a holster. In fact, last month the new summer trail-ride wrangler did it for his newspaper ad."

"Todd here, says he threatened to kill Lonnie Jr. for poisoning his cattle," a red-faced Jesse asserted.

A pillar of smoke soared over their shoulders to the west and the wind carried the distinct smell of burning flesh.

"That's my poisoned cattle burning on the mesa," Cooper stated. The crowd turned to view the smoke.

"Arrest him for stinking up the air. It will ruin real estate showings today and August is our busiest summer month."

"The cattle are burning under Federal and State supervision. The YBarC's land is in San Miguel County so the sheriff's got jurisdiction, not me," the marshal opined.

Cooper didn't see an airborne Jesse Smith, who tackled him off his horse and onto the dull black pavement of the state highway. The Colt 45 skidded into the middle of Colorado Avenue as Jesse rolled off Cooper. The marshal quickly ran over to the loaded gun and picked it up.

Cooper was sprawled on the pavement with sharp pain shooting through his shoulder. "Marshal, watch that trigger. Blue Bob Thompson filed it down. It's gunfighter quick."

Cooper heard Brady yell from the back of the gathering crowd, "Arrest Jesse; he assaulted Cooper blindside."

The marshal pulled Cooper to his feet with his free hand playing for time.

Cooper now squarely on his feet replied, "I don't want to press charges. I'll take my gun now."

The marshal emptied out five bullets and handed it back to Cooper. "You can pick the shells up at the sheriff's office in the courthouse tomorrow. I'll keep them until things cool off. Main Street is my jurisdiction. Jesse, you get back to your office before I have to arrest you. Rest of you back in the bar or go home. Cooper, you ride out now, by god. This town has grown very tired of you."

Cooper was lunching on a can of baked beans when the phone rang at Friday noontime.

"This Cooper Stuart? You remember me. I run the Norwood saw mill. Buddy Whitehorse."

"Yes sir. You and my grandfather did timber business."

"Good memory. I will come straight to the point. The environmentalists over at Telluride are holding up my next Forest Service logging lease over on the Uncompahgre National Forest. I got to lay off sixteen men with families or find some timber 'til the Feds finish an environmental impact review. You want to lease those two YBarC sections of mature Ponderosa on North Mountain?"

Cooper saw a rainbow of hope appear. "How much in it for the YBarC."

"We estimate $300,000 dollars and will guarantee it with fifty percent on the first day of the cut and fifty per cent in two months. We need to sign tomorrow and cut in a week to avoid shutting the mill down. Plus, I'll give you $5,000 cash bonus if you sign tomorrow."

"You have a deal," Cooper grinned.

"Meet me at the Norwood bank tomorrow at 10 a.m. cashier's check will be waiting," and Buddy hung up, happy not to write pink slips on a Friday afternoon.

Cooper called Judy, "YBarC just contracted for $300,000 in a Norwood sawmill timber deal."

"Good news, Cooper. Now can I sell the Hotel and ride the range? That's three hundred thousand plus calf sales plus the cash stash. We can pay the note off at the Telluride Bank," Judy whooped.

"Works for me if it works for you. Guess we will have to rebuild the headquarters house when you move down here."

"You bet, Cowboy. With a big master bedroom with a view of the snowcapped peaks. Whoops, got to go; there's smoke coming from the kitchen. Give Polecat my best at his retirement party tonight. No use to kick sand in his face publicly, your Uncle Harvey would advise."

Cooper visualized the full time dark haired beauty in his bed every night after a hard day on the ranch.

Cooper met Polecat and his extended family of four Norwood generations in the backroom of the Cattlemen's Bar and Grill. As his boot heels clicked across the tile floor, a few murmurs of disapproval were whispered. Blue Bob's pearl handle Colt 45 flashed as Cooper's open sport coat swung with his quick gait.

The dinner conversation was strained but Cooper tried to talk mostly about his grandfather's days with Polecat. Cooper's speech was brief and to the point, thanking Polecat for fifty years of service and awarding him his pension fund of $50,000 dollars that Cooper's grandfather had set up. Then Cooper surprised Polecat by giving him a thirty-five-acre lot on Cougar Ridge that overlooked Miramonte Reservoir. Cooper's grandfather had accepted it as a debt payoff long ago. It was the ranch's only detached small parcel and it was not deeded to the bank. Polecat's family applauded at the announcement because he loved to fish with his grandsons. As Cooper walked out to the bar for a very public drink with his new, 35-year-old foreman Tommy Lee, he made a mental note to record a quitclaim deed for Polecat's retirement lot at the Telluride courthouse.

FIFTY-THREE

Restrained Behavior

T he phone in the Airstream rang at 8:30 a.m. Monday morning just as Cooper walked in
from night hawking the North Mountain herd.

Max's voice barked at Cooper, "TRO court hearing in Telluride at three o'clock today.
I'm borrowing the doctor's Lear Jet to fly up. You pay the fuel. You leased timber without
calling me?"

"Yes, the timber lease is routine YBarC business and when Judy's sells the Fairplay Hotel
the ranch can pay its note off. What is a TRO?"

"Temporary restraining order stopping the dissipation of ranch assets while
you are in foreclosure and appointing a court trustee to manage the YBarC to stop
you from doing it again until you pay the bank in full or the foreclosure is final."

"Can they do that?" asked a stunned Cooper.

"Not in most jurisdictions but maybe in Telluride. Who is Judge Elber?"

"A trust fund lawyer from an old Boston family, and a fly fisherman."

"You and Judy meet me at the Montrose general aviation hanger at one o'clock. We'll
file a Colorado State homestead exemption at the Montrose Court, for you to occupy the
YBarC ranch and its house for life."

"The YBarC is not a one-hundred-sixty-acre homesteader's farm," protested Cooper as
Max hung up.

Cooper met Judy at the Montrose airport just as the Lear Jet taxied up to her Wagoneer.
They stopped at the Montrose County courthouse and filed the Homestead Claim. They
heard the county clerk dialing Telluride as they exited. An hour later they were in front of
Judge Elber's bench.

The clerk read the TRO, which asked the Superior Court to bar Cooper from the YBarC
for dissipating a long-term asset, nullify the timber lease and appoint Polecat trustee until
the note was paid off or foreclosure completed; it was signed Jesse Smith on behalf of the
bank.

Max rose, "I move to dismiss the TRO on behalf of the defendant, Cooper Stuart. This
court has no jurisdiction while the State Appeals Court in Denver reviews the foreclosure.

Notice of this hearing was inadequate and Cooper Stuart is a Colorado homesteading owner and manager of the ranch in question."

"Motion denied. TRO hearings are short notice to prevent irreparable damage. You know that counselor."

"Exception," argued Max.

"Noted. I know you will appeal my decision, counselor," the judge growled.

"I move for a closed session. This is a matter between a corporation and a privately-owned ranch," countered Max eyeing a Montrose based Denver Post stringer who scribbled notes and several local real estate types.

"Denied. Plaintiff, present your case and call your witnesses."

Jesse Smith approached the bench as Buddy Whitehorse, Sam Jr. and Polecat walked into the courtroom.

Jesse Smith asserted, "Cooper leased the timber without bank approval for under market value to raise cash quickly. Also, the ranch's cattle herd, which is its principal cash flow asset, is being given away free to the fired miners, not to mention rustled, and poisoned, which has diminished the herd's value and the ranch's ability to repay the loan once Cooper has exhausted his appeal. The headquarters' house burned and he secreted the insurance proceeds instead of rebuilding the house or paying down the note. Cooper has a bad reputation having been arrested for cocaine possession in Delta County with charges dropped due to a technicality pertaining to a suddenly unavailable informant. He associated with a well-known Telluride town prostitute who died riding fences for the YBarC and he invested money in a condo project with a bankrupt Phoenix-based developer."

Max rose and asserted as he restrained Cooper with his left arm, "This is a hearsay character lynching, not a TRO hearing."

Judge Elber pounded his gavel. "Mr. Smith, present your fact-finding witnesses."

Cooper stared at the judge, starting to fear a "fix" as Max's mouth tightly closed. Buddy confirmed the lease but under cross-examination by Max testified it was fair market value in the recessionary economy, which had lowered timber prices due to slumping lumber sales. Buddy underscored passionately it was done quickly to stop layoffs while he waited for a new Forest Service timber lease to be approved.

Then Jesse called Polecat to the stand. "Cooper Stuart fire you because a part-time Ute Indian employee named Joe Bear Spirit failed repeatedly to show up for work and you asked Cooper to replace him?"

"Yes sir," replied Polecat.

"Cooper give you a thirty-five-acre lot owned by the YBarC at your retirement party Friday night. Another fact in his dissipation of YBarC assets."

"Yes sir," replied a confused and surprised Polecat.

"Cooper a fit ranch manager, in your opinion?"

"No sir," Polecat angrily stated.

Jesse turned to Judge Elber, "The bank proposes Polecat be appointed trustee of the YBarC, the timber lease be vacated and Cooper Stuart and Judy, his bookkeeper, be barred from the property unless and until he pays the note and interest in full."

The judge nodded, "Defense, the witness is yours."

"Polecat, were the cattle rustled while being convoyed to winter pasture in Arizona under your watch as foreman? And are not Utah authorities are still investigating the case?" asked Max.

"Yes, sir."

"Polecat, the poisoned cattle were on Wilson Mesa and under your hands' watch twenty-four hours a day. The sheriff and State Brand Inspector are investigating, I am told."

"Well, mostly yes, sir. We ride regular day checks but only random night hawk checks of the entire YBarC herd. Sheriff has started an investigation. I signed all the paper work before I retired."

"Polecat, you defamed Joe Bear Spirit to Cooper as a no good Ute Injun who was stirring up water rights trouble in Southwest Colorado."

"Objection. They have no witness except Cooper so it's he said - she said," argued Jesse.

"Sustained. You do not have to answer that question Polecat," ordered the judge.

"That all for now, Polecat. Defense calls Cooper Stuart to the stand."

The court clerk swore in Cooper.

"All charges have been dropped by the Delta DA against you, Cooper."

"Yes sir."

"You believe the headquarters fire that killed your mother was arson but the Norwood Volunteer Fire Department ruled it accidental and the insurance proceeds were duly paid to a YBarC operating account to be used to rebuild the house at a future date?"

"Yes, sir."

"You invested your mother's money in a Telluride condo development deal in good faith and recovered all the principal when you found out it was a scam?"

"Yes, sir," and there were gasps in the courtroom.

"The San Miguel County coroner ruled the ranch hand's death in the saddle accidental."

"Yes, sir."

"Joe Bear Spirit had Ute reservation cowhand experience and you asked Polecat to find a replacement hand before you fired Polecat, who is seventy-five years old?"

"Yes, sir."

"Polecat and the cowhands under his supervision failed to stop or discover cyanide-laced salt blocks from being dropped over your Wilson Mesa fence lines."

"Yes, sir. But, when they discovered the dead cattle, Polecat reported it."

"Cooper, you leased the timber in good faith as your grandfather had previously done to Buddy Whitehorse to raise proceeds to pay off the bank note and to help save Norwood jobs?"

"Yes, sir. The $300,000 in timber proceeds plus Judy's $300,000 from the sale of the Fairplay Hotel she has verbally pledged to loan the ranch plus the recovered condo investment money plus the fall calf sales advance will be enough to pay off the bank note."

"Objection. The Hotel sale's proceeds are speculative," asserted Jesse.

"Sustained."

"I will call Judy to testify. Cooper, has your family run the YBarC profitably for four generations?"

"Yes, sir."

"Is it your belief that the bank is only foreclosing to obtain the extensive YBarC water rights for the Ajax Ski Company because you refused their offer to sell out?"

Cooper answered with fire in his voice, "Yes sir, over Jesse's objection, which was upheld by the judge.

"I'm through with Cooper, your honor," stated Max.

"No cross for Cooper. His word's not worth a damn in Telluride," Jesse asserted with a smirk.

"Jesse, you are next for contempt. Shut up," growled the judge.

Judy was sworn in.

"Do you run the ranch's books and money?"

"Yes sir, since Cooper's mom's death."

"Is the ranch now running on a sound financial basis and does it plan to retire the bank note by October one?"

"Yes, on both, sir."

"Are you a blood relative of Cooper Stuart?"

"No, the FAA investigation revealed that my uncle was adopted by Cooper's grandfather during the depression so he is Cooper's uncle, adopted brother of his late father and my mother's common law wife under Colorado law. I inherited his estate, which includes the Fairplay Hotel."

"And you have orally pledged the proceeds of the sale of that hotel to Cooper Stuart to pay off a portion of the bank note."

"Yes, sir. I already have a Breckenridge, Colorado, buyer under contract."

"And you graduated with honors in Ag Management at Colorado State University?"

"Yes, sir."

"You recommended to Cooper three months ago after you brought the ranch's books up to modern accounting practices that Polecat be fired for unauthorized diversion of ranch supplies over a 10-year period?"

"Yes, sir."

Polecat shouted, "That's a lie."

Jesse objected to the question as hearsay.

Judy teared-up as Judge Elber ordered, "Remove Polecat from the room, Deputy Sheriff. That hopefully will keep the rest of the attendees silent."

"Is Cooper a good ranch owner and manager."

"Yes, sir."

"We rest your honor," Max stated.

"No cross, your honor. The bank moves you appoint Polecat its trustee," Jesse moved.

Without hesitation Judge Elber ruled, "TRO is granted. Polecat is the court's trustee. Cooper Stuart is barred from the YBarC until he pays off the note or the bank's foreclosure is completed. The timber lease is vacated, Judy is barred from the ranch and ordered to turn over its books, cash and checking account to Polecat."

"Objection, your honor. There is the matter of the legally filed homestead paper in Montrose." Max walked to the bench and handed it to him.

The judge asserted, "Well, it is dated an hour before the hearing but is in order under Colorado law."

"I grant Cooper Stuart one-hundred-sixty-acres on the YBarC east Wilson Mesa section and he has twenty-four hours to move his Airstream and personal possessions including a horse and saddle off the YBarC headquarters," ordered the judge.

"Objection. The homestead protection applies to the whole YBarC," argued Max. "This is a naked unlawful seizure of the YBarC, my client's home, by this court for the bank, and I believe, for its water rights from its owner Cooper Stuart."

"Denied. I am on fly-fishing vacation for four weeks. You can re-argue my ruling on the TRO here for amendments after I return or appeal my entire temporary restraining order to the Colorado State Appeals Court in Denver, which will take at least a week for a review. Court adjourned." Judge Elber walked out and Jesse smirked at Max and Cooper.

"Fix is on, Cooper. Get Judy and let's get out of here. I will appeal to Denver by sundown for an expedited hearing on the basis of the facts and also Polecat's incompetence as a trustee. You give Polecat a deed to the lake lot?"

"No, there hasn't been time to file one. I haven't released his pension either because Liz was the surviving trustee and it's tied up in her estate."

"Tell him an oral promise of deeded land is not worth the breath expended on it. That's Colorado law because of water rights. His pension's not due because he officially just unretired," Max advised.

Cooper advised Polecat on the Courthouse steps that the deed and pension were rescinded. The deputy sheriff had to restrain Polecat and his son from assaulting Cooper. Max advised the deputy to escort Polecat and his family to their pickups.

Cooper, with his arm supporting Judy, swore softly so that only Judy could hear him, "I will take back every acre of the YBarC for my family and our family to come. Our opponents will have no quarter."

FIFTY-FOUR

The Morning After

Judy removed the Stuart family original deeds, her duplicate set of ranch books, and $48,000 in cash that Cooper and Joe Bear Spirit had recovered from Gary. She departed in a cloud of dust for Fairplay to secure the cash in the hotel safe with a Colt 45 under the driver's seat. Cooper opened the ranch safe for a deputy sheriff. The safe contained Judy's original set of ranch books, the ranch's Telluride bank checkbook, Judy's panties from the strip poker game and a half empty fifth of 20-year-old reserve Kentucky Bourbon. Polecat protested the lack of cash but the deputy inventoried the contents without comment. The deputy let Cooper recover the black lace panties and the Bourbon. Cooper wrote down the old safe's combination for the court and reluctantly handed it to the deputy. Buddy Whitehorse had called Cooper and told him to keep the $5,000 check that was in Jeep's glove compartment as good faith money until the Colorado Court of Appeals ruled on the TRO. He reconfirmed the mill needed the timber and encouraged Cooper to pressure Max for a quick hearing in Denver and to use the local jobs issue.

After five private minutes in the family graveyard, Cooper hooked up the Airstream to the Jeep with the help of Tommy Lee, whom Polecat fired, and they caravanned out of the YBarC with the deputy sheriff. Tommy Lee's pickup pulled Cooper's single horse trailer with his favorite paint. An hour later Cooper and Tommy Lee parked the Airstream on the Wilson Mesa homestead by the burned-out log house. Cooper briefly regretted his decision to burn down a black chapter in his family history. He downed a shot of bourbon, hung the French lace panties on a hook in the Airstream, and buried Buddy's five thousand in cash in a cigar tin by the corral's southwest corner post under a glowing orange sunset. Cooper drove to his inn room with his Colt 45 in the Jeep's secret compartment. He called Judy and asked her to return on Memorial Day, which was two weeks away and the last day of the first Telluride International Film Festival. She happily accepted the invitation. He called Max, who informed him the TRO's Colorado Appeals Court hearing in Denver was on the Wednesday after Memorial Day. It was the first day the judges were back from their summer golfing, camping and fishing vacations. Max confirmed Buddy Whitehorse had called the Governor about the sawmill's impending layoffs.

Cooper walked over to Adrianna's house and to his surprise Joe Bear Spirit answered his knock. "Hello, Cooper. Paper says you're homesteading on Wilson Mesa. Adrianna is in the bathroom throwing up." Cooper frowned but Joe continued, "What brings you here?"

"To set up an account at the Bistro for meals, but come by my room at the inn at eleven tomorrow and pick up a quitclaim deed for half of the YBarC's Delores River water rights as promised."

"Cooper, the judge could jail you for that, according to the newspaper. You're no good to anyone in jail again."

"Judges, all gone fishing. My word is my word. I still own the YBarC," Cooper smiled slyly.

"Okay, Cowboy, our secret not even the throw up queen needs to know," Joe whispered.

Joe stopped by the inn at 11 a.m. and picked up the quitclaim deed that Cooper had hand printed on a standard legal form from the pharmacy. The inn's hippie maid witnessed Cooper's signature, not even bothering to read it she was so stoned.

Joe updated Cooper, "I am departing for the Southern Ute reservation at sunset for a coalition meeting with all seven Ute bands on Wednesday."

Then Joe surprised Cooper with a small gold leaf antique framed oil painting of a modern cowboy, an Indian and a blonde woman on paint horses with a silver Airstream in the background near a snow-covered mountain range.

"It's my last painting for a while, Cooper. It's for the Airstream, your modern teepee," Joe said carefully omitting Sue's name. Ute's believed the mention of a dead tribal member's name could bring back an evil spirit.

"It gets the place of honor over the foldout couch. Thanks, Joe," Cooper avoided mentioning Sue to respect Joe's Ute custom. "It means a lot to me. The YBarC lost its western paintings in the fire."

"See you on the trail," and Joe did his vanishing thing that always amazed Cooper. Cooper headed for the homestead to work on the corral and perimeter fences, tune-up the Jeep, hang Joe's oil painting and clean his guns.

Cooper repaired the corral fence at the homestead during the afternoon. He returned to the inn at midnight so he could pick up some couplings to hook up the Airstream to the well when the hardware store opened at 7 a.m. He dreamed he heard a phone ring and then later a pounding on his door, which startled him awake.

Adrianna charged into the inn room crying wildly, "They killed Joe," she cried hysterically and collapsed into Cooper's arms.

"Not Joe Bear Spirit?"

"They lynched him between Delores and Mancos."

"No way," Cooper said hyperventilating angrily. She cried uncontrollably as Cooper's heart stopped beating.

"Sheriff called a few minutes ago. Joe was driving my Wagoneer. A state patrolman found it run off the highway in an irrigation ditch on a National Forest road. The driver's door open. He followed tire tracks into an aspen grove and found Joe hung from a limb. His body was still warm."

Cooper's heart barely began to beat as he held Adrianna upright.

The phone rang and Cooper moved Adrianna onto the bed and answered it.

"Cooper, sorry to wake you, but this is important. I got a call a half hour ago from the Montezuma's County Sheriff's Department. Looks like your friend Joe Bear Spirit committed suicide."

"Cut the bullshit, sheriff. Adrianna is here. State police called her. He was lynched. You got any facts or are you part of the official cover up to protect Labor Day tourism?"

"No need to talk to me that way, son. There's an investigation underway. Right now, the Cortez boys are calling it a probable suicide regardless of what the state patrol may think."

"I'm going down there now!"

"You best not do that. Tempers high down there. State boys found a quitclaim deed to your Delores River water rights in Joe's jean pocket. They have it at state patrol headquarters in Cortez. A lot of people are very mad at you," and the sheriff hung up.

Adrianna sobbed from the bed, "What did the sheriff say?"

"Folks don't want to believe Joe was lynched. It is bad publicity nationwide with Mesa Verde National Park down there."

"Those bastards," she screamed. "They hate the Utes. They would poison them like your cattle if they could get away with it. Only Indians they like are the dead Anasazi with ruins and pots to loot."

"State troopers found my quitclaim water deed to half of the YBarC's Delores rights in Joe's pocket before the local law could destroy it. Joe had Ute Water Coalition meetings at the Southern Ute Reservation in Ignacio today and then at the res on Sleeping Ute Mountain. I'll call Brady and drive down there. You stay in Telluride. It's too dangerous right now."

Adrianna sobbed uncontrollably while Cooper dressed. Then she confessed, "I'm pregnant with Joe's baby."

"So that's why you were throwing up." Cooper was shocked for the second time in ten minutes. Adrianna cried wildly.

Cooper and Brady were in the Jeep heading to Cortez as the rising sun blinded them. Cooper's memories of Joe Bear Spirit flashed like movie frames through his mind. Joe's intelligence, warrior strength, and courage, whether he was digging a fence line posthole, flying a helicopter, finishing an oil painting or working to solve the Ute's water treaty problems, blazed through Cooper's vision in the early morning intense sunlight.

Cooper and Brady arrived at Cortez in record time. The state patrol and county sheriff had ignored them as they sped by with roof top red lights flashing and sirens wailing in an Anglo conqueror's tribute to Joe. Cooper parked in front of the state patrol district headquarters and counted a half dozen parked white Plymouth Fury police specials. The press was gathered in front of the main entrance. A straw cowboy hatted Cooper left Brady in the Jeep and slipped through the press into the chaos of the reception area. He heard someone yell.

"Take an unmarked patrol car to the Cortez Airport. Jumbo Roberts is arriving in the governor's Lear Jet at 9:30."

Another uniformed state patrolman answered the receptionist's phone, "I know, Governor, it's going to be a rough day down here. I want the National Guard on alert and ready to deploy. The two reservations are already tense. I got maybe twenty-five good lawmen down here but the local sheriff's volunteers are nothing but trigger-happy, Indian-hating trouble. The sheriff's department's still investigating it as a suicide."

A young, crew cut, no-nonsense square-jawed state trooper walked up to Cooper. "You got official business here, sir?" he barked.

"Joe Bear Spirit was employed part-time by my ranch and was a friend," Cooper politely answered.

"Sit down," and he pointed to a gray metal chair.

"Lieutenant will be with you in a minute or two. He's on the phone with the Governor. All hell is breaking loose down here. We pull drunk dead Indians out of wrecked cars and pickup trucks but nothing like this has happened since the turn of the century."

"You Cooper Stuart who signed the deed my patrolman found on the deceased?" the lieutenant dressed in starched gray pants with a side stripe and a brown embossed shirt asked frowning.

"Yes. It was a donation to the Ute Water Coalition."

"You employ him as a cowboy, also?"

"Part-time wrangler and fencer since last winter."

"Follow me to my office. Jumbo wants to talk to you soon as he arrives here."

Cooper followed the lieutenant, who closed a steel door behind him. He offered Cooper a seat in a metal chair in front of a mahogany desk and settled into his high back leather chair. "Crime scene investigation leads to the conclusion he was lynched old west style while standing on a man's shoulder, hands tied behind him, blindfolded, probably half conscious. According to the medical examiner he strangled to death slowly because the rope never broke his neck."

"What else do you know?"

"Not much yet. The Montrose lab is at work on the fingerprints from the borrowed Wagoneer and his belt buckle. We have partial boot prints at the scene. No witnesses yet except a local amateur prostitute saw him at a Mancos, Colorado, cafe bar eating a hamburger and drinking a beer around 11 p.m. last night. She called in ten minutes ago after she heard the radio report. We're bringing her in for questioning. What do you know?"

"I gave him the deed around 11 a.m. at the inn. He departed for a Ute Water Coalition meeting. Today he had a big powwow scheduled with all the Ute bands on the Southern Ute res to prepare for a meeting with state and federal officials after Labor Day. Adrianna, his Telluride employer, woke me up at the inn about 3:30 a.m. with the bad news."

The Lieutenant fidgeted with his eyebrows, "Someone must have recognized him in Mancos. His picture has been in the paper down here over this water rights thing. That bar is dangerous for Utes anytime, though."

"They clearly did not know about the deed or they would have destroyed it."

"Maybe and maybe not. It's being checked for prints. They could have left it as a message to the Utes and to people like you not to mess with their water rights."

"He was followed out of the bar?" Cooper probed again.

"Probably, and forced off Highway 160 just east of Mancos. Then driven up 184 toward Delores, which is deserted after midnight."

"The suicide theory is a local chamber of commerce wish list ending. You calling in the FBI and BIA?"

"Can't and won't. The hanging was not on the reservation. They got no jurisdiction. Besides, Jumbo says he already rescued you from them once. Anybody in Telluride or Norwood want him dead?"

"My foreman, Polecat, hated Joe on sight; the bank and the Ajax Ski Company, if they knew about the deed, but to my knowledge he was keeping it secret until the meeting today."

"Why?"

"The Ajax Ski Company wants the YBarC water rights intact for development of the ski area."

"Well then, I bet a bunch of angry liquored-up local boys done ruined their lives over a water fight. Once I know who was in that bar last night we will start pulling them in for questioning. Get some breakfast, come back see Jumbo at 8:30 a.m. sharp after we brief him and get his orders. Nobody going to sleep here for days."

Cooper and Brady pulled out of the parking lot toward the cafe in downtown Cortez as five tan National Guard trucks with water trailers attached for desert field duty around the reservations turned into the state police parking lot.

Brady observed, "This is big stuff. Like when Martin Luther King was shot in Memphis. They called the National Guard in all over the country."

"Got that right. Joe was well respected for his work for AIM, UWC and for the Ute people. The western reservations will be tense."

After breakfast, Cooper met with Jumbo Roberts alone.

"First, good news Cooper, the NTSB verified that the FBI found Peter Simple's brother's fingerprint on your uncle's plane's carburetor. The FBI arrested him yesterday. The press will have it at noon."

"Thank them all. Uncle Harvey was too good a flyer to have missed the runway even in bad weather. He was practically born in that plane."

262

"Bad news. A tough day ahead with no time to waste. Civil disorder, as they call an Indian uprising now, is possible if not probable. Press knows about the water deed. Someone leaked it to them and the attorney general tells me that Boston blue blood Telluride judge will jail you for contempt of court."

"He's fly fishing in New Zealand," laughed Cooper but added, "Lonnie Jr. set me up. Poisoned my cattle."

"Cows, thank the good lord, are not state police business unless they are rustled and trucked by highway, but dynamite is. ATF says Montrose hardware store records show Y Bar C purchased a lot of it for fence post work last spring."

"Joe used it all up on the escarpment fence line. He was trained to use explosives in the Army."

"We know that, too. Well, Cooper, dead men tell no tales, do they?" Jumbo continued, "We are rounding up patrons of a certain bar now. I'll crack this one today, I hope. If you talk to any of Joe's family or friends, on the res by phone and I mean by phone, please council cool heads. The res is too hot for white men today."

"I will," replied Cooper. The phone rang and Jumbo signaled goodbye with a wave of his large white hand.

FIFTY-FIVE

Redneck Heaven

Cooper and Brady pulled up in front of the nondescript Stage Coach Bar and Cafe in Mancos at lunchtime. Cooper's efforts to reach the Old Medicine Man on the Ute reservation had failed. The phone line into the res had been cut, according to a Mountain Bell operator. Cooper had filled Brady in on the prostitute's call to the state police. A white unmarked Plymouth Fury was parked a block west of the bar watching its entrance. They walked through a rusting iron and pine Spanish style door, which was flanked by glass bricks. The semi-lit long narrow room had a pool table in the back and a cheap red '50s plastic countertop bar on their right with Formica topped matching tables on the left. Two men in jeans and work shirts were shooting pool while five more sat around a table talking quietly. They all turned to stare at Cooper and Brady as a middle-aged alcohol scarred waitress in a too tight thin blue sweater with a clean white apron signaled with her eyes for them to sit at the counter. She put down two menus. Cooper ordered two cups of coffee with doughnuts and Brady began to read the ROCKY MOUNTAIN NEWS. Country music blared from the kitchen behind the counter.

"Fucking Ute don't have no right to hard working farmer's water," an older man in a gray work shirt said angrily.

"You know what UWC stands for?" asked a young pock marked faced laborer.

"No, reckon, I don't," replied the older man.

"Ute whores and cunts," he laughed.

"Give me a Mexican whore any day," and the table erupted in laughter.

"Heard on the radio the dead Injun had him one up in Telluride. Driving her Jeep Wagoneer when he met the devil last night." Brady's hands were shaking as he turned the newspaper's pages.

"That's enough boys," the owner cook yelled from his serving window behind the bar. "We got ski bums from Telluride according to the YZ plates on their Jeep outside and a state cop parked watching my door."

Then a man with big tattooed forearms turned around from the back table, "You snow niggers come down here to see where that Ute died? You know his Mexi whore?"

Brady turned red in the face as Cooper's arm shot across Brady's chest restraining him and replied without emotion, "He was my cowhand. Any of you see him in here last night?"

"Sheriff was already here, snow nigger. That Injun hung hisself," he laughed.

"You own a ranch?"

"I own the Y Bar C."

"You the white Injun loving son of a bitch who gave him that water up on the Delores?" a man in motorcycle leathers asked.

"The same, but it's Mr. Cooper Stuart to you," as Cooper digested the fact he knew about the water deed.

"Then we goanna mop the floor of this joint with your face," and he snapped a switch-blade open.

"You here last night, greaser man? You pull a blade on Joe doing some speed drugs with the boys here? Red line revved up," Cooper challenged.

The 6'2" motorcycle man stood and approached Cooper as Brady bolted out the door.

"You got the same arrogant grin as that Ute trouble maker. I'm gonna cut the smile off that pretty boy face of yours."

"Shut up, Casey," the older man cautioned.

A speed crazed Casey charged knife open, ready to slash as Cooper jumped over the counter like he was escaping a mad bull in a corral.

The door burst open as a state patrolman with Brady following him entered with a shot-gun and ordered, "Hands above your heads everybody!"

The state patrolman's shotgun sprayed pellets into the back of Casey's left knee as he slashed the knife across the counter at Cooper. The owner came out of the kitchen with his hands up.

A half-hour later, five state troopers had everyone handcuffed and ready for transport to Cortez for questioning.

Jumbo was on a radio with Cooper.

"Casey knows something and so does the gray-haired man in the work shirt," reported Cooper after he relayed their bar comments to Jumbo.

"Casey is wanted for Anasazi pot stealing and interstate sales of looted ancient Indian artifacts from Mesa Verde National Park and BLM land by the Feds. Plus, DEA got a drug investigation going on him and his motorcycle pals. They believe speed is being run from the California Hell's Angels to these boys," Jumbo alleged.

"I want to go down to the Ute res and see the Old Medicine Man."

"Stay away. Tempers too hot down there. All roads blocked in and out by the state police and also out by the Ute warriors. Go back to Telluride. I'll call you when we break one of these Mancos boys," Jumbo ordered and signed off.

Cooper and Brady drove back toward Telluride. They took Highway 184 toward Delores and stopped at the gravel road that led to the crime scene. The state patrol had it blocked with two cruisers. Cooper broke down and cursed in anguish.

At the gas station in Delores, Cooper said, "You hitch back to Telluride and look after Adrianna. Get a message to George. We need a meeting. Use pay phones. The Feds are probably all over the Telluride phone lines. I'm going to the res."

Brady protested but Cooper ignored him. He gave Brady $20 and gunned the Jeep away from the pump.

Cooper reached the Southern Ute reservation at Ignacio where he hoped the Ute Water Coalition warriors were still assembled. The late afternoon August sun lit the red orange buttes from the southwest. Four battered pickup trucks drenched in reservation dust blockaded the main road from Ignacio. Cooper had skirted the state police and FBI roadblocks on ranch roads that ran parallel to Highway 172. As the Jeep slowed, its engine produced a rumble through the glass pack muffler. A bevy of rifles were raised to fire a volley at the Jeep as it coasted to a stop and Cooper jumped out hands high in the air with only a small pocket knife hidden in his cowboy boot top. He walked slowly toward an old cherry colored Chevy pickup with a spider web crack in its windshield.

"Halt," a strong hostile warrior's voice yelled. "We will shoot your white eyes out. Are you an undercover lawman negotiator?"

"I am Cooper Stuart, friend of Joe's. He cowboyed for me. I have come to see the Ute Water Coalition members who planned to meet with Joe today."

"You armed?"

"No."

"Spread eagle on the ground. We search first then, talk to the white devil."

Cooper sensed extreme danger too late. He could not run back to the Jeep with a half dozen Ute hunters' rifles beaded on his vital organs.

"You can search me standing," Cooper replied trying to play for time and find an escape route as he reached the front grill of a green Ford pickup.

A warrior stepped out from behind the pickup and in five silent steps reached Cooper. He slammed the hard butt of his rifle into Cooper's stomach, collapsing him onto his knees in disbelief.

"Spread eagle, white fucker, or I'll break you into pieces and stake you out in the buttes for a mountain lion to eat."

A second unheard warrior's moccasined foot pushed Cooper's face into the chocking dust. Cooper slowly moved his legs and arms into spread eagle position, not wanting to take a final disabling blow. The unseen warrior bent over him and a sharp knifepoint scraped his shirt, jeans and boots. Then probed his crotch.

His straw cowboy hat was kicked away as the warrior said, "Running Blue Water, he's clean. Stupid cowboy must be undercover. Let's cut his balls off stuff them in his mouth and send him back to the FBI up the road."

Cooper, face down, spit the dust from his mouth and almost whispered, "I repeat…I am Cooper Stuart, a supporter of the Ute Water Coalition. I gave Joe a deed to half of the YBarC water on the Delores River for use by the Sleeping Ute Reservation."

A voice responded from behind the Cherry pickup,

"He's the one who set Joe up. Promised him water with a phony deed on land the court seized for the bank in Telluride last week. He's a government double agent. Fooled Joe into taking the no-good water deed and then probably called the BIA who had their goons follow Joe and hang him."

The voice floated through Cooper's hazy mind as he still gasped for breath, his ribs bruised or broken. A rifle butt slammed into Cooper's kidneys again and his mind began to shut down.

Another far off voice added, "I saw him at Cortez State Police headquarters early this morning."

Cooper managed to squint one teary dusty eye open and saw the orange globe sinking to the west. A warrior in jeans and deerskin shirt with a bandaged wrist edged-up to Cooper and his dusty moccasin blocked Cooper's view. He tied Cooper's hands and hobbled his feet with a loose rawhide rope.

"Up. Walk to the Jeep," the pony tailed masked warrior ordered. "It will disappear with you."

Cooper, breathing hard, scrambled slowly to his feet and hobbled toward the Jeep as blood rushed to his head. A warrior unzipped the back leather flap of the Jeep's top and signaled Cooper to climb in with his rifle barrel. Cooper prepared to fish the knife out of his cowboy boot and cut himself loose while they drove him onto the reservation. Then grab the pistol from the hidden compartment. As he half climbed into the back of the Jeep a rifle butt slammed into his head and he passed out in a fetal position. That ended his escape plan.

Consciousness returned slowly to Cooper from a very black starry hole in the Universe. He stared straight up at the big dipper in night mesa sky as his vision returned in a bright burst. The moon lit up stark-layered red sandstone walls. Cooper was staked out nude, spread eagle on his back on the hard, rocky canyon floor. Cooper knew survival was short term. He tried to clear his mind with controlled breathing. The tension of the stakes tore at his muscles. Judy's voice visited his mind as it cleared from the violent blow and gave him new strength, but it could not break the rawhide ropes that bound his wrists and ankles to the stakes. His mother's voice brought comfort and strengthened his heartbeat. Judy's vision urged survival. He observed there were no guards in sight but muffled Ute language echoed off the sandstone wall.

About an hour passed as Cooper infused energy into his cold thirsty body. He cleared his mind to use the magic that Joe Bear Spirit had taught him to turn himself into a mountain lion. His gagged mouth forced slow controlled breathing through his nostrils. He wondered why Joe had not escaped his attackers by shape shifting.

Moccasin footsteps approached as a Ute spoke harshly, "I am Running Blue Water. My voice is the last one you will ever know. Hear me traitor to Joe Bear Spirit, the Ute Water Coalition has decided your punishment. It's death the Comanche way. You live your death first without skin, then without sperm, then without a tongue, then without eyes and then holding your guts with your last strength. We would like to hear your screams but houses are too close, so you remain gagged. If you try to shift shape as Joe taught you, a hunter watching from the cliff will shoot you in the heart. You have until the moon leaves the canyon to think about your death starting at sunup."

Time went in seconds not minutes as Cooper tested escape plans with the Ute hunter's gun barrel glinting in the moonlight always pointed at his heart. Finally, he said goodbye to Judy, Joe and Adrianna on the last ray of moonlight to reach his eyes.

The silence broke.

"Skin him from his big toe to his skull. Cut no vital arteries or organs," Running Blue Water ordered.

A razor-sharp knife blade in the hands of the hunter found Cooper's right big toe as pain shot straight up to his heart.

"Stop," an old voice Cooper remembered commanded and the knife moved away from Cooper's toe. The Old Ute Medicine Man continued, "Cooper's spirit called for help. His friend's ghost guided me to this canyon. It is you, Running Blue Water, who's our enemy. Show the warriors the hidden BIA metal box under your deerskin jacket. You had Joe murdered. You sell the drug speed to the Ute students in Durango for the bikers."

Running Blue Water grabbed the skinner's knife and aimed it at the Old Medicine Man as Cooper watched helplessly. The Old Medicine Man, who was wearing Cooper's Swiss watch, hurled a handful of white powder into Running Blue Water's eyes and they burst into flames as the sharp knife fell to the ground. Running Blue Water ran screaming into the canyon's sandstone wall and was knocked to the ground holding his burned-out empty eye sockets. The hidden mic and recording device with the BIA logo fell from his deerskin vest.

"You will always be blind so our people know you are a BIA rattle snake, Running Blue Water. It is you who will never see the rising sun again. You have betrayed the Ute bands. Cut Cooper loose. Give him water. Wrap his toe in soft deerskin. Smash the metal box with your boots and drown it in the Animas River so the BIA and FBI cannot use it to jail the members of the Water Coalition. Continue Joe's work with vision and courage." The old man raised his hand to the first ray of morning sun that broke the sandstone ridge.

Cooper finished a long drink of cool water from an ancient U.S. Calvary canteen then he and the Medicine Man turned into eagles and flew away, leaving the Ute warriors.

FIFTY-SIX

Blood Loyalty

For three nights and three days Cooper lived in a deerskin loincloth under the stars with the Old Medicine Man and fasted in the desert northwest of Sleeping Ute Mountain. He drank only water from a hidden sacred Ute spring and ate only cactus hearts and flowers. The Medicine Man healed Cooper's big toe and bruised body with a paste of desert herbs while he sang the Ute origin chants. Cooper, in deep silent meditation healed his spirit, mind, body and completed mourning Joe Bear Spirit. The Medicine Man sang the history of the natural earth and sky while Cooper meditated and slept. He taught Cooper the Ute star formations as they passed east to west during the long cool nights.

Cooper learned the story of the universe from a man who had no birth certificate, never attended school, had no social security card, no stocks or bonds, no loans or credit cards, no bank or saving account, no television or radio set, had never killed an animal he did not eat and use for clothing, had never cut down a tree he did not use for housing or heat. He traveled only by horse or walked and he had only one wife for sixty years. She was the grand-daughter of Chief Ouray. The only machine he had possessed had been Cooper's Swiss watch that he did not know how use because the sun and stars were his timepiece. He did not even know he was a prisoner of the U.S. Government on a reservation because he could shape shift and time shift to any point in the universe on a perfect pitch chant.

On the morning of the fourth day in the desert the Medicine Man broke his silence with Cooper, "Talk again, Cooper. You have learned the story of the stars and your body is healed."

"I have learned much under the stars at your side. I return not to fight for the YBarC but for the earth."

"Then you have learned the great lesson of the spirit warriors who ride the wind to preserve the soil, the snow, the plants and the animals," the Medicine Man stated.

"I had a vision of skulls of men and cattle littering the high plateaus of Western Colorado again, like the fierce winters and droughts that my ancestors faced."

"Men have come who cannot live in peace with the sky, water, land, plants and fire. They will perish under this sun as they always have," the Medicine Man intoned, staring into the sun. "Go now. Joe Bear Spirit was a messenger from the Gods. You are the chosen link to his earth spirit by the great Ute bear spirit. The bear spirit will avenge his death through your life and power. You leave the desert with the sun and moon and stars as your guide."

"When will we meet again?" asked Cooper.

"Once more. We will both know the place."

In a blue flash the Old Medicine Man vanished and in a yellow flash Cooper was standing by his Jeep in a deserted canyon on the Southern Ute reservation. He had only a deerskin pouch around his neck with a fine white power in it and his loincloth. Cooper's cowboy boots and clothes were stacked neatly in the back of the Jeep with the Swiss watch. He dressed and put on his watch last.

He drove off on a narrow dusty high desert Jeep track and saw only lean cattle grazing. When he reached the highway at a crossroads near Durango, he called Judy from a pay phone in a trading post.

Judy burst into tears when she heard his voice. "Cooper, half of Western Colorado is searching for you. The Utes will say only you disappeared from the southern res with an Old Medicine Man. The Denver newspapers are reporting a BIA Ute informant was blinded the night after Joe's murder. Three men have been indicted from Mancos including a motorcycle gang drug dealer. No witnesses have come forward in the blinding of the BIA agent."

"It's all true. I have been in the desert under the sun and stars with the Old Ute Medicine Man. Call Jumbo Roberts and terminate the search. I am in the Jeep headed for the Airstream. I'll tell you the entire story on Labor Day. I'll meet you in Telluride at the inn. Jeans, no panties."

Cooper's only dime ran out and the line went dead. Cooper walked back to the Jeep and gassed it up, chanting. He kept thinking the Old Medicine Man had never made a pay phone call. He smiled silently thinking the Old Medicine Man liked his wife in a long black Ute-style skirt with no panties on long hot desert walks. Magic is magic but sex is universal.

Cooper woke up the next morning at the inn to a loud banging on his door. "Okay, who is it?"

"Brady. It's urgent!"

Cooper pulled on a pair of jeans and opened the door. Brady stumbled into the room with two Dixie cups of steaming coffee.

"News is really bad. The Federal Bureau of Reclamation has just proposed a dam in Norwood Canyon on the San Miguel River, the last free flowing river in Colorado. They plan to condemn land and water rights if the owners won't sell them to the Feds."

Cooper paused, then said without emotion, "Call George. We'll meet at the Dunton hot springs in three days. Confirm the meeting by leaving an unsharpened pencil in the Jeep's driver side seat. Now the Feds are joining the Lonnie Jr. and Sam Jr. in going after the Y Bar C water."

"How are we going to stop the land grabbing, money grubbing, river damming developers?" Brady asked in a defeated voice.

"The ol' fashioned western way. Get out of here. See you in Dunton," Cooper said coolly and signaled Brady to leave.

Cooper took a long hot bath down the hall and dressed. There was another knock at the door and he pulled his rifle out of its saddle holster, set it upright by the bed and then slowly opened the door.

The State Police Lieutenant from Cortez faced him squarely, his hand on his pistol grip, "We need to talk in private. I have a personal message from Jumbo Roberts for you."

"Come in," Cooper replied warily and retreated to his bed within reach of his rifle.

The Lieutenant stepped into the room and closed the door behind him, "Captain Roberts wants you to know the Simple case is airtight now and the Attorney General's office will press for a conviction for the premeditated first-degree murder of Harvey Stuart and ask for the death penalty."

Cooper nodded in agreement.

"We have arrested three suspects in Joe's murder and will arrest two more tomorrow. The FBI and the BIA are, however, sitting on their hands and not helping on the reservation. Jumbo believes they have lost a key informant on the Southern Ute Reservation. He says you will understand."

Cooper nodded, "Please relay to Captain Roberts - good police work and I expect the death penalty for all of Joe's murderers. The informant was Running Blue Water."

The stone-faced Lieutenant continued, "There was a pay phone call from a café near the southern Ute res to the pay phone at the bar in Mancos during the time Joe was in the bar. Jumbo wants to know if you have any ideas on who made that call."

"The answer is probably Running Blue Water," Cooper replied.

"You either know a name or names or you do not. Withholding evidence is obstruction of justice."

Cooper smiled, "Jumbo will have to answer that question definitively. I was asleep here at the inn that night until Adrianna woke me with the news. I should have been riding shotgun for Joe." Cooper's cold eyes averted to his rifle.

"Finally, Jumbo says stay off the Ute reservations. He cannot help you there any longer. You are a marked man on the FBI and BIA list and they control the res."

"I understand his message. Thank him."

"I want to add the whole department is relieved Senator Harvey Stuart's murderer will be brought to justice." He backed to the door, opened it and departed. His spit shined heavy boots echoed on the polished hardwood floor.

After finishing lunch at Adrianna's bistro, Cooper knocked on her office door but no one answered so he walked over to her house. She answered his knock barefooted and invited him into the pallor. Adrianna was wearing a black velvet robe over her long black Spanish lace nightgown in the dark room. "Why the honor of your visit Cooper? Joe is dead and you have the YBarC to save with your playmate Judy."

"Joe's murderers have all been arrested and charged. I'll drive you down to Durango if you want to meet Joe's family off the res, or Cortez to push state police and DA for the death penalty."

"Joe's family refuses to talk to me. The 400-year-old war between the Utes and the Spanish continues with its timeless hatred. His baby is in my belly, Cooper," Adrianna sobbed. "So talk to me, Cooper. Are you trying to figure out an appropriate response? Joe is in me, Cooper, hiding from all of them. He fooled them again. I am the urn. He's waiting to swim my birth canal and drink my milk," she cried. "Get out, Cooper, I need to cry for awhile."

She collapsed on the Victorian couch. Cooper turned wordlessly and exited through the front door, her cries echoing in his ears down the dusty dirt street. He drove down the valley toward the Airstream. Telluride was going mad. Maybe the mesa would bring hope.

FIFTY-SEVEN

Dunton Hot Springs

Cooper rode his paint up and over the last bit of trail on the flank of Little Cone and looked down on the West Fork of the Delores River, which was a thin blue ribbon at the end of August. The log mining camp buildings around the Dunton Hot Springs looked like a child's play area from almost 9,000 feet. Valleys always looked wonderful to Cooper from high perches on horseback. He could only hear the wind as it stirred the peaks, not the babble of human life and sounds of conflict below. Even the river looked peaceful from the high line trail.

Three hours later Cooper rode across the wooden bridge over the river into Dunton and tied his horse in front of the log cabin-style café and bar. The Idaho license plate confirmed George's presence. Cooper had a cold beer with George and Brady, who had ferried Cooper's Jeep with a horse trailer. A half hour later they were at the target range with Cooper's rifle and three Coors beer cans set up thirty yards away for target practice, which was the cover for their meeting. They shot in order of birth months - Cooper first as an Aquarius, then George as a Scorpio and Brady last as a Sagittarius. Cooper knocked off all three cans on three shots and sent Brady to set them up again.

"We are out of time, George. With Joe dead, the Feds want to dam the river and seize the YBarC water rights with the Lonnies. FAA also just announced a grant for an airport on the old Basque's sheep-grazing mesa west of Telluride. Without Joe, the Ute Water Coalition has fallen apart killing your group's purchase of the Delores River water rights. I can't even set foot on the reservations because of the FBI. The Appeals Court will give me the ranch back, in Max's opinion, but that gives me only sixty days to pay off the bank loan. If Judy can avoid installment payments and close the sale of the hotel in Fairplay by the last day of September and I get all the timber money plus a calf sales advance, we can pay off the note. But Feds will still come after the ranch's water for their dam on the San Miguel," Cooper concluded.

"Got it. Assuming the court gives you the ranch back after Labor Day and we can use it as a staging area, I will meet you then to set a final plan. What do you have in mind?" George probed.

"Range war. I need you and your hard core eco hands, not your attorney," Cooper replied carefully.

"I understand. Also, Lance is dead. He drowned in a rafting accident on the Colorado River in Cataract Canyon on a Class Five whitewater rapid," George watched for a reaction from Cooper.

"Joe was Lance's contact. I've been in the desert with an old Ute medicine man. I hope you can replace Lance. That's a bad assed rapid," Cooper deadpanned, amused at George's cover-up story of Lance's death in the Ajax Ski Company's office.

"Maybe. I may have two helpers who are ready for more than court fights and protests. Both ex-Vietnam Rangers who are tired of seeing Idaho land and rivers carved up by the Feds and developers."

"Can they handle explosives and incendiaries? Your turn to shoot," Cooper replied as Brady approached.

"They can do it all." George took the rifle and hit one can in three shots.

"Not bad for a river guy," said Cooper wondering why George had deliberately missed his last shot to look like an amateur.

"You're up, Brady. If you hit the first two, I'll set up the third can," Cooper laughed.

"I've never fired a high-powered rifle. I'm a fine arts major with a minor in sculpture, grew up in a subdivision with a soccer field," Brady replied.

"Then I'll give you a short course. Just don't pull up the rifle barrel like George did. Keep the rifle quiet on your shoulder, ball in the center of the vee sight on the can's center bottom, hold your breath and squeeze off the shot rock steady. Gun's got no agenda like people. Just point and shoot, the bullet will do the rest. It's a perfect soldier. It doesn't think or have emotion and guilt," Cooper said as George kept a placid face, ignoring Cooper's assertion that he'd pulled his last shot.

Brady shot the remaining twenty-four bullets in the box and never hit a can. The rifle barrel was white hot when he finished.

George and Brady went fly fishing on the West Fork of the Delores River while Cooper went to the log hot springs cabin and stripped down to soak his aching body. The misinformed Utes had inflicted deep pain. Fifteen minutes into a hot-soak, a nude Cooper heard two female voices open the wooden plank door. Two twenty-something women with long brown hair and hiking shorts entered the dimly lit room and eyed Cooper as their sight slowly adjusted.

"We just hiked for two days over Mount Wilson to get here. Mind if we join you?" asked the leggy one as she stripped off her canvas hiking shorts and tee shirt.

"It's a clothing optional community soaking spot," Cooper smiled.

"We're from Montana," she replied, eyeing his sweat stained straw hat on a wood peg.

"You the wrangler in this run-down dude camp."

"No, operate a ranch north of here. Name's Cooper."

"Beth and Carol." They completed shedding their dusty sweaty clothes and stepped into the hot spring pool.

Beth passed a half smoked joint around. Everyone relaxed to a deeper level as the dooby and the eleven percent lithium in the spring water eliminated muscle pain.

A half hour later the group climbed up the springs rickety steps. The women dressed in fresh halter-tops and short shorts from their backpacks. The trio walked over to the cafe bar and ordered a round of cold Coors at sunset. The party started when Brady and George arrived with a dozen large trout for the charcoal grill.

All Cooper remembered the next morning was a blur of grilled fresh trout, dancing to juke box country music and a late night rowdy hot tub. After breakfast George departed for Idaho. Brady helped Cooper load the horse into the trailer and they left for the Telluride Film Festival before the girls woke up.

After a Monday afternoon western movie premier and a Labor Day dinner at The Steak and Brew, drinks at the New Sheridan Bar and a roll in the hay at the inn, Cooper and Judy got a good night's sleep on fresh sheets and rose scented pillowcases. The phone rang in the inn room just as Judy snapped her bra on.

"You up, Cooper?" Max barked. "Appellate courts post their rulings at 8 a.m. You have the YBarC back lock stock and barrel. Old west law prevails. Bank gets the ranch if and only if the foreclosure is perfected. You can lease the timber, cut it, sell hay, sell cows, the art and furniture but you cannot sell the land and water rights without paying off the banks real property first mortgage at closing. You can thank the rural Colorado depression state legislature for drafting air tight legislation to help hard working ranch and farm families when the banks were foreclosing on them."

"We have the YBarC back, Judy. Thanks, and when?" asked Cooper as a smiling blushing Judy pulled on her panties in case Max could somehow detect her nudity.

"Four this afternoon in the company of a deputy sheriff. Bank and Polecat to hand over all records, checkbooks, keys and vacate the property by five. The bank's employees and officers are enjoined from setting foot on the property unless and until they own it as are their agents and attorneys."

"We'll be on time."

"Got to run, Cooper. My wife and I are taking a week's vacation at Cabo to hunt some doves. Stay close to Judy and out of trouble. Buy the girl a gold ring."

At 4 p.m. sharp Cooper and Judy drove the Jeep onto the YBarC pulling the dusty silver Airstream trailer at forty miles an hour. The deputy sheriff was already standing in front of the bunkhouse door and disappeared into the cloud of dust when Cooper braked the Jeep.

Cooper and Judy leapt out of the Jeep and faced an unhappy blinking deputy. "Cooper, that's a reckless driving ticket on a public road."

"Sorry for the dust devil, but it's a dry fall. Please escort Polecat out of here after he hands the books over to Judy."

The deputy frowned but escorted Judy into the bunkhouse office. Polecat, without a word, handed her the checkbook and ledgers. Judy sat down at Cooper's desk and plugged in the electric adding machine and went to work. The deputy emerged with Polecat as Tommy Lee pulled up in front of the bunkhouse in his battered pickup ready to take charge as foreman again. Polecat frowned, "Guess I'm done here. Calves fattening real good on monsoon grass, remuda all in good shape for fall round up, three horses a hand. The hands all staying to work for you against my advice and the fences holding. Only thing I noticed is the level of the San Miguel River never been in my time this low after a big snow winter and regular monsoon summer. Second cut irrigated ranch hay off San Miguel will be fifty percent of normal whereas hay off the Lone Cone ditch will be 120 per cent of normal. Go figure."

Polecat went out a pro, Cooper thought. The late Bill Daniels had known where the San Miguel River water was disappearing. Lonnie Jr.'s pumps were already illegally running year around to make snow and feed the growing demand for water. "Thanks, Polecat. Please brief Tommy Lee in detail and bring him up to date on the hands' assignments. Your pension will be released next month as soon as Max closes out Liz's estate. That's your money fair and square for fifty years of range work."

Cooper did not give him back the lakeside lot. Betrayal in the ranch country came with a penalty. Polecat nodded, knowing he had lost the lot. But he knew in the 1800s a gun hand would have settled his account, not a court of law. He walked away from Cooper without another word and started briefing Tommy Lee on the ranch's current operations. Five minutes later the deputy escorted Polecat off the YBarC forever.

In the office, Judy briefed Cooper, "Books and checkbooks are clean. Looks like Jesse and Sam's bank monitored Polecat's cash flow. There is an infusion of $10,000 cash but no explanation why. Bet the bank just gave you a free undocumented loan. That will offset some of its high interest this year. You need to check the ranch supplies and equipment but I bet it's all there."

"Roger, will do that with Tommy Lee. Then you and I ride the ranch next three days checking the herd. Be ready and saddled at seven so we can reach line shack three before dark." Cooper was off to find his foreman with the adding machine happily clicking in his ears.

FIFTY-EIGHT

Hot Trees

Cooper and Judy had just arrived back at the bunkhouse office after three hot dry windy early September days in the high aspen-groved YBarC rangelands. Their foreheads were wind burned and the bandana tan left their chins lighter brown. They were stripping down to take a shower together in the Airstream when the phone rang. Brady was on the line. "Need you bad at the fire line, Cooper."

"What fire line?"

"An illegal camper in Ilium Valley started a wood cooking fire and the winds gusted over forty miles an hour and blew it into the dry fall brush. The fire is headed toward Telluride up the east side of the valley toward the ski mountain," Brady reported excitedly from a pay phone in Sawpit.

"Why do I care about saving Lonnie Jr.'s ski area from a forest fire?"

"I teach skiing there, Cooper. But the humanitarian reason is the fire may jump both highways out of Telluride in the next two hours and trap a lot of people in Telluride's steep-walled box canyon."

"Adrianna in town?"

"I just talked to her at the bistro. They're preparing sack lunches for the firefighters."

Judy with a bar of rose scented soap in her hand jumped into the conversation, "You have to help, Cooper, or a lot of volunteer firefighters and townspeople could get hurt. You know that terrain and wildland firefighting better than anyone. You know where and how fast that wind will push the fire."

"Okay, okay," groaned Cooper at no one in particular. "I'll call the sheriff. Judy, get dressed and help me pack the Jeep with emergency gear. Be careful, Brady, these hot winds can bring the fire to a hundred feet high moving at ten yards a second. Forest fire can circle you faster than a pro rodeo roper can tie down a calf."

Cooper met the sheriff at the entrance to Ilium Valley by the San Miguel River turn.

"I only have thirty-trained volunteer fireman since the mine closed and seventy or so untrained town volunteers, mostly ski bums, on the line in Ilium Valley. A Forest Service fire commander is due in an hour with the first of his crews plus tankers, I hope and pray. Your granddaddy taught you more about mountain and range grass fires than everyone here knows added up together. What's your plan?" the sheriff asked point blank.

"Split your line or the fire will pin your fighters against the steep west facing Ilium Valley wall with no retreat when it blows up in the noon heat and dry winds. South part of the line of firefighters moves to Ames to protect the hydroelectric plant. Middle line of fighters moves here to hold the highway open down valley for evacuation of town, which starts now. The north part of the line moves up to Highway 145 toward Telluride to clear a blocking line. The fire will climb the Ilium Valley wall by one o'clock unless the wind drops way off. I need a forest service or state patrol helicopter to get up over it." Cooper coughed inhaling smoke as he watched the black gray smoke plume, which rose five thousand feet.

The sheriff keyed his emergency radio channel to move the firefighters. Two Ouray town fire engine companies pulled off the road and the sheriff dispatched them.

His radio cracked, "One firefighter down and burned. That hippie Bluegrass music picker Blue Jay, they think. A summer cabin owner is missing. Did not evacuate according to his wife and the fire burned over their thirty-five acre ranchette lot."

"Follow me to Society Turn where we will set up a command post and meet the state police helicopter from Cortez," the sheriff commanded Cooper.

Cooper followed the sheriff's flashing red lights through the thickening smoke at high speed into the fire zone as loaded vehicles evacuating Telluride passed them. Fire trucks with crews followed them from Montrose, Ridgeway and Grand Junction but Delta had refused to help. At the highway junction near Telluride, command post chaos ruled, to Cooper's dismay, with too many jurisdictions vying for control. Ten minutes later the state police helicopter landed with the Forest Service Wildland Fire Commander on board.

He quickly established a chain of command. "Cooper, let's get up in the air. I'm up from Taos. The Grand Junction Commander is in Idaho on a big fire. I need local knowledge. You already saved me half a day of burn time. Sheriff is the pit boss here."

"You have more crews and some tanker planes?" Cooper asked.

"Next crews are here in four hours and only two more today. Most of Colorado's crews are in California, Idaho and Montana. This big western high-pressure system is burning forests in nine states. Two BLM air tankers from Albuquerque are at the Montrose airport loading water drops now. Should make a pass in half an hour so we need to get up in the air ASAP."

Cooper heard the Telluride town manager yell, "I want to fly in the helicopter. It's my town, not Cooper's."

"You trained in wildland firefighting?" asked the Commander.

"No, but I graduated from Harvard City Management School," he asserted.

"Then go back to town and help your chief marshal evacuate it pronto. Door to door search. There's only one paved highway out now. The fire just jumped State Highway 145, north of the Ophir turn."

After the town manager walked away the sheriff cracked,

"Town managers like wood glue. Always find it when nothing is broke. Always dried up when you need it."

Five minutes later, after a dangerous wind shear lift off, Cooper and the commander were above the fire with the young 'Nam-hardened state patrol pilot. They viewed the almost paralyzing problem as the dry gusting winds drove the fire relentlessly up the Ilium Valley wall toward the thin mesa. A wall of yellow flames was a hundred feet in the air. The ski area base and its outlying ski homes in pine and aspen groves were doomed. Telluride's fate blew in the wind. They watched the fire jump the San Miguel River and the highway at the Ilium Valley road entrance. It closed Telluride's evacuation route to Placerville. Thick gray smoke obscured their view. The fire crews defending Telluride's west flank retreated east toward Sawpit and the state patrol turned back evacuee traffic from Telluride's box canyon.

"Radio the chief marshal to mobilize every 4x4 in Telluride and evacuate everyone over the Tomboy Jeep Road to Ouray. If this wind doesn't drop by sundown, the fire will burn up toward the ski area's north-facing flank and then downslope into town, setting off an inferno. Those new growth pines are tightly spaced," Cooper asserted.

The commander radioed the instructions. The chief marshal estimated five hundred plus people were still in town, including tourists, and only fifty to sixty vehicles capable of clearing Imogene Pass.

The commander ordered, "Women, children and elderly in the 4x4s. Able-bodied men either hike up behind them or report to Society Turn and join the fire lines. Cooper, what will this fire do here late afternoon if no wind drop?"

"Wind will swing straight southwest, die some at sunset but stay hot and gusty off the desert. That means we can maybe hold the fire at the ski area's outlying ski homes. The wind will turn it and force it down the steep front of the north ridge into town. The ridgeline will block the wind some and lay the fire down on the steep terrain. The ski lift chair line up from town will provide a natural firebreak. We make a nighttime stand at San Miguel River along the south border of town," Cooper remembered a similar strategy his grandfather used south of Norwood in Naturita Canyon to keep a lightning fire off the YBarC.

"You bet your cowhands on that, Cooper, if they were on that line?"

"Yes, sir."

"Then I'm all in, otherwise I believe we can lose the entire ski area and the town. Neither would be good for my career," he joked.

"But if it jumps the river we'll lose men," Cooper added.

"I'll order the untrained local volunteers to evacuate next. The wildland firefighting professionals will man the lines after sunset," the commander replied as he received a crisis call from the Telluride Volunteer Firefighters at the Ames hydroelectric power plant, which

Tesla and Westinghouse built. He ordered the two airborne tankers to douse it with their full loads of water.

The helicopter landed them at the command center and left for Montrose airport to refuel. The fire had cut off its avgas tanker truck from the Cortez airport. Cooper borrowed a walkie-talkie from the sheriff and found Brady at the entrance to the Ajax Ski Company's headquarters.

"Come down to the command post and pick up my Jeep and get Adrianna and head over Imogene pass. All untrained firefighters are out of here."

Brady did not argue, "Roger that, Cooper. A fifty-foot wall of flame almost jumped us at the mesa edge. A Hotshot crew saved our ass. I'm on my motocross bike. Will cut to town along the river."

Cooper ears caught the sound of a nearby Lonnie Jr. yelling in a rage at the commander and sheriff.

"You are abandoning the State Highway 145 line. That'll burn my base buildings and a quarter of my ski area. Cooper Stuart behind this?" yelled Lonnie Jr.

"The seasonal prevailing wind and terrain are behind the decision. And it's National Forest land that you lease, so I'm making the call to save most of the ski mountain, the town and every life possible. Two persons are presumed dead so far but it might be a more if Cooper had not been here before I arrived. Now move your trained firefighting employees and their equipment back to the mid mountain cat track and evacuate the rest of them through Telluride over the pass to Ouray," the commander calmly ordered.

"I'll sue you and Cooper for this," an outraged Lonnie Jr. threatened.

"You cannot sue the U.S. government, sir."

The sheriff physically restrained Cooper from advancing toward Lonnie Jr. and yelled over his shoulder, "Get up there on the fire line right now, Lonnie, or I'll have to arrest you for something I'll figure out later. You stay here you can call your insurance agent in cuffs. I hereby deputize Cooper Stuart. You cannot sue the County either."

Lonnie Jr. stomped off, cursing under his breath. There were thumbs-up from all around the command post.

Brady roared up on his dirt bike and turned Cooper's attention away from a retreating Lonnie Jr. Cooper conferenced with the commander's team and it was decided that he would anchor the San Miguel River line at the town border. He was given the authority to pull the fire crews if he determined the fire would jump the river and burn the town. They all would evacuate up and over Imogene Pass via Tomboy Road. Cooper led Brady into town and traded him the Jeep at the riverbank for the dirt bike. The fire crews were already bulldozing a line on the mountain side of the river and clearing brush on the north side of the river.

An hour before sundown the wind started to drop but the box canyon was filled with dense smoke with visibility less than fifty yards. Cooper had confirmed that Brady was driving Adrianna in his Jeep and riding drag in the civilian evacuation of Telluride up Tomboy Road. The smoky road had been snarled from time to time with a breakdown, punctured tires and even a wreck when a 4x4's brakes overheated, failed and then rolled backwards into the line of vehicles. The disabled vehicle had been pushed over a steep cliff on the climb to Ouray to clear the route. The retreat was two hours behind schedule but the marshal's office had assured the fire commander that Telluride was a near ghost town.

A half hour after an eerie sunset the Forest Service radio crackled, "The fire line is holding along the cat track. We lost the base buildings, including the headquarters and the base restaurant. But the wind has shifted due southwest and dropped. The fire line and wind shift are turning the fire and pushing it over the ridge toward the lift tower. Get ready for action in town unless we get a complete wind drop. But Grand Junction airport tower says that's not going to happen tonight," the commander's voice cracked in the smoke.

"Roger that. We'll make a last stand here. Hope we're not Custer at the Little Bighorn," Cooper radioed.

There was no reply. Cooper called the five crew chiefs together and he relayed the report. They moved to defensive positions on the town's southern mountainside with the steely Hotshots deployed to put out spot fires that jumped the San Miguel River. Cooper moved onto the mountainside at the point of the line on the town border, his dirt bike handy.

In complete darkness, as the last taillights of the column of evacuees stalled again near Savage Basin at 12,000 feet, the forest fire roared over the ridgeline with flames leaping fifty feet into the smoky sky toward Telluride. The walkie-talkie crackled again as Cooper heard tanker planes fly over above him.

The commander reported, "One smoke jumper was injured trying to turn the fire. It blew back on them. This is a mean-spirited fire. It is yours now, Cooper. We can and will hold the line up here. Tankers are grounded for the night. One ski area cat and their D10 blade have enough fuel left to keep cutting new fire line 'til midnight. Their main fuel depot blew in the fire but they have two fifty gallon drums of diesel in the lift house for the generators. Two snowcats have already thrown their treads on the rocky terrain."

"Copy that and roger out," Cooper replied.

The fire started its slow burn down a thousand vertical feet toward town, the wind blowing its embers steadily down the steep wooded mountainside with the lift line acting as a break to the east. A Hotshot crew followed it over the ridge, putting out spot fires that jumped east of the lift's ski runs. It was dangerous work under the smoky dark night sky. Thirty minutes later the fire was only two hundred vertical feet from the river when it started to lay down for the night.

The ridgeline blocked the steady southwest wind. The silent dark village of Telluride was front lit in an eerie orange glow behind Cooper as he ordered his last crew to cross the bridge at the town border. Embers fell near them like burned-out fireworks on the Fourth of July. Half of Telluride's buildings had burned in past fires on windy nights over its one-hundred-year history. Its surviving aging dry mining era buildings and run down miner's houses awaited their fate on a September night.

Cooper watched the fire stall fifty yards from the river while the fire crews raced to put out small brush fires on the abandoned railroad bed and on the valley floor where terrified black and white dairy cattle mooed like foghorns in the smoke. Cooper wanted Joe at his side so he could divine the wind's future. Suddenly, the wind shifted due west, gusting straight down the narrow open valley floor toward the steep walls of the dead end canyon.

"All fire crews move down the railroad bed and deploy along the river on town side all the way to the park. The west wind will blow the fire along the river corridor. If it jumps the river and structures catch fire, we are out of here up Tomboy road. It will be a roof top to roof top inferno in town," Cooper radioed.

"I copy that and order it also," the commander radioed.

"My smoke jumper crew's retreating back over the ridgeline. It's too dangerous for them in the dark with the wind shift. You sure you all don't want out of Telluride right now?"

"No," came a chorus of walkie-talkie calls from the crew chiefs, who were redeploying their firefighters along the river.

"Roger that," the commander replied. When the fire hit the riverbank, burning pines fell into the water, producing clouds of dangerously hot steam. Cooper raced the motocross bike along the thinly manned fire line and felt the burning heat on his bandannaed face. He silently cursed Lonnie Jr. for illegally pumping the river too low. All three fire hydrants near the river had long fire hoses hooked up and the Telluride volunteer firefighters were wetting down adjacent building roofs. The Hotshots ran from spot fire to spot fire as willows and pines burst into flames on the town side of the river. Cooper reached the abandoned railroad station as a section of its pine shingle roof burst into flames. A minute later a Telluride Fire Department tanker raced up, hooked up a hose and put the roof fire out before it could ignite the building.

As Cooper reached Oak Street, which defined the west boundary of the business district, the wind gusted to thirty-five miles an hour and a wall of flames twenty feet high blew up along the river. It jumped into town and ignited three houses along Pacific Street.

Cooper radioed, "Telluride Fire Department chief - can you hold the fire on south side of Pacific Street or do we get out of Dodge?"

The captain, a German miner squawked, "We'll douse them good. You keep them wildland crews dousing them spot fires and we'll save this old girl, God willing. I got the Swedes at Oak, the Finns at the depot and the Irish and Italians with me. We all have been here too long to lie down and quit tonight. I have the mining company's enclosed D-12 cat and we'll doze flat anything we can't douse. This wind got to drop by midnight or I will give up beer for a year."

"Roger that, 10-4," replied Cooper.

For an hour, the fire occasionally jumped the river and was pushed back time after time by smoke choked Hotshots.

Cooper had burns on his forearms and left thigh from flaming embers and his radio crackled again, "The fire hydrants just quit. Town water is pumped dry so we have to pump from the river but that limits our range to the south side of Colorado Avenue. If the fire jumps north of there we have to pull out," radioed the Telluride Volunteer Fire chief.

Cooper pivoted to face a tap on his shoulder and the sheriff said, "Last Jeep, which was yours, just cleared the pass to Ouray. If you all want out of here everyone understands."

"We're holding like the center of the Union line at Gettysburg. Can you get us tanker trucks in here from Ames or anywhere? Hydrants are dried up," Cooper replied, choking in the acrid smoke, his eyes dry and burning.

"It's your call on retreat. I'll see if there are any tankers that can get down 145. The commander took most of them up to the cat track on the ski hill and they are trapped there."

The sheriff raced away. Cooper looked over his shoulder to see the roof of the historic Opera House burst into flames. He knew if they lost the Opera House the town would quickly be an inferno. He keyed his radio but paused and said nothing. He raced Brady's motocross bike to the Opera House where a lone tanker crew was already laying down hose. Two volunteer firefighters with mine hard hats raced up the fire escape pulling the heavy hose as a yellow flame with billowing black smoke rose into the orange glow.

Cooper held his breath, finger ready to key the walkie-talkie. A heavy stream of water shot out of the hose and started to knock the roof fire down as black smoke filled the air. Then as suddenly as it had blown in from the hot desert, the wind dropped and shifted due south and the smoke from the Opera House drifted straight into the smoky night sky and the fire started to lay down again on the mountainside. There was a cheer from the firefighters along the river. They knew they could beat the monster now.

Cooper radioed the commander and the sheriff, "The fire is laying down. The wind has dropped for the night. Please have your deputy in Norwood call Judy and tell her I am crispy but okay. She was the one who sent me into this inferno. She is the YBarC conscience."

"Roger that and I will thank her, Cooper. Today I saw your grandfather's courage and wisdom in your eyes. God bless you, son, for riding to help us all."

FIFTY-NINE

Canyon del Muerto

As Cooper sped along Arizona Highway 160 in the midday sun with Judy riding shot-gun and a pregnant Adrianna surrounded by pillows in the back seat, he recounted his forest fire adventures. THE ROCKY MOUNTAIN NEWS had declared Cooper a hero, with praise from the sheriff and the fire commander. The TELLURIDE TIMES had attacked Cooper's and the commander's plan that burned down two of the Ajax Ski Company's base buildings, but left all of the ski runs undamaged. Sam Jr., Jesse Smith, the town manager, the town marshal and Lonnie Jr. led the assault with their quotes. Telluride's opinion of Cooper was now split down the middle with the development community on one side and the work-ing class, including the volunteer firefighters, on the other.

George was on the way from Idaho to meet them at Canyon de Chelly. The Jeep was followed by Blue Jay in his 1948 baby blue Chevy pickup truck with Brady. Blue Jay, Brady's bluegrass music picking friend, had survived the fire in an old gold mining "glory hole" he used to hide his pot shipments. He quoted Mark Twain in the ROCKY MOUNTAIN NEWS article and announced a bluegrass picking and fiddling concert in Town Park to raise money for the Telluride Volunteer Firefighters who had hospital bills to pay. His friend Bill Monroe had agreed to headline it in October with Coors providing the beer and the YBarC the beef barbecue.

Judy stirred from a nap in the passenger seat and asked, "Where are we?"

Adrianna answered, "A half hour from Chinle at the entrance of Canyon de Chelly. You meet your destiny in the Canyon del Muerto…the canyon of death, Cooper," Adrianna prophesied, "We are all caught in the quicksand of your destiny in New Spain."

Cooper felt the cool presence of a spirit in the Jeep. He signaled Blue Jay to wait at the entrance of the Best Western while he did a slow scout of the parking lot in the Jeep as he drove around it with Judy and Adrianna. Cooper spotted an Idaho license plate on a faded green VW van with kayak racks in front of room 212. George appeared on the balcony and tossed Cooper the keys to rooms 210 and 211. Blue Jay pulled in next to the VW van.

After Cooper settled Judy into Room 210 and Adrianna in Room 211, he and Brady met George who briefed them on recent Eco Warrior intelligence.

Cooper asked George for a confirmation about the YBarC water rights if the dam was built.

George replied, "They'll condemn the YBarC's San Miguel River water rights for the dam and then use the National Security Act to take the ranch's downstream Delores River water rights for the National Uranium Reserve for future mining and milling."

"And when the dust clears, they'll lease the Lonnies' upstream rights on the San Miguel they need for the Ajax Ski Company development and snowmaking," Cooper deduced.

"Cooper, you get a green government treasury check and you will be evicted by a U.S. Marshal."

"So what next? We call the Russians and make a deal?" Cooper joked.

"That's treason, Cooper. If I were an FBI informant wired with a tape recorder, you would be finished," George snapped, missing the humor.

"So would you." Cooper pulled a small knife from his cowboy boot to make his point.

"Touché. You all get some dinner and sleep. A Navajo AIM friend is taking me into the canyon tonight. We will stay at his family's hogan. I'll meet you tomorrow with the final plan," George informed them.

"Where in the Canyon de Chelly?" Cooper asked.

"The Canyon del Muerto branch, at a log hogan with an orchard, about a half mile in," George replied with a chill in his voice. "Who will be with you?"

"Brady, Judy, Adrianna, Blue Jay, and the Old Ute Medicine Man," replied Cooper.

"The Medicine Man powerful?"

"He saved my life at the res after Joe's death."

George winced, "Who is Blue Jay, Brady?"

"He's good to fly, George. His band plays the Earth Day concert in Telluride. No worries there," Brady answered.

"Tomorrow," and George opened the motel room door for their exit.

At sunup, while the canyon floor was still cool, Cooper's Jeep led Blue Jay's pickup truck into the canyon. An old Navajo rode with Cooper. Tribal law and BLM regulations mandated that all non-Navajos entering the canyon must be guided. The ancient guide had magically appeared at Cooper's motel room door at sunrise. A tired and very pregnant Adrianna had refused to stay in her room and shared the cramped back seat with Judy. The vehicles sped through the dry riverbed of the canyon past stone ruins high up in the red and white sandstone walls with hand cut steps to them. The group viewed the sacred images of Indian rock art from 2500 years of inhabitants, hunters, farmers and invaders.

The Navajo pointed to tire tracks in the canyon's sandy bottom at turn points to guide Cooper but remained silent. He occasionally signaled a stop and pointed to a ruin or wall of rock art, which he talked about in spotty English but mostly in the incomprehensible Navajo language, which the code talkers had used to confound the Japanese in World War II.

Finally, they turned into the Canyon of Death and Adrianna said, "Well, Cooper have the Anglos in Washington betrayed you, too. Yes or no?"

"Yes," Cooper replied tersely.

"They have betrayed the French, the Spanish, the Mexicans, the Navajo's and the Utes like Joe. They betray everyone in the west at the whip hand of Wall Street and London," she asserted.

"Is she right?" Judy asked.

"Totally. The Lonnies, the bank and Washington plan to seize the ranch's water rights for a nickel on a future dollar, never mind my family's way of life and stewardship of the land."

"Vail now wants my father's mine closed. In the last few months, four federal agencies have harassed him on trumped-up infractions," Adrianna asserted, "and they are planning to create $5 dollar an hour jobs to replace $25 dollar an hour union mine jobs that feed families."

Judy asked, "What's the plan?"

"It's Po'pay's Pueblo Indian revolt in Taos in 1680, not the Ute Massacre at the White River Reservation," Cooper said coldly. "I'm not surrendering quietly."

The old Navajo nodded with war drums in his ears from Cooper's tone of voice. Tears rolled from Judy's eyes.

Deep inside the canyon the old Navajo signaled a halt in front of a hogan with a cherry and apple orchard in its back yard irrigated by a spring. George emerged from the hogan followed by an old Navajo woman who seemed to be the guide's wife. The group had an outdoor breakfast of fry bread and pinto beans. Afterwards, the Navajos entered the windowless hogan to rest in the shade. George took a walk down the canyon while the rest of the group stripped down and soaked in the cool pool as the canyon heat rose to ninety degrees by noon. Adrianna's swollen belly and breasts attracted quick glances. Judy's body was the crowd pleaser but she stayed submerged to the chagrin of the boys.

At two o'clock, when the September sun swung southwest, shadowing the cool pool and the white cliff wall behind it, everyone dressed. George returned just as Cooper's friend, the Old Ute Medicine Man, emerged from the six-sided hogan's east-facing door, a scalping knife in hand. Everyone gasped, except Cooper.

The Medicine Man signaled the group to the wall and spoke first in the Ute language and then in broken English, "Everyone who will go on the raid against the white devils must find a hand print on the wall."

He pointed to his left. The shadowed wall held lightly carved ancient handprints of the canyons inhabitants. He pointed to Judy first and she walked forward and after searching the wall for a long three minutes put her right long fingered hand on a perfect match. Next, he signaled Adrianna who had used her witch's power to instantly find a broad print for her swollen left hand. Her belly pressed against the warm radiating sandstone. Blue Jay, stoned from mushrooms he ate in the pool, spent ten minutes trying handprint after handprint as tension built sprinkled with laughter. Finally, he reached high up and found a perfect match. Brady's small hand instantly found five handprints. The Ute signaled Cooper, whose range-sharp eyes had had 20 minutes to scout the wall. He walked straight to his only matching print and stretched his tall lanky frame and put his hand on the shallow carved print of an ancient. The group giggled in nervous relief.

Finally, the Ute Medicine Man signaled George as the group's attention dwindled, knowing he was the leader of the Eco Warriors. He walked slowly to the wall and bent to reach a print tucked into a crevice in the rock. It did not match because the crevice's shadow distorted it. Cooper's thoughts drifted and he wondered if Judy had a child with him whether her belly and breasts would swell like Adrianna's. Judy smiled, seemingly reading his thoughts and touched the back of his tanned right hand. Adrianna stepped away from Judy when she touched Cooper. Blue Jay palmed a mushroom bud to Brady as the Old Ute Medicine Man suddenly drummed on a log horse trough in front of him with his moccasined foot.

George was frantically smashing his now bleeding hand against miss-matched hand-print after print on the wall. The group's eyes all turned to George as he exhausted the last handprint. He turned wild-eyed and started to dash for Cooper's Jeep. The Ute Medicine Man stepped between him and the path to the Jeep. In two quick strokes of his war knife he cut George's hamstring mussels and he came to a painful stop on the sandy canyon floor. He screamed in pain and knelt, bleeding profusely. Judy fainted into Cooper's arms but Adrianna stared at the attack, her black eyes in witch mode. Blue Jay threw up and Brady sat down crossed legged. The Medicine Man chanted an ancient verse in Ute language and pierced both of George's eardrums with the tip of the sharp steel knife. Cooper stepped forward to stop the massacre.

"Take his watch, Cooper," the Ute ordered.

"He's not wearing a watch," Cooper replied, upset and confused.

"In his ass," the old Ute replied.

The knife flashed, ripping the seam of George's paddling shorts. The sun made the silver metal recording device glisten. The black lettered FBI logo was stenciled on its silver surface. The old one cut the adhesive tape holding it in the crease of George's bottom. It pulled loose as the tiny mic fell from George's square metal belt buckle that hid it.

The old Ute handed it to Cooper and simply said, "The watch."

George turned toward the old Ute and grabbed the knife from his gnarled arthritic hand. He drove it point first into his own heart and fell to the sand floor into a pool of blood. Cooper heard the sound of a helicopter echoing down the canyon. The Ute spoke, "The spirits called me here. The white man's police are searching for you, Cooper. The old Navajo who guided you here was a code talker in World War II. He heard this dead man, who called himself the code name 'Whitewater,' talk to the police in the night by a handheld radio. They have a prison wagon waiting for all of you at the Navajo tribal police house in Chinle by the airstrip. His body will never be found. There are thousands of burial crevices in the canyon. He will join the bones of the pony soldiers who are hidden here for eternity. The Navajo guide will bury him and hide the Jeep and pickup. Follow me in silence. I know the old secret raiding route out of the canyon. The Utes used it to capture Navajo slaves to trade to the Spanish." And he looked toward Adrianna.

The helicopter hovered at the mouth of the thin canyon seeming to listen for a signal. Cooper smashed the transponder recorder against the sandstone canyon wall and pulled the small tape out of it. He opened his Zippo lighter and set the tape on fire. Then he walked over to George and stuffed it in his wide-open mouth.

"Follow and never look down," the Ute commanded. He led the sober group around the canyon bend past the orchard with its ripe small red apples and up a slot canyon with a sandy creek bottom.

Three hundred feet up the slot it narrowed to three feet as they squeezed sideways through it and found hand carved steps in the wall. They started the slow climb out of the canyon. The helicopter thundered over them but the FBI agents could not see them in the dark shadowed slot. They rested by leaning their bottoms against the other wall as they climbed using the ancient hand and toeholds carved into the red sandstone. The Medicine Man chanted as he led them to safety.

SIXTY

The Hole in the Wall Gang Returns

A fter a quiet few weeks, September 21 started the YBarC's traditional cattle round up. After Judy and Cooper had returned to the ranch, life had become very domestic with breakfast and dinner in the Airstream and lunch on the range. The aspen had just started to turn on the north facing slopes in the high country and the night air was crisp. No one had shown up at the ranch headquarters from the FBI, BIA or sheriff's department. The Colorado State Supreme Court was expected to rule on the ranch's foreclosure by Halloween and Max had advised Cooper and Judy to have at least $800,000 dollars in cash by then to pay the bank loan and interest. A good round up and the closing of the Fairplay Hotel sale would save the ranch. Luke Ford, the Fairplay banker, had pledged two hundred thousand new loan dollars for working capital when the Telluride bank loan was paid.

Round up started at 5 a.m. on Monday morning with Tommy Lee in charge. Cooper and Judy joined the nine YBarC hands along with a dozen neighboring ranchers who rode for the week in trade off for the YBarC's help for their day or two round ups. Only the Polecat clan was missing. Blue Jay had volunteered to sing for the round up suppers at the chuck wagon, which Cooper accepted, but he turned down Brady and his three ski bum pals. They did not have time to look for lost or bucked-off ski bums on the vast range. Judy, in jeans and a blue denim cowgirl skirt, looked like a rodeo magazine model with a tan and her jet-black hair streaming out from under her gray cowgirl hat. She handled her quarter horse like the ex-rodeo barrel racer she was. Cooper picked her for his team rider and Tommy Lee sent them to the Lone Cone range with six other riders to bring in 500 mother cows and calves. The cowboys on YBarC quarter horses thundered out of the headquarters, throwing up a cloud of.

Five nights into the round up Cooper and Judy finished dinner at the chuck wagon and walked away from the line shack where the YBarC hands were gathered to drive 496 mother cows and 460 calves back to the corrals for shipment. Cooper and Judy were bone tired, sun burned, wind burned, cut, bruised and scratched up from four twelve-hour days in the saddle. They had chased cows and calves down narrow dusty draws, across streams, through thick red oak, under low aspen tree limbs and in thick sagebrush.

Cooper led Judy to a hidden hot spring in a rock outcropping while Blue Jay's round up songs wafted a quarter mile away through the cool mountain air under a half-moon sky. Cooper stripped off Judy's clothes, enjoying her body in the moonlight. She then stripped him nude and led him by the hand into the pool of ninety degree water. They soaked under the stars.

"Tommy Lee's total calf count's near 1,500 Cooper. Tomorrow is stray day and we should make our final count," Judy reported.

"Good. We can make the note but with cattle prices low, we will need the hotel sale dollars," Cooper reflected.

"They're in the bank, Cooper."

Judy slipped her hand under the dark surface of the pool and found Cooper's magic spot. "No more cattle business tonight Cooper, just pleasure."

"Fine by me," and Cooper's hand disappeared under the surface as Judy giggled.

On Sunday afternoon, Cooper and Judy sat on the top rail of the headquarters' corral fence by the bunkhouse and looked over 1643 mother cows who were bawling for their 1491 calves who had been separated into the shipping corrals. Tommy Lee had presented Judy a count sheet signed and dated. Cooper had posted two armed hands around the clock to patrol the corrals until the calves were shipped. More than a thousand six-month-old calves were being shipped by truck on Tuesday to the family's Kansas broker. Four hundred heifers were staying to be mothers in the spring. For the first time in fifty years the mother cows would not travel by rail to Arizona but winter on hay at the YBarC. It would be a hard frigid winter for the pregnant cows and the ranch hands working in the snow to feed them hay. Judy finished her hour-long eye count and signed Tommy Lee's cattle sheet and dated her signature. Cooper witnessed their signatures with his and the roundup was over.

"Day is done," Cooper said as he smiled at Judy. "Let's go into Norwood, have bourbon and a hot dinner that is not steak, baked potato and canned beans."

Judy smiled to herself as she saw them sitting on the same corral fence together on the same September Sunday with a signed and witnessed YBarC cattle count sheet for the next fifty years.

"Fine by me," Judy replied, "but only after a hot shower in the Airstream and a fresh pair of jeans with a clean shirt." She continued, "Last one to the shower hand soaps the other one's back."

She leapt off the corral fence with cattle count sheets in hand and raced for the Airstream, legs churning while Cooper watched in amazement. He was too sore to win an out of the gate foot race with a twenty-two-year-old full-blooded western woman. But losing was not at all bad, the way he figured it.

SIXTY-ONE

Flashing Red Lights

The ski bums Telluride loved Halloween and the volunteer, commercial-free, community radio station put on its first fund-raising party in the town's Quonset hut gym. Cooper and Judy had been invited as special guests of Blue Jay's band. Cooper exited the Jeep dressed in a Fiji Bula shirt, khaki tropical shorts, carrying a ukulele and with a knife concealed in his cowboy boot. Judy wore her college NCAA barrel-racing outfit with a stuffed toy horse duct-taped to her bottom. Brady dressed as an old miner and Blue Jay wore a sequined Grand Ole Opera shirt. They all followed Blue Jay around the side of the hut where he produced a pint of bourbon.

The hut was decorated with ghosts, witches and goblins. Two hundred Telluridians from 21 to 70 cruised the basketball court floor in costumes. There was the silver duct tape man, the nude gold painted model with her artist husband, two space aliens in shimmering silver aluminum foil suits, a bare-chested blonde mermaid in a boat with wheels being pulled by a fisherman and a most amazing red headed woman dressed as a poet. She was reading a poem written on a roll of adding machine paper, which she pulled out of her vagina.

Cooper spied Adrianna, who wore a Spanish witches outfit and rode a black painted broom.

Cooper pulled Judy over, "Hello Adrianna. Guess you're big pregnant now."

"Feel him kick." She placed Cooper's hand on her stomach.

Judy flushed with anger, but she was determined to keep the peace that had been established after Canyon de Chelly. She pulled Cooper toward the bar.

"Good cowgirl," Cooper whispered his tongue caressing her ear. "Let's get a cold draft beer. The money goes for a good cause. Freedom of speech over the radio."

While Judy was in the women's room, Brady found Cooper,

"When do we meet again?"

"After the court sets a payoff date and when Judy and I retire the note off on the ranch. Clue Blue Jay in after he comes down off his high tomorrow," Cooper replied.

"See you at the ranch," Brady replied.

"Lonnie and the boys are too quiet," Cooper observed.

"They are sub rosa here but FBI agents keep poking around town."

Cooper walked over to Judy and whispered for her to follow him out the front door.

When the phone rang in the inn room at ten in the morning, Cooper answered.

"Cooper, it's Max. The Colorado Supreme Court just ruled the bank has a full legal basis to foreclose but cannot change the original interest rate. Sam has to pay his own legal fees because he illegally raised the interest rate without a default clause in your loan when you paid interest only last year. The YBarC loans never had an interest rate default clause when his father ran the bank and Sam never changed the original note, just rolled it over with a signed addendum each year at prime plus one."

"So what now?" Judy put her ear to the receiver, her soft breasts pushed against Cooper's bare back.

"You need $719,007 at the bank by 5 p.m. tomorrow. The court would not even give you five working days. Sam and the state banking association got to them. No more delays. You have to pay up. The court is making an example out of the YBarC."

Cooper winced, but Judy jumped in, "We have it. Hotel sale money was supposed to be wired into my account by 4 p.m. yesterday. I was going to tell Cooper this morning after I called the bank. I'll pool it with the calf money and fire insurance money and Cooper's cash back from the busted condo deal plus timber money. We can do it with a few thousand to spare. Luke Ford over in Fairplay will set up a two hundred thousand line of credit once we clear Sam's note."

"Marry this girl, Cooper. I'll send you a legal bill. You'll have ten thousand less in working capital plus five thousand for the Lear jet fuel we used. Take the sheriff with you so there are no shenanigans. The court ordered it because of the bad blood. He's receiving a copy of the order. Goodbye."

"We won. The YBarC is ours," Cooper shouted happily.

"Back to bed for a roll in the hay then to Montrose for an engagement ring."

"No, on the roll in the hay, Cooper, but yes on the engagement ring. We need to rocket to the ranch's safe, get the cash, then to the saw mill office to pick up the final lease payment, then to the Montrose bank to get a cashier's check after I have the hotel and calf money wired there from my account in Fairplay," Judy smiled.

"Not just a quickie," teased Cooper.

"Well, Cowboy mount me like a heifer and then it's the trail," and Judy laughing, turned her back to Cooper, bent at the waist, and put her hands on the mattress and opened her feet shoulder width. Cooper had lived on a ranch long enough to figure out the rest.

At five in the afternoon Cooper and Judy left the bank in Montrose with a cashier's check. They had a steak dinner at the Cattleman's Cafe and spent the night under an assumed name at the Best Western. They did not want to be findable by the Lonnie Jr's gang. Tommy Lee and the winter hands patrolled the ranch and night hawked the cattle with loaded Winchester rifles. Cooper slept with his saddle rifle, safety off, by the bed's head-board. Judy had cried happy tears when he gave her a gold Idaho opal engagement ring from the family jeweler on Main Street where the YBarC had an account.

At eleven the next morning they met the sheriff in front of the Telluride bank and he followed them to Sam's open door behind the teller cage.

The sheriff announced, "I have Cooper Stuart, owner of the YBarC, with me and his cashier's check for full payoff of the YBarC note as ordered by the Colorado Supreme Court. I demand a canceled bank note on his behalf according to Colorado law."

Sam Jr. looked up with hatred in his eyes, "I'll settle this with you next election sheriff."

He opened his desk side file drawer and pulled out the note, pushing a Colt 45, aside.

Cooper handed the sheriff the cashier's check and the sheriff handed it to Sam Jr. who frowned and said, "You owe the bank another $1,500 for the October 1 note origination fee for this year and today's early cancellation penalty."

Cooper never said a word as he peeled off fifteen hundred in cash and handed it to the sheriff who counted it and handed it to Sam Jr.

Sam Jr. turned red and took a stamp out of his narrow desk drawer and stamped the note "Paid in Full", then signed and dated the stamps blank lines and entered the cashier check number. "You the witness, sheriff."

"I am, by court order." The aging gray-haired sheriff bent over the oak desktop and signed the witness blank.

Sam glowered at Cooper and Judy, "This bank and town are done with the Stuarts but not the YBarC. Escort them out of my office, sheriff."

Sam handed the sheriff the canceled note and Judy quickly took it out of his hand and she stuffed it into her brown leather shoulder purse.

On the sidewalk, the sheriff frowned and said, "My advice is to stay out of Telluride, Cooper. Get rid of the inn room. I cannot protect you here anymore. They plan to set you up sure as the sun will rise tomorrow, maybe me too. Keep watching your herd and back. Lonnie Sr. always been mean as a snake. I see you going to marry Miss Judy here. That is a fine idea," the sheriff added glancing at the opal gold engagement ring.

Before Cooper could answer, the sheriff's radio squawked,

"Miss Adrianna bleeding real bad. Her life's going away fast with the baby's, too. We have her loaded in the county ambulance at the heath center. Need your approval to lead the ambulance to Montrose Hospital with my lights flashing at high speed," the deputy radioed.

"Lead them, deputy but at a reasonable high speed. I do not need three casualties. I will radio your clearance through Montrose and Ouray counties."

"Can we follow them?" Cooper asked worried.

"At a safe distance. I don't need five of you dead."

"Thanks for showing up at the bank for the YBarC, sheriff."

"Court ordered it. But I did it for your grandfather, son. Go help your friend. Sounds like she needs you real bad." They raced for Judy's Wagoneer and picked up the flashing lights at the town limit.

Sixty mountain miles and an hour later Cooper and Judy pushed through the emergency room doors and heard a nurse say,

"The baby's out, doc, but he won't breath."

Then a loud beep sound stared from behind the curtain. "She's flatlining. We need the heart guy down here now."

Cooper and Judy raced for the curtain but another nurse stopped them saying, "They need to work in there. They both have seconds, not minutes."

Cooper and Judy waited a long half-minute. Then they heard the baby cry.

"He's breathing on the respirator, Doctor," the nurse said.

"She's got thirty seconds or she is brain dead," the Doctor stated.

The beep stayed steady as Adrianna's life drained away.

Cooper saw a spirit in his peripheral vision. The Old Ute Medicine Man walked through the thick white floor length curtains and uttered a chant. Cooper and Judy held their breath. Silence pervaded the emergency unit except for the flatline beep and then they all heard Adrianna's heart beat again.

"A miracle," said the nurse almost crying.

"Indeed, the Indian Medicine Man saved her life. Where is he? What was that brown powder he put in her mouth?" the doctor asked.

Cooper saw the ageless old Ute as he passed back through the thick white curtain. He had come to save his great-grandson and his great-grandson's mother. His work done, he was returning to the desert. Joe's spirit was alive on the earth again. The old Ute could now prepare to join his ancestors in the silence of the vast quiet reservation's desert lands.

The doctor threw open the curtains, "Any friends or relatives here." He looked for the Ute who had disappeared like Joe Bear Spirit always had.

"Friends," Cooper said as he and Judy advanced.

The very red baby was breathing steadily. His flat nose and thick jet-black hair confirmed his Spanish and Ute heritage. Adrianna grasped Cooper's hand, her weak eyes barely focusing. Her mouth tried to ask Cooper a question but it would not move. Cooper knew the answer. "He is Joe Bear Spirit Jr. and his great-grandfather the Medicine Man was here. He helped the doctor and nurses save you and little Joe. The war between the Utes and the Spanish is over," Cooper whispered into her ear.

Adrianna's eyes still tried to search the room.

Judy answered her question, "He is beautiful, Adrianna. He is you and Joe."

Adrianna weakly smiled and fell back into sleep, her witch's earthly powers exhausted.

The doctor stared at Cooper but said nothing. All he knew was it had taken both worlds to save his patients. The doctor held the ancient tiny gold ring he had surgically removed from Adrianna's internal vaginal lips. He put the ring in his pocket. He would return it when she was strong enough. Since he saved her life, he would be protected from the ring's curse.

SIXTY-TWO

Past Crimes

Two weeks later, Cooper and Judy knocked on Adrianna's door in Telluride to visit the mother, baby and drop off a YBarC child's saddle as their present. A young Spanish woman holding the sleeping baby answered the door with tear stained cheeks.

"Hello, ma'am, I'm Cooper a friend of Adrianna and this is Judy. May we see her?" an alarmed Cooper asked.

"I'm her sister Mary. Come in, Adrianna spoke of you. There is a problem."

"Are Adrianna and the baby recovering okay?" asked an alarmed Judy.

"Their health is fine but the FBI arrested her this morning," and she started crying.

Judy took the baby and they followed her to the darkened parlor. When she composed herself, Cooper probed, knowing the answer, "What are the charges?"

"That she was an accomplice to the wounding of the jailer at the Tierra Amarilla, New Mexico, court house raid in 1967. You know of this fight between the Spanish settlers in Northern New Mexico to get their land grants back?" she softly stated.

"I do."

"She was an organizer for the 'Land or Death' movement but she never spoke of her work because my father did not approve. Our family never knew she was in the courthouse with the raiders," she confided.

"So the FBI arrested her knowing she had a two-week-old baby?" Judy asked.

"I don't think so. I hid upstairs in a closet with the baby when we saw their cars stop in front of the house and they came to the door with guns and FBI vests. Adrianna met them at the door and surrendered," she sobbed softly.

"Can you care for the baby?" Judy asked.

"Yes, my father is coming to get me and little Joe or Jose as we call him, after dark," she said almost smiling.

"Good," replied Judy. "Can we help?"

"It is better that you go."

"Does Adrianna have an attorney? Where is she being held?" Cooper asked.

"My father's attorney is helping. The FBI agents were from Denver. We think she is there."

"We'll leave you then if you think it's best. I'll call your family in Red Cliff tomorrow," Cooper volunteered.

Judy returned the still sleeping baby and they departed with the small empty saddle.

The news from Denver papers and radio had been negative for days. Adrianna was being held without bail waiting for extradition to New Mexico, which the Federal Prosecutor was fighting. The FBI feared the Spanish-controlled northern New Mexico state court would let her post bail and might dismiss the charges. But her attorney contended the shooting of the jailer at Tierra Amarilla was a state crime and the Federal Government had no jurisdiction. Little Jose remained with Adrianna's sister. The Denver papers were leading with the story daily and tensions between the Anglo's and Spanish in southern Colorado and northern New Mexico were building. Old battle scars resurfaced.

At first light, Cooper spurred his bay horse and rode out of the YBarC elk hunting camp with a Marlin 306 saddle rifle. Judy stayed in the line shack still asleep in a down bag by the wood stove. Midmorning Cooper returned "elk-less" to meet Brady and Blue Jay to discuss strategy.

Late morning, Cooper heard the buzz of Brady's dirt bike as it approached the line shack. Blue Jay was clinging to Brady as the enduro motocross bike bumped and grinded its way over the rough country, coming into view out of a stand of leafless aspens.

Brady braked to a stop and Blue Jay jumped off and swore, "I would rather walk out of here than get back on the dirt bike."

Cooper laughed, "I prefer a horse myself."

Brady killed the engine and countered, "Easy ride if Blue Jay would relax."

After a swig of bourbon, the meeting began.

Cooper opened, "We need a 'catch-up' now that the YBarC is ready for winter."

Brady asked, "Where do we go from here, Cooper? You have the YBarC back and you'll be marrying Judy. I assume Max can beat the Feds if they try to condemn the YBarC and take its water for the new damn. He sure has beaten everyone in court that has come after you. I hear from my Taos hang gliding friends, a Santa Fe judge will spring Adrianna once she gets extradited back to New Mexico. And we sadly cannot bring Joe back. The bad egg George is dead. Your fallen angel, Sue is dead. The Eco Warriors are lying way low and do not want to come down here for a long time because of the Ute res and canyon of death. Telluride and Nucla are FBI radioactive. I need to make a few bucks this winter so I plan to teach skiing in Aspen with Kara and sculpt. Blue Jay's going on the ski town circuit with his band in their new used Ford van for the winter."

"That all may be true, but I want to settle up with Lonnie Jr. and Sr. now or they will just lay in ambush. They won't stop pushing the damn or polluting the river with uranium waste or over-pumping the San Miguel River for their development plans. Then there are the unprosecuted murders of Bill Daniels and my mom."

"So what do you have in mind?" Blue Jay asked.

"A Winter Carnival parade is scheduled for two days before Thanksgiving that ends at the base of the town ski lift with an Ice Sculpture Contest that Lonnie Jr. and Sr. and the late Lance's dad, the Utah Senator, plan to judge. The Telluride Times said they'd pull the switch to start the lift that was damaged by the forest fire with TV cameras rolling."

"How does that affect us?" Brady asked warily.

"Well you sculpted some in college as I remember so I need you to ice sculpt Lance's head with the YBarC brand on his forehead on a Ute spear point held by Joe Bear Spirit. You'll also ice sculpt a replica of Bill Daniel's missing rodeo buckle which will be on Joe's beaded belt with an FBI tape recorder clipped to it. The base will be engraved 'Best wishes always to Lonnie Jr.' You unveil it for the Lonnies with me standing there in a red bandana and a cowboy hat as our entry," Cooper said evenly.

"So we settle your feud with an ice sculpture?" Brady was skeptical.

Blue Jay sung, "Lord, please let this cowboy ride the range in peace until he joins you in the big blue sky someday."

"Why's the Senator coming, Cooper?" Brady asked.

Cooper replied, "The Senator wants to protect Lance's legacy as a friend to the southwestern rivers and keep the river rafting businesses in Moab, Utah."

"I'm in," Brady said flatly, still in shock. "What do you figure the Lonnies will do?"

"I don't know for sure, but I'll be packing a .45 automatic pistol with extra clips."

"Judy knows about this?" Brady asked.

"No, that's why she is inside baking an apple pie. She doesn't need to know and will not be there," Cooper replied.

"And me? You planning a singing ice sculpture?" asked a perplexed Blue Jay.

"You and the band march in the parade and play at the event. If trouble breaks out, keep playing as loud as you can. If I need an escape route you all scatter and block the town marshal. I'll have a horse tethered at the abandoned railroad terminal."

"Lunch is in the shack. I had Judy make a big one. You are officially here to pick up some elk steaks. But, I missed my only shot this morning, so it's apple pie." Cooper handed a laughing Brady an envelope. "Here's $500 in twenties for Brady since he won't win the prize and $200 for the band."

They followed Cooper into the weathered line shack for lunch and another swig. The smells of the kitchen wafted into Cooper's windburned cold nostrils as he smiled at Judy. He planned to cherish every day with Judy until the Winter Carnival not sure of what fate had planned for him.

SIXTY-THREE
The Raid on Telluride

Three days before the Winter Carnival, Cooper revealed his plan to an astonished Judy.

"So you think both Lonnies will roll over and play dead when they see the ice sculpture next to you?" Judy asked hopefully.

"Nope, there will be a big brawl."

"Guns."

"I will be packing an automatic, army issue. Cannot speak for the 'Loonies.'"

"And your horse will be where?"

"At the abandoned railroad station. Too much chance of a road block to Jeep out."

"And I will be at the YBarC when I want to be in Telluride helping you?"

"Yes ma'am. Tommy Lee and the cowhands will be here to watch over you. Power of attorney is already in the safe. Max drew it up 'til we get married. A new will there, too. Anything happens to me, you inherit the YBarC land, stock and water."

"I want you with the YBarC. You trust Brady and Blue Jay?"

"With my life. They are committed eco warriors. A blue water, green planet is their game."

"If you have to ride out, what about snow in the passes?"

"Brady is scouting with a hang glider tomorrow, weather permitting. Late fall's dry so far and no snow predicted 'til after Thanksgiving."

"Where to once you're across the passes?"

"Blue Jay is dropping the Jeep off with a single horse trailer for a tune-up tomorrow in Silverton. Then I drive to Northern New Mexico on Jeep roads. Will hide out in Costilla, New Mexico, just across the border. A friend of Adrianna's owns a rental hundred-year-old adobe house for elk hunters. She gave me their card last year."

"How do I contact you?"

"By dead letter drop to the Costilla, New Mexico, Post Office. I'll call you from pay phones."

"Wonderful honeymoon, Cooper."

"I'll come back when Max says it's safe. I never, repeat, never will go to jail again. Remember Delta? I would never come out alive. I have to end the range war or you and I will never be safe."

"I know. I love you too much to lose you," Judy said passionately.

Darkness surrounded the Airstream when it rocked from an explosion that startled Cooper and Judy from their sacred sleep. Cooper saw flames leap near the burned-out headquarters house from the Airstream's window.

He pulled on jeans and cowboy boots and picked up a shotgun, racing past a bewildered shivering Judy. "Stay put; it looks like the propane tank by the house blew up."

Cooper reached the front of the Airstream as the propane tank sent up towering flames illuminating the night sky. In a country second he deduced a moron had blown up the wrong propane tank in an attempt to kill him and Judy in the Airstream. Fifty yards from the back of the Airstream the nearly empty propane tank for the burned-out headquarters house blazed sixty feet into the air. Cooper saw the intact portable silver propane tank behind the Airstream's trailer hitch as he rounded it. He stopped, turned off its shutoff valve for good measure and continued to the backside of the Airstream. Only three small patchable shrapnel holes were in the shiny Airstream's aluminum side.

"Cooper, they tried to blow us up." Judy was wrapped in a Navajo blanket wearing cowgirl boots and near tears. "Who is the culprit, Cooper?"

"Got to be the Lonnies. We'll sleep in the Norwood motel. Get some jeans on and we are out of here as soon as the flames burn out."

"You going to call the volunteer fire department?" Judy inquired.

"Nope. The captain would just call it an accident. A leak from the capped line."

Tommy Lee arrived with two hands from the bunkhouse and Cooper winked at Judy and said, "Looks like the propane tank line was not properly capped and something sparked the fumes. We are moving to the motel in Norwood 'til the Airstream can be patched up. Keep a tight day and night watch on the ranch when we're in Norwood."

At dawn, Cooper rose quietly from the sixteen dollar a night motel's sagging double bed with its threadbare sheets. He tiptoed into a hot shower. He kissed Judy goodbye and left for Telluride. He planned to meet Brady to check on the snow accumulation in Bear Creek and the Ophir Pass. When he rode out of Telluride he would only have three hours of daylight to reach the top of Ophir Pass. He did not want the snow pack to be a factor. Judy planned to meet him at the inn in Telluride with his horse in a trailer towed by the ranch pickup truck an hour before the unveiling of the ice sculpture.

Cooper met Brady at the Hoops Hang Glider Landing Field as Brady began to fold up the Wills Wing glider. "Shitty thermals in this cold late fall air. I scouted the route for you. A few snowdrifts, here and there, above eleven thousand feet but no problem riding to the top of Ophir pass. After that, it's downhill to Silverton. Engineer pass is still clear for Jeeping to

Lake City. Will be slow with a horse trailer but the Jeep's V8 will get you across. Sure you don't want company?" Brady asked.

"No thanks, but if I did, Judy would be my out rider. Your dirt bike is too noisy. Scare my quarter horse. Besides, you might get a commission or two once we unveil your sculpture," Cooper laughed.

Cooper parked the Jeep with its empty horse trailer in front of the inn and left the key and a $100 bill under the driver's seat for Blue Jay, who would deliver it to Silverton at first light.

Judy left the ranch alone with a half hour drive to Telluride to meet Cooper. Cooper watched her pull the ranch pickup with his horse and its trailer up to the front of the inn. After looking up and down the street for a marshal, he exited the inn's front wooden Victorian door.

Judy drove the pickup toward the river with Cooper riding close to her on the bench seat. His saddled and bridled horse was in the beat-up rusting white double horse trailer behind them. A blue duster, a blue nylon rain tarp and a winter bedroll were tied behind the saddle. Handmade brown leather saddlebags were filled with dried fruit and jerky. A half-gallon canteen hung from the saddle horn.

Cooper told Judy that a phone call had come from Max early on the cold clear November morning and that he said Adrianna had been released without bail by a New Mexico state court judge in Santa Fe pending a review of the charges against her. The judge had also ruled the Federal Government had no jurisdiction in the matter. Max had told Cooper she was staying in Santa Fe with relatives until the charges were dropped. No one in politics in New Mexico wanted to reopen the case.

Judy pulled up to the abandoned peeling yellow-painted, smoke damaged railroad depot by the river.

Cooper said, "Unload the horse at two o'clock on the nose and tie him on the west side of the station to the old ticket window's steel bars. Leave the saddle rifle under the station's platform by the horse. Then high tail it out of here. Tommy Lee will be back at the bunkhouse by the time you arrive."

Judy, near tears, tried to keep a brave determined look on her face. "I can do that, Cooper, but do you really have to end the range war this way?"

"No other way out for us as I see it. All my love, always."

Judy collapsed into his arms, fear overwhelming her. He caressed her black hair and firm soft cheeks and kissed her goodbye gently. Cooper slid out of the pickup in high country riding clothes, his pistol tucked into the waistband of his bootcut blue jeans. He glanced back at Judy through the cracked windshield of the old pickup truck and she smiled at him, radiating the deep love in her heart.

At two o'clock Cooper walked up behind the tarped ice sculpture while Blue Jay's band was playing country music on a low stage. "Hello, Brady. When do we unveil it?"

"When the judges arrive. All you have to do is pull this rope end and the tarp will fall off it."

"Then bingo! They're face to face with their crimes," Cooper replied.

"I put three all-nighters into this puppy but it felt real fine to be creating again with my eyes and my hands."

"Perfect, but a change in plans. You can go now. I don't want you in the fireworks if things go bad. I forgot my bandana."

"Figured you would boot me out of here so I carved my name in the ice just like a signature on an oil painting. It's my best work ever. I want some of the credit." Brady laughed with relief in his voice.

"Thanks until we ride again. This should get you started in Aspen. Call it an advance on a bronze of my father's head with a polo helmet hat for the YBarC. Plus, you owe me a ski lesson or two." Cooper handed him a white letter size envelope with the $500. "Now out of here. The judges are coming our way."

Brady slipped into the growing crowd of spectators. Long minutes passed while Cooper remembered his happy childhood on the YBarC ending with the tragic death of his mother in the house fire. He smiled, thinking about Judy's love. Then he practiced a visualization of his right-handed pistol draw that he might need later. He remembered the motion from the hundred western movies he had seen. He knew it from birth from the YBarC gun hands' spirits that haunted the log bunkhouse.

"You a fucking ice sculptor, too, Cooper?" Jesse Smith's angry voice boomed.

Cooper turned to face him. Lonnie Sr. and Jr. walked up behind Jesse with Lance's father, the Utah Senator, in tow before they realized Cooper was standing by the covered ice statue. Blue Jay's band struck up a ballad about a gunslinger down Texas way and Cooper pulled the rope revealing the ice statue. Lance's perfectly sculpted YBarC branded head on Joe Bear Spirit's Ute spear faced the Senator and the Lonnies. Bill Daniels silver rodeo buckle was frozen into the hard, clear blue ice facing the Lonnies as the sunrays reflected off the sculpture into their eyes. Joe's face was frozen in an open-mouthed war cry and painted red and black under a thin sheet of ice. "Ute Water Council" was carved into his forehead in gray tinted capital letters.

"This is an outrage," shouted the Senator. "This man has taken the image of my dead son Lance in vain. Who is he? Arrest him," the Senator demanded as the surrounding spectators gawked at the eerie provocative ice sculpture.

"He's Cooper Stuart, owner of the YBarC, and he killed your son in my office!" Lonnie Jr. blurted in shock.

"Just like you drowned Bill Daniels," Cooper mocked.

"I have had enough of you, Cooper!" Lonnie Sr. pulled a .32 police special from his topcoat pocket and aimed it dead between Cooper's eyes and squeezed the trigger. Cooper ducked behind Joe's thick solid ice head. The bullet ricocheted off the hardened steel blue ice Ute forehead and hit Lonnie Jr. in the heart. Blood gushed from the hole in his tan deer-skin leather jacket as he collapsed, mortally wounded onto the frozen ground in front of the rebuilt ski lift. Lonnie Sr., in a trance, fired three more rounds into Joe's icy head, shattering it. He started to pull the trigger to fire his fifth round when Cooper stepped out from behind the ice sculpture and fired one round in self-defense into Lonnie Sr.'s forehead. The old boot-legger died with his eyes wide open as he fell helplessly backward into the Senator's arms.

"Cooper's murdered Lonnie Sr. and Jr. Get the Senator out of here!" Jesse Smith shout-ed. "Get the marshal."

"No way. Lonnie Sr. fired four times at Cooper first," Brady asserted as he stepped out of the crowd. Several spectators nodded in agreement.

"We will hang him high. Marshal, over here! The Senator will back me up. His word is better than a ski bum's," Jesse replied.

"Adios, Jesse. Bury the Lonnie rattlesnakes in their hometown Cortez. The range war is over. Call the sheriff, Brady. Make sure he recovers the bullet from Lonnie Jr. His father's ricochet shot killed him. I only fired one bullet and it's in the old man," said Cooper.

Cooper ran toward the railroad depot building. Over his shoulder, Cooper saw the chief marshal running toward him with his revolver drawn and aimed at his back. Just as the marshal ran past the stage steps, Blue Jay stepped in front of him with a base fiddle case in his hand. The chief marshal crashed into hardened leather framed case and tumbled head first onto the frozen hard ground. Blue Jay fell over his back and the marshal's pistol skittered under the stage.

Cooper glanced back at the chaotic scene before he disappeared around the corner. A minute later he rounded the side of the depot and froze in surprise. There were two horses tied to the bars of the depot ticket window. He looked up to see Judy sitting on her retired barrel racing paint horse.

She smiled, "Change of plans, Cooper. We ride together. Tommy Lee brought him over. Hope you have a fast horse."

Cooper smiled, "He's ranch born like me so he must be fast."

Cooper pulled the saddle rifle from under the depot platform and shoved it into its leather holster behind the saddle. He would explain all to Judy after they cleared the town of Telluride.

"I heard five shots Cooper."

"The range war is over. The Lonnies are both in hell but Jesse wants a lynch mob." Cooper swung into the handcrafted saddle his grandfather had given him as a college gradu-ation present. It had been his father's.

They spurred their horses and headed in full gallop along the San Miquel River toward Bear Creek. They heard the wail of the sheriff's 4x4 as it pulled up to the ski lift. The gallop-ing horses' hooves sure-footed splashed across the too-shallow fall San Miguel River. They turned their horses up the Bear Creek mine trail. Judy rode high and strong in the saddle, her black hair flowing in the cold fall wind, her cowboy hat behind her neck. They turned their horses up Bear Creek. The sound of the hooves on the rocky-hard mining road thundered into the afternoon orange western sunlight. They rode up into the southern San Juan Mountains, the most majestic mountain range on earth. Cooper and Judy were young, free and bonded together in eternal love.

CPSIA information can be obtained
at www.ICGtesting.com
Printed in the USA
FFOW03n1724070218
44911521-45134FF